HOLLY BANKS FULL OF ANGST

HOLLY BANKS FULL OF ANGST

Julie Valerie

LAKE UNION
PUBLISHING

This is a work of fiction. Names, characters, organizations, places, events, and incidents are either products of the author's imagination or are used fictitiously. Any resemblance to actual persons, living or dead, or actual events is purely coincidental.

Published by Lake Union Publishing, Seattle
www.apub.com

ISBN-13: 9781542014069
ISBN-10: 1542014069

Cover design by Liz Casal

Printed in the United States of America

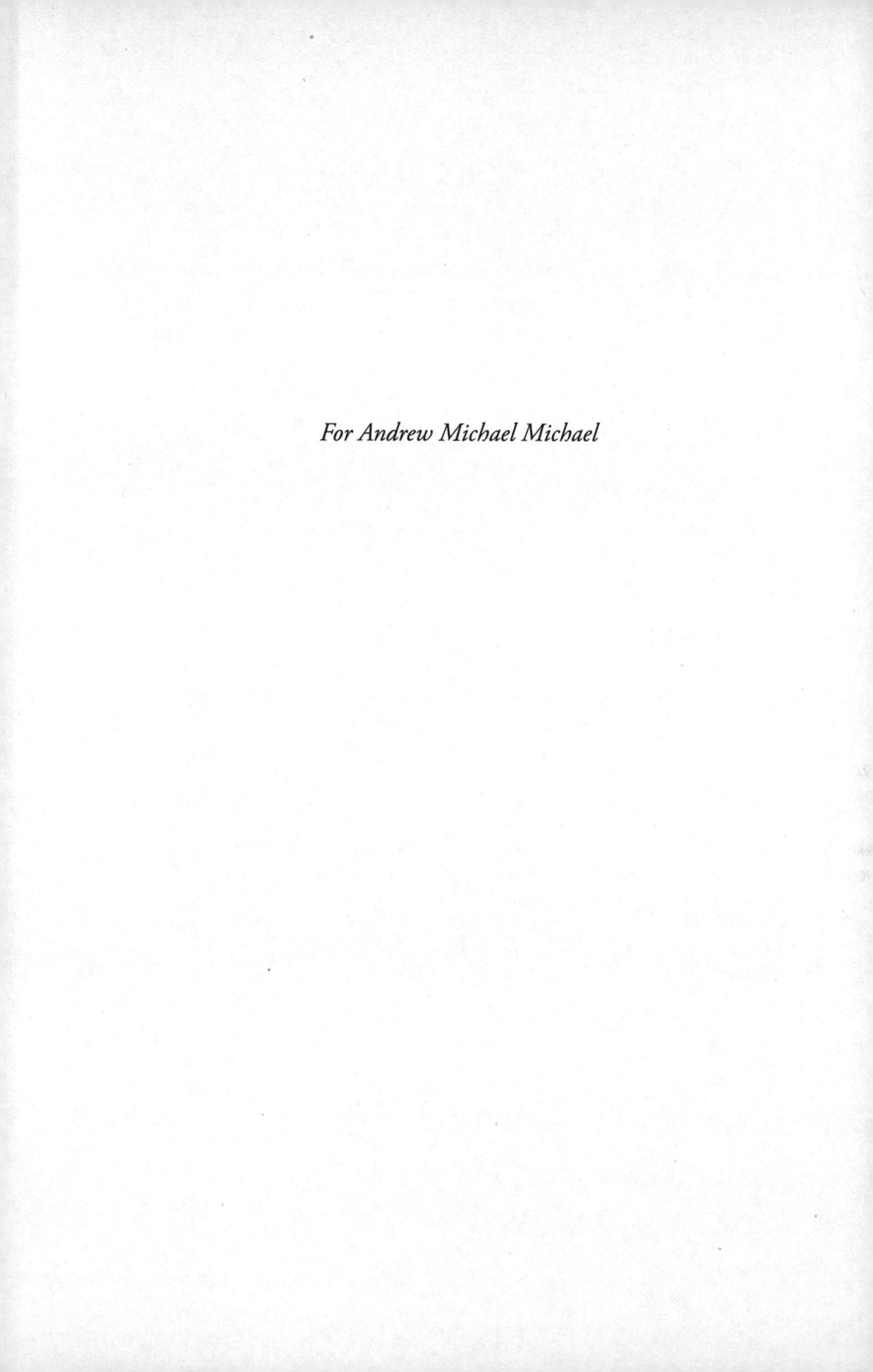

For Andrew Michael Michael

1

—*Welcome to Primm: Take One*—

SCENE 1 – INT. HOUSE – MORNING

HOLLY (V.O.)

Stand by on the set.

Stand by to roll tape.

Roll tape.

Take one.

Action.

Cruel truth? Motherhood on the big screen looks nothing like motherhood offscreen.

"Ella, honey, eat. Eat." Holly poured Gorilla Munch into a Ziploc. *If Ella doesn't eat her waffle, she can eat Gorilla Munch on the bus. Right?*

Is food allowed on a school bus? It was the first day of kindergarten; how was Holly to know? "Two bites, Ella. Take two bites." The bus would be there in six minutes. Maybe five. *Where's her backpack?* "Ella."

"Hmm?"

"Where's your backpack?"

Arms spread across the table, Ella hung over a half-eaten waffle like a lollygagging drunkard unable to rally. *Probably needs a better bedtime routine now that school has started. Add that to the bullet journal, on the things-to-do list. Add "buy a bullet journal" to that list, while you're at it.*

HOLLY (V.O.)

Cue Jack. The ever-handsome, ever-frustrating Jack.

"She's going to miss the bus, Holly." Jack crossed the threshold into the kitchen, wringing his hands in that nervous "Jack" way he did when the world was coming to an end. Bills to pay. The fear the front lawn might dry out and turn brown. Not being able to find a clean undershirt or a pair of matching socks to wear to work. "What happened to the alarm?" Look of utter dismay. "Holly. How did you let this happen?"

"I fell asleep on the couch." *Like that's never happened to you?* Holly brushed past him without making eye contact. "I can't believe you didn't notice I wasn't in bed." If he had noticed, he could have woken her up. Now her neck was crooked, and her back hurt. While spreading peanut butter on a slice of bread, Holly stopped short, knife in one hand, honey whole wheat in the other. She fixed her eyes on something in the distance.

"But where are her shoes?" Jack asked. "Why's her toothbrush on the kitchen table?" He wasn't helping. He was taking up space. "And why is she wearing that? Blue? Ella hates dresses." He waved a hand in Holly's face. "Hello—earth to Holly? You're doing it again."

"What?"

"That Walter Mitty thing. You're a thousand miles away."

"Should I start the film with a breakfast scene? Or is that cliché?" She dragged a slab of peanut butter across the bread.

"Film? What are you talking about?" He tapped his watch. "You should be on the driveway by now."

Off camera: Rumbling sound of a bus approaching.

"Hollythebus." All one word. "Holly—the bus!"

"I overslept!" What'd he want her to do? Yell "run" at Ella? Freak her out? Ella was half-asleep over a half-eaten waffle.

"Mommy? I don't wanna go to keedergarten."

Great. Now Ella's freaked out.

They were still in boxes—newly moved to the Village of Primm. Gilded school district. Land of perfect moms, perfect families, perfect homes. Now Ella would be late for school on her first day of kindergarten. Of all days to oversleep. Of all days to screw up.

Holly closed her eyes. Waited for the voice-over inside her head.

HOLLY (V.O.)
(whispering)

You're never going to make it in the Village of Primm. Other mothers are way better than you are. Write that in your bullet journal. Make that your opening scene.

2

Four days earlier, Friday

Holly and Ella faced a stack of moving boxes that stood like the Leaning Tower of Pisa. The bottom box, the one marked *Fragile*, had a busted corner and was buckling under the weight of the stack. Holly slid the top box from the pile and grabbed hold of a piece of packing tape. Struggle, their chocolate Labrador, lowered her head, kept real still, and growled.

"You can do it, Mommy." Ella counted: "One, two . . ."

"Three!" Holly ripped the tape off the box, Struggle went wild, and Ella moved in to claim her prize: Bubble Wrap. Ella hoarded piles of it all over the house, a weapons cache for making the dog bark and fraying her mother's nerves. Itty-bitty fists snatched. Itty-bitty fingers squeezed. Itty-bitty bubbles went pop-pop-pop!—like tiny gunshots fired in a vaudeville show. Holly wanted to holler, *Stop it, Ella! Oh, for the love of all that's holy, stop popping!* but she couldn't. Because someone was knocking at her front door.

Who was it? A neighbor? Someone welcoming them with a plate of cookies? A cherry pie? She couldn't invite them inside. Nothing but clutter and corrugated cardboard as far as the eye could see. Her home wasn't inviting. It didn't welcome. Didn't say Martha Stewart in the living room. Julia Child in the kitchen. It repelled. Smelled like dog and last night's Chinese takeout. What was she wearing? Awful. Worn-out pair of black leggings and one of Jack's dingy gray T-shirts from his Cosmic Taco collection: *I don't wanna taco 'bout it. It's nacho business.*

"Quick!" Holly fluttered her hands at Ella. "What should I do?"

"Answer it!" Ella pointed.

"Right! Good call." Holly leaped over Jack's suitcase, toppling a lamp on the other side. Struggle was hot on her trail as Holly shuffled toward the door, sliding a rubber band from her wrist to collect her hair into a ponytail. Holly stopped short, grabbing hold of the doorknob as the doorbell rang again, trying to kick free from a hunk of packing tape that was stuck to her ankle. "Ella, call Struggle."

"Come 'ere, Struggle!" Ella was bent at the waist, leaning into a newly opened moving box, tossing everything she could onto the family room floor. Lampshade. Decorative candles. Some random toys thrown in. Ella could tip at any moment and disappear completely into the box, so Holly wasn't surprised when Struggle took one sidelong glance at her and then ran back to the family room to bark at the box that was about to swallow Ella.

Holly swung open the front door and found Penelope Pratt in all her majesty, standing with an outstretched hand.

"Holly Banks!"

Penelope's grip was firm; her shake, determined. Penelope was the Feathered Nest real estate agent who'd sold Holly the house she'd lived in for three days and was now hankering to unpack.

"How are you, Penelope?" Holly stepped over the threshold, joining Penelope on the porch. "I'd invite you inside, but it's a mess in there. I'm still in boxes."

"This is a quick visit, Holly. I'm here to welcome you to Primm."

Oh?

"Welcome to Primm!" Penelope beamed.

"Welcome to my porch!" Did Penelope notice her porch was completely naked, stripped bare of the beautiful items the previous homeowner, Collette, had so carefully selected to welcome her guests? "I wish I could offer you a place to sit, but Collette took that gorgeous bench with her."

Collette had a zillion followers on Pinterest and had used this home to build her online platform as a staging and crafts expert before selling it to Holly and her husband, Jack. Collette had moved her family to a bigger home on Dillydally to start all over again, decorating nooks and crannies until they were Pinterestworthy and ready to be uploaded to Instagram. No Collette at this address meant no more painted wooden bench with two overstuffed pillows, one embroidered with the number 12, the words *Petunia Lane* on the other. No more fragrant flowers in Smith & Hawken baskets hanging from the porch rafters. No flag flapping in the breeze.

"How is Collette?" Not that Holly knew her beyond the sale of this house. Holly didn't know anyone in the Village of Primm except Penelope. "Is she settling in?"

"Completely unpacked. I was just there," Penelope told Holly. "She hosted a tea for a few of the women in my office as a thank-you for some staging projects we've given her. So adorable. She used Bubble Wrap as a tablecloth and served minicakes iced like brown moving boxes stacked on top of each other. Hanging from the backs of our chairs were framed cardboard squares with the words *Fragile* and *This End Up* printed on them." Penelope pulled out her phone and, with a perfectly manicured nail, tapped the Pinterest app and scrolled a moment. "Look." She showed Holly her screen. "She uploaded photos of the decorated table before we arrived so we could pin and like before the first bit of tea was poured. Bubble Wrap as a tablecloth!" Penelope gave a wistful smile. "That Collette. She's amazing."

"She accomplished all this in three short days?" Holly reached for the phone, clicked to view Collette's There's No Place Like Home Pinterest board. "I'm stunned." Utterly stunned. And a bit miffed too.

Holly wondered if it was sad for Collette to pack up her front-porch welcome items and say goodbye to Petunia Lane. From the moment Holly had first seen this porch, she'd wanted to grow old on it, drink sweet tea while leaning back into one of those overstuffed, embroidered pillows. Collette was a tough act to follow. Her porch decor sent clear messages: *Welcome to Primm* and *Welcome to Petunia Lane*. More importantly, it said: *Welcome Home. Welcome to the kind of home you want to create for your family*. Collette's front porch had convinced Holly to buy the house attached to it before she'd even stepped foot inside the front door. That was the power of a porch that presented a proper welcome.

"You're really going to love living here, Holly." Penelope rested her dainty little hand on Holly's arm. "The Village of Primm is a lovely place. Petunia Lane's a charming enclave, and little Ella will love, love, love attending kindergarten at Primm Academy."

Holly hoped so. She and Jack could lose their shirts paying for this picture-perfect suburb.

Holly eyed Penelope. Always so put together. She wore a butter-yellow pantsuit, a striking combination with her coal-black hair, which was pulled into a loose but stylish bun at the nape of her neck. She looked a bit like a honeybee—the Primm Academy school mascot. From her shoulder hung an oversize leather tote bag the color of a caramel latte. The tote's leather was thick and sturdy. It had white edge stitching so tailored and precise Holly was sure this minute piece of detailing was what catapulted the tote to "it bag" status. The tote was gorgeous. Accomplished. A neutral, yes, but a confident neutral. If Holly were a tote bag, she'd want to be *that* tote bag.

From the tote, Penelope pulled a giant cellophane gift bag, tied with a wide silk ribbon and filled with what appeared to be coupons and store flyers. Wait. *Coupons?*

"This is for you," Penelope said. "A gift from the Welcome Wagon Committee." She let a strap slide off her arm, the contents of the tote now fully exposed. “I’m so glad you didn’t buy that colonial in Southern Lakes.”

Holly glanced beyond Penelope toward the sprawling hydrangeas in the neighbor’s yard. “Primm is so—I don’t know—picturesque. I worry I’ve moved to a place where everyone’s trying to keep up with the Joneses.”

“Oh, no, Holly.” Penelope shook a finger. “Don’t worry about that. If you live in the Village of Primm—you *are* the Joneses. Keeping up is never our concern.”

“Oh? That’s odd.” Holly studied Penelope. “If the Joneses aren’t worried about keeping up, what do they worry about?”

“Banishment.” Penelope blinked, with no particular expression on her face. “Banishment from the village. Once you’re in, it’s devastating to be out. Are you a floral or a spice?”

“Excuse me?”

“Your fragrance. I have two samples. One’s a floral; one’s a spice.” Penelope waited with eyes open wide and a smile that showed all her teeth.

“Floral.”

“Here you go.” Penelope pressed a sample of White Gardenia in Holly’s hand, followed by a small box of carpet-and-room deodorizer, a key chain from Feathered Nest Realty, and a whisk tied to an envelope of mulling spices.

“Thank you, Penelope. That’s so kind.”

Penelope began shoving more product samples at Holly. Packets of sunflower seed from the local nursery. A bronzed garden gnome. It was coming at her so fast; she couldn’t hold on to anything. The twelve-by-twelve lunar calendar did her in, and *whoops!*—Holly dropped the bronzed garden gnome on Penelope’s foot.

Penelope took it in stride. “I’m wearing steel-toed high heels, Holly. I’m invincible.” She picked up the gnome, plunked it on top of the pile in Holly's arms. "What was it Dorothy said in *The Wizard of Oz*? There's no place like *gnome*? Ha!"

"This is all very generous. But I'm afraid I might drop something again."

"That's all right, Holly," Penelope said.

But it wasn't all right because the fallen garden gnome called attention to the packing tape trailing from the back of Holly's foot like an unwanted hank of toilet paper. "My goodness. I really stepped in it, didn't I?" She stomped around a bit, mangling the adhesive.

More samples. Hand lotion, a travel stick stain remover, dishwashing detergent, and a fortune cookie wrapped in plastic, the word *welcome* printed in multiple languages. Hands full, Holly tried to juggle her way through this circus act, wishing she could open the cookie and read her fortune.

"This is quite enough, Penelope, really."

Penelope dove into her leather tote bag, retrieved a butter-yellow T-shirt, and then, clutching it by the shoulders, stretched it out so Holly could read *PRIMM* silk-screened across the chest in bold white Varsity font. "Ta-da!" Penelope said. "You're yellow. Team Buttercream."

"Buttercream?" Holly wasn't sure she wanted to be on anyone's team.

"F.U. Frisbee," Penelope explained. "Something the moms do. Helps with stress. You'll see." She pressed a coupon for gutter cleaning into Holly's hand.

"Penelope? Please stop." *Is that it? Is she finished?*

Nope. Penelope thrust a bottle of white wine at Holly, tucking the butt of the bottle behind the samples until it wedged beneath Holly's right armpit. "There," Penelope said, pleased with herself. "Nice and cozy. That's from the vineyard up the hill near the Stone House. Have I told you about the Stone House? The glass artist? Don't believe everything you hear. I'll tell you later. Oh, wait! There's a note attached." She peered down the bridge of her nose. *"From the Petunia Lane Homeowners' Association. Welcome to 'whine' country."*

Holly shifted her feet, tangling both ankles in packing tape. The wine began to slip backward, so she clamped her arm around its neck and wobbled a bit trying to hold on to it. The cork end moved and bobbed like a buoy floating in her armpit. "Thank you, Penelope. My goodness."

She needed to go. *Go, Penelope. Get off my porch!*

"Really, thank you." Holly couldn't hold any more. Tickets to a cherry festival. A sample of dog food. "No more. Please stop." A bottle of Windex with a coupon for window cleaning: BOGO. "Wow. So generous." The wine was slipping. Everything was toppling over. "Please stop." Floor cleaner. "Stop!"

"One more thing." Penelope held a finger up. "I have a few questions to ask." She extracted a small notebook from her tote and clicked a pen. "For the People of Primm section of the *Primm Gazette*."

Holly was reminded of her days in film school: the Welcome Wagon–lady scene opened the *Stepford Wives* book, but in the first film, it was downplayed, and she couldn't remember if the Welcome Wagon lady appeared in the more recent adaptation. She found the whole thing amusing. A welcome lady? Holly glanced beyond Penelope to the pristine homes and manicured gardens that lined Petunia Lane. *I haven't inadvertently moved my family onto the set of a satirical sci-fi horror movie, have I?* She bent forward so she could nudge Penelope in the arm. "You're not a robot, are you?"

"Excuse me?"

"Oh, sorry. Nothing." Holly tried minimizing her bizarre actions, the way Jack so often did, by explaining, "I went to film school. I sometimes imagine—things remind me—never mind. What were you saying?"

Holly answered Penelope's questions, citing Jack's recent job relocation as their reason for moving to the Village of Primm and confirming that Ella was their only child and was starting kindergarten on Tuesday—the day after Labor Day. "I'll be looking for work once Ella gets settled in school." Holly hugged the product samples in a polite, jovial way. "But I highly doubt there's much of a film industry in the Village of Primm, so maybe I'll have to find work in a bookstore or something." She nodded to the bottle of wine in her armpit. "Is the vineyard hiring?" She didn't mention they desperately needed the money because they were in over their heads with this starter home on Petunia. Holly had pressured Jack into buying in the best school district. Southern Lakes didn't have a charter school. The Village of Primm had Primm Academy. And a lot more too. But then, Penelope already knew all that. She was the one who had sold them this bill of goods.

"Very fine. This is excellent, Holly." Penelope clicked her pen, tossed it into her shoulder bag. "I'll get this information to the *Primm Gazette*. Thank you."

As Penelope took leave of Holly's front porch, a black, very square Mercedes SUV with tinted windows rolled slowly past Penelope's car and into Holly's driveway.

"You have a visitor." Penelope appeared impressed. "A G-Class visitor."

"No one I know." *Must be a friend of Collette's who doesn't realize she's moved.*

"Actually, I've seen that car." Penelope glanced back at Holly. "At the vineyard. They have new owners. An investment group. Or something." Penelope clutched the strap of her bag with both hands. Like she was hanging on for dear life but hoping no one would notice. "So that's why calls are coming in for the Stone House. Huh. Oh well." She shrugged, presumably sweeping the Stone House under the rug in favor of making her way down Holly's exposed aggregate sidewalk before the visitor in Holly's drive stepped out to say hello. "There's a certificate for a Welcome to Primm topiary." She pointed to the sliding pile in Holly's arms. "Compliments of Feathered Nest Realty. You can pick it up in the Topiary Park Gift Shoppe. Oh! Bring Ella to the topiary petting zoo. Huge topiary-plant animals you can touch but not climb. Mother Goose, the Three Little Pigs. Other animals, too, like horses lined up for a steeplechase, a turkey, some truly exquisite butterflies. Plume holds court at the entrance to the petting zoo. Ella will love Plume. Everyone loves Plume!"

"Plume?"

"Plume's a peacock. She's the Village of Primm mascot—a matriarch! No—a piece of art. Southern Lakes has pink flamingo lawn ornaments. Primm? Primm has Plume. She's twenty-five feet tall, and her tail feathers—wow. You've never seen so many white begonias. Snapdragons, verbena . . . when the wind blows, you can smell Plume a mile away."

"So Plume's a female?"

"Yes. Huge tourist attraction." Penelope burst with pride. Pride—over a bird. "Huge! But yes. She's a female. Why?"

"Because peacocks are male. If Plume is female—wouldn't she be a peahen?"

"Oh, no." Penelope was certain. "Plume's definitely a girl."

"Then she's a peahen."

"Um." Penelope rolled her eyes up, tapped a finger against her cheek. "Sure." She smiled at last. "If you say so. You know about the event at the school tonight? New Parent Orientation?"

"Oh, sure. Meet the teachers before school starts on Tuesday."

"Exactly. Okay, then." Penelope eyed the Mercedes while hoisting a wayward tote strap onto her shoulder. "My cousin—I told you about her? She's president of the Primm Academy PTA, so I'll be there in a show of support. But Holly"—Penelope lowered her eyes—"if I were you? I'd go to the New Parent Orientation and meet the teachers. But for the PTA portion of the night? I'd arrive late and sneak out early, or you'll sign your life away volunteering for things you couldn't care less about. Box Tops? Pimping raffle tickets? Trust me: the school enrolls the child; the PTA enrolls the mom. Don't fall into that trap. In Primm? It's brutal. But you didn't hear that from me. Wear the yellow shirt." She pointed. "Team Buttercream. It's like blocking a spell cast by a passive-aggressive witch. You'll see. Best wishes with the unpack, Holly. And welcome to Primm!" She pointed to Holly's grass. "Mind if I?"

"Go right ahead."

Penelope lifted the pant legs of her butter-yellow suit to flit across Holly's lawn toward the street, where her Feathered Nest Realty car was parked. To Holly's mind, she looked like a canary. Heels prodding the soil, Penelope took wing with sharp, jerky movements, always aware of the G-Class in the driveway. *Birds can't independently move their eyes without also moving their heads,* thought Holly. *To look at something, they have to turn their heads to face it.*

Holly averted her gaze toward the co-op garden on the cul-de-sac at the end of Petunia Lane. Penelope had said there was a high concentration of Foodie Moms living in the Petunia enclave, and that made Holly a bit nervous. She wasn't a Foodie Mom. She liked food and all—she ate it. But she wasn't a Foodie Mom. Although, hey. Maybe with a little effort, she could become a Foodie Mom. You know . . . fit in. Start her new life on Petunia with a big bowl of quinoa and a tall glass of kombucha. Or kale! That was it. *Kale.* Who knew what might become of her? This move to the Village of Primm had opened up a whole new world—a familiar world, but one that was turned up a notch. She suspected Primm operated a few decibels above the norm. Like an amplified electric guitar played with distortion. You liked it because power chords heightened the experience, making you feel life was being lived with higher intensity.

The man from the Mercedes made his way up Holly's sidewalk, tucking a pair of aviators into the pocket of his shirt. "Beautiful day, yes, Holly Banks?"

How'd he know her name? She'd never seen this man in her life. If she had, she'd remember him: 007 type. Appeared wealthy, tan. Holly gave a swift kick to the piece of packing tape clinging to the heel of her left foot, but all that did was transfer it to the toe of her right foot.

"I'm here for Jack. Is he here?"

"Not at the moment." Jack was at work.

"Give him this?" He waved an envelope, the edges tipped with red and blue stripes. Airmail with postage from somewhere overseas, from a place Holly didn't recognize. "Tell him it arrived this morning." He had a lean but athletic build, took the steps of the porch swiftly, skipping a few on his way up. He tucked the envelope into the pile in Holly's arms, so close she could smell his cologne: clean, but with an edge. "This should get his attention."

"Do you work with Jack?"

"You might say that." Sly smile, long dimples on the side.

If Holly had followed her post–film school dreams of working in the industry, she'd typecast this guy onto the screen of a political thriller. International espionage, something like that.

"Then why are you here? Why not give this to him at the office?" *Is Jack not at work? What's in the envelope?*

"And miss a visit to the Petunia enclave?" He waved a hand toward the co-op gardens.

Who was this guy?

"Would you mind standing on the sidewalk? My dog's about to bark." Holly shifted the items in her arms.

"Of course." He left her porch, continued down the sidewalk. "Tell Jack I'm getting anxious."

"And who shall I say dropped by?" He was bold but elegant. If he was from the investment group that bought the vineyard, if he did, indeed, work in the wine industry—he'd be red. Dry. Something muscular and full bodied. Italian. Barbaresco. Definitely Barbaresco. No—Barolo.

As if reading her mind: "Enjoy the wine."

"Excuse me?"

"The bottle in your arms. It's an award-winning chardonnay." Beside the lamppost at the end of her sidewalk, he slid his sunglasses from his pocket. "That was a good vintage. You'll find vibrant aromas of pear, green apple, and white flowers. With just the slightest touch of oak." He slipped the aviators on, walked around the front of the Mercedes to open the driver's side door. "Tell Jack I'm waiting for his call." He slipped into the driver's seat.

Moments later, he was gone.

3

Friday night

"Sorry I'm late." Holly felt a room of on-time moms judging her as she bumped her way across a row of knees—*excuse me, excuse me, excuse me*—toward an available black-pleather flip-down seat in the expansive auditorium. The Primm Academy New Parent Orientation was well underway with a good showing of new parents. "Husband was late," Holly told a mom. "I hit traffic on the way over," she told another. *Why am I explaining myself? I don't even know these women.*

Holly took a seat, then took a swig of her to-go cup of vanilla hazelnut coffee as a woman dressed head to toe in powder pink waltzed across the stage to take the microphone from Principal Hayes. To Holly's mind, the woman looked like a tall Reese Witherspoon or maybe a blonde Alexis Bledel. She moved with the confidence of a Hollywood celebrity not yet rocked by personal scandal.

The woman seated next to Holly leaned in. "My Realtor, Penelope Pratt, told me the Southern Lakes PTA voted for term limits, so their president serves only one year and then passes the baton to another parent." She glanced once over her shoulder before whispering to Holly, "But in the Village of Primm, a PTA president running unopposed can serve the school for years and years. So it's more like a dynasty."

The woman beside Holly clearly didn't know how to whisper because two moms in front of them joined the conversation. One said, "I'm an incoming kindergarten mom, but my son's in third grade here. Primm's PTA is the engine behind school rankings. That woman up there strengthens the school *and* surrounding property values." The other said, "It's true. I thought about moving to Southern Lakes, but in the end, I just couldn't do it. The whole town credits high property values to the work of one mom—her." She nodded toward the stage. "The president of the PTA."

"Who happens to be Penelope's cousin," Holly added, pointing with her vanilla hazelnut. "Penelope told me the same thing. I thought it was a sales pitch."

"Well, I almost bought a colonial in Southern Lakes," the woman in front of Holly said. "It was a lot cheaper, had a bigger kitchen and more closet space."

"Me too!" The woman beside Holly covered her mouth. "I wonder if we were looking at the same house. Oh, but then our kids would be going to Southern Lakes Elementary."

Everyone exchanged a mutual rolling of the eyes. Thank God *that* didn't happen.

"Why is your shirt yellow?" one of the moms asked Holly. "I thought we were supposed to wear pink."

"Penelope gave this—" Holly swept her gaze across the room, shocked to realize she was surrounded by shirts exactly like the shirt she was wearing—the word *PRIMM* in Varsity font blazoned across every chest—except everyone else wore pink. Did she miss the memo? Holly spotted Penelope at the back of the room. Penelope was wearing yellow. Penelope and Holly were the only two women in the entire room not wearing pink. Where was Team Buttercream?

The woman onstage pointed a remote control at the ceiling behind her, lowering a giant screen. As it descended, the woman's larger-than-life face slid onto the screen, filling it from top to bottom. All eyes in the auditorium fixed on that close-up shot: flawless skin and a turned-up nose, blue eyes squinting above a brilliant smile—a wad of pink bubble gum hidden at the back.

"Can everyone hear me?" the woman at the podium asked. "Is this mic on?" Tap, tap, tap. "Oh. Ha! Ha! It is. Thank you, everyone, thank you." Her voice amplified, her eyes slowly scanning the room before coming to rest on Holly's shirt. From the woman's point of view, Holly sat front and center, about six rows into the audience. Everyone was clapping except Holly because she couldn't clap without splashing her coffee. "I see everyone read the tip sheet in the *Proper*."

Tip sheet? What?

"Great show of pink. Thank you, New Moms. Thank you for your show of support for this *school* function." Slight twitch of the eyebrow.

Holly followed the woman's line of sight as it moved from Holly's yellow shirt to Penelope's. Penelope smiled at the woman, waved hello with the slightest wiggle of her fingers, triangulating the tension.

Undaunted, the woman at the podium produced a smile so piquant, so rehearsed, so tightly polite it spoke volumes: *We're not children. We're moms. We know our colors. Yes?* "Warm welcomes are so important in the Village of Primm."

The mom sitting beside Holly leaned, a slow creep to the left, positioning herself as far away from Holly as she could get.

"And newcomers? Newcomers are always welcome." The edge of the woman's lips curled into a pinched position of authority. "Welcome, New Moms." Because, clearly, *she* wasn't a New Mom. She was an Established Mom. A been-there-done-that, zero-tolerance, scheduled-playdate mom. The double entendre type, a mother bird both for and against the concept of free-range chickens. "Welcome to the Village of Primm and to New Parent Orientation at Primm Academy. I see we have lots of incoming kindergarten and transfer families in attendance." She gazed down upon her flock, her face enlarged to Orwellian size on the screen behind her. "If there's anyone in the auditorium who doesn't know me, or hasn't met me but wants to know me, or pretends to know me but hasn't met me, or has met me and knows me, or knows my family, or knows of my family . . ." She tucked a lock of honey-blonde hair behind one of her diamond-studded earlobes. There was a twinkle in her eye, and something . . . something that gave the impression she was about to make a grand announcement—winning numbers to a lottery, a list of ingredients for a secret cookie recipe. Instead, with arms spread wide, she declared, "My name is Mary-Margaret St. James, and I am the proud, proud president of the Primm Academy PTA!"

Bingo! It was her—Penelope's cousin: the woman who, as Penelope had said, made everything in Primm, well, prim. Holly sat up to get a better look at the woman responsible for Holly shelling out top dollar for her modest home on Petunia Lane. Holly didn't see a cape. No tiara. So what made her so special?

"She's a bit over the top, don't you think?" Holly noted to the other moms near her.

"I paid good money for my home," the mom beside Holly whispered, "and I'm not about to go underwater if this school district tanks because Mary-Margaret St. James decides she wants to quit the PTA or move to Southern Lakes or some other such thing. If she's our parent-teacher president and whatever it is she's doing is working—and apparently, it is working—then sign me up."

Holly folded her arms across the *PRIMM* on her yellow shirt. "I was just saying I'm sure you or I could do as good a job as she does." In the end, Mary-Margaret St. James was probably no different from any other mom: flawed—and hoping no one would notice.

A folded piece of paper arrived at Holly's arm, passed by a row of moms.

Yellow is a protective color.
Trust me. You'll see.
—Penelope
P.S. Get out while you still can.

Penelope sold a ton of houses in Southern Lakes and the Village of Primm. Holly knew because she had stalked the two housing markets every time she logged into Feathered Nest Realty. But as far as Holly could remember, when she and Jack were looking at houses with Penelope, Penelope made it appear as if Southern Lakes were built on a cemetery next to a nuclear power plant. It clearly wasn't—but Penelope gave that impression. According to Penelope, Southern Lakes parents were more concerned with having a good time than with having a good school. According to Penelope, the affordability of Southern Lakes came at the expense of standardized test scores. According to Penelope—

From the podium: "For those of you taking copious notes, and I know you all are, that's Mary-with-a-hyphen-Margaret, St. James with an *S*, *T*, and a period. St. James. Mary-Margaret St. James. That's me! But then, you know that." She winked from the podium and extended an arm to wave like a beauty queen on parade. "I'm sure you've all heard of my husband, 'My Love,' Michael St. James? My Love is a *huge* philanthropist in the Village of Primm. Everyone knows My Love. My Love, Michael, sends his best wishes." Big smile. Hand placed gently over her heart. "From our happy family to yours: we wish you a happy, memorable, A-plus-plus school year. From My Love and me, Mary-Margaret St. James, to you."

She took a moment to gaze upon the crowd. To slowly scan the room, giving everyone the chance to *feel* Mary-Margaret and My Love's love. And then: "Anyhoo. Changing topic. If you're new in town and you're wondering how the PTA operates at Primm, I'm here to tell you, we're not like other PTAs. For one, we've severed all ties to any national parent association and are now completely independent of anyone or anything that's 'official' or regulated. We felt too constricted by all of those silly 'official' bylaws and guidelines imposed on us by all of those 'official' parent-teacher organizations. So I decided, and we all voted to break ties with them. Now, we have the freedom we need for the rules we all want. That's what makes us special." Polite clapping from the crowd.

"And now," said Mary-Margaret, "the moment you've all been waiting for: the moment I announce this year's theme, a theme that I created, with a slogan you won't soon forget. Are you ready?" She nodded yes to the crowd. "Yes? Ready? Okay." Big smile from Mary-Margaret. "Here it is: *No one can do everything*," she said, with eyes opened wide, "*but* everyone *can do something*!"

Holly tapped the arm of the woman beside her. "I know that. I've heard that before . . ."

"No one . . . can do everything . . ." Mary-Margaret waited. Presumably to let it all sink in. "But everyone . . . can do something."

Holly whispered, "She didn't make that up. She lifted that from Helen Keller."

"Let's think about that for a moment. Shall we?" Mary-Margaret paused for a moment of reflection, then pointed the remote and, with the press of a button, loaded a video onto the large motorized screen behind her. The lights in the auditorium dimmed, reminding Holly of her days in film school, of an auditorium like this one where Holly was surrounded not by moms—though she realized some of them could have been moms, too—but by dynamic, creative storytellers studying the art of cinema, filmmaking, and script writing. Holly let her mind wander, pretended she was back in Professor Keegan's screen-writing class about to analyze the heroine's journey in *The Wizard of Oz*. She forgot all about the quote stolen from Helen Keller (or was it Max Lucado? Edward Everett Hale?) and instead got comfortable in her seat and settled in with her coffee.

FADE IN:

EXT. PRIMM ACADEMY GATES – MORNING – ESTABLISHING

Sun is shining in the Village of Primm as a montage of images captures the essence of Primm Academy, from the school gates to the crest to the large wooden doors. The Primm Academy alma mater plays softly in the background as the camera dissolves to:

EXT. PRIMM ACADEMY FLAGPOLE – MORNING

Surrounded by SCHOOLCHILDREN, MARY-MARGARET ST. JAMES, Primm Academy PTA president, wearing a pink blouse and crisp white skirt, hoists the American flag up a flagpole. Patriotic music plays. Camera zooms to close-up:

MARY-MARGARET

Welcome to Primm Academy. As a nationally recognized school of excellence, Primm celebrates the continued partnership between the independent PTA, the school, and the families whose lives are enriched by an active school community. Always striving to provide an outstanding educational experience for our children, the Primm Academy PTA encourages every parent to get involved and to remember: no one can do everything, but everyone can do something.

CAMERA: CLOSE-UP SHOT

MARY-MARGARET
(smiling at schoolchildren)

Children, tell your parents your important message.

SCHOOLCHILDREN
(speaking in unison)

No one can do everything, but everyone can do something!

MARY-MARGARET
(saluting the camera)

Ask not what Primm can do for you. Ask what you can do for Primm. May God bless you. And may God bless the United States of America!

The crowd in the auditorium erupted into applause as the projector rolled back into the ceiling. Holly checked the expressions on the faces of the moms sitting near her, the moms who, only moments ago, were trading snarky gossip but now appeared mesmerized.

Mary-Margaret leaned into the microphone. "At this time, I'd like to dismiss the dads. Thank you for coming to tonight's meeting," Mary-Margaret cooed. "We know you're busy and this isn't your cup of tea, so you're free to go. Leave it to the moms to run school functions, the PTA, the class parties, after-school activities, fund-raising, teacher appreciation, playground duty, backpack check, carpool, homework, snack schedule, field trips, holiday parties, health screenings, the science fair, Paint the Playground Project, library book drive, graduation ceremonies, Technology in Our Classrooms Initiative, Box Tops, and the Raise the Flag fund-raiser. You're free to go. Thank you. Thank you, dads, for making an appearance at tonight's function."

What? Holly scrambled for her phone, fired a text to Jack.

HOLLY: Unbelievable! PTA president dismissed the dads.

JACK: What?

HOLLY: The dads left—well. Most of them. Why do they get to leave?

JACK: I have no idea. I'm not there.

HOLLY: Why are moms assigned to school duties? Why am I here and not you?

JACK: Because you're better at it. Relax.

HOLLY: I am relaxed. But I want to be home with Ella right now. Why does everyone assume I should do the school volunteering and not you? You're Ella's parent too.

JACK: Holly. Come on.

HOLLY: What?

JACK: You're the mom.

HOLLY: So?

JACK: So that's how it's done. That's how it's always been done.

HOLLY: Seriously, Jack?

JACK: What?

HOLLY: Are you really going there?

Heeding Penelope's call to "get out while you still can," Holly stood up and began her *excuse me, excuse me, excuse me* across the kneecaps toward the aisle.

"*Whoopsie daisy!*" Mary-Margaret gasped from the podium. "Looks like someone is trying to sneak out of a PTA meeting early. Will someone stop that mom from leaving?" said Mary-Margaret, following up with a polite chuckle and then snapping, "*Stop that mom.*"

Holly turned. "Me?"

"Yes, you, Team Buttercream."

Surrounded—not by orange Oompa Loompas but by a sea of seated pink people blinking up at her—Holly felt like Dorothy in *The Wizard of Oz* after crash-landing in the Village of Primm, insisting she wasn't a witch at all.

"Oh, no. I don't play Frisbee." Holly channeled Dorothy. "I'm not a Frisbee player at all."

"You can't leave now," Mary-Margaret implored. "I'm not through with my announcements."

"But—the dads just left." Holly felt her face and neck turn red.

"I know the dads just left. I dismissed them. Moms run the school. Not the dads." Mary-Margaret shook her head as if this were the most obvious thing in the world. "If dads ran the school, nothing would get done. Except, maybe, a barbecue. Or something. Flag football . . ."

Fine.

Holly returned to her seat—*excuse me, excuse me, excuse me*—then sat and stewed, completely humiliated.

Mary-Margaret said, "Despite my selfless, tireless recruiting over the summer, no one has signed up to serve as secretary of the Primm Academy PTA. I certainly hope it's not because of what happened to last year's secretary . . ."

Holly wondered, *What happened to last year's secretary?*

"I'm sure she's perfectly happy in Southern Lakes," Mary-Margaret added, with just a tinge of pity in her voice. "And don't let anyone tell you she was banished from the Village of Primm. It wasn't banishment. It wasn't! She wasn't banished. So don't say *banished.* Her grass was simply greener on the other side of the fence. That's all. She wasn't banished. So don't say it. Banished. That's what you don't want to say. Anyway. Will *you* be the next Primm Academy PTA secretary?" She pointed to a mom in the crowd and then pointed to another. "Will you?" Pulling the microphone to her lips, she lowered her voice an octave. *"Ask not what Primm can do for you. Ask what you can do—"*

ZZZPT! From the microphone came a *RurrrrRing!*

"Whoo! What was that? Can everyone hear me?" Mary-Margaret scratched the top of the microphone. "Oh. Ha! Ha! Okay, it's still on. Thank you." She looked to her left. "Where's Principal Hayes?" She scanned the room. "Did he leave? Is he here? Because this microphone . . . did everyone hear my last announcement? I need a secretary. I need someone by my side, each and every day to help *me* help *you*." She pointed to someone in the front row. "You. With the glitter notebook. What's your name? You can be my secretary. Do you like glitter? Because I like glitter."

ZZZPT! RurrrrRing!

"Ahhhhhhhh! *Ouch.* Gosh. That hurt my ears." She extended her lower lip to pout. "Can someone help me with this microphone? It doesn't seem to be working all of a sudden."

Holly turned to scan the back of the room for a tech person. Was someone messing with her microphone? Being silenced would drive someone like Mary-Margaret nuts: a fate worse than death—or banishment from the village, since that seemed to be a concern around here.

ZZZPT! RurrrrRing!

"Hello?" Tap, tap, tap. "But . . . I don't understand," Mary-Margaret whined. "What's wrong with the microphone?" Tap, tap, tap. "Hello? Are you there, crowd? It's me, Mary-Margaret."

4

During the break

A quick break in the New Parent Orientation meant Holly had a chance to slip out and get home to Jack and Ella and relax. Holly held tight to her coffee, slipping deftly through the crowd of moms and toward a side door. She wished she could render herself invisible. She pushed a hip into the exit door's silver exit bar—*weeeoooweeeoooweeeooo!*—triggering the alarm.

From across the room came a loud "Stop!" Mary-Margaret rolled onto her tippy-toes and began snapping her fingers.

Weeeoooweeeoooweeeooo!

"Stop that mom!" She rushed through the crowd toward Holly as everyone turned to look. "She's trying to escape!"

"Escape?" Holly shook her head at a nearby mom. "I'm not trying to escape. Sorry, everyone!" She had to holler to be heard above the alarm. "I didn't mean to—" She pulled at the exit bar. "I wasn't trying to—I was just—" *Weeeoooweeeoooweeeooo.* "I can't make it stop."

"Coffee mom!" Mary-Margaret picked up the pace and began running across the auditorium. "You! You with the yellow shirt!" *Weeeoooweeeoooweeeooo.* She crossed the entire length of the room in seconds flat.

Holly threw her arms up—then lowered them. What was she doing? Hands up? She wasn't under arrest. *Weeeoooweeeoooweeeooo.* "I thought it was an exit."

Weeeoooweeeoooweeeooo.

"Why are you trying to escape?" Mary-Margaret grabbed the exit bar—*weeoo*—yanked it shut. Alarm stopped. "Goodness." Mary-Margaret wiped her brow. "You need to switch to decaf." She swung around to face the crowd with arms extended to reassure them. "Everyone settle down. I got this." She returned to Holly. "You're not from around here, are you?"

Holly started to say, "I live on Petunia Lane," but Mary-Margaret interrupted her after the word *Petunia* and said, "You can't leave now. You haven't volunteered for anything."

In script writing, if one character interrupted another character, the first character's dialogue ended with a space followed by two hyphens.

```
                    HOLLY

     I live on Petunia --

                MARY-MARGARET

     You can't leave now. You haven't
     volunteered for anything.
```

But Holly suspected something else was going on with this conversation. Mary-Margaret hadn't interrupted her; she had flat-out ignored her. She didn't give one hoot that Holly lived on Petunia Lane. Forget the two hyphens; what Mary-Margaret did was gloss over all Holly's words—practically her entire sentence. Holly might as well omit all her words and just leave the hyphens. Maybe add a hyphen. And some punctuation marks.

Like this: "---."

Or this: "---?"

And this: "---!"

"Do you collect Box Tops?" Mary-Margaret tapped her foot. "We need a Box Tops Mom."

Holly wondered, *Why the panic? Why the pressure to volunteer?* Couldn't Holly do this another day? No offense to Mary-Margaret, but Holly had only lived in Primm a few days. She wasn't used to jumping right in. She thought she'd take a month or two to unpack, settle in. And besides, with Ella starting kindergarten, Holly needed to find a job. It would be foolish to commit to anything right now. And truthfully? The high-pressure sales tactics triggered something in Holly: fight or flight. Holly chose flight.

Holly told Mary-Margaret she had to get home, but it came across like this: "---."

"I think you're brave for wearing yellow to a pink event." Mary-Margaret pointed to the *PRIMM* on Holly's shirt. "I love that! It says you're confident. Secure. You don't care what people think. I admire that. I'm drawn to secure people, and secure people are drawn to me."

Mary-Margaret grabbed a pink PRIMM T-shirt from a nearby table. It was exactly like the one Holly was wearing, except pink. "Here." She pushed it toward Holly. "I assume Penelope's already recruited you to play for Team Buttercream? Oh, but you should know: colors matter on and off the F.U. Frisbee field. You don't have to play for the Pink Erasers to wear pink to a school event. We're women. We should support one another. What's your name?"

"---."

"Well, I support you, Polly."

"---."

"*Molly.* Sorry." Mary-Margaret moved quickly to a nearby table to grab a few clipboards. "Here. Sign the Anything and Everything clipboard. No, wait." She put the Anything & Everything clipboard down to pick up another. "Sign the Available on Short Notice clipboard. Volunteer for something, and I'll forgive you for wearing a confrontational shirt to a PTA meeting. You know you practically declared *war*, don't you?"

"---."

Holly had told her no, she didn't realize she was declaring war at a PTA meeting, but Mary-Margaret ignored her. *Who is this woman? Is she a narcissist? Is she that self-absorbed?* Holly had met people like her. She was the guy who'd take you out to dinner at a sports bar so he could cop a glance at the game on the TV screen above your head while you tried to hold a meaningful conversation with him. *Uh-huh. Uh-huh. Yup, yup,* he'd say. She was the boss who'd call you into her office to ask your opinion about something but then check email while you were talking. Politicians were the worst. Shake their hand at a political rally—they smiled and nodded and then moved on to the next person in line. You could prepare what you were going to say to someone like that, but when it was your turn to speak, they glossed right over you. Like you weren't even there. The world was full of people like Mary-Margaret.

"So you're new here?" Mary-Margaret offered Holly the clipboard. "Volunteering is a great way to meet other moms. These clipboards are like online dating sites. You simply sign up, and then *presto!* Instant friends."

"---."

"Never mind. Don't sign," said Mary-Margaret. "Because *I'll* write your name on the clipboards. I'll pick something extra, extra special."

Holly started to walk away, but Mary-Margaret followed her.

"Do you like to volunteer before school, during school, after school, in the evenings, or on the weekends? Because the PTA accommodates all schedules. At-home moms, at-work moms, at-home working moms, at-work homing moms . . . whatever you are. Whoever you are. We're here to help *you* help *us*."

The conversation felt like Holly was on social media. Everything was *talk, talk, talk,* but no one was listening. Mary-Margaret kept uploading post after post after post—and couldn't care less if Holly was an authentic part of the conversation.

Penelope Pratt waltzed over. "How are you, Holly?" Penelope placed a hand on Holly's arm. "Settled in?"

Holly hated that question. Of course she wasn't settled in—because she didn't have any storage. Holly didn't know how she'd missed that little detail when they were looking at houses. All she saw was Collette's bright-white porch with that wooden aqua-blue initial hanging from the front door knocker on a beautiful silk ribbon, and she thought, *I want that.* Well, not that exactly—not that initial. Holly wanted her own swirly initial on a chunky silk ribbon hanging from a door knocker on a bright-white porch. And she wanted a coir welcome mat with a trellis motif like Collette's. And she wanted a pair of polka-dotted red rubber boots like Collette's, to sit next to that beautiful welcome mat. Porches ruled the world of first impressions. They set the tone for what came next. Holly had even made a mental note to tuck fresh white daisies into the red rubber boots once she found a pair—she'd wanted everything Collette had. She still wanted everything Collette had. Holly made a silent note never to look at Pinterest again. Or Facebook. Or Instagram. Or Houzz. Or whatever else came next.

"If you need any help with decorating or home organization," Penelope offered, "Feathered Nest has many services for homeowners. I sell real estate, but I'm also a professional home organizer." Pointed to her shirt. "Think hearth and home? Think yellow."

"Thank you, Penelope. But I think I'm good. I just need a few more days. To unpack." Unpack everything. Paint. Hang drapes. Hang window blinds. Maybe get a new couch. Maybe then she'd find time to label the sections of her utensil drawer like Collette had: *Knife. Fork. Spoon.*

Penelope's coal-black hair was (yet again) pulled into a loose bun at the nape of her neck, and she was wearing yellow. How did *she* get away with wearing yellow to a pink event? And why was pink a school color? Pink wasn't one of the academy's colors. The academy colors were gold, black, and white. If anything, it was Penelope who looked most like a Primm Academy Honeybee with her coal-black hair and pale-yellow attire—not Mary-Margaret.

"What Penelope is trying to say is . . . moms tend to take sides," Mary-Margaret explained. "In Frisbee and in life. Some moms focus their energies on their homes, others on school . . . Gym Moms versus Sports Moms—similar in concept, but in reality, the two can be quite different."

"Holly, you have my card. Excuse me," Penelope said, taking her leave.

Penelope's skillful exit was so clean and so swift Holly decided she'd try it. Chin up, Holly touched Mary-Margaret's arm, excused herself, then marched toward the door at the other end of the room. But Mary-Margaret stopped her, pulling her back into a web of excessive blather.

"Sign your name. Somewhere. Anywhere. Please. That's all I ask," Mary-Margaret said, tossing Available on Short Notice onto the table, grabbing Miscellaneous Tidbits, and pushing it toward Holly. "Pick anything. Doesn't matter. The break is almost over, and I'm needed at the podium. Hurry. Sign up, and then I'll leave you alone. Volunteer. Volunteer! *Volunteer!*"

Fine!

Holly snatched the clipboard. Signed her name. Handed it back.

"Oh. My. Gosh." Nose down in the clipboard, Mary-Margaret opened her eyes wide. "You signed up to send in *napkins* for the next kindergarten class party? *That's it? Nothing else?*" She looked at Holly. "That's totally lame. A pack of napkins weighs like, what? An ounce? It's not even heavy or troublesome for your child to lug into school. You simply chuck it into their backpack the morning of the Presidents' Day Picnic. *Whoopee!* On Presidents' Day? My child? In addition to carrying a backpack, a laptop, and a cello, my child will lug a gallon of apple juice and a veggie tray to school for her country. Meanwhile, you think you're outsmarting everyone. You think you're the only one to figure out the napkin strategy? Even the teachers know about that. Napkin Moms are everywhere. Napkin Moms smile and chitchat during school functions, proud their yellow and black napkins are on the spelling bee table; then you know what they do? They go home and let the teachers and all the other moms do the real work." She jerked her chin toward Holly's coffee. "Your type usually shows up hugging a cup of coffee. You know what I always say? Moms who sip on mocha frappa soon head home to take a nap-a."

"---."

"Don't walk away from me." Mary-Margaret grabbed Holly by the arm. "I'm not done explaining."

The auditorium was spacious, but there were pockets of moms gathered everywhere. Mary-Margaret must have sensed nearby moms were listening, because she changed her demeanor, clearing her throat to speak more softly. "At *Primm*, sending in napkins is not volunteering. Finding nut-free, sugar-free, egg-free, gluten-free, free-range pumpkin bread recipes to bake for the Pilgrims and Native Americans Festival when your child isn't even allergic—*that* is volunteering. Handling the paint table in a classroom filled with kindergarteners making fingerprint pictures of themselves on oyster shells is volunteering."

Mary-Margaret led Holly to a nearby row of seats. Presumably so no one would hear them. "Did you know," Mary-Margaret said, "that during Johnny Appleseed Week, I'll give up three afternoons of my life visiting each and every second-grade math class with a wagon filled with apples that I personally handpicked with them during the field trip to Pip's Mountain? The kids always vote on the best-tasting apple. Granny Smith? Always a close second, but in the end, too sour. Fuji? Never makes the list. And yet, there I am. Year after year, producing a ginormous graph chart of second-grade apple preferences—when we all know Red Delicious will win. For parent-teacher conferences in

November? I'll stay up all night scooping out cantaloupes and muskmelons with a baller so I can fill an intricately carved watermelon for the refreshment table. You know why I do that? To serve others. So when you leave your teacher conference in tears because your child needs remedial help in reading, I can say, 'Here. Here's a fruit cup.'

"And every October, and then again in May, I'll set up sixty science fair projects in the cafeteria before the four p.m. start of the science fair. You know how messy that is? *Volcanoes?* Smelly, moldy bread experiments?"

"---."

Mary-Margaret ignored the reason Holly gave for not volunteering and instead added, "The year I was chair of the science fair? I dropped a lizard cage, and the screen popped off. Hundreds of crickets escaped down the hallway jumping for their lives. Have you ever picked up a Chinese green water dragon with your bare hands? Well, I have. And I was in four-inch heels. Jimmy Choos. I could have broken my ankle." She led Holly to believe a tear was about to fall from the outer edge of her left eye. "But that's what I do. I can't help it. I'm dedicated." Mary-Margaret dabbed at said tear with the tip of her finger. "I love my children."

Seriously? Holly rolled her eyes, folded both arms across her chest. "---."

"I'm sure you love your child too." Mary-Margaret's voice wandered off a bit, like she didn't quite mean what she just said.

I'm done. Holly surveyed the room. *Anything. I'll say anything—just get me outa here.*

"---."

"Yes, I have given a lot to Primm Academy," Mary-Margaret agreed. "So polite of you to notice. Now will you please sit back down? The break's almost over, and I still have announcements to make. I haven't found anyone to serve as my secretary. Yet. Now, please, Polly," Mary-Margaret urged. "Sit down."

"---."

"Holly. Fine. Whatever." Mary-Margaret set the clipboard on the table as a woman at the podium announced the ten-minute break was over and invited the room of mothers to take their seats. "But hear this." Mary-Margaret leaned in, inches from poking her finger into Holly's chest above the word *PRIMM*. "You're either a School-Volunteer Mom or you're not." Mary-Margaret took a step back to regard Holly. "What kind of a mother *are* you?"

Holly squirmed. A bit. Okay, a lot.

"And don't tell me you're too tired or too busy to serve our beloved community because I'm tired, too, you know," Mary-Margaret added. "Imagine being *me* for a day. Me, Mary-Margaret St. James. I'm the president of the Primm Academy PTA. Do you know how much pressure that is? I have to run this place. But more than that, I have to manage all of the moms. Moms! That's like, next to impossible because moms run everything. They run companies, their households, their husbands, their children. Do you have any idea how hard it is to micromanage the micromanagers?"

Mary-Margaret returned to the podium to address excuses moms gave to avoid volunteering. "If you have to work? We have opportunities that fit your schedule. Can't find a babysitter? Then bring the kids. Feel you've already paid your dues? Well, haven't we all!"

Holly managed to take a seat on the far side of the auditorium, away from the other moms and next to the main entrance—next to the door that was propped open—the door *without* the security alarm.

"Because the truth is," Mary-Margaret told the crowd, "we can't build a future for our kids in a school where only twenty percent of the moms do all the work."

Holly relaxed her back, slithered down her seat until her knees touched the floor and her head disappeared from view. On the floor now, she took to her hands and knees, crawling her way down the row of empty seats, up a side aisle, and toward the open door. As she crawled, she cupped her vanilla hazelnut in one hand, making sure it didn't spill.

"Eventually, that semitruck will arrive with six hundred pounds of cookie dough, and someone's gotta unload it onto the pallets," Mary-Margaret was saying, "organize it by flavor, match it to the order forms, and deliver it to the children in their classrooms. I can't be expected to do it all by myself. Not me, not Mary-Margaret. Our children depend on us. Us. That word is plural. Not singular."

Hidden from Mary-Margaret's view, Holly scurried on all fours like an overly exuberant baby just learning to crawl.

"No one can do everything," Mary-Margaret reminded everyone. "That's why everyone—everyone should do *something*."

With a quick turn to the right, Holly crawled past the threshold of the door and arrived in the foyer outside the auditorium. She'd made it. She was in the lobby. *Free! Free at last!*

"PTA dues may be *tax* exempt." Mary-Margaret was still talking. "But moms are not *work* exempt."

Holly rose to her feet on the tightly woven gray floor mat, standing on the words *Primm Academy.* She brushed any dirt off her knees, then leaned back to take a long, slow swig of coffee. *"Psst!"* A handful of moms signaled her, silently applauding her escape. One mom flashed a spiral notebook, scoring Holly's exit a perfect 10.

Holly waved, feeling like a celebrity, proud of her death-defying escape from Mary-Margaret's PTA meeting. It was a bold move, but someone had to do it. Just as she was about to give her new fan club an enthusiastic two thumbs-up, Holly heard Mary-Margaret at the podium say, "Because let's be honest. It's not fair that some moms let other moms do all the work. Truthfully? It's a bit selfish, don't you think?"

Great. Now I feel like a jerk.

And then, from the podium: "Wait a minute. Where's Polly? The mom in yellow? She didn't leave, did she? I sure hope not. My meeting's not over yet."

5

Saturday

Cable guy was young. Midtwenties probably. Short, spiky brown hair, squat in stature. Seemed nice. "Twelve Petunia Lane? Install for Banks?" He passed Holly a business card from Primm Cable.

"That's me." Holly swung open the front door. "Thanks for coming out on a Saturday."

She led him down the hall toward the kitchen, which overlooked the family room, where Struggle stood where Struggle always stood—beside Ella. Struggle was so focused on the *My Little Pony* horse Ella was playing with she didn't notice the strange man in their house. Some watchdog. Should've gotten a German shepherd.

Holly told the cable guy, "That's a new TV, and if I don't get the Hub network, I can't get *My Little Pony*, and if I can't get *My Little Pony* . . ." She tipped her head toward Ella.

"I have a loose tooth," Ella told him, wiggling the one on her bottom right.

"Cool." He gave Ella a thumbs-up. Tossed a treat from his pocket toward Struggle. To Holly, he said, "You know the Hub network is owned by Hasbro." The expression on his face was one of grave concern. "The toy company. You do know that, don't you?"

"Um. No? No, I didn't know that." Holly scratched at a spot behind her ear. "What's wrong with Hasbro?" *There's so much to keep track of when you're a mom. BPA-free containers, safety recalls, deer ticks.* "Oh!" She snapped her fingers. "Toys made in China. Melamine! Is that it? No? Hmm . . ." She snapped her fingers again. "Trade deficits!"

"You're funny." He set his cable bag down, strapped on his tool belt. "Cable is moving away from creator-driven entertainment and toward company-owned networks."

"Oh, dear Lord, no." Holly covered her mouth with both hands, feigned concern, then fessed up. "Sorry." She winced. "I went to film school, but I have no idea what you're talking about. Is Hasbro a front for organized crime or something? Because all I want in this world right now is to sit my daughter in front of the TV so I can unpack. School starts Tuesday. I need the TV—I don't have a babysitter. The only person I know in Primm is Penelope Pratt, and I doubt she babysits."

"My name's Caleb." He shook Holly's hand. "Now you know two people. But I don't babysit, sorry. Where'd you go to film school?"

"Northwestern."

"American Film Institute." He shrugged. "But I had to drop out because I ran out of money. What have you done?"

"Beg your pardon?" Holly knew where this was going. He wanted to know if she'd produced anything he'd seen. Well, guess what: she hadn't. Ella was the only meaningful thing she'd done with her life. "Oh, I. Um. Actually, I . . . ," Holly stuttered, wishing she knew how to answer his question.

"The Wilhelm Klaus Three-Minute Film Festival is coming to Primm in October." He pointed a pair of pliers at her. "You should go. Winner gets ten thousand dollars. Do you submit your work to festivals?"

"Me? Um. No. Not lately." She walked to the couch to pull one of Ella's pink T-shirts from a pile of laundry to fold it. "I've been meaning to, but . . ."

"Oh. But you should still go." Caleb twisted something into something. "You can watch. They always need people to watch."

Before she could respond, Jack ran down the stairs, clearing the steps in rapid succession. Thump, thump, thump. "Holly. Ready to start?" He tapped his watch, noticing Caleb reaching behind the TV. "Oh, hey. How's the cable coming? Any ponies yet?" He checked his watch again. All this watch checking. "Doesn't it start in a few minutes?"

"No ponies, Daddy," Ella whined. "No Fluttershy, no Rainbow Dash, no—"

"Nothing yet, Jack." Holly tossed the folded T-shirt onto the pile. "We're working on it."

It was Saturday, and Jack was working. Lately, Jack worked every day. When he couldn't, he'd get absolutely antsy and want whatever it was that was keeping him from work to hurry up and go away. He had moved to Primm to start work in a new office *with Bethanny* a month before Holly and Ella arrived. Holly knew what was going to happen: he'd unload a few more boxes, then skip off to work again, and Holly'd have to face the daunting task of finishing the entire unpack by herself. She loved her husband. She also *knew* her husband.

"No Applejack, no Pinkie Pie . . ." Ella counted on her fingers.

"Ella, honey, shhh. We're almost done." Holly touched Ella's sweet cheeks. "She's exhausted," Holly explained to Caleb, immediately wondering why she cared what the cable guy thought.

"Holly?" Jack tapped his watch again. "Boxes. Garage. Can we get started? I'm meeting Bethanny at the office in two hours."

Bethanny. Holly was so sick of hearing that name. "Go ahead and get started," she told Jack, feeling agitated all of a sudden by the thought of his advancing his career while she moved further and further from the person she once was. Wilhelm Klaus Three-Minute Film Festival? Apparently, it was something she should *watch*.

Holly folded her arms across her chest. She wasn't looking at Jack, so she wasn't surprised when he asked, "What's the matter with you?"

"Nothing's the matter with me."

They hadn't been connecting lately. Maybe it was the stress of the move, Jack's new job, and Ella starting kindergarten. Or maybe it was the stress of using their savings for a down payment on an eighteen-hundred-square-foot expanded cape with no storage and no place to unpack anything except onto another pile that sat on the floor.

"Oh, Jack," Holly remembered, "there's an envelope on the counter for you. Someone hand delivered it to the house yesterday." She checked the expression on his face. "Sorry," she added. "I forgot to tell you."

He looked concerned. Walked immediately to the kitchen to retrieve the envelope.

"Okay. I think we're in business." Caleb pointed the remote, and the Hub network flashed onto the screen.

"Yay! Pinkie Piiiiie!" Ella rang out, taking her seat on the floor in front of the TV.

Holly grabbed Ella's sports cup from the counter beside Jack. The moment she arrived beside him, he shoved the envelope into his pocket.

"Why'd you do that?" she asked, trying to read the look on his face.

"What? Oh, that." He shrugged. "That's nothing." Tucked both hands in his pockets. "Work stuff."

"Work stuff?" said Holly. "Seems pretty top secret to me."

"Well, it's not." Jack averted his gaze, away from the inquisitive look on Holly's face.

"Work shouldn't be a secret." Holly turned her back on Jack, returning to the family room to give Ella her sports cup. *What are you hiding, Jack?*

"She still drinks from a sippy cup?" Caleb asked.

Holly's back stiffened. Who was this guy? "It's not a sippy cup," she pointed out. "It's a sports cup."

Caleb swung his gaze toward Jack. "I heard sippy cups cause tooth decay and speech delays."

"Holly?" In Jack's voice, Holly heard the sound of grave concern. "Did you know about this?"

"Speech delays? From a cup?" She waved them both off. "Give me a break."

Jack was always saying Holly didn't push Ella enough, that she didn't "guide" her toward achieving milestones according to a set schedule. But she was a *child*, for crying out loud. Not a product scheduled for manufacture.

"What's a speech delay?" Ella looked up at Holly.

"Nothing, sweetie." Holly knelt down to give Ella a kiss on the lips. They were so thin, so sweet, and her breath still smelled like toothpaste. Holly was going to miss that little tooth when it fell out.

She handed Ella the sports cup as Ella reached up to squeeze Holly's cheeks and get right up close to say, "Pinkie Pie keeps her pony friends smiling allllll day."

Holly closed her eyes. Felt a little sting in her nose as she tried not to cry. Ella started kindergarten in a few days. *Kindergarten.*

"My sister's a speech therapist and won't let any of her kids drink with a sippy cup past the age of two," Caleb told Jack. "And she has five kids."

"Five kids? Wow." Jack raised his eyebrows.

Holly could tell he was impressed with Caleb's sister for having five kids. But Caleb's sister could be a horrible mother—how would Jack know? He'd never met Caleb's sister. And five kids didn't make her the expert on *their* child. "Well, I only have one child, Caleb, but I'm not willing to ruin my carpets because someone else decides Ella should give up her sports cup."

"Holly." Jack was taken aback. "Why are you so defensive?"

"I'm not defensive." Holly folded her arms across her chest. Both Jack and Caleb were staring at Holly, that odd look men got. "*Fine.*" She moved focus from Jack to Caleb. "Ella still sucks her thumb."

"No, I don't," Ella said, which was a total fib.

"I think Caleb's got a point." Jack began wringing his hands together. That "Jack" thing Jack always did. "She probably has a loose tooth because she sucks her thumb *and* drinks from a sippy cup. We should eliminate both. Go cold turkey."

"Her loose tooth started when she fell on the playground, Jack. The dentist never said anything about her thumb causing her teeth to fall out ahead of schedule."

"I still think we should stop the sippy cup," Jack said. But by *we* he meant *her*, Holly, because she was the one home with Ella all day while he was at work. "And the thumb," he added, getting fidgety. "We need to stop that too."

"But it's not a sippy cup," Holly insisted. "It's a *sports* cup. Sippy cups are plastic and have butterflies and Elmo on them. Her sports cup is aluminum. It has a soccer ball on it." Neither of them responded. "Soccer is for older kids. Soccer is a sport. So this is a sports cup. For older kids." Right? And besides, they just moved. Less than a week ago. Force Ella to give up her thumb? Make her switch to drinking glasses in the middle of all of this chaos and moving debris? That was *insane*. Why would Holly take that on? "I'm kind of busy right now, Jack."

"Doing what?"

"*Excuse me?* Look the flip around, Jack. We just moved everything we own across the country."

"Well, don't get mad at me." He scowled. "I'm just worried about her speech delay."

"She doesn't have a speech delay!"

"But she might get one"—Jack lifted an eyebrow—"if you keep giving her sippy cups."

Holly glared at Caleb. "How are you doing with our hookup? Almost finished?"

"I don't know why you're so upset about this," Jack said. "This isn't about *you*. It's about our daughter."

"Well, no spit, Sherlock. I know it's about our daughter."

"Did you just say *spit*?" Caleb asked, as the hint of a smile spread across his face.

"Actually, yes. I did say *spit*." *Mutha fricker had better not be laughing at me.* Jack was checking his watch again. Holly graduated film school but had never submitted three minutes of anything to anyone. "I'm a mom, Caleb. I don't say bad words." At least, not out loud.

The phone rang, and Holly snatched it off an end table. "Hello?" She refused to look at either Caleb or Jack.

"I need a gift for my casino host." It was Greta, and their connection was bad, making it sound like she was talking from the bottom of a bucket. "He comped me three nights, with meals, and tickets to Cirque du Soleil. I'm thinking necktie."

"Necktie?" Holly headed toward the kitchen, pressing a finger in her ear. "Don't buy your casino host a gift, Mom. You shouldn't even have a casino host." Not this again. She leaned against the oven, hoping Jack wasn't listening. "Seriously, Mom? He's only giving you things so you'll gamble."

"I think he likes me."

"Where are you? Are you calling from the casino? You need to go home. Right now. Call your sponsor." Holly tucked her head to whisper: "Because I'm not bailing you out this time, Mom. I'm not." Jack *flipped* the last time they bailed her out.

"Would wine make a better gift?"

"Mom, no. Please stop. This is crazy talk."

"I've never actually seen him wear a necktie, and he's always gifting me with bottles. And nooooo, before you go jumping on my head and start gnawing on my skull like a rabid squirrel, I don't drink the wine he gives me," Greta said. "I give the wine to Atticus, the maintenance man in my apartment complex. Hush money. He's letting me keep a stray cat without paying a pet deposit."

"Mom."

"Red or white? Come to think of it, I'd rather see Céline Dion. Reminds me of the time I—remember the wig?"

"Seriously, Mom? You're going there with me?" Jack was acting secretive, boxes to unpack, cable wasn't hooked up properly, they still needed curtains in the front living room window . . .

"Never mind, Holly. Forget I said anything." Greta lowered her voice. "Because you know what I'm talking about."

Holly stayed quiet rather than engage.

Greta continued, "I never understood why you were so embarrassed. It was just a wig! Big deal. It was a slumber party . . . I was a fun mom! Most kids would *kill* to have a fun mom at their slumber party."

"You were drunk, Mom." Why did she always bring stuff like this up?

"Maybe I should see Cirque du Soleil. Reminds me of that high school musical you were in. What was that called? The one with the jugglers and Hula-Hoops?"

"*Pippin.* And thanks for reminding me—now I can't get that 'Magic to Do' song out of my head. I was the follow spot operator, remember? I'd come home traumatized because I had to shine a light on the guy who stood me up for prom." Leaning against the oven, Holly looked out across the kitchen to watch Ella playing with her *My Little Pony* setup in the family room. "Why am I always reminded of obscure things from my past when you call?"

"Because I'm your mom. I'm a portal to your childhood."

"Don't say that."

"Why not?"

"Because if I'm the portal to Ella's childhood, then every little thing I do between now and the time she's an adult will either enhance or spoil the portal. I do something good? Portal's good: Ella looks back with fond memories of her childhood. I do something bad? Portal's bad. No fond memories. Just a mom who kept screwing up." Holly blew out a long, slow exhale. "Like spray-painting the walls of a subway station. It's either art—or graffiti. Either way, it's hard to scrub off."

"Why would you want to scrub it off?"

"Forget it, Mom. You wouldn't understand."

"Something bad's about to happen. Isn't it?"

"What? No." Holly looked past the mess in her kitchen toward Jack playing with Ella in the other room. Since when did Jack get G-Class visitors? There was something odd about the man from the vineyard: *Tell Jack I'm getting anxious.* Oh? Anxious? About what?

"You're worried about Ella's first day of kindergarten. Aren't you?"

"Me? No. Why? Should I be?"

"Absolutely. A thousand things could go wrong."

Like making a horrible first impression at New Parent Orientation? "What kind of a mother *are* you?" Mary-Margaret had asked.

"I have to go." Holly moved to hang up the phone. "I love you, Greta Vogel—you old bird." Holly called her mom by her full name as a way of saying *I love you.* (*Vogel*: German for *bird.*) Just something they did.

"Graffiti is art, Holly!"

Of course it is, Mom.

After they hung up, Holly showed Caleb the front door.

"I'll bring a flyer by the house," he offered. "You should enter the Wilhelm Klaus Film Festival. Get back into it."

"Who says I'm not into it? I've kept up with it." Did she sound as defensive as she felt? And why was he looking at her that way? "I do plenty with film." Poker face. More like a bald-faced lie. She hadn't done squat with her film career since graduating college. Except, maybe, *watch.*

"Wilhelm Klaus." Caleb passed an invoice to Holly. "In Primm. That's *huge.*" Both hands in the air—for emphasis. *"Huge."*

Wilhelm Klaus? In Primm?

"Think about it," said Caleb.

And Holly had nothing. No demo, no script, no *logline.* Nothing. But so what? *Life gets busy—that's all.* And Holly was a mom. Ella was her first priority. So what if years of her life were lost to laundry, dishes, and picking up toys? She loved Ella. "You don't know a thing about me," she told him.

"I think I do." There was something tender but amiss in the way his eyes searched hers: an unspoken understanding, but also a challenge. Something. He took his leave, out Holly's front door, across the porch that fared better under Collette. Holly'd done nothing with Collette's porch despite plans to lay a welcome mat the moment she arrived in Primm. Maybe she sucked at beginnings. Maybe Holly's act one lagged a bit.

CAST LIST

HOLLY BANKS . . . . . . film school grad

CALEB THE CABLE GUY . . . . . . film school dropout

What'd he know? He was probably a gamer. A YouTuber. Something. Probably lived in a basement. Not bothering to uncross her arms, Holly gave a swift kick to close the front door, separating herself from Caleb, from the reminder of Collette, and from the Village of Primm beyond her front porch. The Village of Primm, no doubt, was waiting to welcome her with open arms. At least, Holly hoped it was. Mary-Margaret had singled her out at New Parent Orientation. Penelope had thrown her under the bus by telling her to wear yellow. "Get out while you still can," Penelope had warned. Penelope—the woman who recruited Holly to live in Primm. Holly assumed Ella would feel welcome in kindergarten, but would *Holly* feel welcome in Primm? From the doorway of her new home on Petunia Lane, Holly grew increasingly unsettled. About Jack. About Bethanny. About the G-Class visitor. His envelope. Wilhelm Klaus.

Maybe Greta was right. Maybe something bad was about to happen. Something really, really dreadful. Like a tornado. Or a house landing on a witch. *There's no place like home. Right?*

6

Monday, Labor Day

Topiaries were everywhere. On porches. In shop windows. Flanking entry doorways to smart cafés. Persnickety little plants. Holly wondered if other plants admired them. Or made fun of them. Seemed a cruel thing to do to a plant: shape it into something it would never become were it left to its own devices.

Bicyclists filled the bike lane to the right of Holly's red Suburban. She suspected that what she and Ella were seeing were tourists making use of the fleet of Tiffany blue cruiser bikes Penelope said were available for rent from Papyrus, Parchment & Paper, the indie bookseller in town. Tiffany blue cruiser bikes to borrow. Imagine! Holly suspected the tourists came for the Topiary Park but stayed for the charm.

Up ahead of them, a trolley car slowed to a stop beside a gas lamppost and a triple-sphere topiary that stood six feet in height in a stately black urn. An elderly gentleman with a book in the crook of his arm and a blue Great Dane beside him raised two fingers to signal the trolley driver. Holly's eyes shifted from the open-air trolley's copper railings and intricate wood paneling to the rare steely-blue coat on the dog—a color no other breed could boast. The only way to get a blue Great Dane was to breed two Great Danes that both carried the recessive blue gene—very rare. The elderly gentleman looked right at Holly and tipped his hat, presumably to acknowledge her patience as the trolley stopped to let him board. Holly nodded, unaware of the clout he held in the village, unaware of the muck they'd both find themselves in by week's end. The old man nodded back, bending first to lift an old typewriter from the bench beside him. From what Holly could see, the typewriter was antique, highly ornate, with what appeared to be enameled roses on the body of the typewriter above the keys. Probably quite valuable.

They followed the trolley to the renovated train station in the trolley lot next to the Topiary Park but missed the opportunity to introduce themselves to the man and his rare blue Great Dane. Ella held Holly's hand, swinging it as they strolled the length of a cobblestone sidewalk beside an eight-foot-tall wrought iron fence along the front entrance to the Topiary Park. Consumed by a thick drape of creeping ivy, the fence obscured the park beyond it, but as they reached the enormous entry gate, the ivy was cut away, exposing a white enamel oval sign edged with black cast-iron scrollwork and carved with ornate black calligraphy: **Village of Primm Topiary Park.** Chiseled into a limestone mantel at the top of the archway above them were the words *Cnaeus Matius Calvinus*. Holly didn't know what that meant but loved the implied majesty.

Ella reached out to touch a bean-like seedpod hanging from the wisteria. "Don't touch that," Holly warned, wondering why anyone would grow wisteria within reach of children. "Every part of the wisteria plant is poisonous." The wisteria reminded Holly of the television series *Desperate Housewives*. When she was in film school, she made a replica of that neighborhood in prop class. The neighborhood was an actual set at Universal Studios Hollywood named

Colonial Street. *Leave It to Beaver*, *Buffy the Vampire Slayer*, *The 'Burbs* . . . they were all shot there. So were others. Film crews had been modifying that street for years.

Holly shielded her eyes to look up at the sky. Above them, wispy, pillowy clouds appeared sleepy, like they were taking naps across a sky the color of Crayola's parakeet blue.

Next to a large kiosk map of the Topiary Park sat a girl who looked to be about sixteen, clearly bored with her job watching tourists ogle and point at high-maintenance bushes. When she rose from her chair beneath a cluster of spiral-cut trees to take Holly's money, Holly pointed to a poster of what appeared to be a ginormous peacock made entirely of plants. "Is that the famous peacock?" Holly asked. "And can you tell me where to find him?"

"He's a she," the girl said, snapping her gum, handing Holly her receipt. "Her name's Plume."

"Oh, yes. Quite right. But then, Plume isn't a peacock." Holly squeezed Ella's hand to make sure she was paying attention. "If Plume's a girl, then Plume's a peahen. Peacocks are boys."

The girl opened a folded map to point to a drawing of the grounds just as Holly was spotting a few itty-bitty words at the bottom of her receipt: *The Village of Primm Topiary Park, a limited liability company incorporated in the British Virgin Islands.*

"The British Virgin Islands?" Holly jerked her head back. "That's nowhere near Primm. That's not even in the United States."

The girl shrugged. "Don't ask me. Ask Hopscotch."

"Hopscotch?"

"Are you a tourist? You're joking, right?" At first, the girl laughed, but when she realized Holly wasn't kidding, she stopped and dropped her jaw. "You don't know who Merchant Hopscotch is? Merchant Meek Hopscotch the Third? You must live under a *rock*. Are you from Southern Lakes?"

"No." Holly shot a glance at Ella. "We're from Boulder City."

"Ha!" The girl snorted. "Funny. Everyone knows who Merchant Hopscotch is. He goes by his middle name, Meek. He's old money. Owns everything. Lives on The Hill . . ." She folded her fingers into air quotes. "'The Hill' overlooking 'The Lawn,' two locations so important to the Village of Primm the word *the* is always capitalized." She pointed in the direction of Hopscotch Hill, an enclave of prominent historical homes positioned high on a hill above the village. Holly knew this neighborhood. If you googled *Village of Primm*, the homes that appeared on the Chamber of Commerce website were all Hopscotch homes. Holly knew because she'd stalked the website before moving here. It linked to another website Holly stalked, the Feathered Nest Realty site, where pictures of Holly's home when Collette owned it were marked with a blue ribbon for "award-winning interiors." Penelope lived on Hopscotch Hill. So did her cousin, Mary-Margaret St. James.

"If you do see Plume," the girl added, "don't worry about what's happening to her. She's insured."

"Something wrong?" Holly asked. Ella looked concerned.

"You'll see," she said.

Ella and Holly took their leave, wandering through maze after maze of carefully manicured boxwoods with tiny green leaves that swooped up, then down, curved left, curved right, forming endless rows of green. Some formed tightly shaped squares as large as six feet across, while others formed small spheres the size of soccer balls. Their path zigzagged, then opened into an endless labyrinth with holes in the hedges they stepped through to discover courtyards adorned with koi ponds, birdcages, and water fountains. They saw glass houses, a bird sanctuary—huge bird sanctuary—live musicians, and a woman drawing caricatures using a peacock feather as a quill.

"We need to bring Dad here, Ella. He'd love this."

"He's at work." Ella pulled a tight, tiny green leaf from a nearby boxwood.

"Maybe he'd like to come when he's not at work," Holly offered.

"He's always at work." Ella flicked the leaf.

Holly pulled out her iPhone, sending a swift text to Jack.

HOLLY: You sure you can't get off work to join us? It's Ella's last day of summer.

HOLLY: We're at the Topiary Park—the famed tourist attraction Penelope told us about. Remember? Tourism is the heartbeat of Primm, blah, blah, blah . . . Stimulates the local economy? Tax revenues? Hold on a sec. I'll drop a pin.

Holly dropped a pin. Sent it to Jack. *Swoooosh.*

She watched Ella for a moment, glints of sunlight in Ella's auburn hair. *Kindergarten.* Such a big girl. It hurt—like, physically hurt. The sadness Holly felt every time she remembered Ella wouldn't be home with her during the day: she'd be in kindergarten. The emotional pain was manifesting into something she felt on a physical level: a swelling in her heart, an aching in her bones. Holly had been thinking about her mom a lot this week. Holly was Ella's age when her parents split up. What Holly remembered from her first week of kindergarten was much different from what most people remembered. Holly didn't remember bright colors and happy songs. Holly remembered her mom crying at the kitchen sink.

"According to the map"—Holly spread it out in front of Ella—"at the entrance to the petting zoo stands Plume." Holly read the description. "'Plume's tail is a majestic array of Liberty Classic white snapdragons, white begonias, purple pigeonberry, sky-flower and golden dewdrop, blue lisianthus, fragrant verbena, English ivy, and others, including sweet viburnum.'" She kept reading. "'See list at bottom left for additional flowers.'"

Now seated at a small round table near a bank of windows in the park's tearoom, Ella leaned back in her chair, face to the ceiling, arms spread wide, lips puckering over and over again like the fish they'd seen in the koi pond outside the tearoom. Holly showed Ella Plume's picture. Plume stood with her tail feathers down, trailing behind her like the train on Kate Middleton's wedding gown, not up and spread fanlike like you'd expect. Plume was a noble peahen at rest, pausing to appraise surrounding topiaries, a giant among lesser plants.

"Says here she's twenty-five feet tall, forty feet long, and the widest point of her tail is at the end, where it spreads to a whopping twenty-four feet. Wow, Ella." Holly had to give it to Primm. No wonder neighboring towns couldn't keep up. "That's some bird."

Eventually, they finished their drinks—milk for Ella, hibiscus tea for Holly—then headed next door to the gift shop to inquire about the Feathered Nest Realty gift Penelope'd mentioned the day she paid a visit to their home on Petunia Lane. Entering the Topiary Park Gift Shoppe was like stepping inside an enchanted music box lined with peacock feathers—emerald greens, soul-piercing blues, Plume *everywhere*. On T-shirts, scarves, jewelry, umbrellas. The only thing missing from the gift shop was a prominently displayed picture book retelling the *Tales of Primm*, a certain beloved *peahen* adorning the cover. Surely, Primm was home to a children's book author hidden in a turret somewhere or in a dusty attic room above the village bookstore. Holly was a newcomer, but as far as she could tell, the topiaries across town paid tribute to Plume, linking the villagers to the Topiary Park, pointing the way to the blessed bird like tiny lines on a compass. Plume. Holly wondered, checking her map, *Where is this Plume?* Holly wanted to see Plume.

When Holly had told her mother she was getting a topiary plant as a housewarming gift from Penelope, Greta asked if she could name it. Holly thought Ella should name it, but she said fine. So without even seeing it, Greta named their topiary Anna Wintour, equating the care and keeping of topiary with the serving of an aloof fashion icon. Holly couldn't help but agree with Greta; the editor in chief of *Vogue* often did look like an elitist insect because she was always wearing those dark, bulbous sunglasses indoors and in dim light, giving her the distinct appearance of a fly, magnified. Holly had heard the compound eye of a fly was actually thousands of teeny tiny eyes, giving the fly a broad field of vision. Eyeballs and insects gave Holly the creeps. Eyeballs on insects? Holly shuddered just thinking about it. Topiaries, on the other hand, reminded her of *Edward Scissorhands*. Holly loved Tim Burton. Loved every film he'd ever created—wished she could crawl inside his brain and have a look around. She'd probably find crazy things like spools of thread and an opera singer. Maybe an octopus. Holly decided she'd renew her subscription to *Filmmaker Magazine* when she got home. To keep tabs on what Tim Burton was up to. And *Vogue*. She'd subscribe to that too. Why not? Wouldn't hurt to see what the elitist insect was hocking as fashion this season.

"I'm excited about our special gift from Penelope, Ella. Aren't you?" Holly squeezed Ella's hand, then presented the gift certificate Penelope had given her to the woman behind the counter.

"Oh, you must be the Banks family." The woman placed her hands in a position of prayer, elbows out, the way a woman working in a bird sanctuary would, as she escorted Holly and Ella to the picture window, where a round cloth-covered table sat. "You're the last of the new families to arrive." She swept her arm toward the waiting topiary. "Here you are. Your very own Village of Primm topiary."

There, in the middle of the Feathered Nest Realty table, stood a three-foot-tall topiary with a single twelve-inch ball tightened with tiny vibrant green leaves—perfect in every way—sitting pretty, perched on top of a sturdy wooden triple-ply trunk. *How'd they get that trunk to braid like that?* Painted on the white, packed-with-moss porcelain cachepot was their family name:

Banks
Petunia Lane
Village of Primm

Holly wanted to pinch herself. In Boulder City, it was buckbrush, prickly pear cactus, and prairie sage. But here, in Primm . . .

"Is it real?"

"Oh, yes." The woman with the hands held in prayer nodded. "She's real. Same base-plant material as Plume." She broke her statuesque posture to rest a hand on Holly's arm. "Your family name was hand painted by the park calligrapher. He created the sign on the ivy-covered gate at the entrance."

"Yes, I remember that sign." Holly placed a hand against her heart.

"Is she—" Ella whispered, tugging on Holly's shirt. "Is she ours? Our very own poodle plant?"

"Ella, honey. That's Anna." Holly gave Ella a squeeze. "That's Anna Wintour, Ella. Our special topiary."

"Wow," Ella said against Holly's side, pressing herself into Holly's leg, wrapping her arms around Holly's waist. "Is that Plume's baby?"

"I suppose she is." Holly nodded, reaching for the white parchment envelope propped against the topiary. "May I?" Holly asked.

"Yes, of course," the woman said with a slight, slow nod. "Open it."

On the outside of the envelope, in the same lettering as on the topiary pot, was their family name, along with the words *Petunia Enclave*. *We live in an enclave!* According to Penelope, Southern Lakes didn't have any enclaves. Southern Lakes had boroughs.

Holly slid a single notecard made of heavy card stock from the envelope. Below the Feathered Nest Realty logo, printed at the top in stately silver ink with raised embossing, were the words:

Welcome, Banks Family.

Welcome to the Village of Primm!

—Penelope Pratt, Feathered Nest Realty

"Such a lovely gift." Holly pressed the notecard to her chest. "Thank you."

"On behalf of Feathered Nest Realty, the Topiary Park Gift Shoppe, and the Village of Primm, you're quite welcome." The woman lifted the topiary, slowly, with as much honey and ginger as she could muster, placing it into the crook of Holly's arms. "Take good care of . . . Anna, did you say?"

"Yes, Anna." Holly appraised the calligraphy on the white porcelain pot. Gazed at the topiary's tight, perfectly shaped sphere. *Hello, Anna.*

Ella leaned onto tippy-toes to get a better look at Anna.

"So what d'you think, Ella? Should we keep her?"

Ella blew Anna a kiss.

"Oh, I almost forgot." Sliding her hand into the pocket of her apron, the woman produced a Feathered Nest Realty card. Magnetic. The kind you could hang on your refrigerator. "When you have a moment, text *911ENCLAVE* to this number." She peered through her reading glasses, down her nose, and toward the number. "You'll receive Enclave Alerts from Penelope." Hands back in prayer position, to Ella, the woman said, "Take good care of Anna." To Holly, she said, "Welcome to the Village of Primm, Banks Family." Off the praying woman went to help an overwhelmed mom with a crying baby hoist a bronze replica of Plume onto the back of her stroller. Tail feathers mottled with umber patina, the statue looked heavy and quite a bother, but who was Holly to judge? Maybe she, too, wanted a piece of Plume.

Holly handed Anna to Ella. "Be careful."

Ella, barely three and a half feet tall, hugged the base of Anna's porcelain cachepot, Anna's slender twig body leading upward to a twelve-inch round topiary "head" that was now eye level with Holly.

Holly texted "911ENCLAVE" to the number on the card, and *presto!* A message appeared.

Penelope Pratt
Feathered Nest Realty

—ENCLAVE ALERTS—

Drive safely! Primm Academy starts Tuesday. Go Honeybees!

(Text "BA-BYE, SUMMER!" to 125VILLAGEROWE to launch an onslaught of school emails.)

Mortified by lifeless mulch? A small investment will bring new life to your mulch beds.

Deliveries scheduled for enclaves: Hobnob, Chum, Ballyhoo, and Pram

(Text "CHA-CHING" to PRIMMULCH to place your order.)

F.U. Frisbee is this Saturday!

Swim Moms vs. Gym Moms—11 am

Team Buttercream vs. The Pink Erasers—12 noon

Winecraft vs. PokeMOMS—1 pm

(Avoid injury by playing sober. Review tournament rules by texting "F.U. MOMS!" to FU-PRIMM!)

And please, please keep Plume in your prayers. Something is eating her face.

(For the latest gossip text "YUCK.IS.IT.HEAD.LICE?" to PRIMMLOVESPLUME.)

~

Hmm. Still no response to her earlier text to Jack. *What's he doing?*

Holly and Ella left the gift shop, carrying Anna with them through a sprawling system of tree houses placed high in the trees and connected by eco-friendly suspension bridges. Everywhere they walked, they saw families. Some noticed Anna Wintour and welcomed them to Primm, but for the most part, Holly and Ella passed like ghosts or nameless tourists, unseen by others.

"Ella, take your thumb out, please." Holly tugged at Ella's wrist, almost pulling her loose tooth out. "Wow, Ella. That's ready to come out."

Ella wrapped her arms around Holly's waist to nestle in, stepping on Holly's toes with her sparkly lavender Mary Janes. Holly set Anna down so they could sway to the tinkling sounds of a nearby wind chime made entirely of glass beads, copper pennies, and antique spoons. She pressed the fleshy tip of Ella's nose, treating it as she would the bulbous shutter-release button on her camera. If she could, she would tuck a photo of Ella at age five into the face of Father Time, hoping to jam his second hand—stop it from ticking. Ella was like a sprinkle of fireflies. "Stop growing, Ella," Holly whispered. "Stay with me awhile." She bent down to kiss Ella's cheek. "Are you sleepy?"

"Just my eyes are sleepy," Ella assured Holly. "Not my whole body." Ella tucked her thumb between her lips.

"No thumb, sweetie." Holly pulled it out; then she bent down to brush the tip of her nose against Ella's.

When Holly stood upright, she heard a *bzzzt,* turned to look, and—*thwap!*—got whacked in the head with something large, black, and plastic. It clipped her shoulder, then crashed to the ground. "What the—?" Holly rubbed her head.

"That's a spaceship!" Ella bent to touch it.

The pilot of the unmanned aircraft rushed toward them. "Sorry. Sorry. Sorry!" He waved a remote control in the air. "I'm so sorry," he panted, retrieving the downed object.

About two feet round, with four sets of tiny propellers, it had a tiny camera mounted to its center.

"That's a drone." Holly pointed, not sure how she felt about it.

"Really sorry," he said. "I must have lost control."

"You certainly did." Holly scowled. "Never thought I'd be the victim of a drone attack."

"Me too," Ella chimed in, her little voice scolding him as if she were an adult and he were a child. "We were just minding our own business." Ella stomped. "Standing here, trying to give our eyes a nap. And then, blam." Ella clapped. "You hit my mommy."

"My apologies," he told Ella. "Truly. I never meant to interrupt your nap." He offered his hand to Holly. "I'm Caleb."

"I know who you are." Holly shook his hand. "You're with Primm Cable. You were at our house on Saturday."

"Oh, yes, that's right! You're the film school mom."

"And you're the sippy cup man."

"I was just grabbing some aerial shots of Plume," he explained. "Her area is closed to visitors because she's so sick."

"Plume is sick?" Ella blinked.

"Ella. Plume is just a plant," Holly reminded her.

"But Plume is Anna's mommy," Ella whined, anxiety rising. "You said she was—when we were back there."

"Ella's right," Caleb said. "Plume is like a mother to us all."

"'A mother to us all'?" Holly rolled her eyes. "Isn't that a bit much?" She flashed a smile at both Ella and Caleb. "I'm sure Plume will be back on her feet real soon."

"Let's hope." Caleb directed his worry toward Ella. "They're flying in experts to take care of her. Her face is starting to rot."

"No!" Ella gasped.

"And if she dies, the whole town will mourn." Caleb adopted a look of grave concern.

Is this guy an actor too?

"Hey, I probably got a clear shot of the top of your heads just now. Camera's mounted right here." He showed Ella the tiny camera mounted to the drone. "Sorry I hit you." He reached out to touch Holly on the arm. "I don't know what happened. I must have hit the down button on the remote. Are you hurt?"

"I'll be fine," Holly said. "Just surprised."

"Can I buy you a cup of coffee? They're selling cherry pies to promote next weekend's Cherry Festival on The Lawn."

"Can we, Mommy? Pleeeez?"

"We're good. But thank you." Holly was speaking to Caleb but shaking her head to Ella. They weren't staying for pie. They didn't eat pie. No one in their family ate pie.

"Oh, hey." Caleb patted the pockets of his khaki cargo pants. "I think I've got something you might be interested in." After much searching, he pulled a folded piece of paper from one of his side pockets. "I thought I had an extra. Here: the Wilhelm Klaus film contest I was telling you about. Wilhelm Klaus. Can you believe it? All the way from Germany in, like, six weeks. Bringing a troupe of German puppeteers too. They're performing Grimm fairy tales for the children of Primm this Halloween."

Ella rolled up onto tippy-toes to have a look as Holly read the flyer.

Wilhelm Klaus Three-Minute Film Festival
Win $10,000 and dinner with THE Wilhelm Klaus
Germany's most celebrated filmmaker
Any Genre | Any Style | Any Technology | Any Level | Any Age
www.WilhelmKlaus.com/three-minutes-to-personal-glory/

"Keep it." Caleb smiled. "I have another one at home." He tipped an invisible hat to Ella. "Enjoy the topiaries," he said to Holly, turning on his heel to walk away, disappearing through a rabbit hole carved into the hedges.

Holly studied the flyer in her nail-bitten hands. Holly knew all about the German film industry. She told Ella, "My roommate in college left Northwestern to attend the University of Television and Film in Munich." Holly fingered the edges of the Wilhelm Klaus flyer. "We kept in touch at first, but over the years . . ."

Ella kissed Holly's arm.

"Well." Holly folded the flyer, shoved it deep into her pocket. "Enough about that. It's Labor Day! We have hamburgers to eat." She picked Anna Wintour off the ground, set her on her hip, then reached out to take Ella by the hand. "And then you, my darling, need to get a good night's sleep so you're ready to catch the school bus tomorrow for your first day of kindergarten."

"I don't want to go to kindergarten. I want to stay home with you."

Holly's heart sank as Ella's hopeful eyes searched Holly's. To Holly's chagrin, Greta's ominous warning came to mind: a thousand things could go wrong. Holly bent for a bittersweet kiss on Ella's sweet cheeks. "Me too, Ella. Me too."

7

Later that afternoon

Jack arrived with supplies for their Labor Day cookout, and Holly left to run some errands without Ella. Ella needed school shoes and a cloth bag to carry her lunch. They'd talked about buying Ella an electric toothbrush after her tooth fell out, but Holly got it in her head she wanted to buy it before school started. When Holly arrived home, she found Jack in the kitchen. With Bethanny.

"You're home!" Jack was jovial. Too jovial.

No wonder: a confident, sexy woman with tousled, beach-waved caramel-ombré hair stood in the kitchen wearing a cobalt—*no, excuse me, azure*—off-the-shoulder peasant blouse with a sassy flounce at the bottom.

Jack's smile. All teeth. Pasted on his face like an ad for teeth whitening.

And Bethanny. Racer skinny jeans in a low-rise, figure-hugging cut with near-perfect whiskering and fading throughout, mending details at the knee. Tobacco-colored ankle boots. Alex and Ani bangle at the wrist.

Holly shot Jack a look that said, *She's your boss? What the frock, Jack?* No wonder he was always working.

"Holly, this is Bethanny Baylor. Bethanny, this is my wife, Holly." He slunk backward. Literally, took a step backward—like he was afraid of them. And well, he should have been. Because Holly was imagining a full movie sequence playing out in her kitchen: Holly and Bethanny as Yu Shu Lien and Jen Yu in *Crouching Tiger, Hidden Dragon*, reenacting the masterful, perfectly choreographed courtyard sword fight. Sorry, Jackie Chan: for all your lifetime achievements, the best kung fu sword fight—best *any kind of sword fight*—in movie history was, of course, between two women.

"Bethanny," Holly said with forced, overly controlled speech, "how lovely of you to join us."

She needed to be polite. Bethanny was Jack's boss, after all; she meant a great deal to him—and them. But it wasn't lost on Holly that Bethanny was also the woman responsible for moving them across the country on such short notice. If it weren't for Bethanny, Holly'd still be in Boulder City in an established, unpacked house surrounded by a neighborhood filled with kids Ella knew and loved playing with. Ella'd have no problem transitioning into kindergarten were it not for the move to Primm. Yellow? No one gave a flip about yellow or pink in Boulder City. A shirt was a shirt; you could wear whatever color you wanted. Would there have been a PTA in Ella's school? Sure. But Holly was fairly certain it would be a *normal* PTA and not some high-octane army of overachieving school moms.

Holly petted Struggle, who greeted her with a wagging tail and a tennis ball. Holly tried tugging the ball from her clenched teeth, which proved difficult because Struggle never let go.

"I apologize for the moving boxes," Holly told Bethanny. "As you know, Ella and I just arrived a few days ago." Holly set her car keys on the kitchen table. Studied the lines on Jack's face. *My house is an absolute wreck. Frick you, Jack—this is embarrassing.* She gripped the tennis ball, yanked it from Struggle's mouth, tossed it down the hallway.

"It's wonderful to finally meet you." Bethanny offered her hand for Holly to shake. She seemed nice. Despite having ridiculously pouty lips and no wedding band.

Struggle scampered back, dropped the ball at Bethanny's feet to then stick her nose in Bethanny's crotch.

"Whoopsie." Bethanny twisted, swooping her arm across Struggle to dislodge her snout from her nether regions. "No, no."

"Struggle!" Jack lunged at the dog, pulling Struggle from the space between Bethanny's legs.

Holly asked Bethanny, "Would you like something to drink? Sparkling water? Iced tea?" The lighting in Holly's kitchen felt garish. Felt like last call in a bar. Time to sober up and "see" each other for the first time.

"Oh, that won't be necessary," Bethanny demurred. "I brought coffee." She pointed to a cardboard drink holder, and *yup!* Holly counted two (not three) take-out coffees from Primm's Coffee Joe. Each cup had an initial written in Sharpie marker: *B* for Bethanny. *J* for Jack. Together they read *BJ. Such a lovely acronym.*

"Where's Ella?" Holly asked Jack.

"Watching the ponies."

"Again?" *Don't park my daughter in front of the TV so you can spend time with Bethanny.* She canvassed Jack. *Leather belt. Blue shirt pressed and tucked into a pair of linen pants. You never dress like that for family burgers on the grill.* Holly looked at his feet. *Allen Edmonds Voyagers? Seriously, Jack? No. Where are your leather no-brand flip-flops? This is* not *happening.* Holly regrouped, cognizant of the fact Bethanny was his boss. Holly needed to be polite.

"Mommy!" Ella ran in, waving her well-loved Pinkie Pie pony in the air. "I lost my tooth!"

"Wait. What?" Holly asked Ella with a sharp glance toward Jack. "Her first tooth?" she asked him. "And I missed it? How. How'd that happen? I was only gone a few hours."

Ella pulled her lower lip down, used Pinkie Pie's foot to point, and sure enough, there was a space on the bottom row where her tooth once was. *Nooooooo!* Holly missed it. She freaking missed it.

Ella smiled at the woman standing in Holly's kitchen. "Bethanny pulled it."

"Excuse me?" Holly bent to Ella's level. "I'm sorry, honey. What did you say?"

"Bethanny pulled it."

Holly closed her eyes. *Bethanny pulled it.* Bethanny Baylor. She stood upright. "You pulled my daughter's tooth out?" So what if she was Jack's boss. "Her first tooth?"

"Well, I. It was . . ." Bethanny glanced at Jack for help. "Um. I'm sorry; I guess I wasn't thinking. One minute I was touching it. And then it happened."

"One minute you were touching it," Holly clarified, with a brief check on Jack, "and then it happened?"

"I'm really sorry, Holly." Bethanny wore the same expression Struggle wore when she got caught piddling on the carpet. "Truly. I'm sorry."

"So am I." Holly folded and then unfolded her arms. She didn't know where to look. Didn't know who to look at. She was afraid she might cry. Instead, she started blinking. Blinking, blinking, blinking.

"What's the matter, Mommy?" Ella tugged at Holly. "Your eyes are soggy."

"I'm fine, sweetie. Fine." *I won't cry in front of Ella. I won't.*

"I should check on the burgers." Jack glanced apologetically toward Holly, unable to make full eye contact.

Coward.

He made a fast dash toward the deck. "Excuse me."

"Ella, honey, give Mommy a hug." Holly pulled her into her arms. "I'm so proud of you. Great job." She gave her a squeeze, kissed the top of her head. "Now go play. I'll be there in a minute."

Ella skipped off with Pinkie Pie, leaving Bethanny Baylor the Tooth Puller alone in the kitchen with Yu Shu Lien.

"Well, that's strange. Will you look at that?" Holly pointed to her keys. "What are my keys doing on the kitchen table? They belong in the foyer."

Ella's first tooth. Ella's first *mutha freaking* tooth!

Holly snatched her keys, then walked them to the side table near the front door. But of course, Jen Yu followed. Bethanny. Bethanny Baylor. Who belonged in an office. Not in Holly's home.

"You have such a welcoming foyer," Bethanny said, fishing for something to say in Holly's almost empty hallway. Tight quarters for a kung fu sword fight, but still.

"And I love your coatrack. And this banister." Bethanny touched the banister that led to the bedrooms upstairs. "Is it original?"

"You mean, like a baby tooth?"

"I'm so sorry." Bethanny shrank, appearing sincere. "I never meant to—"

"Yes, well." Something got caught in Holly's throat. She tried clearing it. Studied her ceiling, blinking back tears. "I'm overreacting—it's just a tooth." Holly's nose stung.

"It's more than a tooth," Bethanny whispered, taking a step toward Holly to touch her arm. "It's the first tooth. And I'm sorry. I made a mistake."

Holly closed her eyes. Fanned her face with her hands. Swallowed a few times.

"Jack is a valuable member of the team," Bethanny blurted.

"Yes. Well. I, um . . ." They both needed to stop talking.

Finally, Holly came up with, "I'm so thrilled he's working in the Village of Primm office now. His office back home was so close to everyone we knew and loved; it was hard keeping work and family life separate. He used to coach four-and-under soccer. Ella and I would join him for lunch. But here, here in Primm, he's able to focus solely on work. And well, that works out great, because Ella and I don't know a soul. So it's forcing us to leave the comforts of home. You know—branch out. Meet new people." Where was she going with this? "Our social calendar is completely empty. But Jack's work. Jack's work is. He's so busy these days."

"I think a screw might be missing from your coatrack." Caught in the middle of pointing, Bethanny flinched, as if acknowledging she knew it was a stupid thing to say.

"Yes. A screw is missing. But then, I love my coatrack," Holly told her. "I love everything that belongs to me. Like my coatrack, my dog, my keys—my husband. And I love teeth. I love teeth a lot. Although I have to say, I'm not sure Ella will understand if Jack works tonight. It's Labor Day, and we always cook out—as a family. On Labor Day. And well, she starts kindergarten bright and early tomorrow morning, so she shouldn't be watching television right now, but . . . well, if you're here, she's not getting much attention from her dad, now, is she?" Holly paused, letting the words sink in. Maybe she'd gone too far. Instinctually, she knew she'd gone too far.

Bethanny's shoulders slumped. "Oh. Oh, yes. Of course. I understand. I'm sorry," she said again, rattled by the circumstances. "I should go."

"Are you sure? It's no problem," said Holly, walking Bethanny the remaining few steps toward the door. "We have plenty to eat." Holly opened the door, sweeping her hand toward her front porch. "Perhaps you'd like a hot dog?"

"Good night, Holly. It was lovely meeting you."

"Yes." *You wore skinny racer jeans to my house. Brought BJ coffee to my husband.* "Good night, Bethanny."

Holly closed the door, not sorry her front porch was naked. Collette may have wanted visitors to feel welcome when it was her front porch, but Holly? Holly wouldn't want to encourage a woman like Bethanny.

Holly contemplated a Pinterest board filled with front porches that warded off women like Bethanny. She'd call the board Bitch Pulled My Daughter's First Tooth Out.

"What happened?" Jack appeared in the hallway, wringing his hands together. That "Jack" thing Jack always did. "Where's Bethanny?" End-of-world things like—

"I sent her home."

"Because of a tooth?"

"No, Jack. Because it's Labor Day." *Why do I have to explain this to him?* "This is my house."

"She's my *boss*, Holly. You act like I'm into her."

"Well, are you? And why'd that guy with the envelope come to our house the other day? I want to know what's going on." Something bad was about to happen. Holly could feel it.

He turned his head to stare at a spot on the wall.

"Fine." Holly folded her arms. Decided the sword fight she wanted to have first would be with Jack, the crouching tiger. And then Bethanny, the hidden dragon. "Tell Bethanny number twelve Petunia Lane belongs to me. I own that coatrack." *Even if it is missing a screw.*

"Holly," he said calmly, taking a step toward her.

"She pulled Ella's first tooth out."

"It wasn't like that."

"Oh?"

Holly's phone rang. She pulled it from her pocket.

"You suck, Jack." She pointed. "You know that? You suck. *Hello?*"

"Holly Tree. It's me."

"You *always* call at the worst times, Mom."

"I'm in a pickle."

"A what? Where are you?"

Jack crossed his arms, leaned a shoulder against the wall. Like he was settling in. Like a call from Holly's mom meant he had to get comfortable because something *big* was about to happen: Greta was on the line.

Greta said, "I'm at Caesars Palace."

"Mom." *Why is this happening?* "You're not supposed to be there."

"Now hear me out, Holly. I'm in a pickle. An actual, honest-to-goodness pickle. A six-foot-long, bright-green pickle."

"Kill me."

"It's a pickle costume. I'm handing out flyers for the Céline Dion concert tonight. Imagine. Me! A pickle on the Las Vegas Strip."

"Why, Mom. Why?" Holly's head hurt.

"I'm working off a marker," Greta whispered, as if pickles had secrets. "But don't worry—it's a small one."

Through gritted teeth. "*Another* marker, Mom?" Holly thought she might scream.

Jack groaned. Took the phone from Holly. "Greta, listen to me. I deal with this all the time at work. Owing someone money isn't a crime, but if you sign an IOU for more than two hundred and fifty dollars with no means of paying it back—you've committed felony theft under a 1983 Nevada law. Felony theft. Casino markers are legally binding. Do you understand me? Do not leave town again without arranging payment. I can't fly to Vegas for you. I've got a lot going on at work." He handed the phone back to Holly without giving Greta a chance to respond. Holly couldn't blame him for being angry, but she hated the fact that now *she* was the one causing strife between them because of *her* mom and not because of *his* bringing Bethanny home to pull *their* daughter's tooth out.

"Mom. I'm back."

"My entire body is a pickle," Greta explained. "From my ankles, to up over my head. I'm looking out a teeny tiny green screen cut into the pickle face. Can you believe they're paying me to wave at people? Smells pickley in here."

"The fact that you're a pickle is not my problem," Holly muttered. "Who's the parent, Mom? Who's the child? Hmm? You or me?"

"Yeah, yeah, I know."

"I thought you were on probation. I thought they blocked you from pulling lines of credit." Holly wanted to scream. Her marriage couldn't handle another loan to bail her mom out. She sneaked a peek at Jack. *He's angry? No. I'm angry. About Bethanny. I get to be angry. I call "being angry" first.*

"Have you been going to your meetings? Where's your sponsor? Did you call your sponsor?"

"He's standing right beside me."

"Oh, thank God." Holly exhaled. Covered the phone to whisper to Jack, "She called her sponsor. He's with her right now." Hopefully, Greta's sponsor would speak to casino management and sort this whole thing out. Greta was registered with the local GA. Hopefully, Greta had her meeting card on her.

Holly asked, "So what did your sponsor say?"

"Not much."

"What do you mean 'not much'?"

"I mean 'not much,'" Greta told Holly. "He can't talk."

"Why can't he talk?"

"Because," said Greta, "he's a hot dog."

WESTERN UNION ONLINE

Money transfer control number: 8720461849
Recipient: Greta B. Vogel
1610 Clairmont Court—Apartment 2B
Sender: Holly Banks
12 Petunia Lane
Amount $2021.80 (two thousand twenty-one dollars and eighty cents)

Message: This is a loan, and this is the last time. Do you hear me? And get a new sponsor. Your sponsor sucks. I was going to use that money to get CURTAINS and a BOOKSHELF. I need lamps. COFFEE TABLE! There's this mom named Collette and she used to have my front porch. And Bethanny—forget it. Mary-Margaret St. James! Call Ella tomorrow. She gets out at 3. And stop doing this. I'M SO FREAKING ANGRY RIGHT NOW!

8

Monday night

For the rest of the evening, Holly iced Jack, refusing to talk or make eye contact. Inviting Bethanny over without so much as a warning—his fault. Speaking to her mom the way he did? His fault. But mutha frucker—Ella's first tooth? His. Freaking. Fault! And he knew it. He eventually stopped with the *I'm sorrys* and went to bed, leaving Holly to flip mindlessly through hundreds of cable channels only to realize there was nothing on TV. Sometime after midnight, she went upstairs, Struggle trailing behind with nails that needed clipping: click, click, click, the sound of Struggle's steps on the wooden stairs.

Entering with Struggle, Holly slipped inside Ella's bedroom and thought, *There she is, my Ella Cinderella, sleeping with a matted Pinkie Pie pony tucked beneath her arm, baby tooth beneath her pillow. Tonight? I'm a tooth fairy. Tomorrow? I'm a school mom. Packing Ella's lunch, packing her backpack, walking her to the bus stop, waving goodbye for the first time, watching as she rides away from me. Tomorrow? I'll spend the majority of my day without her. Tomorrow, and then every day that follows for an entire school year, I'll have no idea what she's doing at any given moment, no idea who she's talking to, no idea how her day is going.* For Ella, it was a beginning. But for Holly, it felt like the end. Biggest job she'd ever had, most important thing she'd ever done and would ever do, would fundamentally change—tomorrow.

Tomorrow, Ella would leave, and Holly would be home alone, the sights and sounds of *My Little Pony* falling silent in the house because Ella wasn't there.

Struggle hopped onto the foot of Ella's bed, and Holly sat on the edge, watching Ella as she slept. Ella was five years old. *Five.* She was four last week, three the week before, then two. Last month, she was a baby, and Holly had cradled her in her arms, nursing her to sleep. As far as Holly was concerned, the moment Ella was born, the world grew big. Earth swelled ten times its original size.

"I'm going to miss you, Ella," Holly whispered, using the tip of her finger to sweep a lock of her hair from her forehead. "And I hope I never embarrass you." *Like my mom did.*

Greta, the memory of her lurking at the school gates while Holly was out for recess, seeped its way into Ella's bedroom, morphing the beautiful glow cast by the nightlight into a harsh mustard light that flickered against the wall. Holly leaned over to push the nightlight farther into the socket as memories of Greta, always drunk back then—a one-woman wrecking ball, both joker and wild card—tainted the moment she was having with Ella, pulling her back. Pulling her back through the portal. Reminding her. Haunting her.

When Holly was in kindergarten, playing at recess, a Hula-Hoop around her waist, Greta had staggered over to the school wearing pajamas and a trench coat: drunk. She began calling Holly's name: *Holly. Ais me; hit's your mom, Holly.* Horrified, Holly walked away from the school gates and toward the building, desperately twitching her hips, focusing on each step as she walked, hoping no one in her class would point, ask who that woman was, and find out she was Holly's mom, broken and slouched against a chain-link fence, calling her name as if it were a desperate treasure that kept slipping from the edges of her tongue. *Holly. Ais me; hit's your mom, Holly. Comes to me, Holly; comes to Mommy.*

Sitting on Ella's bed, Holly reached out to rest her hand on Struggle's back, then closed her eyes. Holly felt shame. Still did. Couldn't seem to shake it.

"I'll be a good mom for you, Ella," Holly whispered, combing Ella's hair from her forehead, watching her breathe as she slept. "I promise—I'll be prim." Holly patted Ella's shoulder lightly, careful not to wake her.

Holly. Ais me; hit's your mom, Holly . . .

She needed to shake this off. It had been a bad day; that was all. She was tired. Moving was stressful. Change was difficult.

Holly tucked a dollar beneath Ella's pillow. Slid Ella's tooth into her pocket.

"I have loved every moment of every day we've spent together," Holly whispered, bending to kiss Ella on the forehead. She kept thinking, *I'm happy for you. But I'm going to miss you so, so much.* "You're my whole world, Ella Bella," Holly said, nose stinging, tears welling up in her eyes. "You're my Pinkie Pie."

Struggle understood. Struggle cried too. Whined—whimpered—something. Holly reached over to pet her. *Those sad Labrador eyes.*

I should go. Get some sleep.

Holly traced the tip of Ella's nose, remembering how little her Ella once was. For the coming silence, for the coming loneliness, Holly blamed Pinkie Pie, Twilight Sparkle, and all the little ponies in Ponyville. She knew she shouldn't; it didn't make sense; but she did. Because Ella loved them. The *My Little Pony* world created by Hasbro and shown through—what was it Caleb said, a company-owned network?—was part of the world Ella and Holly had created. And now Ella was leaving it. Growing up. Leaving Holly and those stupid ponies behind.

Holly left Struggle at the foot of Ella's bed, slipped from Ella's bedroom, and headed downstairs, Ella's tooth burning a hole in her pocket. *What should I do with it? Save it? Put it in my jewelry box? I don't want Ella to find it, or she'll know there's no tooth fairy. But I don't like holding a piece of Ella that's not attached to her, and I can't bear the thought of throwing it away.* Instead, Holly placed it with another living thing: Anna Wintour, their family topiary. Anna would keep Ella's tooth safe.

It felt like a seed in Holly's hand as she pressed the tiny tooth finger deep into Anna's soil. With Ella's tooth beneath the moss, Holly made a wish, for luck, for Ella, for Holly, for Holly's new life—as the mother of a little girl who lived in Primm. "What kind of a mother *are* you?" Mary-Margaret had asked. *Long live Anna,* thought Holly. *Long live Plume. And long live motherhood in the Village of Primm.* With the planting of Ella's first tooth as the seed of a promise, Holly vowed she'd do this right. Vowed she'd be a great mom to Ella in this new town, this mom town everyone so affectionately called the Village of Primm.

~

Too alert to sleep, Holly carried her laptop to the family room couch. Scanning a website that posted astrological forecasts, she learned Mercury was retrograde. *Retrograde? What is that?* Clicking through, she caught the words *FREE! FREE! FREE!* blinking in red letters around a box inviting her to ask a psychic a *FREE! FREE! FREE!* question. So Holly entered her email address and then, to prove she wasn't a robot, transcribed a series of fuzzy letters and numbers. Finally, she typed her question inside a box:

> Is there a secret power in the universe I can tap to help me cope with my child starting kindergarten? Because this particular milestone in her childhood is upsetting me more than I think it should. One more question. (And I'm hoping you won't charge me $$$ for this because it still fits in this tiny little box, so I'm thinking it still counts as one question and not two.) Here it is: If you're a psychic, shouldn't you know I'm not a robot? Yours truly, Holly Banks.

She hit send, clicked off the astrology website, then settled in to watch a *Cutthroat Kitchen* rerun. About an hour later, she checked her email.

~

EMAIL—Time Received: 2:24 a.m.

TO: Holly Banks
FROM: Psychic Betty, Psychic Hotline Network
SUBJECT: Your FREE "Ask the Psychic" Question

Today's planetary alignment gives you the ability to make wise choices and seek useful information. Thank you for submitting a question to the Psychic Hotline Network. I am Psychic Betty, your online psychic. Exercise extreme caution if your child starts kindergarten between August 20 and September 10. But other than that, the answer is: NO. The universe does NOT have a secret power you can tap to help you cope with your child starting kindergarten. Have you tried vodka?

—Psychic Betty

Click HERE to ask another question.

Click HERE for coupons to Dizzy's Seafood.

~

Holly clicked "here" to ask another question, and a box appeared, asking her to prove she wasn't a robot by answering the following: 23+2 =

So easy! Twenty-five. Any robot would know that. Holly typed her question:

> Yes, she starts kindergarten between August 20 and September 10. Why? Why should I exercise extreme caution? Now I'm starting to panic. And why do I have to keep proving I'm not a robot? Maybe you're proving you're not a real psychic. P.S. I don't think I should have to pay for this question since my first question wasn't answered to my satisfaction. (This is Holly Banks. You might remember me?)

Holly waited.
And waited.
And waited.
And waited some more.
And then finally, another email.

~

EMAIL—Time Received: 2:51 a.m.

> TO: Holly Banks
> FROM: Psychic Betty, Psychic Hotline Network
> SUBJECT: Your Second FREE "Ask the Psychic" Question
>
> Thank you for submitting a question to the Psychic Hotline Network. I am Psychic Betty, your online psychic. Mercury retrogrades August 20 to September 10. I know you're not a robot because a robot would never ask for two free questions.

And a robot would never imply that I'm not a real psychic. That hurt my feelings.

—Psychic Betty

Click HERE to ask another question.

Click HERE to subscribe to my newsletter.

Click HERE to follow me on Twitter.

Click HERE for coupons to Dizzy's Seafood.

~

Oh, good gravy. This is ridiculous. Holly clicked "here" to ask a final question, proving she wasn't a robot by typing what she saw on the reCAPTCHA screen:

@ss s@ndwich

Her final question:

Okay, Psychic Betty. What is Mercury retrograde? I am willing to spend one dollar exactly—NOT A PENNY MORE—for the answer. AND IF YOU TRY TO TRICK ME—actually, scratch that. Never mind. I'm sorry. And I'm sorry I implied you weren't a real psychic, Psychic Betty. I never meant to hurt your feelings. I guess I'm just having a bad day. Another woman pulled my daughter's first tooth out. I thought I'd enjoy being the Tooth Fairy, but truthfully? I'm sad.

P.S. This is Holly Banks.

Holly waited.
And waited.
And waited.
And then . . .

~

EMAIL—Time Received: 3:16 a.m.

TO: Holly Banks
FROM: Psychic Betty, Psychic Hotline Network
SUBJECT: Hurting My Feelings

Don't worry, Holly Banks. I forgive you. But then, I'm a Pisces, so I'd forgive a garden slug.

My psychic powers indicate you are going through an emotional time right now. Most likely, your suffering is caused by planet Mercury and the negative influences of Mercury retrograde.

If you'd like, I can be your online psychic, and you can email me directly and not have to continuously prove you're not a robot. I charge $1.00 per email. If you are a robot and you want to email me directly, same rates apply. If you are a garden slug, well . . .

Meanwhile, meditate on this:

FEELINGS ARE NEITHER RIGHT NOR WRONG. THEY JUST ARE.

Now, sit still. Sit very, very still and don't move . . .

Let your feelings take you where they want you to go.

Shhh . . . Listen . . .

They want you to go to Dizzy's Seafood.

Hushpuppies. Half price. You heard it: HALF PRICE. Woof!

Click HERE to order a candle.

Click HERE to order a crystal.

Click HERE to order Dizzy's Seafood.

9

Tuesday, first day of kindergarten

SCENE 2 – INT. HOUSE – MORNING

HOLLY (V.O.)

Scene Two. Fixed discovery shot. Use the front porch as an unobtrusive vantage point, characters walking in and out of the shot.

MAN (V.O.)

You sure? Wilhelm Klaus hates fixed discovery shots.

HOLLY (V.O.)

Wilhelm Klaus hates voice-overs, but this is my film. I'm using the front porch as a story motif.

MAN (V.O.)

Oh. Should we lose the dog?

HOLLY (V.O.)

Struggle? No. Keep Struggle. Struggle's good. On second thought, mount Camera Two in the hallway. Camera Three on Bus 13.

Stand by on the set.

Stand by to roll tape.

Roll tape.

Scene Two.

Take One.

Action.

Camera One: Front porch.

Holly *swung* open the door, Ella in her arms. A look of determination on her face. To the bus driver: "Wait! Stop!" Holly waved frantically. "We're here!" To Ella: "Ella, listen to me: you're going to run out there and get on that bus." She set Ella down, guiding each foot into a shoe. "It's gonna be great." Over her shoulder toward the kitchen: "Jack!" Holly yelled. "The backpack!"

Camera Two: Hallway.

Holly turned to find Jack rounding the corner of the family room, gripping Ella's backpack like a football.

Jack. In a panic. *"Why is it happening like this?"* He drew his arm back and threw a Hail Mary pass to Holly—delivering the pack into her outstretched arms. "It's her first day of kindergarten. What are we doing, Holly?" He grabbed his head with both hands, elbows out—that two-seconds-left-on-the-clock thing he always did when watching football. "Why, Holly? Why is it like this?"

Camera Three: Sound of bus rumbling. BUS DRIVER honks the horn.

Camera One: Cut to front porch.

"That's your bus, Ella." Holly hoisted the pack onto Ella's shoulders. "Run out there." The anxiety they both felt. The panic. "Go on. Run out there." Holly felt it in her chest. Felt a tightness in her breath. She signaled the bus driver. Gave Ella a little shove. "You can do it. Off the porch. Come on, Ella. Please?"

"It wasn't supposed to be like this, Holly." Jack appeared in the doorway as Ella pulled from Holly to cling to Jack. Jack's face morphed from frazzled, end-of-world things to right now, at this moment: not anger, more like disappointment. Almost pity—for Holly. For not being able to get her daughter on the dang bus. Something. It was awful. Struggle barked, announcing to the world just how much her human, Holly, sucked at life.

Camera Three: Cut to bus door being opened.

BUS DRIVER

You coming or not?

Camera One: Cut to front porch.

"Ella, please. I know this isn't perfect, but we've gotta go, honey. *Please.* The bus is here. It's right there." *Get off the porch, Ella. GET OFF THE FREAKING PORCH.* Like something from the pages of a 1950s Dick and Jane early reader: *See Jane? See Jane forget to set the mutha freaking alarm on the first day of kindergarten? Run, Jane. Run!*

Camera Three: Bus driver closes door, starts to pull away.

Camera One: Cut to HOLLY on front porch; stays with Holly for the remainder of the scene.

Bus leaving the curb. Holly: *"Nooooooo!"* Off the porch she jumped, running barefoot across the lawn. "Stop! Stop! You saw us. You freaking saw us!"

Holly ran into the street, arms waving above her head.

Up Petunia Lane the bus drove, filled with little Petunia children.

Except for Holly's. Holly's child wasn't on Bus 13. Holly's child was on the front porch, sucking the thumb she shouldn't be sucking. Holly's husband—never mind that. Holly's *dog*? Barking. At Holly. She snatched a hank of grass from her lawn and threw it at the bus. See Jane? See Jane suck at motherhood?

Collecting her wits, Holly sneaked a peek at the other mothers on her street. Petunia Moms chatting. Petunia Moms waving to other

Petunia Moms as they waltzed down their sidewalks and up the steps of their cheerfully decorated front porches. All of them: clones of June Cleaver. Pictures of success. Women who, only moments ago, had executed seemingly effortless, storybook back-to-school mornings for their children. Holly? Not so much.

Shoulders slumped, Holly felt like she was in one of those idyllic Random House Little Golden Books with the gold foil binding, illustrated by a picture book artist like Mary Blair or Gustaf Tenggren. *The Poky Little Puppy. The Little Engine That Could.*

In Holly's Little Golden Book, the women of Petunia Lane were cast in muted watercolors and dressed in tailored garments: clean lines, pointed busts, cinched-in waists, and voluminous skirts. Holly? She was cast in garish Technicolor.

"If my life were written onto the pages of a Little Golden Book, its title would read *The Little Mommy That Couldn't*," muttered Holly, snatching a second patch of grass to throw toward the bus as it crested the hill at the top of the street, en route to distant bus stops, en route to on-time moms waiting with ready-for-school kids.

Bye-bye, bus!

The back of it looked like a smiley face about to wink at her—black bumper smile stretched across a pale-yellow face below round rear-headlight eyes. The way it barreled up the hill on its merry little way made Holly feel like the bus was mocking her, 1950s–nuclear family style: *Golly gee, Holly, seems you failed to get your daughter on me on the first day of kindergarten. You're a stinker of a mom. Yes sirree! You're a true stinker.*

"Stay there, Ella." Holly ran past Jack and Ella, back inside the house to grab her coffee and keys from the kitchen counter. "Struggle. Stop barking!"

Back on the porch, Holly told Jack, "People miss the bus all the time."

"But it's the first day of kindergarten."

"I'm sorry. *Jeez,* Jack. Will you drop it? Where were you? Hmm? You could have helped. Why'd you leave everything to me? That's so unfair." Struggle through the open door. "Struggle!" Freaking barking. "Will you stop?"

From Ella: "I don't wanna go to school. I want to stay home with yooooou."

Holly placed her hands on the top of Ella's shoulders, turned her around, and calmly pointed to the red Chevy Suburban on the driveway. In a controlled voice: "You're going to school, Ella. And I'm going to drive you."

To Jack: "This Friday night"—Holly lifted a finger—"if I make it through the week with the house unpacked and Ella on the bus each morning, we're opening the pinot noir: the grand cru from Burgundy, the bottle your company gave us when you signed the agreement to move us to the Village of Primm. You hear me? Friday night. We're drinking the Gevrey-Chambertin."

"That's a hundred-dollar bottle—"

"We're drinking it."

"Got it." Jack nodded. Grabbed Holly. Hugged her. "You can do this."

"We can do this," she corrected. "Not 'me.' 'We.'"

Holly closed her eyes, took a moment to feel Jack's embrace. Could she? Could she do this? Ella would be fine; she'd adapt. But as far as school moms went? Holly worried Holly might flunk kindergarten.

Gevrey-Chambertin. Gevrey-Chambertin.

Holly pulled away from Jack, stepped to the side to look at the floor of her naked front porch. "We need a welcome mat. Collette had this place looking so nice."

And then I showed up.

~

After driving a few blocks, Holly stopped at the corner of Dillydally and Castle Drum Tower. A scant seven cars separated Holly's SUV from Ella's school bus. And great news: the Dillydally and Castle Drum Tower bus stop had to be one of the most populated bus stops in Primm because it stood at the courtyard intersection between two enclaves: Dillydally and Castle Drum Tower. A large sparkling-white gazebo stood at the center of the courtyard, staked at the roofline with a circular row of flags known collectively as the Flags of Primm. The courtyard was one of only two locations in Primm with a gazebo showcasing all the enclave flags; the other flagged gazebo was known as the South Gazebo, and it stood in the center of town at the southern end of The Lawn. Each triangular pennant flag was poly burlap in make, burlap in color, with the name of an enclave embroidered in black above a touch of elegant black scrollwork at the pointed end of the flag. Enclave names were spelled out, with three exceptions: Castle Drum Tower's flag read *CDT*; the Gilman Clear enclave was simply *Gilman*; and Parallax, though not especially long, so fit wasn't an issue, was rendered with two *Ls* and nothing more, to match the gilded *Ls* in the cresting of the village carousel.

"Ella?" Car still running, Holly shifted into park.

"What?"

There were still plenty of Dillydally and Castle Drum Tower kids at the bus stop, moms and dads snapping photos as one by one, the mixed-age smattering of kids boarded the bus.

"Grab your backpack. You're boarding that bus." Holly ran around to open the passenger-side back door and unbuckled Ella.

"What's happening?" Ella, wide eyed, kept shaking her head no. "Where are we going? Is the car broken? I'm scared. What's happening. Mom? What's happening?"

"We're catching that bus."

Holly set Ella on the street, then hoisted Ella's blue backpack onto her tiny frame. "And I want you to know this is perfectly normal, Ella.

People catch buses this way all the time. But don't tell Daddy. Okay?" She took hold of Ella's hand. "Okay, now. Run." Off they went.

They were almost to the bus when the last Dillydally Tower child climbed the steps, and the bus driver closed the door. *Dang it.* Red traffic light about to turn green, Holly let go of Ella's hand. "Stay here." She hoisted her onto the grass. "Stay on the grass. Don't step onto the sidewalk, and definitely don't step into the street." Holly ran fast to bang on the bus door. Bang, bang, bang!

Nothing.

Holly banged again. Bang, bang, bang!

Door opened. A thin elderly bus driver peered down at Holly. "Can I help you?"

"Yes," said Holly, out of breath, signaling for Ella to join her. "My daughter needs a ride to school." Panting. "To Primm Academy. You forgot us."

He looked beyond Holly's shoulder. "Where'd you come from?"

"Petunia."

"This is Dillydally and Castle Drum Tower."

"Yes, I know, but you drove past my house. I was in the grass, waving my arms and yelling for you. Please? Can you please take my daughter to school?"

Loud enough for Holly to hear, as Ella arrived to grab hold of Holly's leg, one of the bus stop moms remarked, "I don't think you can board your child from anywhere in town. I'm pretty sure that's against the rules."

"Oh, hush up," Holly snapped, placing an arm on Ella's shoulder. *Probably a crafty, overachieving Dillydally mom. Collette type. Always burning up social media with photos of their perfect world.* Holly had seen a wallpapered bookshelf with parchment-covered books just last night. *Who does that?* To the bus driver: "Please? It's her first day of kindergarten."

"I'm sorry, ma'am. But what you're doing is very dangerous." In Holly's face, with little Ella by her side, he snapped the door closed, leaving them high and dry on the street. Traffic light turned green, and off he went. *Dang it!*

"Do you need a ride?" a mom offered. "I'd be happy to drive you."

Holly turned, and sure enough, the offer had come from Collette. Perfect Pinterest Collette.

"Oh, no, that's okay. Our car is right over there." Holly pointed. "But thank you. I, um . . . I lost track of time this morning because I was busy making a bulletin board for my family." Lie. "Upholstery nails, burlap, black silk ribbons." *What am I saying?* "I had trouble stretching the burlap across the canvas." Total lie. All of it. A total lie.

"Mom?" Ella tugged at Holly.

"Shhh, not now, sweetie."

Ella, holding fast to Holly's arm, was shaking. Holly didn't know if she was tired from running or shaking because she was scared of being so close to so many moving cars. *Whoops. My car! It's blocking traffic.* "Gotta go! Come on, Ella." Holly scooped Ella into her arms and ran with her toward their SUV as the cars in line behind their Suburban began honking. "Thanks anyway, Collette. Stop in sometime for a cup of tea!" Cup of tea? What was she saying? She hardly knew Collette.

They ran to the car, hopped inside, got buckled, and then drove down Village La-La, past the shops, past the bookstore, past the World of Primm and Drunken Plaid, and past Primm's Coffee Joe, where a musician they'd met the day they went to the Topiary Park sat outside playing his guitar. *Gary-Gee! That's his name.*

When they pulled into the grand cobblestone circular drive in front of Primm Academy, Ella's bus—Bus 13—was parked right in front of them.

"Yes! We made it." Holly clapped. Triumphant, she turned to face Ella in the back seat. "Woot! Woot! We did it, Ella. We made it."

Couldn't be more perfect. Now Ella could slip into the line and walk into the school with her bus mates—pretending she caught the bus on Petunia Lane. Pretending none of this ever happened.

"I don't want to go to school," Ella said, all wide eyed and frightened. "And who's that lady?"

A woman dressed in school colors, probably a teacher's assistant charged with working drop-off, walked toward their car, smiling and waving with gusto. Holly gave her the once-over. She seemed nice. White blouse with short capped sleeves exposing long, thin arms. Tailored black pants with a stylish gold belt that looked like a wide ribbon tied just above her right hip. From this distance, Holly could almost make out the shimmer of a honeybee hanging from a pearl necklace.

"She looks scary." Ella fidgeted.

"Scary? No way. She's wearing low-flat shoes. She's harmless."

"What if she's mean?"

What if she's mean? Is that what Ella is afraid of? Oh gosh, what if Ella gets inside and her kindergarten teacher is mean? God doesn't make mean kindergarten teachers, does he?

On the way to their car, the smiling woman passed a matching set of topiaries flanking the school gates.

"Ella, trust me. This woman is not mean."

"How do you know?"

Holly pointed at the woman's head. "She's wearing a headband."

"So?"

"So you've got nothing to worry about. Only nice people wear headbands."

Holly stared at Ella. Ella stared back.

"Is that true?" Ella asked. "Only nice people wear headbands?"

"Totally true."

As the woman with the headband opened Ella's car door, the look on Ella's face confirmed Holly's worst fear: Ella was petrified.

"I love you, Ella. You're going to have so much fun and meet lots of new friends." Holly plastered a golly-gee smile on her face as she watched Ella's face morph into sheer panic. "It's okay, Ella. Kindergarten is *fun*! If you're happy and you know it, clap your hands." Clap. Clap. Ella looked miserable. "If you're happy and you know it, clap your hands. If you're . . ." Holly wanted to cry.

"Good morning," said the headband woman to Ella. "My, you look pretty today in your blue dress. What's your name?"

Ella furrowed her brow and growled a deep, throaty growl—like a grizzly bear or someone possessed by the devil. "*I. Am. Pinkie Piiiie*," she bellowed.

The headband woman took a step back, surprised to hear a sound like that coming from such a little girl.

"Ella, that's not nice." Holly had hoped she'd be able to turn her morning around and everything would sparkle like a Mary Blair illustration in a Little Golden Book. But Ella—Ella was channeling demon-possessed Linda Blair in *The Exorcist*. "Apologize to the nice lady. Tell the nice woman your name, Ella . . . and use your *human* voice."

"*Nooooo*," Ella roared, eyes bulging, nostrils flaring, "*I'm not going to schoooooool!*"

What was happening?

Ella lowered her chin to her chest, then ordered Holly, "*Drive awayyyy, Mommyyy!*"

"I—I'm so sorry." The way Ella was acting, Holly half expected her to levitate. "I don't know what's gotten into her."

"Drive. Mommyyyy."

"She was fine this morning." Holly felt desperate. "I fixed her a plate of french toast." Total lie. "Played a little Beethoven"—another lie—"drove her to school . . . not because she missed the bus or anything—because it was a special day."

"I'm not going to SCHOOOOOOL!"

"Ella, honey. Stop that. Go with this nice woman. She'll help you inside."

"*NOOOOO.*"

Seriously, Ella?

"*NOT GOOOOOING.*"

The headband woman remained calm and upbeat. "Let's unsnap your seat belt and grab your backpack. Oh, I see you have a black puppy dog on your backpack. Looks like Terrier."

Holly's little *Exorcist* spawn growled, "*Don't touch the puppyyy,*" clearly competing against Linda Blair for Best Actress in one of the highest-grossing films of all time and the first horror film to be nominated for Best Picture—but that wasn't important right now. What was important was Ella. Who was practically foaming at the mouth. "NOT GOINGGGG."

"Kindergarten is fun, Ella. I promise." Holly reached for Ella, trying to squeeze her hand to encourage her to leave the car. Ella acted like she was about to get a katrillion immunizations all at once in her right shoulder with the way she leaned left to avoid the woman. Was this normal? Shouldn't Ella be a little bit curious about starting school? Was she *that* unprepared? *My gosh. Is this my fault?* Holly knew she wasn't supposed to do this, but bribes usually worked with Ella. "Go to school nicely, and we'll get some ice cream after school, Ella. I promise."

"I want another Pinkie Piiiieee."

"We'll get another Pinkie Pie, Ella, but you have to go with this nice woman and stop carrying on."

"You prooomise?"

The headband woman pulled Ella's puppy dog backpack from the car and hoisted it onto her shoulder. She unbuckled Ella and then pulled Ella delicately, but firmly, from her booster seat and onto the pavement. The woman told Holly, "This behavior is perfectly normal."

Normal? Holly thought Ella's head might spin around. Expected she'd have to relive the greatest projectile vomiting scene in film history—pea-green *Exorcist* vomit—sent from the depths of hell, the kind that turns a person's eyes evil and rips fire out of their belly. *Rrrrrooooooaaaaarrrrrr!*

Ella stood on the pavement pushing hot air through flared nostrils, grumbling as if something evil seethed inside her.

"Lots of children do this," the headband woman said.

"Oh, really?" Holly didn't mean to sound incredulous. "Because I'm wondering if I should start carrying a vial of holy water with me."

"Excuse me?" Taken aback, the headband lady twitched her head ever so slightly. Either she had no idea what Holly was saying, or she did know and thought Holly was a horrible mother for saying such a thing. What kind of mother made holy water jokes about her own child?

"I'm noooot going inside."

I mean, come on. Who is this child? Satan's Mini-Me? This isn't my *child.*

"You can't make me!"

"Ella, honey, stop that." Holly gave a stern look to Ella. "Be a good girl for Mommy."

"Nooooo."

"All of this is really strange because Ella never misbehaves," Holly told the woman. "She's an absolute angel at home."

"I don't like french toooooast!"

"She'll be fine," the woman said.

"I. Hate. French. Toooooast."

"I'll take her inside, and we'll find something to do right away." The headband woman showered Ella with a smile. "Maybe we'll draw a picture. Do you like crayons?"

"I like PINK ANDDD YELLOWWWW." And with that, Ella tried to plop down on the curb, but the headband woman was too fast for her and instead scooped Ella into her arms. Well, *that* unleashed

Armageddon. Yelling, screaming, depths of hell, Ella flailed about trying to escape as the poor woman wrestled to keep hold of her. Arms, legs, all of it. Movements so chaotic it looked like Ella was trying to take flight.

"LET ME GOOOOOO!" Ella thundered. "I HATE CRAYONS." But it sounded more like *I ATE CRAYONS*. Which Holly would be fine with right about now because she could at least blame Ella's behavior on an upset stomach.

This wasn't how it was supposed to go. Holly was supposed to prepare her child for school, both socially and emotionally. She felt—she didn't know what she felt. Guilt? Worry? Embarrassment? *Anger?* Why wasn't Ella walking through the gates of the school like all the other Primm children? *Seriously, Ella? Could you at least try to be prim? Because I'm pretty sure demon possession is not allowed at the academy.*

The poor woman's headband had been knocked silly and now sat askew; a hank of her hair hung across her left eye. Either thanks to nerves of steel, great training, or both, she remained calm, a consummate professional. She told Holly, "Call the school in thirty minutes. We'll send a teacher's aide from the guidance office to her classroom to check on her."

"I WANT MY TOOTH BACKKKK. I ONLY GOT A DOLLAR."

The woman was cool as a cucumber. Holly wished she could be like that, cucumber-like, but she wasn't. She was egg-like. Cracked easily, usually served scrambled, and could make you sick if you weren't careful.

"I. AM. PINKIE PIIIIIIIIIE!"

And then—the woman quickly released Ella, placing her firmly on the ground.

"Did she just bite you?" Holly's jaw dropped. *Please say no. Please say no.* "Did she?" Ella hadn't bitten anyone since she sank her teeth into a kid at a park in Boulder City when she was three. And then there was that one time when she was almost four and bit a kid at the library during story time. Okay, so maybe she bit him twice, but the bites were a week apart, and he deserved it both times—sort of. And Holly was sorry if that mom dropped out of Mommy & Me Story Time because *Ella* couldn't control herself. But Ella—Ella had never bitten a *grown*-up.

"I'm so sorry. Did she bite you? She bit you. Please tell me she didn't bite you. She did—didn't she? She bit you?"

"Yes." The woman inspected the top of her arm for broken skin.

"Anything?" asked Holly. Thank goodness, no. Just teeth marks the size of a tiny shark's. "Ella. Apologize right now. Biting is *not* okay." Holly pleaded with the woman. "I'm so sorry. I'm as surprised as you are. Ella's never bitten anyone. Ever."

"It'll be okay in a few minutes," the woman said.

How is she still pleasant to us? How? My rabid kid just bit her bicep.

"Ella will be fine once she gets inside. Trust me," the woman told Holly. "Kids always do better once the mother leaves."

Wait. What? "Is that true?" *That's a horrible thing to say.*

"Usually. Yes. I'm afraid it is." The woman closed the car door with a reluctant smile, separating Holly from the child she'd brought into this world—a demon spawn, true, but she was Holly's demon spawn.

Holly could barely see the top of Ella's head. Barely see the little blue barrette she had fastened above her ear while urging her to finish her waffle. The barrier between them was just a car door, but apparently the barrier worked because through the closed window, Holly watched the woman say a few words to Ella, and then, miraculously, as if the skies opened up and a ray of sunshine beamed down from the heavens to light upon Ella's head, Ella was cured. No more demon possession. No more Linda Blair.

Ella took the woman's hand and walked up the cobblestone sidewalk as if nothing had happened. At least Holly was right about one thing: people who wore headbands tended to be nice people—despite telling mothers their children did better after they left.

Holly watched the two of them walk hand in hand up the cobblestone sidewalk and toward the grand front entrance that welcomed the children of Primm to the first day of school. The headband woman pulled a tissue from her pocket to wipe Ella's cheeks. Stopping beside a pair of matching topiaries to wait at the back of a line, Ella turned to give Holly a tiny frightened wave. Holly pinched her arm. So this was it: kindergarten. Holly's baby girl—all grown up.

10

Moments later

With Ella in line on the sidewalk, there was nothing for Holly to do at the moment except wait for the buses in front of her to pull out. Then she'd go home and take a shower, try to figure out what she was supposed to do with herself now that Ella would be gone all day every day. Holly reached for her phone to call Jack but didn't have it because she'd left the house in such a hurry.

Holed up in her red Chevy Suburban, she passed the time watching Mary-Margaret St. James place an apple and a pencil into the hand of every child who disembarked from a bright-yellow school bus. The kids walked in single file beside the stately brick-and-iron gate, down the cobblestone sidewalk, and in through the same heavy wooden doors that Ella was in line to enter.

At least a dozen moms, fanned out behind Mary-Margaret, worked countless bushels of apples, handing off what must have amounted to over one thousand pencils and pieces of fruit, if Holly's student head count was correct. Kindergarten through twelfth grade, about four classrooms per grade, twenty-five kids in each classroom. The apple passing resembled a bucket brigade, the kind used by firefighters before the invention of hand-pump fire engines. But they weren't firefighters passing buckets of water to extinguish a fire. They were chipper, hardworking school moms dressed in the school colors of gold, black, and white, passing shiny red apples and pale-yellow pencils to eager schoolchildren. Intercepting each and every child to bestow a greeting, an apple, and a pencil certainly slowed the unload, but what could be more perfect? The moms' flawless execution, the way they bent and reached in choreographed, synchronized assembly, astounded Holly. This dance of the mothers of Primm should be set to music, she thought. A ballet. No! A lilting instrumental jingle you'd expect to hear in a sappy nuclear family television show: *Gee, Wally, I sure do like apples.*

She relished her front-row seat on opening day at Primm Academy because the two buses in front of her hadn't unloaded, so her SUV was perfectly positioned at the centermost point of the academy's front circular drive. Mary-Margaret was a scant two bus lengths away, a safe distance for Holly to study her from while not feeling she needed to interact. Like she was on safari, the lioness fascinated Holly, but she didn't want to get too close. She nursed her vanilla hazelnut coffee, remembering how the mothers fell into orbit around Mary-Margaret the other night, while all Holly wanted to do was escape. How did one mom manage to position herself as the sun in the center of Primm's little solar system? As PTA president, Mary-Margaret reigned supreme over all the school moms at Primm Academy. According to Penelope, as a founding member of the Magnolia Society, Mary-Margaret reigned supreme over all the philanthropists in the village. That was a lot of power. Maybe Mary-Margaret was the sun.

Good gravy, you'd think these buses would unload a little faster. And then she saw the culprit behind the slow unload: an equally slow volunteer mom staging photographs of the children as they stepped off the bus. Mary-Margaret: greeting, apple, pencil—wait for it . . . *smile.* Next child. Greeting, apple, pencil—wait for it . . . *smile.* Holly sipped her coffee, admiring the photographer and the dedication of the moms in the apple brigade. She should volunteer for something at the school. She was grateful for the school moms. Had Ella made the bus that morning, she would be enjoying an apple and a welcome pencil. And yet, somehow, Holly couldn't bring herself to sign on the dotted line when Mary-Margaret asked for help the other night.

Outside Holly's car window, over the din of school buses and kids, she heard Gary-Gee playing his guitar outside Primm's Coffee Joe—catchy acoustic tunes, folksy renditions of "You Are My Sunshine" and "Zip-a-Dee-Doo-Dah" played into a microphone that fed into a large speaker. Holly and Ella had stopped to sing with him the other day after leaving the Topiary Park during one of those fleeting moments when Holly found herself believing their new life in the Village of Primm would be perfect. She knew that wasn't entirely realistic—nothing and nowhere was perfect—but she desperately wanted a happily ever after for this once upon a time in their family's life.

Taking a quick sip, Holly choked on her coffee. *Did Mary-Margaret just point at me? Why is she snapping her fingers? What'd I do?* Holly looked over her shoulder. *There must be some mistake. Why is she leaving the apple brigade? Don't leave the apple brigade, Mary-Margaret. Someone might need you.*

She tried to ignore it. Mary-Margaret must be walking somewhere else—toward the flagpole—not toward Holly. Holly leaned back in her driver's seat, trying to act chill as she focused on the bumper of the bus in front of her, but the sight of Mary-Margaret marching down the cobblestone sidewalk, past the open gate flanked by those perfectly manicured topiaries, made Holly feel like she was back in film school. She couldn't help but imagine Mary-Margaret as the Queen of Hearts, stomping about in a comically blind fury, about to swing her Tudor rose in Holly's direction and command, *Off with her head!*

Mary-Margaret was practically shouting. "Used car park thar!" Something.

What was she saying?

"You!" Mary-Margaret snapped and pointed. "Used car park thar!"

What's going on? Why the panic? Holly hated panic. Hated confrontations. She found herself fighting the urge to throw her SUV into drive, pull onto the grass, and gun it past the flagpole, then out onto Village La-La, tires screeching, leaving behind the pungent smell of rubber as it hit the road. But she couldn't go anywhere because she was trapped. Bus 13, with its wide black bumper, was a thick line across Holly's windshield, and there was another bus behind her.

Holly wished Ella would let go of that woman's hand, leave the line, and jump into the back seat, clapping and saying, *Move it, Mommy. Move it, move it, move it!* Like Holly was Butch Cassidy, and Ella the Sundance Kid. Like this wasn't reality. This wasn't Primm Academy, and they didn't live in the Village of Primm, and Mary-Margaret St. James wasn't rushing toward Holly at this very moment. Holly'd give anything to be on a movie set, pulling off a bank robbery, a casino heist, a dramatic escape from kindergarten. Holly and her little Ella, driving off into the sunset. Holly with her coffee; Ella, her sippy—er, *sports* cup—of watered-down white grape juice.

"Excuse me. Woman in the car!" Mary-Margaret brushed past Ella, who was still standing near the pair of triple-sphere topiaries. Mary-Margaret stepped off the sidewalk and onto the circular drive. "Yoo-hooo!" She got closer. Closer . . . closer.

"*Me?*" Holly mouthed, pointing to her chest. She was a bit alarmed by Mary-Margaret's brazen attention. Holly didn't want to be noticed by anyone in Primm yet. She wanted to unpack her house, get settled with school, enjoy a little peace and quiet, and *then* venture into the mom world. The privacy she was enjoying was kind of nice right now.

Mary-Margaret marched toward Holly—and by default, so did the school crest embroidered in golden threads on the left breast pocket of her starched white shirt. Mary-Margaret's walk was prissy but efficient. Elbows bent, hands clenched, hips swinging from side to side in her tailored black pencil skirt. Holly wondered, *How long does it take for Mary-Margaret to get dressed in the morning?* Holly had visited all three clothing stores in Primm—Prim & Proper, the World of Primm, and Drunken Plaid. None of them had clothes that nice, and that said a lot. Where'd Mary-Margaret shop? Was everything custom made? Holly had read about devils who wore Prada.

Knock. Knock. Knock. Mary-Margaret rapped her knuckles on Holly's driver's side window, and all Holly could think was, *Spit cakes! I haven't showered.* Why would she? She was just driving Ella to school. She was planning to return home, take a shower, and begin her day. She couldn't deal with Mary-Margaret right now. Not like this.

Knock. Knock. Knock. "Roll down your window. It's me: Mary-Margaret St. James."

Mary-Margaret peered down a thin nose. Bright-white teeth with a wedge of pink bubble gum in the way back. Her hair was smooth, styled, fixed with a golden grosgrain ribbon. Holly's mousy brown hair needed a root touch-up to cover sprigs of early gray and was also fixed—beneath a baseball hat. Why? Because she'd stayed up late last night stalking Collette's boards on Pinterest while emailing a psychic named Betty. Holly couldn't deal with this right now. She wasn't prepared. Wasn't fully awake. Wasn't interested in reality but couldn't harness the power of her imagination to escape into film.

"It's me, Mary-Margaret St. James. Open up! Roll down your window." Knock, knock, knock. Thin fingers. Bony knuckles. "You can't park here." *What do you mean I can't park here?* Holly gestured to all the buses. *This is the drop-off lane, right?* And then it hit her: "Used car park thar." Mary-Margaret had been saying "You can't park there."

"You're in the bus lane," Mary-Margaret scolded, arms folded. "Cars aren't allowed. Only buses. Roll down your window, Fruit Roll-Up." Mary-Margaret spoke through Holly's closed window, overenunciating every word. "What. Is. Your. Naaaaaame?" *Wait. Did she just call me a Fruit Roll-Up?* Holly rolled her window down. Immediately, Mary-Margaret was in Holly's face. "You look familiar," Mary-Margaret said, hands on hips. "Oh yes! I remember you—at the meeting the other night—you left early."

Holly told her, "My name is Holly Banks." And Holly knew Mary-Margaret heard her, but Mary-Margaret was such a narcissist she ignored Holly. Talked right over her. Like she wasn't even there because Mary-Margaret was the only one that mattered in the conversation.

"What's your name?"

"---."

"Polly Banks. That's right," Mary-Margaret said. "I remember now."

Mary-Margaret was so close Holly smelled her perfume. Gardenia. Tuberose. Something.

"Sorry, Polly, you can't park here."

Mary-Margaret shook her head at Holly as Holly decided she smelled of gardenia. Tuberose was sharp, almost bitter. Gardenia was sweeter, creamier.

"No cars in the bus lane. Didn't you read the back-to-school handbook? You're mucking up drop-off on the first day of school." Mary-Margaret exhaled as if Holly were the lamest mom in the world. "That happens, I guess." Another pause. "You don't know how things work around here. Do you?" She twitched an eyebrow.

Holly opened her mouth to reply, but—

"You need a back-to-school handbook. Can't live without one. Lemme guess. You left before I handed them out. I'll try to find one for you—in my free time. It *is* the first day of school, and I *am* the president of the Primm Academy PTA. I'm really busy, you know."

Holly looked out her windshield, hoping the buses in front of her would pull forward and bring a natural end to their conversation. No such luck. The apple brigade was still in full swing, indicating the first bus in line hadn't finished unloading yet. Mary-Margaret kept tabs on the apple brigade too; the sight of moms working like a machine appeared to bring her much pleasure.

"Hard to believe, isn't it?" Mary-Margaret said. "The children—they grow up so fast." Mary-Margaret used Holly's mirror to check her hair. "But not us. We stay young. Well, at least, I do."

"---."

"Crossing guards. I agree." Mary-Margaret nodded. "We need crossing guards so drivers like you, my little cupcake, don't cross the line."

Cupcake?

"Wow. This is a big red sports utility vehicle!" Mary-Margaret's eyes scanned the length and girth of Holly's car. "Looks like you're driving Clifford the Big Red Dog. What kind is it? A Suburban Godzilla something?"

"---."

"Okay, Emily Elizabeth—take your big red dog and run along. Ha!" Big smile.

Speaking of smiles, the bus in front of Holly looked like a bright-yellow face emoji with no expression. Just blinking red eyes and a straight black bumper mouth. Bus 13. The bus Ella would have taken if they hadn't missed it.

"Try squeaking past it on the left. Because you can't stay here. You're ruining morning drop-off on the first day of school. That bus in front of you is packed with children, all hopeful and happy, ready for the first day of school at Primm Academy. *Hip! Hip!*"

"---?"

"Hip. Hip. That's what we say at Primm Academy." Mary-Margaret placed her delicate hand over her heart, covering the gilded school emblem. "The 'hooray' is implied. It's something we feel in our heart."

Ha!

"What's so funny?" Mary-Margaret whined. "Now let's go! Let's move this thing." Snap, snap, snap. Through Holly's window, Mary-Margaret's bracelets jingled in Holly's face.

"Try scooting past that bus. Just pull up and try getting around it on the left side," said Mary-Margaret. "I'll direct this Suburban Godzilla. But you really should know: it smells like sour grape juice in there."

Excuse me?

"And I see there's a bunch of crushed-up Cheerios and Goldfish in your back seat. You should probably have it detailed. I find I'm more organized when my car is clean. Right. Car detailing—I'll try to get you a coupon. Now let's get you out of the bus lane. Okay, I'll direct you . . ."

"---."

"Nope!" Mary-Margaret put her fingers in her ears. "No way, I insist. You can trust me. I'll direct you." She skipped to the front of Holly's SUV, placing herself near the left rear corner of the school bus, positioning herself safely to the side of both vehicles. Mary-Margaret motioned which way she wanted Holly to turn her steering wheel—and Holly was the fool who listened. Holly was the fool who let herself be led by a woman who said, "Hip, hip!" because she felt the "hooray" in her heart.

"Slowly, slowly, slowly, a little bit more," Mary-Margaret coaxed, "a little bit more . . ." Like she was a traffic cop—in heels. "You can trust me, a little bit more, a little bit more. Punch the gas . . . good, press your foot down; punch it some more." More hand signals. "Good. Turn your head and look behind you if you want to. I'll watch your front. That's right. A little more gas, more, more. Good, now come forward; punch the gas; come forward . . . punch the gas. Forward. Forward. More gas. Forward. More ga—"

Bang!

"Aaaaahhhhh! Sweet cherry pie! Look what you've done!" Mary-Margaret raced to Holly's window. "You just hit a school bus on the first day of school. *Are you crazy?* I can't believe you just *did* that!"

Whatthe

frrrrrruck

just

happened.

Mary-Margaret hooted and hollered. She wouldn't stop. She signaled the apple brigade. "See this mom?" She pointed. "She just hit a school bus. Someone! Quick. Call 911. Call 911!"

Why did I trust her? How could I be so stupid? Holly closed her eyes, desperately hoping this was just a dream, a figment of her imagination, one of those Walter Mitty moments, a momentary lapse into one of those silly film sequences she imagined when under stress.

Holly opened her eyes. And dang it, this wasn't the movies.

I hit a school bus?

Me?

Me.

I hit a school bus.

Holly covered her face. She looked at the crunched and shattered front right end of her Suburban, now caught beneath the back left corner of the bus bumper. She'd been inches away from not hitting the bus. Now there was a streak of red paint on the black bumper announcing to the world Holly was there.

Holly was certain the bus driver would want to talk to her. She was sure the principal would want to talk to her. *But I didn't hit it that hard. Did I? No, I couldn't have.*

Holly checked the pack of kids gaping down at her from the rear window of the bus. They appeared to be—fine—thank God. Actually, they were laughing and pointing at Holly like she just did something really embarrassing like walk out of a bathroom with toilet paper stuck to her shoe. She didn't know what to do, so she sort of gave them all a pathetic little wave and two thumbs up. Like she was the clown hired to entertain them on the first day of school. Holly mumbled to herself, "Get me outa here. Someone—anyone. Help me!"

Afraid of what she might see, she glanced out her driver's side window and down toward the village square. Gary-Gee had stopped playing

"Zip-a-Dee-Doo-Dah." Why? Why did he stop playing "Zip-a-Dee-Doo-Dah?" It was such a nice song. *Wait. What?* He turned his mic up. Now he was strumming "The Wheels on the Bus." No! Not *that* song! Suddenly, that was all Holly could hear. Over and over, ringing in her ears. She covered her ears. *I'm going crazy. Mary-Margaret—the Village of Primm—they're making me crazy.* Holly felt her cheeks heat up. *I'm red faced. I know I am.* Patrons sitting outside Primm's Coffee Joe turned her way and pointed. Everyone knew. Everyone saw it. Everyone was talking about her. Someone's yappy little dog was barking at her. Holly hated yappy little dogs. Why was that dog barking? *Stop barking, dog!*

Looking out her passenger window, over to the cobblestone sidewalk—to Holly's horror, the apple brigade ground to a halt; apples and pencils hung in the balance. Little children with outstretched hands went unnoticed by the moms. If this were a real bucket brigade of water to douse a fire, the flames would rage out of control because now—especially with Mary-Margaret carrying on—none of the mothers could focus. Their well-oiled machine was broken, and Holly was the louse who broke it. Her heart sank. *I've broken the apple brigade. Me. I did that.*

Mary-Margaret, running in circles, pointed: *She hit a bus! That mom hit a bus!*

There was nowhere to turn, nowhere to look, so Holly clutched hold of her rearview mirror, twisted it toward her reflection, and pretended she was checking to see if something was caught in her eye. Pretended to check her contacts. Something. "You know what?" she said to herself as she tugged her lower lid down to stare into her own eyeball. "You suck, Holly Banks. You're a bad mom." And then, Holly looked. And she saw Ella's face, and Ella's face saw Holly's: Ella. Ella had seen the whole thing.

No! No! NO!

Holly rolled the passenger-side window down as fast as she could. "Ella!" she hollered. "Ella, it's okay. Mommy hit your bus, but no one's hurt. It's just a fender bender."

Mary-Margaret was at Holly's window, eyes huge. "You just hit a school bus on the first day of school. Who does that?"

"---!"

"Well, I'm sure you're sorry," Mary-Margaret said. "Who wouldn't be? Tell you what. You go talk to the bus driver and Principal Hayes about this fender bend—*no!* This accident—*no!* This senseless-collision-that-never-should-have-happened, and then maybe the PTA won't suspend your driver's license on school campus. Or distribute your face on a school flyer with the words *Danger to Society* in big bold letters that even the kindergarteners can read." Mary-Margaret gasped, covering her mouth and pointing toward the school office. "Oh! Oh, my goodness, will you look at that?"

"---?"

"*That.* Bree-with-an-E Snelp. Who clearly needs help—because she's running? In heels? Bree never runs. Ever." Mary-Margaret stared at Holly. "You must have scared her. That's not good. Bree-with-an-E wears Spanx. If she gets out of breath, she could faint and hurt herself. Then you'd *really* be sorry."

"---?"

"It's a nickname. Bree-with-an-E is the school historian; she's a Scrapbooking Mom and a freelance writer for the *Primm Gazette*," Mary-Margaret said. "Why won't you get out of your car? You hit that bus three minutes ago. Get out. Do something. Why are you still sitting there clutching your steering wheel? You look absolutely panicked. Just a minute." Mary-Margaret waved to Bree-with-an-E. "Over here! We're over here!"

Bree-with-an-E arrived, completely out of breath, bulky camera hanging from a strap around her neck.

Mary-Margaret grabbed Bree-with-an-E by the shoulders. "Thank goodness you got here when you did, Bree-with-an-E." Kiss, kiss. "Yes, of course I know what happened. I was here. I was an innocent bystander, minding my own business," Mary-Margaret reported. "Bree-with-an-E, you know who this is, don't you? The escape artist who sniper-crawled out of my meeting."

Whoops! How does Mary-Margaret know about that? She knows I crawled out?

Mary-Margaret pointed at Holly's vanilla hazelnut. "Honestly. An open cup of coffee?" She snickered. "With all the social injustice you're bringing to our quiet little school," she told Holly, "I sure hope you're drinking free trade."

Mary-Margaret shook her head at Bree-with-an-E as Holly glanced slowly in Ella's direction. She couldn't see her; the line had moved. Ella must be inside.

"Get this, Bree-with-an-E: she won't get out of her car. It's like she's trapped inside, frozen to her seat." Mary-Margaret placed both hands on her hips. "I give up with this one. Honestly, I do."

Holly tried telling Mary-Margaret there weren't any signs indicating cars couldn't use the bus lane. But Mary-Margaret yipped at Holly and said something about crossing guards.

"It's in the handbook," Mary-Margaret said. "No one drives a car into the bus lane. Everything's in the handbook."

"---."

"Well, if you didn't sneak out of the meeting like a spy from the Southern Lakes PTA, you would have been given a handbook! And guess what? Since you left early, I signed you up. Congratulations. You're now a kindergarten Room Mom. Next time, don't crawl out of a PTA meeting on your stomach." Mary-Margaret narrowed her eyes. "Escapees never truly escape—now do they?" Without skipping a beat, she added, "And yes, I know there was a stack of handbooks on the table beside me Friday night, but I forgot to give you one because you had me so flustered by your refusal to sign a school spirit clipboard. Who's ever heard of a mom so determined to avoid volunteering? Are you sure you're not from Southern Lakes?"

Holly wanted to throw up. Seriously, she felt nauseous. This whole thing was being blown out of proportion. Holly needed to inspect the damage to her car and the bus. Instead, she said something Mary-Margaret promptly ignored.

And then Mary-Margaret told Bree-with-an-E, "At the meeting Friday night, after twisting her arm, she offered to send napkins to a class party. *Napkins!* I know, right? So lame!"

"---?"

"What? I'm not overreacting," Mary-Margaret said. "I never over-react. But guess what? The commuter traffic can't get around the buses because the buses can't get off the street to enter the bus lane. Listen." She cupped an ear. "Everyone's starting to honk. The entire town will be affected. People traveling on Village La-La will be late for work. Essential people like brain surgeons, NASA scientists, ambassadors to foreign countries, PTA presidents, people like that. Think of the impact on the local economy." Mary-Margaret paused. Her eyes widened. "Oh, my goodness. *Hip! Hip!* This is great for you, Bree-with-an-E. You can write an article about this, and it'll end up on the front page of the *Primm Gazette*. It will. I know it will." She added, "My grandfather, Merchant Meek Hopscotch the Third, publishes the *Primm Gazette*. I'll call him. Like, pronto. Oh, congratulations, Bree-with-an-E!" Mary-Margaret gave her a big hug. "The front page!"

"---."

"Excuse me, Bree-with-an-E," Mary-Margaret said. "I'm being interrupted." Mary-Margaret glared at Holly like Holly was a child. "Yes? What is it? What's so important?"

"---."

"Yes, I know you want to go home. You always want to go home. But you can't. You're trapped. I suppose you could step out of your car and stand out here with us."

"---."

"No? Why not? Do you have environmental allergies that prevent you from leaving your car? Like, maybe you're allergic to your kid's school?"

"---."

"No? Are you sure?"

"---."

"Are you sure you're sure?"

"---."

"Are you sure you're sure you're sure?"

"---!"

"Okay, okay, you don't have to *yell* at Mary-Margaret!" Mary-Margaret turned to Bree-with-an-E. "Bree-with-an-E, did you bring your camera? Of course you did. It's the first day of school, and you're a Scrapbooking Mom. Scrapbooking Moms document everything."

Mary-Margaret said to Bree-with-an-E, "You should probably photograph her now before the police arrive."

Wait. *What?* No.

"---!"

"Of course I need to call the police," Mary-Margaret said, matter-of-factly. "There's been an accident. An accident involving *children*."

Holly looked at the *children* on the bus. They clearly couldn't care less. The bus driver? He probably cared, but the bus in front of him was still unloading, so Holly assumed he couldn't leave the driver's seat until he pulled forward and unloaded all his kids, or the kids on his bus would be unsupervised. *How long does it take to unload these buses?* It was possible there was so much commotion on the bus on the first day of school he didn't realize he'd been hit from behind. Who knew? It could happen.

"She's not even wearing a seat belt," Mary-Margaret said. "And she won't get out of her car. She won't budge." Mary-Margaret leaned in to grumble in Bree-with-an-E's ear. "I just found her, sitting here with an open cup of hot coffee. In the bus lane! Probably texting while her car was still running. Texting while carpooling. So dangerous! Let's take a mug shot before the police arrive," she told Bree-with-an-E. To Holly, Mary-Margaret said, "Get ready to say cheese!"

But then, suddenly, Mary-Margaret stopped. "Wait a minute."

She leaned through Holly's car window to get a closer look.

"Oh. My. Gosh." Mary-Margaret's jaw dropped. She pointed.

Freaking crud, thought Holly. *Just when I thought my morning couldn't get any worse—*

"Bree-with-an-E, look!" Mary-Margaret started in. "I've never seen anything like this in all my life. She looks normal from outside the window. In fact, if she were driving down the street, you wouldn't think anything was strange about her at all. But now that I'm standing next to her, when I lean in the window to take a closer look—no wonder she won't get out of the car. Look what she's wearing! Pink and brown piggies? Those aren't *pants*—those are pajama bottoms. What kind of a mother drives to school wearing pajama bottoms?"

Mary-Margaret snatched Bree-with-an-E's camera, and Holly swore, if she were a cartoon character in the Sunday paper, she'd be drawn with a red face and squiggly lines around her head. If Holly were a comic strip, right about now, she'd be shouting all sorts of comic strip obscenicons and grawlixes at Mary-Margaret.

"@#$%&!"

"@#$%&!"

"@#$%&!"

But Mary-Margaret didn't care.

Because she was Mary-Margaret.

"Say cheese!" Mary-Margaret sang.

CLICK!

Moment of truth? Cameras didn't lie: Holly wasn't like Plume. Other mothers were like Plume. Topiaries were fanciful living sculptures. Holly? She was a ficus tree. No! A spider plant: easy to grow but sprawling, shabby, and unattractive. Moving to the Village of Primm was a mistake. Holly was her mother's daughter. *Ais me, Ella, hit's your mom. Comes to me, Ella; comes to Mommy.*

If this morning had been filmed, if this morning were Holly's submission to the Wilhelm Klaus Film Festival, she'd open with an expansive aerial shot of the village, capturing all the beauty and motherly perfection that was Primm. And then she'd zoom in on herself—the troll crouched low in piggy pajamas, desperately clutching a vanilla hazelnut coffee. Holly wished she'd never met the megalomaniacal Mary-Margaret St. James. When Holly was with Mary-Margaret, she lost all confidence. Lost her voice. She became this "---." and this "---?" and this "---!" She became so small, so passive—*poof!*—you hardly saw her on the page. Holly was a flawed, hapless underdog lost in an unfamiliar land, powerless when facing the silver-tongued antagonist.

Poor Ella. Her childhood portal? Lined with piggy graffiti.

Holly wondered which was worse:

Being a bad mom?

Or becoming your mom?

11

After the commotion

Once inside the front foyer of Primm Academy, Principal Hayes directed Holly to a wooden bench outside the school office, instructing her to wait while the students finished entering and he had the chance to read morning announcements. Outside, the buses unloaded from Village La-La at the entrance to the circular drive, because Holly's SUV sat pressed against Bus 13, blocking traffic from entering. Principal Hayes was very precise, telling Holly, in no uncertain terms, "Sit here. Do not leave."

"It's not *my* fault," Holly told him, pointing to the front courtyard, where Mary-Margaret dashed about, handing out Ticonderoga pencils and Red Delicious apples. "*She* made me do it. It's her fault."

"I'll be with you in a moment." Principal Hayes disappeared into the school office.

Holly started counting black and white floor tiles, wondering what Ella was doing. Wondering what Ella was thinking. She leaned over the edge of the wooden bench to peer down the hallway, and then, wouldn't you know it, in through Primm's front wooden doors, *she* sauntered in: Mary-Margaret St. James. Had they been batwing doors from an old western, and had Mary-Margaret been Clint Eastwood—a pale-riding, ethereal drifter pushing her way into the joint on a cloud of dirt and smoke—Holly would be choking on plumes of dust as a cameraman, trained to film a shot like the great Sergio Leone, captured first a panoramic shot and then a close-up of Mary-Margaret's baby blues as they stared down at Holly, the dying man on the saloon floor in *Unforgiven*, the pathetic soul at the receiving end of Mary-Margaret's cocked-and-loaded gun. *I don't deserve this,* Holly would say, referring to the bus, the sign-up sheets, the humiliation.

Holly shook her head, snapping out of it. *I gotta stop doing this. Life isn't a movie. Mary-Margaret isn't an ethereal drifter. Every "kill" is not a moral question for Mary-Margaret the way it was for Clint Eastwood's character. Mary-Margaret is a volunteer school mom. There's no killing in the PTA. Showdowns, yes. But no actual killing.* At least, Holly hoped not.

"Whew!" Mary-Margaret breezed her way across the ceramic tiles, swinging a basket like she was a leggy fashion model working the catwalk. "I'm going to need more pencils." She winked at Holly as if nothing had happened, as if she hadn't just coaxed the front end of Holly's SUV into the back end of Bus 13. "Ticonderoga." Mary-Margaret spoke with wistful breathiness. "World's best pencil, don't you think?"

Holly didn't respond. She wasn't going to offer her point of view only to be ignored.

There'd be no statements from Holly. "---."

No questions. "---?"

Not even the occasional interjection or exclamation. "---!"

Although there were lots of interjections Holly'd like to exclaim right about now. She'd love to hurl all eight parts of speech at Mary-Margaret—dump a bucket of punctuation marks on Mary-Margaret's head.

But Holly kept her cool and kept her mouth shut. She folded both arms across her chest and simply glared at Mary-Margaret, devil incarnate, so she'd know Holly hadn't forgotten about the bus—or the photo Mary-Margaret just took of her carpooling in pajama bottoms. But while Holly crumpled her eyebrows, showing Mary-Margaret her evil eyes, resolving to punish Mary-Margaret with her silence and utter lack of concern, Mary-Margaret blathered on about pencils. Holly sure hoped Mary-Margaret wasn't ignoring the fact that Holly was ignoring her.

"Why aren't you in the Community Helper Annex with Officer Knapp?" Mary-Margaret pointed at Holly with a pencil. "The time-out chairs in the annex are upholstered. Easier on the tushy."

Time-out chair? Holly wasn't in a time-out. Was she? No, of course not. Holly was a grown woman.

Mary-Margaret blew on the tip of her pencil like it was the barrel of a smoking gun, then turned on her heel and sauntered down the hallway toward some distant supply closet filled with more pencils. *Good riddance.*

Holly slipped over to the windows to check on her SUV. From Holly's view, the front right headlight needed replacing, and there was a bit of bodywork to be done. *Seriously? I didn't hit it that hard.* Bus bumpers must be made of kryptonite. Holly needed to call Jack and tell him she wrecked the Suburban.

Bree-with-an-E burst into the sunlit foyer, furiously scratching her arms. She nodded hello to Holly as she rushed past the row of floor-to-ceiling windows.

"Are you okay?" Holly asked, scurrying after her, hoping she'd stop. Holly wanted that photo. Holly needed that photo.

"I'm fine," Bree-with-an-E snapped. "Why wouldn't I be? Because I worked all summer on the Crayons-to-College Symposium scheduled for this weekend and now no one's coming to it because they're all going to that stupid Cherry Festival on The Lawn? Is that why you're asking?"

Actually, Holly had no idea Bree-with-an-E was running the—what'd she call it? The Crayons-to-College Symposium?

"Because I'm fine, thank you. I'm just"—she raked her nails across her arm—"I'm just a bit . . ." She scratched the back of her neck. "I think it's hives."

"Bree," Holly said, sweet as sugar. "I'm so sorry about your hives, but would you mind deleting that picture Mary-Margaret took of me?"

"Is that all you care about? A *photo*? The kids are starting their education today. Soon, they'll surrender their crayons in pursuit of a college education, and all you can think about is a *photograph*? I suppose you're skipping my event too?"

"What do you want for it, Bree? Name your price." When Holly thought about politicians and Hollywood celebrities who, over the years, probably paid tons of money to stop incriminating photos from being circulated, it made her wonder what it would take to get an incriminating photo away from a mom. What was considered a lot of money in the mom world? What offer could Holly make that no mother in her right mind would refuse? "I'll give you fifty bucks."

"I don't need your money," Bree barked. "I need a nap."

That's it!

"Deal!" Holly jumped at the chance. "A nap. Let's shake on it. You give me that photo, and I'll give you a nap. I'll come over to your house this afternoon and do whatever you want me to do so you can sleep. I'll watch your children, clean your house."

Bree scratched her elbow, presumably considering Holly's offer. Holly suspected if Bree wasn't careful, she might rip her skin off.

"Who are you?"

"Holly Banks." Holly extended her hand to shake Bree's, hoping the hives weren't contagious. "I live on Petunia Lane."

"That was a rhetorical question." Bree ignored Holly's offer to shake hands. "I know who you are."

"So. Can I give you a nap? Because I'd really love to—in exchange for that photo. I'll even do your dishes and fold your laundry so you can sleep, sleep, sleep. Want me to drive your carpools?"

"Carpools? No. Absolutely not," Bree said. "I'll tell you what. I'll give you the photo if you run the Crayons-to-College Symposium this weekend."

"What? Me?" Holly stammered. "Why, I—what?"

"Exactly," Bree snipped, stomping down the hallway, fingernails raking her skin. "No one can do everything. But me? Me? I have to do everything."

Primm's sound system left something to be desired. A loud crackle pierced the airspace, followed by that familiar horrid whine you heard when the frequency distorted as it came out of a speaker. The voice of Principal Hayes, heard through tiny brown boxes mounted throughout the school, asked everyone to please stand to say the Pledge of Allegiance.

Holly stood to face the American flag hanging beside the office door, right hand covering her heart, pink and brown piggies covering her legs. She began when Principal Hayes began, but he spoke so incredibly slow it really dragged on.

Principal Hayes: "I." (Pause.) "Pledge." (Pause.) "Allegiance." (Pause.)

Was he speaking slowly because he was teaching the pledge to the younger grades? Holly figured most families didn't pledge allegiance to the flag over breakfast. They certainly didn't in their home. By the time they were finally saying "to" (pause), "the" (pause), "flag," Holly's attention had drifted to the announcements on the large bulletin board beside her.

An enormous sun cut from bright-yellow paper smiled down on Holly, casting its paper rays on the red, white, and blue flyers pinned to the board. Upon closer inspection, Holly realized the entire board was dedicated to volunteer opportunities for parents. Each of the five cascading paper rays of the sun had a phrase written on it in Sharpie marker. Five rays of sunlight from left to right:

/ No one /
/ can do everything /
/ but everyone /
/ can do something. /
/—Mary-Margaret St. James /

Room parents needed. Parents needed for playground duty and cafeteria duty. Parents needed to lead Girl Scout troops, Cub Scouts, and an after-school soccer league. One flyer asked for eight parents to run a chess club after school on Wednesdays and Fridays. According to the flyer, if eight parents didn't sign up to run the program and lead the instruction, students would be denied the opportunity to play tournament-level chess. *Really?* Holly assumed most homes in Primm had a chess set lying around. Couldn't the kids play chess at home? Did they really need eight parents, twice per week, for two hours of chess instruction? She did some calculations. That was thirty-two cumulative hours of volunteer parent labor, per week, for six weeks. That was like a full-time job if done by one parent, and most parents already had plenty to do outside of the world of competitive chess. *And get this: the cost to enroll your child in the chess program costs more than it would cost to buy a nice chess set. Am I wrong? Or am I cynical? Probably cynical.*

A group of moms gathered, congregating on the eight-foot-wide welcome mat inside the front wooden doors of the school. One of the moms carried professionally made posters advertising the Cherry Festival on The Lawn. The other mothers held freshly baked cherry pies—presumably for the teachers' lounge?

With no one else in the front foyer at that moment but the five of them, Holly had no choice but to say "hi" and "hello" to the Pie Moms. Turned out they were really nice. They answered back with typical mom-like greetings. "Exciting day, isn't it?" "So sad summer with the little ones is over." "Goes by so fast." That sort of thing. They were everything you'd imagine pie-baking moms to be: relaxed yet polished, genuinely nice, and pretty, like angels. Pie angels. And while they were busy being their perfect little selves, Holly managed to blurt, "Where does Dorothy from *The Wizard of Oz* weigh a pie?" The Pie Moms exchanged glances, and then one of them said, "I give up. Where?"

Holly sang out the punch line: "'Somewhere over the rainbow, weigh-a-pie . . .'"

Reaction from the Pie Moms? Nothing.

Not a word.

Nothing but silence.

It was awful.

And then one of them laughed—the one carrying the posters. So the others laughed too. And then Holly apologized, acknowledging the joke was stupid—and for the singing. Holly apologized for that, too, but the mom carrying the posters said, "No, no. It's okay. Don't apologize. It was funny. My name's Emily." She extended her hand to shake Holly's. "I'm the Pie Mom for this year's Cherry Festival on The Lawn. I run the pie auction. It's like being the Cookie Mom for the Girl Scouts."

She was so sweet, so warm, so—pie-like.

"This is Suong-Lu and Peyton," Emily told Holly, pointing to the other mothers as they took turns nodding and smiling at Holly. Their eyes twinkled. Every last one of them exuded a wholesome glow. Emily finished, "And this is Jhone. Together, we're the Pie Committee, delivering pies across town to promote the Village of Primm Cherry Festival on The Lawn. It's this weekend in the town square between the two gazebos. Are you coming?"

"Oh, gosh, yes," said Holly. "Wouldn't miss it."

"The town runs the Cherry Festival, but the pie auction is a fundraiser for the school."

"Oh yes, I know all about it," Holly assured them. Because Holly was informed, Holly was one of those moms who knew everything. (Not.) "I read about it in the back-to-school handbook," she told them.

"Really?" Emily tipped her head to the side. "That's odd."

Spit cakes. I'm busted.

"I didn't know it was in the handbook." Emily checked with the Pie Committee. Suong-Lu shrugged her shoulders.

"Oh, gosh, yes. Page . . . twelve," Holly said. "Something. Maybe page sixteen. I can't remember." Now she was lying to Pie Moms. *How have I stooped so low?* Nowhere to hide, no way to escape, she felt fidgety, so she—*quick!*—tugged a few flyers from the bulletin board. Then—*nope!*—changed her mind and decided instead to slowly lower her body, until she was sitting once more on the bench.

"Page sixteen?" said Suong-Lu. "Are you sure?"

"Sure, I'm sure." Holly doubled down. Because clearly, she had no conscience. "I read about it last night. During one of my highlighting sessions." *Highlighting sessions?* "I always highlight school items in yellow. I mean—*pink!* And then I go back through with Sharpie markers to color-code items that need transferring to my calendar." *What am I saying?* "And I love cherries," Holly gushed. "And pies too. Pies are the best." Holly assumed they were about to ask her to buy one. She'd be happy to buy one, but she'd probably throw it in the trash once she got home.

Holly crossed her legs, trying to act all prim and proper, which was ridiculous considering her attire on the first day of school. *I'm hopeless. Poor Ella, she deserves so much better. She deserves a Pie Mom. Not a lowly Pink and Brown Piggy Mom like me.*

"Would you like to be on our Pie Committee?" Emily asked.

"Me?" Holly stammered, nearly knocking the flyers from her lap. "Pies? Sure. I love pies." Holly hated pies. Jack hated pies, and Holly was pretty sure Ella would hate pies, too, but she wouldn't know because Ella had never eaten a pie.

"We'd love to have you. We're running short on pies. Do you think you could bake one—or two pies, maybe?" Emily the Pie Mom grimaced. "We could use the help. Last year's sale didn't go as planned, and we have a lot of pressure on us this year. What do you say?"

Emily clasped her hands together, praying Holly would say yes, so hopeful in her pretty blue shirt, classic white pedal pushers, and brown leather sandals. Her look was clean, crisp, and casual.

Holly wished she could be like that. Polished. Confident, yet relaxed. With Old Glory hanging over her head, both literally and figuratively, Holly figured, what was more American than motherhood and apple—er, cherry pie?

"Sure," Holly said. "I'll do it. I'll bake some pies." *I'll do it for my country*. What could possibly go wrong?

"That's wonderful news!" Emily clapped. "Thank you so much. How many can you make? Can you make two? Or maybe three?"

"How about six? Make it a half dozen." Holly wanted to make her mark, stand out.

"Six? Wow. That's great. Six is great. Thank you." Emily swooned.

"You know what? Since it's a benefit for the school, make it a dozen. Better yet, make it a baker's dozen. Thirteen. The world needs more pies." Holly collected the flyers from her lap, tapping them into a tidy, orderly little pile. "Now, if you'll excuse me, I need to get these posted to the bulletin board, or I'll be late for the gym." Holly pretended she was the steward of the volunteer bulletin board. Like she was Bulletin Board Mom, hoping her piggies would pass as yoga pants.

Emily handed Holly a Pie Committee sign-up sheet and a pen.

What's with all the sign-up sheets at Primm? Are they contracts? Legally binding?

Under the appropriate columns, Holly scribbled her name and the number thirteen, then told her new friends from the lovely Pie Committee, "One person tries to do everything—no, wait. Um. One person can't do anything—no, that's not right." Holly copped a glance at the sun's paper rays cascading across the bulletin board. "No one can do everything," she announced. "But it never hurts to try!"

"We're meeting later this week at the North Gazebo to go over last-minute details before the big event. Can you come?" Emily asked, all hopeful and wide eyed.

"Oh, sure." Holly waved. "Happy to come. I love meetings."

It's easy to volunteer. You're not doing *anything the moment you sign up except, well, signing up*. That was the easy part, and Holly suspected that was the part that got moms into trouble. One minute you were signing up; the next, you were wondering why you signed up.

As the Pie Committee set off down the hallway toward the teachers' lounge, Holly's heart rate started to rise. She felt dizzy. A million thoughts entered her mind like fast-rolling film credits:

Betty Crocker!

What have I done?

Pies?

I can't make pies.

She placed two fingers against her carotid artery to check her pulse. Couldn't find it. No pulse. *Am I dead? Was it all a bad dream?* Holly sat down. Tried to slow her breathing.

"God?" she said out loud.

No answer.

I must be alive; still on earth. So this wasn't a bad dream. I really did say I'd bake thirteen pies for a cherry festival. Mutha fricker.

12

Still not over

After twenty minutes of Holly's waiting on the stiff wooden bench, Principal Hayes escorted Holly to the Community Helper Annex, a long gray trailer behind the athletic fields with a security camera mounted above the door.

Hayes told Holly to have a seat and wait for Officer Knapp, the school's attending police officer, who would take care of the paperwork. Then Holly could leave. "I apologize for the wait, Mrs. Banks, but it's the first day of school." Hayes pushed his black-rimmed glasses from the bridge of his nose to his frown line and straightened his necktie, which was embroidered with honeybees. "After Officer Knapp signs the paperwork, let Rosie McClure in the front office know you're leaving campus."

Hayes left. Holly sat.

Three hours of Holly's life passed—*three hours!*—and Officer Knapp still hadn't shown up. She was wasting her life away in a mobile trailer. The long rectangular kind with deck steps and a white metal doorframe. Inside? More gray. Gray walls, gray flooring, gray metal desk. She was starving, absolutely famished, because she hadn't eaten anything since dinner the previous night.

For the umpteenth time, Holly contemplated leaving the school grounds to go home, take a shower, change into normal clothes, and then come back to deal with the situation. But here's the thing: there were twelve black-and-white closed-circuit security monitors mounted to the wall not far from a television set that had all the best morning talk shows on. Not only that, but there was a coffee maker in the corner, so Holly made herself a few cups of coffee while waiting for Officer Knapp. She was quite comfortable in her own little world: she spun in the swivel chair behind the desk, watching TV while keeping a watchful eye on the security monitors for glimpses of Ella. Was she angry she'd been waiting so long? Sure. But there wasn't a mom in the world that would pass up a chance to spy on her child on her first day of kindergarten. Holly would fly a surveillance drone over Ella's head if she thought she could get away with it. *Mom drones. Now there's a technology.*

On the video screen, for a fleeting moment, Holly spotted Ella walking down a hallway. "*Awww*," Holly whispered, touching the screen because she couldn't touch Ella. "Hey there, Ella Bella. Look at you!" She traced Ella's image. "I miss you, baby girl."

Holly's index finger banged into the outer rim of the monitor as Ella walked out of view. She flipped dials and pressed buttons, until at last, she managed to swivel one of the cameras to tune to the inside of the library, and *whoa!* Out of nowhere, the Cat in the Hat's face appeared on her screen, filling it completely.

"*Aaah!*" Holly jumped, knocking her coffee off the desk and onto the floor. An oversize stuffed animal, propped on the counter of the library, the Cat in the Hat had to be six feet tall—maybe taller. Not as tall as Plume, but a cultural icon nonetheless.

Holly couldn't see Ella because the camera had limited range and was capturing the top of the librarian's head as she checked books out for a line of kids. Holly could hear most of what was going on in the library. A woman offscreen but near the camera was reading a book, presumably to Ella's class. Holly turned up the volume on this particular monitor—the monitor that brought familiar words from two books Ella and Holly loved to read together. Holly closed her eyes and listened to a reading of Leopard Print's *Little Kids, Little Zoo*, a story about a teacher who gathered her children on the first day of kindergarten, only to realize the children were little animals escaped from the zoo. Followed by Jenna Denny's *Rabbit Home*.

Whoever was reading was doing a bang-up job of capturing the lyrical magic of Jenna Denny's words. Holly knew the exact page, could see capital letters and the illustrations in her mind when the homesick little rabbit reached his breaking point while on an adventure and started to cry. *Rascally rabbit out to roam . . . Rabbit, Rabbit, HURRY HOME!*—when *bam!* Mary-Margaret appeared on the monitor, her face filling the screen.

"Aaah!" Holly jumped.

"Yoo-hooooo!" Mary-Margaret waved at Holly through the security camera. Eyes, cheeks, dimples. She was at the door of the annex smiling into the security camera mounted above the door.

Holly swiped her tears, her nose, then—click!—killed the security monitors, afraid Mary-Margaret would accuse her of spying on her own daughter. Ha! Ridiculous. Like that would ever happen . . .

"Knock-knock. Anybody home? It's me, Mary-Margaret St. James!"

Mary-Margaret opened the metal screen door wearing a new outfit: a petal-pink skirt with a crisp white blouse, pink shoes, and a pink hair ribbon. Did she go home? How did she manage a wardrobe change on the first day of school? Earlier, in the bus lane, she was dressed in honeybee school-mascot colors: gold, black, and white. Come to think of it, the entire apple brigade was dressed in gold, black, and white. So was the headband lady. Who was circulating *that* memo?

Mary-Margaret lowered herself to perch on the chair beside Holly. On Mary-Margaret's lap sat a thick ivory pastry box, the edges of its scalloped lid embossed in pink. A soft brown ribbon was tied gently around a flower of some kind. An orchid, thought Holly.

"It's a *Paph. pinocchio* lady-slipper orchid blossom in full bloom," Mary-Margaret told her.

"Oh, yes, of course." Holly cleared her throat. "I knew that."

Slipped beneath the satin ribbon, just below the orchid, was an ivory calling card with embossed initials in the same soft pink found on the scalloped edges of the box: M-M St. J. *Ugh! Even her monogram is high maintenance. M-M St. J.? Imagine texting that. Your thumbs would cramp.* But Holly had to hand it to her: moms wrapped a lot of gifts over the course of a lifetime, and even on their best days, most packages didn't look like *that. Paph. pinocchio* lady-slipper orchid blossom? In full bloom?

"How are you? Feeling overwhelmed today?" Mary-Margaret asked, placing a hand on Holly's leg.

Holly started to say something about the spilled coffee and lack of paper towels:

"---."

But *poof!* She disappeared from the conversation when Mary-Margaret said, "You've gone all morning without a bra. Haven't you?" Mary-Margaret's eyes spanned the width of Holly's faded college T-shirt. "That's too bad. 'The twins need support!' I always say."

Holly informed her she was wearing a bra—a sports bra.

"A sports bra?" Mary-Margaret acted a bit startled. "But that's not a real bra. That's an ace bandage with straps." She played with her soft brown ribbon for a moment. "But women love them! My gosh, do women love them." Mary-Margaret shrugged. "Women wear sports bras even when they're *not* working out. Why is that, do you suppose? Why do women dress to look like they've just worked out? We all know that's a big fat lie." She reached into her handbag to retrieve a lipstick. Reapplied. "Do you remember the song 'Dancing Queen' by that Swedish pop group ABBA? I picture you as the dancing queen, twirling around topless, but wearing your sports bra—so incredibly happy to be wearing a sports bra! Maybe you're even spinning around, waving a long, flowing scarf behind you. I see that. I'm picturing that right now."

What the hel-icopter is she talking about? ABBA? Seriously?

"Do you know the song? 'Dancing Queen'?" Mary-Margaret asked. "I love disco. It's coming back. I'll sing it for you."

No, Holly pleaded. But once again, Mary-Margaret ignored her.

"Wooo-hooo-oooo!"

Holly covered her ears. *What's wrong with this woman? Is she on drugs?*

"---?"

Mary-Margaret's shoulders slumped. "Of course I'm not on drugs. How could you say such a thing?" Now she was pouting. "At least I'm not wearing a sports bra," Mary-Margaret added. "Sports bras aren't real bras. They smash your ta-tas until your ta-tas aren't ta-tas anymore. They're blah-blahs. Imagine the bumper stickers: Save the blah-blahs? That's ridiculous. But don't you worry . . ." She leaned in to wink, flashing her pearly whites. *"Wooo-oooo-oooo!"* and began to sing. "Dancing Queen." Of all songs. *"Wooo-hooo-oooo!"*

Holly couldn't take it anymore. "Stop singing!" she hollered. *"Oh, for the love of God, STOP SINGING!"*

"My goodness." Mary-Margaret straightened her back. "That's the first time I've heard you speak up for yourself. And not just a little bit. You really let me have it. Odd that it took my singing a song by a Swedish pop group to bring it out of you, but okay . . ."

You'd think Holly would have something pithy to say after yelling at Mary-Margaret, but she didn't. The two women sat in silence for quite some time.

Holly could hear birds chirping outside of the annex. Birds. Imagine that.

Eventually, Mary-Margaret leaned over to whisper, "My Love owns the most extensive collection of singles and LP microgroove vinyl records this side of the Mississippi." She counted using her fingers. "My Love owns an Elvis Presley first commercially produced single in mint condition. The Beatles' 'I Want to Hold Your Hand' with the WMCA Good Guys promotional picture sleeve printed on the B side. In his ABBA collection—in unopened, pristine, original packaging—My Love owns the ABBA Gold 1992 and 1999 Australasian editions."

Mary-Margaret brought on the big smile: "We fell in love listening to ABBA . . . 'Dancing Queen,' 'Fernando,' 'Waterloo,' 'Mamma Mia,' 'Take a Chance on Me.' His ABBA collection jumped in value thirty percent when ABBA was inducted into the Rock and Roll Hall of Fame."

As Mary-Margaret's smile faded, she strummed her fingers on the top of the pastry box, presumably singing the words to a distant ABBA song in her mind. "I think 'The Winner Takes It All' is so sad. Don't you think it's sad? I think it's about divorce." She went somewhere in her mind, losing herself in thought. "Oh, for goodness sake. Forget all that!" Snapping out of it, Mary-Margaret waved a flippant hand in the air. "I think you should call everyone in the school to apologize."

"Apologize? For what?"

"For the bus. You drove like Princess Peach in *Mario Kart* high on golden mushroom speed. This isn't a video game, you know. You shouldn't live your life in an altered reality. It's not healthy."

"*I'm* the one living in an altered reality?"

"You know, you really shouldn't drive your child to school in your pajama bottoms," Mary-Margaret said. "For two reasons." She pointed a finger at Holly. "One, a woman shouldn't have a category of her wardrobe called carpool clothing. You wouldn't invite someone into your closet saying, 'This is my evening wear, my casual sportswear, my resort wear. And over here . . . over here is my *carpool* wear'? No one does that. Don't be that mom."

"Goodbye. I'm done." Holly stood to leave. "Moving to Primm was a mistake."

"A mistake?" Dismay in Mary-Margaret's eyes, both hands on hips. "Mistake? How can you say it's a mistake to live in the Village of Primm? You're not comparing us to Southern Lakes, are you?"

"Maybe I am."

"But the Village of Primm is so pretty. Did you see our welcome sign? It's so pretty. It says: *Pretty People Live Here.* Well, it doesn't really say that. But it should. Primm has gazebos and flags and white picket fences. Primm has Plume!"

"So?"

"So? Southern Lakes doesn't have Plume. Southern Lakes has pink flamingo lawn ornaments. Southern Lakes doesn't host a Cherry Festival on The Lawn. Come to think of it, I don't know what they host. Probably hot dog eating contests . . . with men who crush beer cans on their foreheads—I don't know."

"I like hot dogs."

"But—that town is messy. Dogs have the audacity to play off leash. Southern Lakes kids leave toys strewn about. In the yard, on the sidewalks, all over driveways . . . you know what that is, don't you? *Toy litter.* Have you seen their *lawns*?" Mary-Margaret's eyes opened wide. "They have crabgrass. *Crabgrass!* And please don't say you like crabgrass. Why would you like crabgrass? No one likes crabgrass." She appeared genuinely distraught. "You don't like crabgrass." She blinked her baby blues at Holly. "Tell me you don't like crabgrass."

"Honestly? I've never thought about it before." *So what if the grass is greener on the Primm side of the fence. Crabgrass is a small price to pay for a more relaxed motherhood.*

"Oh, what's really wrong, Popcorn? Why would you choose Southern Lakes over the Village of Primm?" Mary-Margaret fingered the ribbon on her box. "It's your sports bra, isn't it? Feels like a boa constrictor? Probably cutting blood circulation to your brain."

"Sorry, Mary-Margaret, but no. My sports bra isn't strangling me. Nor is it clouding my judgment. And my name isn't Popcorn or Chef Boyardee or some other name you picked up on aisle five. It's Holly."

"Then what is it, Bok Choy? What's wrong?"

Holly glanced at the security monitors. The screens were black because she'd shut them down when Mary-Margaret waltzed in. Ella was somewhere in that darkness—but Holly couldn't see her. She couldn't hear her. Couldn't touch her. Holly had no idea what Ella was doing at that moment. "Maybe I'm not feeling very welcome in Primm."

"But why? Didn't Penelope bring you coupons?"

"She's already welcomed me to Primm. And I should have invited her in for a cup of tea, but . . ." *Do I tell her? Do I tell Mary-Margaret I didn't welcome Penelope inside my home because of* Collette's *overachieving? Why am I letting these women get under my skin?* Stupid Pinterest. Holly hated Pinterest. She plopped down. Hated Houzz too. And Facebook. Happy family photos. Instagram . . . Stories. Why was everything in your face all the time?

Mary-Margaret patted Holly's knee. "Cheer up, little buckaroo. We moms try so hard to do so much for so many, but sometimes"—she shrugged, tossing her hands up—"we screw up. That's all you've done. You've screwed up. Multiple times, actually. At least you don't have to worry about leaving your car in the bus lane. Because I called a tow truck."

"*You what?*" Holly sprang from her chair.

"You're welcome."

"*You had it towed?* Why'd you do that? Who are you? The Wicked Witch of the West?"

"Well, don't yell at me! You left me no choice—it's been sitting out there for three hours." Mary-Margaret wiggled in her seat. "And don't call me the Wicked Witch of the West." She looked offended.

"I'm sorry," Holly told her. And she was. That was mean.

"Because I'm clearly Glinda. See?" Mary-Margaret rolled her hands down the front of her outfit. "I'm wearing pink!"

"In the 1939 film version," Holly pointed out, "Glinda is the Good Witch of the *South*. But in the original—in Baum's 1900 children's novel—she's the Good Witch of the *North*."

Mary-Margaret blinked once, but other than that, she sat perfectly still. Blank stare. Nothing on her face moved. No twitch. No flinch. No wince. Nada.

"I went to film school."

"Whatev." Mary-Margaret handed Holly a slip of paper. "I bumped into Officer Knapp at Primm's Coffee Joe two hours ago. He's supposed to work out of the Community Helper Annex but uses Coffee Joe as a satellite office. He's in it for the parfait Joe sells with the thin blue line of blueberries. He's very busy—not really. Not since that murder that one time. Years ago. One murder in the entire history of Primm. Still unsolved. Not really. There were two murders. One solved. One not. Or maybe there were three? Unspeakable things. Secretive little village. Anyhoo. Have Principal Hayes sign that, and then you can leave."

"Thank you." Holly looked at the piece of paper.

"Do it fast. There's a wrecker out front."

"You're joking," Holly said matter-of-factly.

"Not joking."

Frock her. Holly made her way toward the door. *Towed?* If the Village of Primm was Oz, then Holly wanted anarchy. She wanted to be Dorothy so she could snatch the Tin Man's ax and hack a few bricks loose from the yellow brick road, then hurl them at the Pink Witch. Holly hadn't told Jack she hit the bus yet—and now her car was being towed? Towed?

Wait. Mary-Margaret was laughing. *She's playing me. The Pink Witch is playing me.*

Holly reached up to press the vein in her neck. Still couldn't find her pulse. *I'm dead, right? This is just a dream?* And then she realized if she was dead—and Mary-Margaret was sitting beside her—then she didn't make it to heaven. She was somewhere else.

"Am I in hell?" Holly asked.

"No, silly." Mary-Margaret brightened. "You're in the Village of Primm!"

"Why do you do this to people?"

"You really want to know?" Mary-Margaret confessed, "I'm bored."

"I'm leaving." Holly got up to leave. "I've been here long enough."

"Sit down," Mary-Margaret urged, lifting the gift box to present it to her. "I went home this morning and baked you a batch of my special peanut butter cookies. And here they are. Have one. Have two! It's a secret St. James recipe, and I want you to have them. They're called peckled peanut butter cookies. Because they're peckled with love. My husband, My Love, loves them. They're still warm. Try one."

Holly took the box. She'd been wondering what was inside . . .

"It's all yours." Mary-Margaret pointed to the elaborate packaging. "All of it. It's all yours." She reached over to untie the ribbon for Holly. Lifted the lid, handed Holly a cookie.

Holly took a bite. It was good. Really good, in fact, and Holly was hungry.

"Our friendship got off to a bad start. I want to start fresh," Mary-Margaret explained. "Fresh like fabric softener. You and me, me and you, you and Mary-Margaret St. James, starting fresh. Fabric softener fresh."

The cookies were scrumptious.

"Tell you what." Mary-Margaret dipped her hand into the box to give Holly another one, which Holly promptly ate because the cookies were so dang good and she was so dang famished. "I'll be lilac. The scent of lilac suits me. It's elegant. You?" Mary-Margaret handed Holly a third cookie. "You can be lavender. You're definitely more lavender smelling. Of the two fragrances, lavender is more generic."

Holly looked at Mary-Margaret through lowered eyelids.

"Generic is good," Mary-Margaret assured Holly. "Think of pharmaceuticals. Everyone wants generic. It's cheaper. Anyway, stores sell candles in both fragrances, but trust me—there's a huge difference between lilac and lavender. Huge!"

"Actually," Holly said between bites, "they're essentially the same."

"Oh, no. That's not true. Lilac is much higher end. Lilac is couture," Mary-Margaret explained. "And you're spitting. A bit. You're spitting cookies as you talk."

"But they're fragrances," Holly pointed out, wiping her mouth with the back of her hand. "How can one smell be more expensive than the other? That's ridiculous."

"Trust me. The next time you're in a store, you'll think of this conversation, and you'll buy lilac. I know you will. Power of suggestion. Mary-Margaret inside your head. *Peekaboo!* You'll hold both candles in your hand, and you'll start to think: they're both purple, so they're the same, right? But then, all of a sudden, you'll find yourself second-guessing it. Moms do it all the time. The pictures on the candle labels. Which is prettier? The lilacs? Or the lavender? You'll take a sniff. Lose precious moments of your life over this huge decision. Your child will urge you to hurry up, but you'll stand there, frozen in the aisle, wondering which purple is the better purple."

"No I won't. Purple is purple."

"And then I'll pop into your head and say *peekaboo*!" Mary-Margaret giggled. "It's me, Mary-Margaret St. James! I'm inside your head!"

Holly pressed another cookie into her mouth.

"Wow, Lavender, you're really hungry."

"Don't call me Lavender." Holly waved a finger at Mary-Margaret. "Don't do that. I don't want to be a Bree-with-an-E. I hate nicknames."

Mary-Margaret handed Holly another cookie. "Wow. Look at you go! You're like the Cookie Monster. 'Me eat cookie. Nom-nom-nom.' No, really. It's okay. Eat! I'm accustomed to watching people gorge themselves on my baked goods. Wow. Your stomach is growling. Did you eat breakfast? Because it's past lunchtime. How's your blood sugar? Should I be worried? Lavender." She placed her hand on Holly's knee. "While you're busy eating the entire box of cookies, I thought I'd tell you your good news. I signed you up."

"Signed me up?" Holly asked. "For what?"

"For the PTA, silly."

"THE WHAT!"

"Congratulations, Lavender! You're the new secretary of the Primm Academy PTA!"

"Nooo!" Holly yelled, sounding as if she were standing at the bottom of the Grand Canyon, opening her anguished soul to the universe. "Not the PTA!"

"There's a meeting tomorrow. Can you bring cupcakes?"

"No, I can't bring cupcakes!" Holly snarled. "I don't want to be on the PTA. I want to be a wolf. So I can dress in Grandma's clothes and eat you. Face first. Why did you sign me up?" Holly howled. "I just got here. I'm not unpacked." She counted on her fingers. "I don't know a soul. Ella's only in kindergarten. What do I know about the PTA? I don't want to be on the PTA."

"But—why are you overreacting?" Mary-Margaret whined. "I thought you'd be happy." Mary-Margaret leaned backward. "Whoa. Lavender, what big eyes you have. Why are your eyes popping out? I'm sorry to break it to you, but you're not a scary wolf. You look like a Muppet."

A what? A freaking Muppet?

"You're Cookie Monster with big bulging eyes." Mary-Margaret thought a moment. "No, wait. Ha! Ha! You're not the Cookie Monster." She pointed to Holly's legs. "You're Miss Piggy!"

Holly snatched another cookie, ripping it with her teeth. She'd probably eaten six already. Intended to eat a lot more. Planned to binge eat her way through this horrible day. *Secretary? No way. I'm not serving as anything for anyone. I'm not.*

"Think of it, Lavender. You're stepping onto the Primm Academy stage—as a *newcomer*—welcomed by me with a nickname *and* a title!" Mary-Margaret winked. Nudged Holly with her elbow. "Very strategic!"

Hmm. Holly would like to meet other mothers . . . maybe make a few friends.

"Think of all the time we'll spend together," Mary-Margaret said. "We'll become great friends. Best friends!"

Whoa! No, thank you. And yet . . . is she right? Is a position on the PTA strategic? Would it give me status? Clout with other moms? Clout with Ella's teachers? Do I want this? Do I want a little celebrity? It would be a great way to meet other moms. Become more involved; become one of them. Holly knew this: her own mother would *never* serve on a PTA. Holly should take the position for that reason alone.

But then she moved quickly to her initial gut reaction, which was no, definitely not. She wasn't good at these things. She'd make a fool of herself somehow. She'd forget the PTA pledge, something. Was there a PTA pledge? Holly didn't know.

"I'm very sorry, Mary-Margaret. And I thank you for the kind offer, but I can't do it. I won't do it."

"Too late. I suggested it to Principal Hayes as community service for hitting the school bus," Mary-Margaret informed Holly. "He thought it was a great idea."

"That's the stupidest thing I've ever heard of. Community service? *On the PTA?* There's no such thing." Holly shoved another cookie in her mouth, spitting a little when she said, "And besides, if you sign me up, I'll just quit."

"If you quit, I'll tell everyone in town you're a quitter. Slow down with those cookies. You're eating like . . . Cookie Monster—unchained."

Holly took a few bites of cookie and then swallowed. Cookie, cookie, cookie. Nom, nom, nom.

"Slow down, Lavender. You're chewing so fast."

Cookie, cookie, cookie. Nom, nom, nom.

"Actually, you're sort of spitting at me right now. Will you please stop?" Mary-Margaret jumped up, brushing cookie crumbs from her pink skirt. "You're spitting. Really spitting. That's so gross." Mary-Margaret's expression showed her disgust.

Holly had seen that look of disgust. Had seen it on her friends' faces when her mom stuffed bananas down her shirt at the grocery store. Greta made Holly's friends look like that. When she was drunk. When she did things. That night she drove across town to catch Holly's dad with another woman. That night she was arrested. That thing she did. Back then. When it was bad. Even now, Jack got that look when Greta called asking for money.

"Swallow, please," Mary-Margaret told Holly, eyebrows pinched above her nose. Was Mary-Margaret mad? Or just shocked by Holly? "You really should swallow," she said, hands on hips as if scolding a child. "Lavender, please."

She better freaking stop calling me freaking Lavender.

"Slow down, Lavender. You're getting crumbs all over your time-out chair. Meeting is tomorrow." Mary-Margaret tidied up, getting ready to make her departure. "Cupcakes?"

Holly said no with a shake of her head.

"Great." Mary-Margaret smiled. "Then it's settled. Bring three dozen."

Holly shook her head again. "No cupcakes. I won't do it." Holly felt savage, crushed another cookie into her mouth as Mary-Margaret hitched the thin strap of her school tote bag onto her shoulder.

"Nut-free, gluten-free, and egg-free, please."

"No!" Holly mustered, her mouth full of cookie. *Does this woman ever listen? Must I bully the bully? Pursue the aggressor? Do I have to overexaggerate everything in this town just to get my point across?* Holly found herself standing in front of Mary-Margaret, arranging clumps of cookie inside her mouth like bullets inside a NERF N-Strike Elite Retaliator Blaster gun. The way Holly saw it, they were alone in the annex—so no one knew she was doing this, except Mary-Margaret. And besides, Mary-Margaret got to act bat-flipping crazy all the time; why couldn't Holly? Holly would never actually spit cookie crumbs at Mary-Margaret . . . would she?

"I know what you're thinking, Lavender," Mary-Margaret said, challenging Holly with that slight twitch of her eyebrow, that curl of her mouth. "I know what you want to do." Mary-Margaret eyed Holly's mouth, apparently aware cookies were being stockpiled behind pursed lips. "But you don't have the guts," Mary-Margaret snarled, an excited wide grin spreading across her face.

I get it now. Everything's a game to the bored Mary-Margaret St. James. Mary-Margaret pushes, hoping someone in this village will push back. But no one does. Well, guess what, Mary-Margaret? I'm pushing back.

Holly added cookies to her mouth and started to chew, slowly. They were moist. Chewy. Formed perfect little balls inside her mouth. It was bold, Holly knew. But what the heck? She was facing a prison sentence as Mary-Margaret's secretary, facing a nickname she might never live down. Lavender? No thank you. If Holly didn't take Mary-Margaret down now, there'd be no telling what Mary-Margaret might do to her.

"Madam Secretary"—Mary-Margaret slipped from her chair, moving with precision and stealth toward the annex door—"you might want to rethink this." She was smiling a wicked smile. Appeared absolutely thrilled by what Holly was suggesting she was about to do—absolutely thrilled.

Holly? Holly couldn't tell if they were enemies or forming some kind of twisted friendship. This was how young girls acted—thrilled by a ridiculous, daring stunt that solidified a friendship. But Mary-Margaret wasn't Holly's friend. They were grown women. Moms. They were supposed to live by rules, proper codes of conduct.

"Lavender," Mary-Margaret taunted, "you're bringing the cupcakes to the PTA meeting tomorrow. I can count on you, right? You won't let me down."

Holly shook her head. Stuffed her mouth with another cookie. Her cheeks puffed out. "Not bringing no dang cupcakes. And my name's not Lavender. My name . . . is Banks," Holly muttered, pressing cookies against the inside of her lips, cookies ready to storm the gates. "Holly. Banks."

"Whatever you say, Lavender." Mary-Margaret inched her way toward the annex door. Swift. Like a jackrabbit.

But Holly was cocked and loaded. She rounded the corner of the desk with the pastry box in one hand, packing cookies into her mouth with the other. She formed perfect chewy bullets in her mouth. One after the other. Holly's heart raced. *What's happening. What's happening?*

"Let me be the first to congratulate you on your new position, Lavender." Mary-Margaret reached for the door. "Wow. PTA secretary. You're going to be *so busy* this year." She punched the door handle with the side of her fist—*and then took off!*—out the door and down the steps.

Holly followed in hot pursuit—spitting cookies in rapid fire. Bam! Bam! Bam! It was such a release, both literally and figuratively. *I'm a Hasbro Nerf gun. No! I'm the dancing queen. No! I'm Cookie Monster—unchained. Nom-nom-nom.*

Mary-Margaret was about twenty feet ahead of Holly when she lost her footing and fell, hitting the pea gravel with an *oompf!* "Lavender," she croaked. Smile on her face. Crawled a few paces before rising to her feet again. "Lavender, have mercy!"

Holly pushed another cookie into her mouth. Tossed the box. Mary-Margaret ran, and Holly gave chase, two women wearing the wrong kind of footwear. They ran like platypuses, strange creatures with appendages that baffled the observer and only seemed to get in the way. The limited circumference of Mary-Margaret's pink pencil skirt compromised her running stride—legs chopping across the field like blades on scissors, feet sharpening to points in a pair of sling-back heels. Holly's sports bra and piggy pajamas made her the dancing queen, but she had to curl every muscle in her toes to keep her flip-flops from falling off. Never mind that her mouth was chock full of peckled peanut butter cookies. It hurt to run with toes clenched like a fist; Holly's shoes kept slipping off. She improvised by running with a sideways gait, like a lumbering giant, the way the Hunchback of Notre Dame would run if given the chance and inspiration.

Wind whipping through their hair, they both stumbled at different times and at different places on the soccer field, at first falling with a clumsy thud, then scrambling to their feet to resume the chase.

They were halfway across the field when dozens of sprinkler heads rose from the earth to water the grass—and them: two spasmodic, galumphing school moms sprinting as best they could across campus, a PTA president and her would-be secretary. They were wild. They were moms. And they were setting a *horrible* example for the children.

Mary-Margaret reached the building first, slammed against an entry bar to open a door, rushed inside, and then pushed the door shut before Holly could catch her. Out of breath and with cookies in her mouth—Holly unloaded everything she had all over the door's glass panel, firing peckled peanut butter bullets like she was "Momma Ragu" Sauce, a hit woman in the Sicilian Mom Mafia.

What just happened? What in the world possessed me to chase that woman? Cookies spent, Holly bent over, hands on knees, gasping for breath. *Do wild animals end a chase wondering what just happened?*

Safe and sound on the other side of the door, Mary-Margaret—the Pink Witch in this strange Land of Oz—clapped and squealed with delight, mouthing to Holly through the window, "Don't forget the cupcakes!" She flipped the safety lock on the door, then skipped off down the hallway, leaving Holly locked outside, sucking air, examining her life, her choices, her actions. Some of the children in a side-facing row of classrooms gathered at the windows to stare at Holly bent and panting beside the emergency exit. *Please, God. Let Ella have a front-facing classroom. Please. Please, I'm begging.*

Above Holly, in the alcove of the brick doorway, a black security camera with a blinking red light and penetrating eyeball lens zoomed in to center its sights on Holly. *Freaking pig pajamas. From now on, I'm sleeping in black yoga pants.*

When Greta had humiliated Holly at the school gates, she'd worn a trench coat over her horrendous attire, so there was a chance no one had realized how disheveled their situation was at home. Holly's home on Petunia wasn't disheveled. It was just messy, and she needed to finish unpacking. And yet, there she was—in piggies—chasing another mom across a schoolyard, firing cookies from her mouth.

Greta had an excuse: her world was falling apart. Those days were dark—but Greta kept the lights on, kept full custody, and by the end of Holly's third year in school, Greta was sober and on the way toward rebuilding her life.

Odd. The further Holly ventured into Ella's first day of kindergarten, the closer Holly came to forgiving her mother.

13

Moments later

As the walkway swung closer to the building, Holly hopped off to take a shortcut by squeezing through bushes and pinching past a spot where a tall black gate met with the side of the building. Cutting around the front corner of the school, she emerged about a hundred feet from the same double doors Ella had disappeared through a few hours ago. No *Cnaeus Matius Calvinus* above the doors like the gates at the Topiary Park, just the words **Primm Academy Est. MCMXLVII**. Holly couldn't read roman numerals. Looked like MOM XL V11 to her, although she thought it might read 1947. Wouldn't surprise her a bit to learn the academy opened its doors the year Christian Dior's "New Look" swept the cultural zeitgeist with its nipped-in waistline, pointed breasts, and expansive skirts. *War's over, gals. Time for elastic-boned corselettes!* Nor would it surprise Holly if the school opened in 1957, when Chuck Berry's "School Day (Ring! Ring! Goes the Bell)" topped the charts. Or 1967, the year Twist 'N Turn Barbie released with a new head mold and long, rooted eyelashes. Any of these would make excellent cultural references in a film set in the Village of Primm the year the academy opened and moms rushed the gates. Maybe that should be Holly's Wilhelm Klaus story line: Postwar Barbie Moms with Impossible Waistlines Take on Primm. Set to a Chuck Berry soundtrack.

Holly's Suburban Godzilla was right where she left it. Only now, it had orange traffic cones surrounding it in a perfect circle, some cones stacked horizontally on top of other cones—hold up. Holly took a closer look: the traffic cones were arranged like the sarsen stones at Stonehenge. What the—

Holly marched into the school office, assaulted by the smell of freshly applied perfume. Gardenia. Rose. Something. Smelled like someone blew up a floral cluster bomb and tiny particles of flower were hurtling through time and space, Holly caught in the cross fire. "Excuse me," she choked, waving her hand beneath her nose to block the smell. "I'm here to see Principal Hayes about an incident with a bus. I need to see him now because I have to get home right away. Can you page him? Call him on the phone? Something?"

The woman behind the counter delivered a blank stare. That was all Holly got. Holly wanted to say, *Oh, I'm sorry, did I interrupt? Because you're acting like I have no business asking you to do anything. Now get me the principal!*

The woman tossed her pen onto the counter. Ho hum. Checked her watch. La-dee-dah. Blew the words *Principal Hayes?* like she was so incredibly annoyed that Holly was standing in front of her in the first place. *It's the first day of school, for crimìny's sake. Be a little more cheerful. And besides,* thought Holly, *I'm a parent at this school. Wasn't she hired to help me?*

Women like this drove Holly's mother nuts. "They use what little power they have in this world just to torture us," Greta would say. "If there's a counter separating you from another woman, you'd better believe that woman will throw her power around." Holly had vivid memories of hanging on to her mother's hand for dear life as she stormed out of a post office or, so help them, the Department of Motor Vehicles. That place was the worst. Lots of power behind those counters.

The woman punched a couple of phone extensions with the eraser on her pencil but came up with nothing: no Principal Hayes. She walked around the counter toward the back administrative offices: nothing. "Principal Hayes?" she called out with no effort whatsoever. No gusto. No nothing. What was she, a sloth? "He's not here," she said.

"Hmm," Holly mocked, slapping an index finger against her cheek the way the woman had. "What should we do now? Maybe we should try harder to find him?"

"Oh, yes, but you see, I'm expecting a UPS package." Returning to her post behind the tall laminate counter, the woman slipped a lipstick and mirror from her purse and began applying it—right in front of Holly.

Was she immune to Holly's sense of urgency? Holly was soaking wet from the soccer sprinklers. Her flip-flops covered in mulch. What was this woman doing? Applying lipstick? Running her tongue across her teeth? Puckering her lips into a handheld mirror? "Seriously?" *Unfreakingbelievable.* "What the monkey. That's so unprofessional."

The woman stared back at Holly, folded both her arms. "I just told you. I'm expecting a UPS package." She repeated, overenunciating, "*A U-P-S package.*"

So Holly borrowed a play out of her mother's handbook and stabbed her index finger on the counter. "I demand service!" She was about to stomp her foot when she noticed closed-circuit security monitors behind the woman's desk. Six of them. One tuned to record events happening in the hallways, another tuned to record exterior doorways, the rest tuned to the classrooms. *Ella.* Maybe Holly could catch a glimpse of Ella. "Can I check on my daughter? Maybe see her on one of those screens?" Holly pointed. "Her name is Ella Banks."

"What seems to be the problem?"

"No problem," she lied. "She got on the bus this morning—so excited to start kindergarten! I just want to make sure she's okay. Do those dial up to different classrooms?"

"Maybe." The woman folded her arms. "But for now, why don't you have a seat on the wooden bench outside." She began primping again, unbuttoning the top button of her silk blouse to reveal a string of pink freshwater pearls and a lot of, um, flesh. The pearls, they were so pretty—organic, irregular shapes, colors that glistened from pink to peach. Holly didn't own anything like that. She had a few silver necklaces and a bracelet or two worth about fifty bucks, but most of Holly's stuff was, well, as Ella would describe it: yuckity.

Even the school office was beautiful. Like something out of a magazine, it was so polished and welcoming. Bright windows with deep windowsills, beautiful blue tone-on-tone wallpaper, plenty of fresh white flowers in vintage silver trophy cups. Artwork made by children. Classical music played. It was more beautiful than any room in Holly's entire house. Freaking school office—probably had its own board on Pinterest.

Holly returned to the bench she'd sat on earlier in the morning, plopping down beneath the American flag and the volunteer bulletin board that basked beneath the glow of Mary-Margaret's sun. Holly vowed to wait no more than five minutes. No more!

She waited, worrying about the cost of repairs, worrying about car insurance premiums, worrying her reputation with the other mothers would be shot before she even got the chance to say hello. She worried about PTA cupcakes and cookie spitting caught on film. She worried about cherries, and pies, and wondered how cherries got inside pies, and how pies sold at festivals, and what if her pies sucked so bad they didn't sell at auction? Then what? She'd disappoint Emily the Pie Mom. And Suong-Lu the Pie Mom. And Peyton. And Jhone. And all the Pie Moms that came before them, like Betty Crocker and that freaking Martha Stewart with all the pie baking *she'd* done over the years. Holly worried about Ella, alone on her first day of kindergarten, alone in the Land of Oz. Ella could be in art right now, or music, or the cafeteria, who the heck knew. *It's fourth period. Where's my daughter? I don't know!*

Holly needed a happy place. Which she got at that very moment, because in through the front doors of Primm Academy walked the most beautiful creature Holly had ever seen. Tall, dark, and handsome—and carrying a large brown package and a handheld device for collecting signatures—in came . . . the UPS man.

Oh my. Oh my indeed.

Because, good gravy, was he hot! *Thank you, Village of Primm!*

Penelope had never mentioned him. If Holly were Penelope, she'd hire this guy to deliver real estate flyers all over Southern Lakes. **FOR SALE** signs would spring up overnight, and a mass exodus out of Southern Lakes and into the Village of Primm would ensue, Holly was sure of it. Oh, but maybe the uptight Village of Primm didn't *want* the laid-back families of Southern Lakes moving into their gilded school district.

Know what? Who cares! Because he was delicious: everything the bodice-ripping covers of racy novels delivered. Only he was real and in the flesh. Longish dark hair; dark, smoky eyes the shape of almonds (a werewolf maybe?); olive skin (was he Greek? Italian? from some island in the Mediterranean?); and a jawline as rugged as the Alaskan coastline (cliché, yes, but true). And he clearly didn't know his own strength because he swung open the heavy wooden doors of the school with such force the bulletin board flyers behind Holly ruffled beneath their thumbtacks.

Holly grabbed the large phallic box he was holding, grabbed his handheld device, and signed her name with gusto. *Look at me! Just a-signing away!*

He thanked her. And she thanked him. Watching him leave, Holly tipped her head ever so slightly to the side until every last gorgeous morsel of that man left the building.

Freshwater Pearls rushed into the front foyer. "Where is he? Is he here?" Pearls spotted the package in Holly's hands. "Is that my map?" she snapped, snatching it from Holly. "You signed for my map?"

14

Finally

Thanks to Principal Hayes, Holly left the school with an address of an auto repair shop in Southern Lakes that also had a few cars on their lot to rent. Leaving her Suburban Godzilla at the auto repair, Holly took possession of a brick-red Buick sedan that had crazy high mileage and worn seats that slumped where your butt sat. The smell inside the Buick was a mix of stale cigarettes, pine air fresheners, and the deep fat used to fry onion rings. *Do I detect a cat smell?* Holly checked the back seat. Vacuum tracks across the velour seats, occasional traces of cat hair.

"Are you sure no one's tried living in here? No dead bodies in the trunk?" Holly asked the man holding the clipboard. Not wanting to contaminate Ella's booster seat, she asked him for another car, but none were available, and she couldn't wait. She was running out of time and still hoped to swing home to grab a shower and change her clothes before Ella got home.

The man wore jeans and a dreary brown T-shirt with a navy-blue train car and the words

ferroequinologist
hung like an iron horse

He told Holly, "The last person to rent this car was a distinguished Panamanian man with business dealings in China. Car was fine for him."

"Is that so?" *Honestly? I couldn't care less—just tell me it's not infested with bedbugs.*

"His family left China to build the Panama Railroad in the nineteenth century," he added.

Oh, please, no. He's not going to talk my ear off, is he? Holly did have one question for him: "What's that mean?" She pointed to the word *ferroequinologist*, hoping for a short answer.

A broad smile spread across his face. "Well," he began. "A ferroequinologist is someone who studies trains." He tapped a thumb across each syllable on his shirt. "*Ferro* means iron. *Equine* means horse. Iron horse. I'm a rail fan."

Do I look bored? Because I am.

With no other way of getting home, Holly signed on the dotted line and climbed into the brick-red Buick, hoping she wouldn't arrive home covered in fleas. She started her slow slog home by clutching the steering wheel and peering over the dashboard. She felt uneasy, as if she'd forgotten how to drive, familiar buttons not in the familiar places. The car sat so low to the ground, its sagging seats so worn, she swore her feet were almost level with her waist. How was this okay for a distinguished Panamanian man with business dealings in China? This awkward position coupled with the rank smells reminded Holly of the time she watched her film school roommate's dog drag its butt across their living room floor.

Holly was sitting at a traffic light beside a Wendy's in Southern Lakes, when who did she see? Jack. Eating a sandwich. But wait. *Who's he with?*

Holly leaned toward her passenger window, squinted a bit, and yup. *It's them. He's with Bethanny.* Miles and miles and miles from the office, apparently not working, but certainly enjoying themselves over a tray of fast food. Jack must have been telling one of his oh-so-charming, overly animated jokes because his arms were up, and then they were down, and Bethanny's head fell back, and she laughed and laughed and laughed. Qualms. That's what Holly had. Holly had qualms about the way her husband's arms were moving, qualms about the way that woman tossed her hair, qualms about the suspicious circumstances surrounding what she knew was her husband's number one single combo—no cheese, no onions—medium size with a Dr Pepper. He'd have exactly four packets of ketchup on his tray for his french fries, and if a pepper shaker was within reach, he'd pepper his fries into oblivion. But Holly was the only woman who should know that. Bethanny shouldn't know that. And yet, now she did. Bethanny knew what Holly's husband ordered at Wendy's. And Jack knew what Bethanny ordered. This was not okay with Holly. Nor was it okay with Holly when Bethanny reached across the table to take one of Jack's fries and eat it. Seriously? Was another woman eating Jack's fries? Yes, she was, and Jack wasn't stopping her. *That's not okay. That's way too intimate. Get your freaking hands off my—*

When she was growing up, Holly's mom had so many qualms about Holly's father. They looked it up in the *Oxford English Dictionary*: *qualm* was from the Old English *cwealm*, meaning *death* or *plague*, a word that worked its irksome way through the Old High German *qualm*, meaning despair. This uneasy, sudden pang of doubt and despair Holly felt prompted her to swing the jalopy she was driving—the rattletrap, the banger, the beater, the motley tin lizzie spawn that was her rental car—into the parking lot and . . .

Dang that Jack! I'm not a jealous person. So why am I doing this?

Holly whipped, a safe distance for spying, into a parking space and then, through the restaurant window, watched them eat as if she were watching a movie at an outdoor drive-in theater. Holly became Jennifer Aniston, with no popcorn but a front-row seat, as Brad Pitt and Angelina Jolie ate their seductive dinner in *Mr. and Mrs. Smith*. Everyone knew what came next for Brad and Angelina in that movie:

gunfire, hot sex, and an explosion that literally blew their house off its foundation. Fifty million in box office sales opening weekend. Worldwide sales of over 475 million. Jennifer? Her Hollywood ending? Not so good. And okay, it didn't work out for Brad and Angelina either. Which proved there were no winners when a dinner like that was eaten. Was Holly jumping to conclusions? Or witnessing something she'd sensed but didn't want to face?

That's it. Can't take it anymore—I'm going in for a Junior Frosty.

Holly killed the engine, pulled the keys from the ignition, but dang it again, she couldn't go inside because of her pink piggies. When Holly was in kindergarten, and her dad was in Miss Mayfield, her mom let six months pass without dying her roots. Eventually, if Greta pulled her hair into a ponytail, she had the head of a brunette and the tail of a blonde. As much as Holly wanted to disrupt Jack and Bethanny's fast-food evildoing, she wasn't getting out of this Buick litter box to storm into Wendy's sporting leather flip-flops and a sports bra that made her ta-tas look like blah-blahs. She wasn't doing it.

Holly drew the bill of her baseball hat low, near her eyebrows, so Jack wouldn't recognize her. She'd cry if she could catch her breath. She'd kill them with Bethanny's black plastic salad fork if she thought she could get away with it. *Who orders a salad at Wendy's?* Instead, after a few minutes of watching their quickie meal at a quickie restaurant, Holly stabbed the key back into the ignition, revved up the engine, and drove herself home, butt dragging like a dog with worms. *Wish this were someone else's movie. Wish I wasn't Jennifer Aniston.* Why was the girl next door always blindsided by the sultry salad eater with the heart-shaped ass?

Leaving Southern Lakes to rumble into the Village of Primm, Holly passed the white gazebos with enclave flags a-flying, topiaries, and freshly cut lawns. Holly's dad never cut their grass because he didn't live at their house past Holly's sixth birthday. Ella was five. Was it true what they said? You knew when you knew? Because Holly knew Jack.

Jack ordered a Wendy's number one single combo—no cheese, no onions—medium size with a Dr Pepper, but was that "just" a meal? Or was that a *combo* meal?

Holly wasn't sure what she knew, but she knew how she felt. She felt angst. She felt agitated and angry. Miserable, dejected, disappointed, crestfallen. She felt glum. Gloom. Doom. And woebegone. That was it! She felt woebegone.

Such an odd little word: *woebegone*. Like someone took a three-word command, or wish, or desire—woe, be gone—and smashed it, like a marshmallow between graham crackers. Or a bug. *Ugh*. That was it. A bug.

15

Home at last

Holly reunited with her phone to find an Enclave Alert from Penelope, a series of phone messages from Mary-Margaret, an email from Online Psychic Betty, and an email from Rosie in the school office . . .

Penelope Pratt
Feathered Nest Realty

—ENCLAVE ALERTS—

Two items.

ITEM #1: FIRST DAY OF SCHOOL

Congratulations to the children of Primm for this morning's successful start to school! One morning down, 179 more to go!

At Feathered Nest Realty, hospitality is the cornerstone of our success.

Hospitality Tip: If your home hosts a Primm Academy bus stop, consider providing a quaint, cloth-covered hospitality table so neighboring parents and children feel warmed and welcomed as they wait for the happy yellow bus to come toot-tooting along. Remember! It may be their bus stop, but it's YOUR driveway!

Try these tasty bus stop treats:

Cherry-Hibiscus Plume-T™

Proceeds from the cherry hibiscus line of Plume-T™ will fund "The Travailing Puppeteers!" scheduled to give a travailing performance at the upcoming Wilhelm Klaus Film Festival this October.

CranBran BranMan ManMuffins™

Ditch the donuts. This is the Village of Primm. Serve CranBran BranMan ManMuffins™.

Measured Shell Edamame

As the "Soy Wars" rage (tempeh vs. tofu?), edamame is headed for world domination! They're actually boiled green soybeans—but don't tell the kids. Love soy? Text "TEMPEH" for recipes. Speaking of tempeh, to understand the plight of the picky eater and their many fears of texture, google: TRYPOPHOBIA IMAGES. No, really. Google it. Think you don't have Trypophobia? (You will!)

ITEM #2: PLUME

It's worse than we thought. Topiary Park officials report Plume's condition grew dire overnight. DO NOT—I repeat—DO NOT bring your children to visit Plume. She is in no condition to receive visitors. Her face fell off earlier this morning, and her tail feathers are starting to wither. Botanist Billy O'Malley shared this at this morning's press conference:

"Plume is now in full isolation, wrapped where she stands in a drape of reinforced cotton landscaping mesh. All of the animals in the Topiary Petting Zoo have been quarantined for fear of cross-contamination. Portions of the Topiary Park are now on lockdown. Risk of a village-wide bug infestation is HIGH because Plume is 'tightly planted.' If not dealt with, this infestation may reach epidemic levels not seen in Primm since the Primm Academy Head Lice Infestation of 1978."

"It appears someone in the Village has put a hex on our beloved Plume," said Officer Knapp this morning from his table at Primm's Coffee Joe. "Which begs the question: Who'd want to kill Plume?"

Advice from Feathered Nest Realty:

1. Embrace your topiaries. Give them a little hug.

2. Park officials have increased security, standing guard 24/7 like the guards with the tall fuzzy hats at Buckingham Palace. Please, send donuts. Better yet—send CranBran BranMan ManMuffins™.

~

[FIRST PHONE MESSAGE ON HOLLY'S PHONE]

(Beeeeeep.) Greets, Lavender. Hip! Hip! Mary-with-a-hyphen here. Answer your phone, silly girl. Glad you're finally home from pris—I mean, jail—I mean, time-out. Time-out for grown-ups. Ha! Community Annex. I only have a few PTA items to discuss—wait a minute. Another call coming in. Sorry. Have to take it. [CLICK.]

[SECOND PHONE MESSAGE]

(Beeeeeep.) Yooo-hooo? Lavender? Mary-Margaret here. Welcome to the Primm Academy PTA! I have a few questions now that you've committed to a year as my secretary . . . okay, a few short questions, no biggie. Okay.

How fast can you type? Do you know shorthand? Do you know Excel, PowerPoint, Word, HTML, HP-HELL, PDF, XYZ-PDQ, MP3, Google Plus, Google Minus, and Google Division? How about web design?

Do you tweet? Do you twerk? Does anyone follow you? Does anyone like you? On Facebook. Does anyone like you on Facebook? If yes, how *many* people like you? And forgive me if I'm stating the obvious—I know you're a mom—so I assume you have a blog?

Ah! My goodness. Another call coming in. Gotta take it. [CLICK.]

[THIRD PHONE MESSAGE]

(Beeeeeep.) Hip, hip, Lavender! PTA Executive Board meetings are mandatory. So whatever else is going on in your life, set it aside. Never miss a PTA meeting. I hope this won't be a problem. It won't be a problem, will it?

Will it?

Will it?

Okay, that's it. No more calls from Mary-Margaret St. James. [CLICK.]

[FOURTH PHONE MESSAGE]

(Beeeeeep.) You are coming to tonight's Back-to-School Scrap and Swap, aren't you? It's a PTA fund-raiser, so you can't miss it. I'd feel guilty if I missed a fund-raiser. But that's just me. I'm not implying that *you* should feel guilty. Unless you want to. In that case, go right ahead! Feel guilty. Who am I to stop you?

My advice? Come tonight and put your best foot forward with the Scrapbooking Moms. They're like a militia. Seriously. They'll probably organize a group photo tonight so they can document who *wasn't* there. And after all you've been through in the last twenty-four hours, do you really want to be exploited in a grand display of craft wizardry? I mean, really. Humiliation on archival paper lasts forever. Your shame will never yellow. (Beeeeeep.) [CLICK.]

[FIFTH PHONE MESSAGE]

(Beeeeeep.) Sorry. Your phone keeps cutting me off. You should think about getting a new one. Anyway. Scrapbooking Moms are absolute power players when it comes to school projects. Ever notice how many posters and hallway projects are assigned ahead of school concerts and special events? Administration wants the halls to look good when the parents arrive so they don't get itchy and start complaining about curriculum. Hallway projects have a calming effect on parents because they feel better walking through hallways covered in color-coded drawings of dissected frog guts. They like knowing their child took a sharp pair of scissors and cut off the head of a US president. It's patriotic. Wait. Did I just say "cut *off* the head of a US president"? I meant to say "cut *out* the head of a US president." *Oops!* Silly me. I'm a registered Independent, by the way.

Lavender. Come to tonight's Scrap and Swap Fund-Raiser so you can start building an arsenal of scrapbooking supplies your child can use on her homework. Tell your husband scrapbooking supplies are school supplies. Because who do you think makes the best periodic table of elements every September? Not the science kids. A love of chemistry has nothing to do with it. It's always a scrapbooker's kid. You know why? Think about it. The periodic table of elements is all letters. Scrapbooking Moms hoard alphabet stickers. But they don't call them *alphabet stickers*. They call them *alphas*. Ironic, isn't it? (Beeeeeep.) [CLICK.]

[SIXTH PHONE MESSAGE]

(Beeeeeep.) Gosh. What's wrong with your voice mail? It's so full. Who's calling you? I really need a reliable secretary. Anyway, as I was saying, don't forget your scrapbooking goody bags for the goody bag swap tonight. I've seen Collette's, and they are a-ma-zing! Make sure yours are amazing because I'm hosting a competition. Cherry Festival on The Lawn is this weekend, and we need to improve our baked goods packaging if we want to increase sales and profits. Last year's pie auction was a disaster, and we can't let *that* happen again. And you'll never graduate to bake sale packaging if you don't master goody bags first. Baby steps. But that's just my opinion—turns out I've got lots of them. Ha! Ha! Silly me. [CLICK.]

[SEVENTH PHONE MESSAGE]

(Beeeeeep.) One more itty-bitty thing. No biggie. It's tiny. Just a little something I almost forgot. Don't eat any more of those peckled peanut butter cookies I brought you. It's not my fault, so don't blame Mary Margaret St. James. Blame the United States Center for Disease Control. They're the ones announcing a nationwide peanut butter recall. Apparently, there's been an outbreak of E. coli or Ebola or early-onset balding or something. One of those *E* diseases. So scary. Probably from one of those farms that grow free-range peanuts or something. Anyway, people can die from that. I hope you don't die from that, but if you do die, don't blame me because it's not my fault. It's never my fault. [CLICK.]

[AUTOMATED VOICE MESSAGING SYSTEM]

We're sorry. Mailbox is full. Press 9 to delete all messages. Repeat. Press 9 to delete all mess—

~

EMAIL—Time Received: 1:11 p.m.

TO: Holly Banks
FROM: Psychic Betty, Psychic Hotline Network
SUBJECT: Is Your Life Going Downhill?

Ever fear the cosmos has launched a sinister plot to muck up your life? Well, you're right. It has! It's called Mercury retrograde, and it happens three times per year.

Are you finding communications with loved ones have become strained? Do you feel your mind is playing tricks on you? Do you feel lonely, sabotaged, overwhelmed? Well, you're not alone. Because Mercury rules communication and clear thinking, you may find yourself misspeaking or saying things you'd never typically say. Disagreements in conversation frequently occur. Try silencing yourself around your spouse and coworkers. That's right. Slap that hand across your mouth because there's no telling what might come shooting out of it. You're probably screwing things up left and right. But hey, it's not your fault! It's Mercury's fault!

Having engine problems? Car won't start? Feel you've "bought a lemon"? Because Mercury rules transportation, during the retrograde period, a person's ability to catch a plane on time is compromised. Luggage is lost, and it's hard to find a good mechanic.

But hey, it's not YOU!

It's MERCURY!

When planet Mercury "retrogrades" it appears to be moving backward in the sky. Just like your miserable life!

But don't fret. For survival tips, log onto Psychic Betty's Psychic Hotline Network.

Hold your next party at DIZZY'S SEAFOOD!

Click HERE for half-priced shrimp.

~

EMAIL—Time Received: 1:23 p.m.

TO: Holly Banks
FROM: Rosie McClure, School Office, Primm Academy
SUBJECT: Lots of things, too numerous to count.

Ms. Banks, this is Rosie McClure from the school office. I believe we met earlier today? You signed for my map.

I hope this doesn't sound terse or insensitive, but your daughter, Ella, was brought to the school office during lunch today because she had no lunch. Nor did she have any money to buy lunch. Perhaps this detail slipped your mind? I gave her money from the school's petty cash account and made sure she had something nutritious to eat. Please come to the school office at your earliest convenience to settle your daughter's account. It's only the first day of school, and already she has a negative balance.

On another note, you may want to have her evaluated for kindergarten readiness. She's been crying for you for most of the morning.

Perhaps you should come to the school to pick your daughter up? Use the carpool lot, not the bus lane, please. I've added a $10 cleanup fee to Ella's account for the cookie mess you spewed all over the door. You also traipsed through the Science Department's endangered boxwoods and ivy garden. Do you have something against sidewalks?

You can wait for me on the wooden bench outside the school office. You know, the bench beneath our nation's flag? That one.

16

Back to school again

Holly felt certain, with the notable exception of Mary-Margaret St. James, there wasn't another mother in town going "back to school" as often as she was on Ella's first day of kindergarten.

Ella appeared so innocent and vulnerable in her blue dress and little doggie backpack, waiting for Holly on the wooden bench beneath the American flag, the volunteer bulletin board, and the paper sun with the streaming petition to volunteer. The moment Ella's eyes met Holly's, Ella yelled, "Mommy!" and leaped to her feet, running the length of about fifteen black and white ceramic tiles. Holly knelt down on the large welcome mat where the Pie Committee once stood, her arms stretched wide to receive Ella as she crashed into Holly with such force Holly fell backward. The two of them, a pile of emotions sprawled out on the mat, smothering the word *welcome*.

Ella's arms and legs wrapped around Holly so tight you'd think Ella was trying to climb inside Holly's rib cage. Holly didn't bother standing upright or wiping away Ella's tears. She didn't care that Pink Freshwater Pearls from the school office stood in the doorway, watching. After the day they had? Nothing mattered. Nothing. Nuclear proliferation? Who cared? Climate change? Didn't matter. Trans fats? *Zzzzzz.* Ella was Holly's baby girl, and she'd had a bad day. That was what mattered. The End. Fin.

Holly signaled Freshwater Pearls to give them a minute as she sat, rocking Ella, kissing her neck, smelling her scent, running her fingers through Ella's hair.

"Mommy's here. Don't cry, sweetie."

"I don't want to go to kinner garnen."

Ella sucked her thumb.

"I know it's hard, Ella. New things are hard."

And dang it, Ella wasn't supposed to suck her thumb. But Holly didn't want to deal with that right now because Ella needed comfort—Ella needed her thumb.

"Aim sleeves back plack on my cooks."

What? "Ella, honey, I can't understand you." Holly pulled Ella's thumb from her mouth, wondering if now was the best time to pick this battle. Jack's voice crept inside Holly's head, reminding her she needed to be consistent. Every dang parenting article by those stupid dang child psychologists popped into Holly's stupid dang head. Ella had turned five in May. Holly knew she shouldn't suck her thumb or drink from a sippy cup. She didn't need Jack or the magazines—and especially not the cable guy—telling her that.

Holly gave a sidelong glance at the checkered pattern of the black and white floor tiles, so grateful she'd had time to drive home, take a shower, and get into some real clothes. White jeans, a heather-gray shirt, and a pair of black Doc Martens. Maybe all of this was her fault. Maybe Ella'd be ready for kindergarten if Holly'd weaned her off thumb-sucking earlier. But what was Holly supposed to do now? Trust the mothering instincts that told her now was not the time to take Ella's thumb away from her? Or be consistent, as Jack said, and help Ella break the habit? Holly hated moments like this. Motherhood was so confusing.

So Holly stalled, knowing full well her stalling would give Ella a few moments to comfort herself, and *then* Holly'd insist she take her thumb out of her mouth because *then* Holly'd know she was a "good" mom. *Because, hey: I'm consistent! I make my daughter face her fears without the use of an emotional crutch.* And besides, if your own mother didn't give you a moment of grace when you were so distraught you were sucking your thumb, who on earth would?

"Tell me about your day, Ella." Holly paused, listening to Ella suck. "What happened?"

Like mother like child, Ella paused, too, resting her head against Holly's shoulder. Eventually, Ella slid her thumb out of her mouth, pulling it out so fast it made a wet, sloppy sound. Ella pulled back from Holly until they were arm's distance apart, took a deep breath—and then let Holly have it.

"Ainsley's-backpack-was-on-my-hook-so-mine-was-on-the-floor-but-it-can't-be-on-the-floor-or-someone-will-trip-but-I-didn't-make-anyone-trip-they-just-tripped-by-themselfs-but-my-teacher-said-mine-needed-to-be-on-a-hook-but-I-couldn't-hook-it-because-Ainsley-hooked-it-and-I-don't-have-a-mat-to-sleep-on-and-the-purple-broke-and-I-didn't-have-a-lunch-and-I-don't-like-center-time-and-I-was-thirrrrrsty-but-didn't-have-a-water-bottle-because-you-didn't-pack-me-a-lunch."

Holly combed Ella's hair with her fingers. "Tomorrow will be better, and every day will get easier and easier . . ."

"When-the-purple-broke-I-couldn't-finish-the-balloon-so-the-number-six-doesn't-have-one-and-I-couldn't-finish-so-I-put-it-in-the-'finish'-cubby-but-it-wasn't-'finished'-it-was-'worked-on'-so-that's-not-'finished'-that's-called-'worked-on'-but-I-couldn't-finish-because-of-the-purple." Ella came up for air. "And the six. So I need a new purple or I'll *never* finish."

"I'll get you a new purple, sweetie. What's a purple? Is it a crayon?"

"It's *broken*!"

"Okay, okay. It's broken. But maybe we can fix it. Is it a crayon?"

"I wanna go home." Ella put her thumb into her mouth, falling back into Holly's arms, burying her face deep into Holly's chest.

"I know, baby girl. I know." It was close to dismissal time. Soon, the entryway would fill with people. "Let's get you signed out, Ella. You'll feel better tomorrow. Tomorrow, we'll both try this again."

Freshwater Pearls walked with them into the office. Pearls, now somewhat cordial, counted Holly's bills, tucking them into the petty cash box behind the counter to settle Ella's lunch and Holly's cookie bill. Pearls, of course, had a real name. It was Rosie McClure.

Holly didn't have a nickname growing up. She was simply Holly. Wait, that was not entirely true. Her parents sometimes called her Holly Tree. "Holly Tree? You finished your homework?" Now with screen names, usernames, profile names, avatars, gravatars, *Holly* became HollyBanks224@email.com or HBanks or HollyB. Holly chose @EndofRope as her Twitter handle because, well . . . she never wanted to be on Twitter in the first place, but her mom pressured her to open an account. A good Twitter handle for Jack? @WorkHusband or @lunch @Wendys @BethannysTable. @sshole.

"I'm sorry about earlier," Holly said to Rosie. "For signing for your map. You were looking forward to seeing him."

Rosie shrugged.

"You like him, don't you?" Holly asked.

Rosie didn't make eye contact.

Holly handed Ella an organic, sugar-free lollipop from the glass jar on Rosie's counter. "I can understand why you would like him," Holly offered. "He's very cute."

Rosie looked to be about Holly's age. *She must be single, and apparently not happy about it.*

"Can we start over?" Holly pushed her hand across the counter, hoping to shake Rosie's. "I'm Holly. Holly Banks."

Rolling onto her tippy-toes, Ella slapped her little hand onto the counter too. "And I'm Ella. Ella Banks."

Rosie warmed a bit and smiled. "I know who you are, Ella." Rosie shook Ella's hand. "Nice to make your acquaintance again, Ella."

Rosie paid no attention to Holly—to Holly's hand, stretched across the counter—which was unfortunate because this was a big moment for Holly. Holly's mom would never do this. Greta would never reach across a counter to call a truce with a woman perceived to have more power.

"How was your day, Ella, Ella Banks?" Rosie asked, a delicate lilt in her voice. "You're in Miss Bently's class, aren't you? Miss Bently is lovely. She's new here, too, but she's already one of my closest friends. Did you finish your lunch?"

"Yes."

"Did you eat the apple I gave you?" Rosie leaned over the counter, still holding Ella's hand. Rosie appeared to have a natural rapport with children and seemed especially keen on Ella. *Must be Ella's big brown eyes, cute little nose, and soft, sweet cheeks,* thought Holly.

"Miss Rosie, do you like *My Little Pony*?" Ella's inquiry came with the tip of her head as she scratched her nose with her free hand.

"Oh yes, very much," Rosie said. "I like Princess Celestia. Coruler of Equestria!"

"I like Pinkie Pie." Ella smiled, a gap where her baby tooth once was.

Meanwhile, Holly's outstretched hand was being ignored, so she dragged it like a limp fish across the counter and stuffed it into the front pocket of her jeans. What in the world was going on? Did they forge a friendship earlier in the day? They were talking about *My Little Pony* like they'd known each other their entire lives. *Hey! Rosie might be the perfect person to help Ella transition into kindergarten—like having a family ally in the front office.*

And that was when Holly heard Rosie say, "If your mommy forgets to pack you a lunch, I want you to come to the office to see me, okay,

Ella? I don't want to hear from Miss Bently that you went without eating."

"Excuse me?" said Holly, trying not to throttle Rosie. "Mind if I interject?"

Rosie glanced at Holly, then returned to Ella. "I want Ella to know that I'm here for her. If she needs me."

"My child is fine." Holly took Ella's hand from Rosie's, guiding her gently but firmly toward the door. "My child doesn't *need* you." *Freshwater Pearls.*

Ella swung her gaze up at Holly, presumably to get a read of Holly's facial expression. Ella looked as perplexed as Rosie did about the sudden turn of events—how a conversation about ponies that was going so well for *them* suddenly took a nosedive with Holly.

Holly focused on Rosie. "Are you suggesting I don't feed my child?"

"No, not at all."

"Because I forgot her lunch bag—it happens; I'm human. It was on the kitchen counter. Fully packed. And I feel really, really bad about leaving it behind."

Rosie fell silent.

"But I'm not a bad mom. I'm not." Holly spoke without confidence. Afraid her words could be disputed. "I had a bad morning. That's all."

"Yes, of course." Rosie softened. "We all do."

Although, there's a real chance I might actually be a bad mom. Not everyone is a good mom. Holly was cynical. Suspicious of other women. She was clearly disorganized, kept a messy house, and couldn't, for the life of her, finish unpacking a few stupid boxes. She didn't bake pies—but she'd lied and said she did. The other night, when all the other mothers were more than happy to sign their names on the polka-dotted lines, when pushed—and only because Holly was pushed—the most she was willing to contribute was napkins. *Napkins!* She was selfish. And probably lazy. Holly assumed other mothers would do all the work.

As if reading her mind, Ella wrapped her arms around Holly's waist and gave her a squeeze.

"I'm not a bad mom," Holly said again, trying to convince a woman she hardly knew.

"No, of course not." Rosie spoke softly. "There's no such thing."

Holly's shoulders relaxed. "Thank you. Thank you for saying that."

And Holly thought Rosie meant it, but couldn't know for sure. Rosie's eyes flitted briefly to Ella, whose face was buried against Holly's leg. Was it possible that while Holly worried about being a bad mom, Rosie wished she were a mom? *My heart breaks for women, for women like me and for women like Rosie.*

Holly told Ella to say goodbye to Rosie. Ella did so, then left the school office to wait for Holly on the bench.

"I can check on Ella tomorrow," Rosie offered, nodding toward the bank of security monitors behind her desk. "I'll call you if I see Ella's having trouble."

"I'd like that, Rosie. Thank you."

Rosie reached across the counter to offer her hand to Holly.

Holly gladly shook Rosie's hand, two women now united in one cause: helping Ella navigate the yellow brick road into kindergarten.

17

Moments later

Holly and Ella left the school, skipping a bit down the cobblestone sidewalk toward the side parking lot where the rental car was parked. Holly felt happy. She and Ella made a friend, and they made that friend together. Which was a good thing, because they could both use a little welcoming to the Village of Primm right about now. The Topiary Park ran a succulent-of-the-month program, shipped from a private nursery at the edge of town. Maybe Holly should send Rosie a thank-you gift. Like a teacher appreciation gift but for the front office. The website said the succulents were shipped UPS and required a signature—maybe Rosie would enjoy a few months of succulent deliveries. On second thought, maybe Holly would too.

While Holly fumbled with the two keys, Ella pointed. "All of the windows are open, Mommy."

"Oh, I know. I'm wondering which is the ignition key and which is the trunk key." Since passing the Peloton enclave, she'd been driving with all the windows down. Truthfully, she might have been stalling a bit by fiddling around with the keys; it stank in there.

"Why are we driving this? Where's our car?" Ella asked. "Oh, wait. I know." Ella tipped her head and rested her hands on her hips like she was scolding Holly, but in a playful way. "You wrecked it."

"You saw that, didn't you?" Holly winced, hoping Ella was okay with things, hoping the portal to her childhood was still painted in bright colors—like the colors of the sky over the Topiary Park. Crayola's parakeet blue.

Ella climbed in, and Holly helped her get buckled.

"It smells like Band-Aids in here." Ella pinched her nose. "Can we get some chicken nuggets? I don't like school food."

"Why? What were they serving?"

"Fish solopia."

"Tilapia?" Holly got herself situated in the driver's seat.

"That's it. Good, Mommy. You got it."

"What else did you eat? Anything for dessert?"

"Cherry pie." Ella brightened.

"Really? What did you think of the cherry pie?"

"I loved it!" Ella clapped. "My mouth was so happy my lips grew a smile."

Well, I'll be danged. Holly started the car. *Ella likes pie.* Holly smacked a small yellow bug from her dashboard. *Must have flown in the open window.*

"There's another one!" Ella pointed to the dash, and Holly slapped it dead. *Man, what a disgusting car.* Holly looked toward a triple-sphere topiary flanking the entry to the Primm Academy Atrium. *Something wicked this way comes. Hope whatever's eating Plume isn't taking over the village.*

WESTERN UNION ONLINE

Money transfer control number: 0421464892
Recipient: Greta B. Vogel
1610 Clairmont Court—Apartment 2B
Sender: Holly Banks
12 Petunia Lane

Amount $994.00 (nine hundred ninety-four dollars and no cents)

Message: Again?!? MOM! Stop. I can't keep doing this—YOUR ACTIONS are putting a strain on MY MARRIAGE. The fact that YOUR stray cat got "knocked up" is NOT my problem. I AM NOT PAYING FOR A CAT DOULA! I'm not. You hear me? And I think it's APPALLING that you're asking for money to restring your ukulele. NOT MY PROBLEM! This $994 is a LOAN, and it's to be used for one reason and one reason only—FOUR NEW TIRES. You got that? That's it! And next time—don't order first and then wonder how you're going to pay. DON'T USE THIS MONEY FOR ANYTHING ELSE. No slots, no blackjack tables, AND NO MORE CACTUS GARDENS! I don't care how old, or how rare the stupid cactuses are. Cacti. Whatever.

18

Later that night

Ella sat watching her ponies, meatloaf was baking in the oven, and Jack still was not home yet. That meant Holly would be late for tonight's Scrap & Swap Fund-Raiser at the school. *Thanks, Jack. How was that Wendy's number one single combo—no cheese, no onions—medium size with a Dr Pepper?*

Holly pulled Ella's school folder out of her backpack, and out dropped her school supply list. *Mother fletcher!*

"What the hell-o kitty kind of sh—what a buncha horse hockey." Holly clenched the list with both fists. "What's a 'plastic no-prong' folder? I've never heard of such a thing," she muttered. "Zippered, solid-color, canvas pencil case with a front pocket and three holes? Isn't that a bit specific?" Holly read further. Ella already owned a pencil case, but it didn't have a pocket. Couldn't she use that?

Primm Academy Kindergarten Back-to-School School Supply List

- 24 Ticonderoga pencils SHARPENED. ***NO LEAD OR MECHANICAL PENCILS!***
- 2 large Pink Pearl erasers, 1 white Magic Rub art eraser, 24 pink pencil-top erasers

- 2 highlighters. One yellow, one green, one blue.
- 1 black Papermate Flair pen—felt tip only
- Crayola (please, no store brand or Roseart) 24-pack classic, 8-pack basic. Labeled. One each for the class and student. Class box not labeled.
- 6 plastic no-prong folders
- 2 clear pencil pouches with three holes (clearly labeled with student's name in BLACK permanent ink)
- 4 low-odor black dry erase markers (LOW ODOR)
- one white athletic sock
- 2 two subject notebooks, wide ruled three hole punch, spiral WITH TABS (no color)
- 1 red three subject spiral bound wide ruled notebook (THREE HOLE)
- 4 tennis balls—cut the letter "X" into them (Do not send excess balls to school. No storage.)
- large bag large cotton balls (air spun white not needle punched)
- 4 large bottles Elmer's Washable School Glue (***ELMERS ONLY!)
- 7 Elmer's disappearing purple—LARGE. (***ELMERS ONLY!)
- 6 pocket folders vinyl solid color (red, blue, yellow, green)
- 4 folders no pockets, not labeled, not vinyl, no holes
- easy close Ziploc—boys quart; girls gallon
- Scissors specifics: Fiskars, 5-inch blunt—rounded tips
- 2 each: tissues, paper towels, 50-count white napkins
- 2 bottles alcohol-free, scent-free hand sanitizer (MUST HAVE PUMPS!)
- Optional: Friday headphones for computer lab

The list was riddled with incomplete information, typos, and quantities that didn't add up, and Holly didn't understand half of what she was reading. It didn't seem very Primm to her. Was this a mistake? All the other papers in Ella's backpack were close to perfection: no typos, printed on crisp white paper with the Primm Academy gold, black, and white school crest at the top. Holly flipped the paper over, thinking this must be a piece of scratch paper Ella had used at an art table. "Ella, how old is Miss Bently? Is she my age or Cousin Sophia's age?"

"Sophia's."

Then Miss Bently was right out of college. "Did she give you this list?"

Ella crumpled her eyebrows, shrugged her shoulders. "I don't know."

"Ella." Holly pointed at Struggle. "Get that out of Struggle's mouth."

Struggle wagged her tail, a stuffed green dinosaur hanging from her mouth.

The dinosaur, one of the kindergarten classroom "pets" this year, had traveled home in Ella's backpack to live with her family for the week as part of an ongoing first-semester homework assignment about emotions and using a thesaurus to describe those emotions. Strict instructions made the assignment very clear: no computers. The children had to use an actual physical thesaurus and sit down with a grown-up to receive help sorting through the printed index of a reference book while discussing their feelings.

Then, together as a family, they had to make a poster illustrating how their family expressed that emotion in healthy ways.

Then, around their drawing, photograph, or whatever, they had to record all the synonyms they found in the thesaurus for that particular emotion onto the poster board.

No problem.

Except, Holly wasn't fully unpacked yet. Had no idea where to look for (as the assignment called it) their "family thesaurus," hadn't seen or used an actual thesaurus in years, and suspected they didn't even own one in the first place.

"Struggle! Drop that." Holly clapped from the kitchen. "Ella, take it out of her mouth."

Miss Bently's dinosaur, Tyrannosaurus Thesaurus, ruled over the herd of take-home dinosaurs that, a lot like Snow White and the Seven Dwarfs, all had names. One was named Sleepy, another Surprised, another Hungry, and so on. Lucky for the Banks family, the dinosaur Ella brought home was Happy. Happy should be an easy emotion to describe during the first week of kindergarten, right?

"Struggle!" Ella leaned over to swat Struggle on the snout. "Let. Go. Of. Happy! *Mmmmom*!"

Holly walked over with a stern "No!" and shook a finger. "Bad dog."

Struggle lowered her head, pulled her ears back, and then, reluctantly, released Happy into Holly's hand.

Holly handed the dinosaur back to Ella. "You have to keep Happy out of reach of Struggle. Struggle grabs hold of things and doesn't let go. You know this, Ella—that's how she got her name." Holly pointed to a nearby rubber cog. "Git your cog, Struggle. Git your cog."

Ella tucked Happy into the neck of her shirt, began dancing to an episode of *My Little Pony*, but the TV kept flicking on and off. It had been doing this for days. Holly took the remote, pressed a few buttons. "I'll call the cable guy, Ella. He'll fix it." Tossing the remote onto the couch. "Ella, honey? Don't stand so close to the television. It's bad for your eyes."

Ella spun around, squinting. "What?"

"It's bad for your eyes."

Back in the kitchen, Holly checked the meatloaf. Called the cable company.

"Primm Cable," a man answered.

"I need someone to come out to check my TV. We keep losing our signal. Is Caleb available? Young guy? Maybe midtwenties?"

"That's me. I'm Caleb. Happy to help. What's your address?"

"Twelve Petunia Lane."

"Film school mom?"

"That's me." *Nice to be remembered.*

"I'm booked for the rest of the day, but I'll come out late tomorrow morning. What seems to be the problem?"

"We keep losing the signal for the Hub Network, and my daughter likes watching—"

"*My Little Pony.*"

"Right. *My Little Pony.*" Holly cleared her throat. "I hate that cable is moving toward company-owned networks. It's so . . . I don't know. *Commercial.*" *See? I went to film school. I'm cool. I'm hip. I know about these things.*

"You haven't traveled to Area 51 lately, have you? Nineteen forty-seven Roswell UFO incident?"

"In Nevada?" Holly tucked a finger in the ear opposite the phone. "Are you serious? I just moved from there. Boulder City." She waited for a response, but it never came. So she asked, "Government cover-up?" Still no response. "I don't understand," she told him. "Hello? Are you still there? What does this have to do with my cable connection?"

"You tell me."

"Wait. What?" *This is so bizarre.* "I'm confused."

"That's what they all say . . ."

"I'm not following you."

"Someone might be following you," he warned.

"What?"

"Just kidding! Have you decided anything about the Wilhelm Klaus?"

"No. Not yet."

"Maybe there's a three-minute film you can dig up from your portfolio to submit," Caleb suggested. "You went to film school."

"I did. Go to film school," Holly said. "But I've been, um . . . busy. Doing stuff. You know, lots of things. Over the years. Like children's literacy . . . and immunizations—art. We do lots of art. In crayons. Science things like museums . . . of science. And developmental! Those things. Like bikes and stuff." Her voice wandered off. "Busy things. That moms do. You know, because it's important. And tough! Boy, oh boy, is motherhood a tough job." She needed to shift focus. "So. You have a YouTube channel?"

"Everyone has a YouTube channel. How else are you going to get your film work out there?" He practically laughed at her. Like he was saying *duh.* "So I'll come tomorrow and fix your cable."

"Tomorrow. Okay. Sounds good." She traced the edge of her countertop. "And after you fix the TV, can you stay awhile? Have some coffee?" Maybe this was too forward. "Not . . . not *that* kind of coffee. I'm not hitting on you or anything. I have questions."

"About your cable?"

"About the film industry. About getting back in. Freelance. Nothing big." She grimaced, closing her eyes, feeling like a fool, an imposter. "Definitely freelance. Nothing big."

"Yeah, sure. I'll bring my micro–spy camera equipment. I got great footage for my project with it. We can talk about Wilhelm Klaus."

"Sounds great." Holly exhaled, feeling . . . a bit giddy. Someone to talk film with? That was new. She hadn't had that since film school. "We can talk about Klaus." Wilhelm Klaus. A better topic to think about than combo meals at fast-food restaurants. "Yeah, that sounds good. See you tomorrow." She hung up.

Holly snatched the school supply list off the table, held it up to inspect both sides. *Is this stupid thing a fake? Because if Mary-Margaret's behind this—I'm not letting her get away with it.* Holly snapped a picture of it with her phone. Contemplated reporting Mary-Margaret to Principal Hayes. Bullies should be reported. Even fully grown bullies. Especially fully grown bullies.

~

EMAIL—Time Sent: 5:49 p.m.

TO: Principal Hayes
FROM: Holly Banks
SUBJECT: Seriously? Have You Seen This Back-to-School Supply List?

Principal Hayes,

Please see attached back-to-school supply list for Kindergarten Room K-9. Am I to assume this list comes from an actual teacher at Primm Academy? Or could it be the work of someone who enjoys torturing others?

You decide.

~

Penelope Pratt
Feathered Nest Realty

—ENCLAVE ALERTS—

THIS MAY BE HARD TO STOMACH

Please, please, please check your topiaries. I am sorry to be the bearer of bad news, but a few hours ago, Plume's stomach disconnected from her body and fell on top of Botanist Billy O'Malley.

As you can imagine, the stomach of a twenty-five-foot-tall topiary peacock is quite heavy.

Luckily, a forklift operator rallied and lifted Plume's belly off Botanist Billy O'Malley. Botanist Billy O'Malley's wife, Sally O'Malley, said Botanist Billy O'Malley was taken by trolley to the triage center at the trauma treatment center. Some time ago, Sally O'Malley reported Billy O'Malley was in stable condition—surrounded by wife Sally, brother Willy O'Malley, and Billy O'Malley's triplets: Molly O'Malley, Milly O'Malley, and lil' Billy O'Malley III.

Not to worry, the O'Malley family lives on Dillydally, and the Dillydallys always rally around Dillydally daddies. It is troubling whenever stomach contents are spewed. No doubt, this experience was especially troubling for Botanist Billy O'Malley, who, after thirty-seven years of working next to plants, found himself inside one.

BEFORE THINGS GET UNDERWATER—IF YOU NEED TO SELL

We here at Feathered Nest Realty care about YOU and your homeownership. Let's hope these bugs don't kill the entire Topiary Park—or the Village of Primm will lose its most valued tourist attraction. (No offense to the new owners of the vineyard—yes, you're a tourist attraction too.)

If the Topiary Park goes belly up, I don't want to THINK about the resulting loss of tax revenue and its impact on real estate taxes and home values. Surely, with the loss of commercial business revenue, our real estate taxes will have to rise to cover the costs of our beloved community and school. I suppose if we all collectively drink more vineyard wine our taxes won't go up . . . (Something to consider?)

But if our mom-and-pop economy goes bye-bye, who'll be knocking at our doors? WALMART. All that acreage—Walmart would level the Topiary Park and put up a parking lot! That would forever change the face of Primm. Right now, our biggest parking lot is at the school, and at least that's hidden from view—and painted with educational, enriching art like world maps and the solar system. We're bug bites away, people. Bug bites.

Reports from the Peloton and Blythe enclaves point to suspicious, widespread bug activity across the village. Blythe residents aren't feeling carefree these days, and one Peloton resident noticed the topiary on her front porch—so overwhelmed by the little buggers—crawled right across her front porch and traumatized her cat. Sally O'Malley, advising from Botanist Billy O'Malley's bedside, said the Blythe and Peloton residents should start dousing their topiaries with gasoline and setting them on fire.

Could this be the beginning of the end? Is this—the Apocalypse?

SCRAP & SWAP FUND-RAISER

This next Enclave Alert is brought to you at the request of my (dear) cousin, Mary-Margaret St. James, from Hopscotch Hill. Please attend tonight's Scrap & Swap Fund-Raiser at the school and please wear your pink PRIMM t-shirt—as Mary-Margaret feels this is a SCHOOL function, and SCHOOL functions are coded as PINK, her favorite color. I, however, feel scrapbooking is a FAMILY event, centered around the HOME, and should, therefore, be a YELLOW event requiring a YELLOW shirt. And yes, the school mascot is a golden honeybee—which could be construed as yellow. But no, apparently (according to Mary-Margaret), there's a huge difference between gold and yellow. I say wear whatever you want and see what happens. Anarchy is the bed maiden of the apocalypse. On to more pressing issues. Like the swarm of bugs invading our village, that dastardly Walmart wanting to break ground, and the obvious need to stimulate the economy by drinking more vineyard wine.

F.U.!

Team Buttercream and the Pink Erasers face off in the summertime finals at this weekend's F.U. Frisbee Tournament. Location: South Gazebo. Cherry Festival on The Lawn. Be there. And be sober. (Please.) We all remember what happened last time. NO ONE should feel it's within her rights to get SO SMASHED playing F.U. that she feels the need to climb on top of the South Gazebo, dislodge her enclave flag from its bracket, and then wave it above the crowd, shouting—

Well.

You know what she shouted.

So no more tequila at the tournaments. Whenever a group of moms drink tequila—the F.U.s always get out of hand.

19

Later that night

Where's Jack? He was supposed to be home by now.

Holly scanned the school supply list again. Four tennis balls? What would a kindergarten teacher possibly do with four tennis balls? The more she scanned the list, the worse her stomach felt. Was it anxiety? She almost felt nauseated. Holly opened the fridge to refill Ella's sippy—sports cup. "You know what, Ella? You don't need this cup anymore. Let's throw it away."

"No!"

"Okay, fine. We won't throw it away. But let's put it somewhere special and only take it out for special occasions." Holly reached for a juice glass. "You're a big girl now. You're in kindergarten."

Ella eyed Holly with suspicion but, for now, agreed to the new drinking arrangement.

"Tell me about the Leopard Print *Little Kids, Little Zoo* play in your classroom. Are you doing that this week? As a get-to-know-you activity?"

"Yup." Ella took a sip from the juice glass.

"How exciting, Ella. That's really great," Holly said, genuinely upbeat. Not just because the flyer said her daughter had a part in a play but because Ella needed a teacher costume and that should be easy to pull together, considering they were only halfway unpacked.

Ella started in: "Little frog, on a log, who is next to me? Little duck, with a cluck, is quacking next to me. Little duck, with a cluck, who is next to me?" As she recited the lines, Ella slyly walked her juice glass out of the kitchen and into the family room.

"Get back here, Ella." Holly lifted an eyebrow. "I didn't give you permission."

Ella slowly, carefully turned to carry the glass back to the kitchen table.

"Thank you." Holly took the glass from Ella's hands and placed it firmly on the kitchen table. "Say hello to Anna."

Ella waved. "Hi, Anna!"

"Now go back and play."

Holly figured she'd keep Anna inside the house for a while. Protect her from the bugs.

By the end of yet another episode of ponies, after the meatloaf cooled to room temperature, was covered with plastic wrap, and placed on the top shelf of the refrigerator, Jack walked through the door, tossing his keys on the kitchen counter. Struggle ran to his side in seconds flat, showing up for her daily dose of petting and *good girls*.

"Jack." Holly, a tangled mess of school supply panic mixed with conflicted feelings about fast-food dining, gave her crayon to Ella to finish coloring. "Be right back." She kissed Ella's forehead, then left her in the family room with Happy the Dinosaur and her *My Little Pony Pinkie Pie's Adventure* coloring book.

Should she say something about the Wendy's number one single combo—no cheese, no onions—medium size with a Dr Pepper now? Or wait for later?

"Look at this school supply list. I'm freaking out." Holly shoved the list at him. "The scissors I have for Ella are no good. I have to go out and buy a specific type of scissors. Five inch, blunt, Fiskar." Holly stabbed the list with her index finger. "Specifically Fiskar."

"Ahhh, yes." Jack smiled, exuding an air of nostalgia. "The annual school supply list." He scanned the list. "How was the first day of school? Where's Ella?" He squinted his eyes, held the supply list at arm's length.

"Jack." Why was he late? He was wearing gym clothes. "I thought you were at work. You were at the gym? You told me you were coming home early. I've got a function at Ella's school tonight."

"Oh, that. Sorry. I had to work out." He said it so . . . flip. Like . . . *Big deal. You've got nothing better to do. Me, on the other hand, I'm Jack. I get to come and go as I please.*

"You're not sorry." Holly took the list from his hand. "Don't say you're sorry if you're not sorry. You said you'd be home early." She leaned in. "You smell like cologne. Did you take a shower?"

"Hmm?" said Jack. "Oh, sure. After my workout."

"You never shower at the gym." Holly touched the sleeve of his shirt. "And your clothes aren't sweaty."

"Holly, stop." Jack was annoyed. "What are you saying?"

Ella dropped her crayon and ran with Pinkie Pie—comb still lodged in Pinkie Pie's hot-pink mane. "*D-aaaaaaa-ddddd-yyyyyy!*"

He swooped Ella into his arms, then folded her into a great big bear hug as Struggle struggled to suppress her instinct to bark.

Struggle hated it when anyone picked up, hugged, or play wrestled with Ella. Whining while taking sidelong glances at Holly, Struggle pleaded telepathically with her to make it stop: *You have to help, Holly. You're her mother*. Holly knew Struggle knew they weren't going to hurt Ella, but her protective canine instincts were quite strong where Ella was concerned. Having an absolute fit, Struggle jumped about, trying *not* to rescue Ella by biting Jack in the @ss.

"How's my sweetie?" Jack asked. "How was your first day of school? Tell me all about it. And hey, we need to eat ice cream tonight! To celebrate."

"Mommy hit a school bus," Ella said. "Now she drives a smelly car."

"I heard." His eyebrow twitched.

"Why are you looking at me like that?" Holly asked, snapping her fingers at Struggle, signaling she needed to *sit!* and settle down. "Are you *mad* at me? It was an accident."

Jack kissed both of Ella's cheeks, back and forth, cheek to cheek, back and forth.

"It's not like I did it on purpose," Holly mumbled. Struggle was now by her side, plunking down with a groan to lie at her feet. "Not like I chose to miss the bus and then *hit* the bus."

"I didn't say you did." The sharp and sudden rise in Jack's voice sent Holly a clear message: *Let's not fight in front of Ella.*

Holly turned her gaze toward Anna Wintour, sitting in her white cachepot in the center of their kitchen table, so prim, so pretty. The lettering on her pot: *Banks. Petunia Lane. Village of Primm.* It seemed like a dream, a mirage of a perfect family, in a perfect home, with a perfect school for a perfect child. *Perfect* meant happy, thought Holly, and *happy* meant she wasn't her mom.

"Forget it." Holly folded, then shoved the school supply list deep inside her back pocket. Grabbed her keys. "I have to go. I'm late."

"Holly, what? Wait. Why are you leaving?" Jack set Ella down. "Did I do something wrong?"

Holly spun around. "So let me get this straight. Are we fighting in front of Ella or not?"

"Whoa, Holly." He put his hands in the air like he was the bad guy and Holly the cop. And well. Maybe he was the bad guy. Athletic shoes, athletic socks, gym shorts, shirt. *Showered.* An hour late.

"Dinner's on the top shelf of the fridge. You might want to heat it up." Holly stuck her finger in Anna's soil to see if she needed water. She closed her laptop. Started gathering her stuff off the kitchen table. "I'll be home later."

"Holly." He gave Ella one last squeeze and a kiss.

Ella ran back to the family room to finish combing Pinkie Pie's tangled mane. Struggle followed.

"We need to talk," he said.

"Is this about Bethanny? Because I know about your lunch. I saw you."

"What are you talking about?"

"Today. At Wendy's. I saw you."

"So?" He folded his arms across his chest. Was he being defensive? Did he have something to hide?

"So. I was in the parking lot." *Fool.* "I saw the whole thing. *She was eating your fries.* Jack."

He acted confused and bewildered. Like Holly was crazy. Like he had no idea what she was talking about. "So why didn't you come inside?" he asked. Like that was the most pragmatic thing in the world for Holly to do.

"Oh. And ruin your happy meal?"

"We were eating."

"You were, like, peppering your fries and waving your arms around all *ha ha ha*!" Holly demonstrated. "And she was tossing her head back and laughing all *ha ha ha*!" Holly twisted her face and laughed like that twitch did. Bethanny. Holly didn't like to cuss, but she was so mad right now—she didn't care. Not twitch. →Bitch←. There. She said it. *And so what. Because it's the truth.* →BETHANNY'S A BITCH.←

"Quit your job," Holly told Jack. "Find another one."

"Quit my job?" His voice sharpened. "I can't."

"Why not. Because you can't leave Bethanny?" Wendy's number one single combo—no cheese, no onions—medium size with a Dr Pepper. Holly wanted to cry. *I'm not going to cry. I'm not.*

"Noooo," he said, like Holly was stupid. Like Holly was a child. "I can't afford to quit. Because I'm stuck. Because we have bills. Because we bought an overpriced 'expanded' cape in Primm and not the colonial we could afford in Southern Lakes. We're not saving." He counted on his fingers. "My 401(k) is a joke. We're not getting ahead on anything. I work—to pay the credit cards. If I get a little money—it gets wired to your mom. Because she's a child. Meanwhile? The child in the other room? My child?" He pointed. "Better get good grades or be amazing at sports because we'll never have enough money to send her to college. You want curtains? We can't afford curtains. We've bailed your mom out twice since buying this house, and we just got here. Funding your life? That's why I can't quit my job. Because I'm stuck." He snarled. "Stuck in Primm, when—at best—we should be in Southern Lakes, and we both know we can hardly afford that, but no. You wanted the better school."

"Funding my life? Funding *my* life? This wasn't my idea. I never wanted to move, Jack. You moved us. I was happy in Boulder City."

Jack had told her to quit her job when Ella was born. He told her he had it all taken care of. That he could support them. Holly never launched her career. Caleb the Cable Guy was further ahead than Holly was, and he was at least ten years younger. And Jack thought he was funding her life? *I don't have a life.* At least, not one that was her own. Holly gave up film. She dropped it. Set it aside. For him, for Ella, for their family.

Something wild and untamed unleashed itself inside her, and horrible words rolled up from the part of her gut that wanted to kick him in the balls. But instead of screaming like she should, like she wanted to, the words slipped out in a barely there whisper: "I hate you." Holly started to cry, unable to breathe. She shook her head no as if disagreeing with the very words she was saying as they came out. The tears. Wouldn't stop. And her chest. Her chest ached. She said it again: "*I hate you.*"

She'd never said anything like that to Jack. Ever. She felt

sad

about

those

words.

She felt like a series of lowercase letters on a piece of loose-leaf paper, all lined up to spell *woebegone*, but in one brief second, one fleeting moment, a pencil eraser dragged a line through her, and her lowercase letters became less than, and they fell, toppling one by one, off the thin blue line to dangle a bit, and then finally, the little bits of letters—the *w*, the *o*, the *e*—teetered. Got brushed off the page, leaving the space behind white, but with sad blue lines, empty lines. Lines running forward and backward with no place to go. No start. No finish. Woe, be gone.

Holly didn't curse. At least, she tried not to. There were things she wouldn't say, things she said instead. Silly replacement words like *fluck* and *mutha frucka* and *bullspit*. Those words didn't hurt. They didn't insult or inflict pain. At worst, they made her look strange for using them. But the words she just said to Jack—those were words she had never said. Never spoken, even in anger. Until now.

Hate was the most deplorable word in the English language. It was worse than a tiny four-letter word. It was worse than all the curse words combined. Something burned Holly's face—a heat she felt on her skin. A sad-from-the-eyes-and-shoulders-and-back feeling she felt as her chin quivered and the tears rolled, and Holly grew small inside and shriveled up. Like a crumpled piece of paper, or a baby bird that fell from the nest and landed twisted below, or a knot that was knotted up and tucked inside. Her stomach hurt. She was a little girl again. Only, she was Ella. And it was Ella's first day of kindergarten, but it was Holly's first day, too—because Holly's parents had done this. Holly's parents had fought in the kitchen, and the words they said were never erased. They stayed on the page. Holly was probably in her family room at the time. Coloring or playing house with her dolls like Ella was now. Something. But Holly was there. Listening. She was sure she was listening. Her parents' words were inside her. She swallowed them. They became her bones.

Holly felt more words roll up from deep inside. Still a whisper, but different this time. "I'm sorry you feel that way," she said to Jack, but really, Holly was talking to herself. *I'm sorry you feel that way,* she said to the little girl inside her—the little girl stuck in kindergarten. Stuck in that place. In that time. *I'm sorry you feel that way. Because you were five. You should have been playing. Carefree. Not pensive because someone smashed your "woe be gone" like a marshmallow or a bug. You should have danced. Been silly. Your portal should have been vibrant and happy, like a fistful of crayons labeled parakeet blue, pink rocket pop, marmalade, and limoncello yellow. Not gray. Not rocky slope. The walls of your portal shouldn't have been seaweed or shadow flint. You deserved happy. You deserved cloud-like, puffy and cotton. I'm sorry it was arcus clouds and ominous chaos, the fear you might suffocate beneath dark skies looming above, pressing down. You never had a chance. You were small and fragile. Soft cheeks. Hopeful eyes that looked up.* Inside, it was always small child and fragile. That feeling Holly had? That burden she carried? Its name was Angst: an arcus cloud from a long-ago sky.

Holly shook those thoughts away. This wasn't about her childhood—was it? This was about her marriage. Real problems in real life. Today, now.

Holly left the kitchen, left the hurt look on Jack's face. She rushed past the family room and toward the front door. Ella looked up from the combing of Pinkie Pie's mane. "Mom?" Ella called out to Holly. "Why are you running?" Like living in an echo chamber. *Mom? Why are you running?* Ella's words, they hung in the air.

"Going out for school supplies, Ella Bella!" Holly tried to sound chipper. Tried speaking above a flood of memories. "I'll be home soon!"

Beyond her front door, Holly heard the sound of a distant lawn mower—but it wasn't her dad's mower. Because Holly's dad had moved away, become two weeks in the summer and every other Christmas. What would Jack become? Wednesday nights? Every other weekend?

I'm sorry, Ella. Echo chamber. Portal. *I'm sorry.* The sound of the lawn mower—everything. Everything reverberated in her ears. *Tzzzzzzt!*

She was just about to leave their porch when she heard, "Hollywait." It came out like that. One word: *Hollywait.* With it, Holly felt Jack step onto their front porch, joining her in the place Holly once found so welcoming. That porch. That place. Now? Space. Once destination. Once arrival. Now? Departure. A porch of inhospitable. A porch of "not now" and "go away." A porch of "confront the problems in your marriage." *Don't hide behind the little girl you once were. Become the woman you are.*

"I'm done," she told him, stopping at the top of the porch steps. "I have to get Ella's school supplies." She didn't want to cry. Maybe she hadn't seen anything—it was lunch. A number one single, no cheese. Nothing more. She didn't see anything. She didn't. There were no onions. Jack never ate onions.

"Holly, stop. Please. Listen." He reached for her upper arms to center her attention, to get her to look at him, but she stepped back before he could touch her. "I'm sorry." He pulled his hands back, holding them in the air in a sign of surrender. "About what I said. About you and Ella. And your mom. I shouldn't have said it. I'm sorry."

"I don't want to pay her gambling debts," Holly spat. "I don't enjoy that. But yes, I do want curtains—for privacy. For simple, basic *privacy.*" Collette? Holly wanted to pin *her* to a Pinterest board. For publicizing a front porch on social media. For making Holly feel inferior. "Worn-out bedsheets aren't living room curtains, Jack. That's what we have. A bedsheet in a window. I'm not a bad person." It was all so stupid.

He turned to face the co-op gardens at the end of their street, giving Holly a chance to catch her breath and collect her thoughts. Her face felt hot. Her stomach felt twisted. She needed to switch gears and started thinking about . . . her neighbors' . . . mulch. How it matched. How every single house on Petunia Lane was lined with the same expensive mulch. Mulch beds that swooped, dipped, and curved, forming tributaries of bark that collectively formed a sea of beautiful amber-brown cedar. Cheap mulch provided color and contrast. Expensive mulch provided color and contrast but also replaced nutrients to the soil, repelled insects, emitted a scent that was pleasant to humans, and, more importantly, increased property values through great curb appeal. All the mulch beds on Petunia Lane were exactly the same. From the same supplier, delivered the same day. Expensive. Now how'd that happen? Overzealous homeowners' association? Perhaps. But it didn't matter. When Penelope's Feathered Nest "Mulch Alert" for the Petunia enclave came—and Holly knew it would—what if they couldn't afford the amber-brown cedar? What then?

He took a shower at the gym. Why? He never does that. Was he even at the gym? She checked the expression on Jack's face. What was he thinking? Was he about to admit it?

"We're under federal investigation."

What? "Who is?" Holly asked. "We are? You and me?"

"The company. And maybe me—for working there." He released a long, slow exhale, like he'd just confessed something, like he was glad he'd finally gotten it off his chest. "Offshore shell companies."

"Offshore *what*? What does this have to do with curtains?" Was this a dodge? Was he making this up? Because Holly had seen him. He was eating a hamburger. With Bethanny.

"Seven of our clients are under federal investigation for money laundering, insurance fraud, and tax evasion. Three of them live in Primm."

"I'm so confused." Holly covered her face. Took a moment. To think. To take this all in.

"I wanted to tell you, but I signed a confidentiality agreement."

He was almost pleading with her. Why was he pleading with her? Was he apologizing about the agreement without actually apologizing?

"I've known this would be my new role when we moved. That I'd be working on something I swore I wouldn't tell anyone about—not even you." He looked bruised. Defeated. Run over by a bus. "I've known all along. I'm sorry."

"We moved to the Village of Primm because you might be under federal investigation?"

"Sort of. I mean, I'm not in trouble, yet. At least I don't think so."

"Jack." Holly could hardly form words. "I thought you were having an affair. You're always working. You're so secretive. You told me you were being *promoted*."

"Well . . . I was. Being promoted. But not exactly. More like I've been given a chance to bail the company out of a tight spot. And hopefully save my job."

"Your job?" They'd have no income. And then what?

"My job?" He laughed a laugh that was filled with disbelief. "More like my career. Everything I've ever worked for. If this doesn't go our way, the company will be compromised, and everyone involved will be ruined. Tarnished reputations. It'll hit the papers. And the evening news in most markets. I'll be finished. No one will want to touch me."

"We can't afford this house without a job, Jack. Why did we do this? All of our savings." The lawn mower sound Holly heard earlier stopped, the cutting complete. Holly needed to win the Wilhelm Klaus. She needed that prize money. Not that it would fix everything, but it would bridge the gap. Whatever that gap might be. Her thoughts trailed toward the cul-de-sac, toward Petunia's community gardens. She wasn't a Primm Mom or a Petunia Mom. She'd known that. But now, she'd give anything to be one. Anything. Rose-colored glasses? Yes, please. Holly didn't want crabgrass. She wanted prim. She wanted proper. Topiaries. Gazebos with enclave flags. A thriving PTA. She wanted Ella catching Bus 13 every morning, on time. Because Holly got her there, backpack packed. Nutritious lunch inside. "We'll have nothing," Holly said. "We'll lose everything."

"I know." He rubbed his temples. "It's bad. It's really bad, Holly. I can't sleep. I take, like, twenty antacids—before breakfast." He pressed his palm to his chest. "I get these . . . panic attacks. Like I can't breathe."

"I thought you were an auditor. Offshore shell companies? Tax evasion? Jack—you have a master's degree in tax law. How could you let this happen?" She needed to sit, but her front porch was empty. Naked. But not barren—because they were talking. Not flat, desolate scrubland. But where was Collette's wooden bench? Where were her pillows? Holly needed pillows with the number *12* and the words *Petunia Lane* embroidered on them. She needed pillows to anchor her. Seriously? Why didn't Collette leave her *freaking* pillows? It wasn't like she could even use them at her new address. "Are you in legal trouble?"

"Hard to say. It's not illegal to incorporate a company in the British Virgin Islands. It's how you use that company that becomes questionable in the eyes of the law. Bethanny and I are tasked with pulling a package together that demonstrates our company had no knowledge of our clients' illegal activities. That we set up those shell companies according to US law. The firm needs to establish distance. Clear its name. Or all of the partners in the firm are going down. Reputations and careers ruined. Including mine."

"So you've done nothing wrong, and the company's done nothing wrong."

"Correct. I mean, sort of." He squeezed his eyes shut. Real tight. Then opened them. "There are teams in offices across the United States focused only on retracing a particular client's steps. Bethanny and I are one of those teams. If we can map the money trail, prove the firm didn't take part in anything that was illegal, and if we cooperate fully with federal investigators, then I think we'll be in the clear. I think."

"Are you having an affair?"

"Absolutely not."

"But you're always with Bethanny." Holly's face felt hot.

"Holly, I'm trying to distance myself from what could be a really bad situation—legally, and for my career. I'll have zero chance of providing for you and Ella if my career tanks. I'm trying to keep my job—my reputation. Honestly? I don't have *time* for an affair. That's the last thing on my mind."

"Why did you take a shower at the gym?" Holly pressed. "Your clothes are perfectly clean. Did you work out?"

"The clothes I worked out in"—Jack pointed toward the front door, toward the hallway that led to the kitchen—"are stinking up my gym bag. I took a shower so I could relax and not run up our water bill."

"But I saw you. She was eating your french fries."

"No offense"—he sounded angry—"but if I was going to have an affair, I wouldn't take her to Wendy's."

"Where would you take her? Burger King? Chick-fil-A?" *Because Wendy's is our place for fast food, our number one single combo—no cheese, no onions—medium size with a Dr Pepper.*

"I wouldn't."

"You wouldn't take her to dinner? You'd just sleep with her and toss her out? You're that shallow, Jack? That cruel?"

He reached for her hands, pulled her into an embrace and then squeezed—hard. "I wouldn't take her to dinner," he said, "because I wouldn't have an affair. I'm not made like that, and you know it. Jeez, Holly. I took a vow."

"Were you really at the gym just now?"

"Will you stop? Of course I was at the gym." He released her. "If I don't relieve some of this stress, my heart will attack me." He lifted her chin. "Holly?" His eyes searched hers. Like he was about to kiss her but saw something and changed his mind. "You look pale. Almost. Gray."

"I think . . ." Holly's face, now her stomach. It felt . . . "I feel sick. Like. A lot sick."

"I'm sorry," he said. "Now I feel bad."

"Don't. It's not you. Well, okay, it is you. But it's something else too." Ugh. *My stomach.* "I think I ate something. Cookies maybe." Was Mary-Margaret telling the truth? Was there a nationwide peanut butter recall? "And I have to bake thirteen pies for this weekend's Cherry Pie Festival."

"Pies?" He took a huge step backward. Like that was the most shocking thing either of them had said on this front porch.

"What's so funny?" *That's offensive, Jack. Why'd you step back like that?* "Now I'm pissed."

"Pies?" he said. Just like that: "Pies?" Why was he grinning? He just said he was in dire circumstances. What? Now he was laughing?

"Stop laughing." She swatted his arm. "It's not funny. It's an auction for the school. I'm on the Pie Committee."

"*Pie* Committee?"

"Don't make fun of it, Jack. I'm serious. There's this Pie Mom, Emily. Seriously, Jack? Stop laughing. I might be secretary of the PTA now too." She bent over, placed her hands on her knees. "And I flunked clipboards, so I'm probably Room Mom for Ella's class." She started breathing heavily. *Who's having a panic attack now?* "Since we're both confessing, I hope there's room on the credit card because we'll be getting a bill for the bus I hit this morning."

"Big day," he acknowledged, teary eyed and with pinkened cheeks from laughing. He helped her stand upright.

"Yeah, well, what do you expect?" She shrugged. "I'm a school mom."

"School moms kick butt."

"Yup."

They fist-bumped.

Number twelve Petunia Lane? Jack and Holly? They fought. Holly figured every couple in every house argued from time to time. Amber-brown cedar mulch. Shred it up, spread it around. When mulch happened, they'd deal with it. But offshore shell companies? Money laundering and insurance fraud? Tax evasion? Life in the Village of Primm was almost perfect. But newcomers? Apparently, they'd reached their limit. The point of no return. Today was rough. Tomorrow? As yet unknown.

"Jack. I love this house. I love Primm. We could be happy here."

"I know we could. I'm sorry."

"Then we need to fight," she said.

"Kick some balls."

"You and me against the world. Like Angelina Jolie and Brad Pitt in the closing scene of *Mr. and Mrs. Smith*."

From the front porch, with their home behind her, Holly pretended she was Angelina, lifting a high-caliber weapon to her shoulder, cocking her head to take aim at a world that was closing in on them.

Jack scratched his head. "Um, I hate to disappoint you, but I think they die in the end."

"No they don't." Holly peered down the scope of her gun, setting her sights on a neighbor's mulch bed.

"I'm pretty sure they do," he said. "They're in a department store, surrounded. Outgunned and outnumbered."

"But that's the magic of movies." She lowered the high-caliber weapon from her shoulder. "Don't you remember? They stick together—move in unison. The gunfight's perfectly choreographed: a metaphor for sticking together, for building a kick-butt marriage. They take on the whole world. They win, Jack. They beat the odds."

Holly contemplated the sheer nakedness of her front porch. It had been naked too long.

"I want to get back into film," Holly told him, flat out. "I don't know how, but it's what I want. Something I have to do."

Jack stepped closer, collecting her into his arms.

She wrapped her arms around him, leaned her cheek against his chest. "I hear this voice-over inside my head, and I can't silence it. I see a script forming, as if it's being written on the page as I'm living my life.

It's like it's pushing itself out of me. Like it wants me to do something with it, but I don't know what."

"You have to live your art, Holly."

"But that sounds so crazy. What art? I don't have any art. I'm a mom. I hardly got through the first day of kindergarten."

"No offense, but you're always staring off into space."

"But where does that come from?"

"Seriously? You don't know?" He leaned his head back to get a look at her. "That's your art. Your truth, trying to get out."

"Stop. I know I do that Walter Mitty thing. But it's like—lately, it's gotten really intense. It's like, one minute, we move to Primm, and the next minute, I can't stop seeing everything around me as a set. I see characters. And story lines."

"Maybe Primm's your muse. Give it a voice." He spoke matter-of-factly. Like this was the simplest answer to the simplest question in the world.

"But . . ." The answer wasn't simple to Holly. "What am I supposed to do?"

"The only thing you can do. Take it seriously. Get started."

"But then I'll have to finish. And once it's finished, I'll have to show people." Holly felt woozy. Closed her eyes, pressed her head against Jack's chest. "Wilhelm Klaus is coming to Primm. What if I show him my work and he doesn't like it?"

"It's not about Wilhelm Klaus. It's about you."

"But he's huge—he's like . . . the Steven Spielberg of the German film industry. Or George Lucas."

"So?"

"So I want him to like it. But he's coming in, like, six weeks. I won't be ready."

"Then forget about Wilhelm Klaus. Shoot a film and upload it to YouTube. See what happens."

"I'm not doing that. I hate social media. And what if no one watches it? Or worse—what if they make fun of it or hit that stupid thumbs-down button."

"Then take another film class. Find equipment you can rent. Practice. Do different things. You'll figure it out."

It might have been the cookies, but Holly suspected it was the conversation that was making her dizzy. In an arc shot, usually used to convey a big event with far-reaching consequences, a moving camera circled the characters a full, dizzying 360 degrees. J. J. Abrams used an arc shot on Skellig Michael off the coast of southwest Ireland to film the final scene of *Star Wars: The Force Awakens*, in which Rey reached out to hand the hooded Luke Skywalker a lightsaber.

"Live your art." Jack kissed her forehead. "It's certainly living you."

Jack said *live your art*, and Holly's porch became Skellig Michael. Holly became Luke, and Jack became Rey, and Jack climbed the mountain to hand Holly her lightsaber—daring her to come out of hiding to do what must be done. *So cool.* A wicked grin spread across her face as she heard the orchestra play the closing score: "The Jedi Steps and Finale" by John Williams. A week ago, this porch belonged to Collette, but all she did with it was add a bench and some pillows. So dull. Now it was Holly's porch: Skellig Michael. Tomorrow? For all Holly knew, her porch might slip under the sea and become a stage for a courageous little mermaid risking it all to find her voice amid Technicolor fish and a prince. You never knew—Holly's porch could become *Jaws*. The *Titanic*. What Holly's porch became was up to Holly.

20

Tuesday night

Late again but not wanting to miss it, Holly stopped at a convenience store on her way to the Scrap & Swap Fund-Raiser to buy Gatorade and antigas, antidiarrheal remedies. Now, as she sat in the parking lot of Primm Academy—her third visit to the school in one day—she kept wishing she could wait a few minutes to let the medicines and electrolyte-replenishment start to work, but she was already late. The event had started more than an hour ago.

"Jack, I feel horrible," Holly breathed into the phone, leaning her head against the steering wheel of the rental car.

"Then come home."

"I can't. I have to at least make an appearance."

"That's crazy. Come home."

Holly took another swig of her Gatorade. "Don't say that. I'm not crazy." *Pa-leez don't tell me I'm crazy.* Holly paused a moment. *Should I tell him? Oh, what the heck. He dropped a bomb on me today. Offshore shell companies? That's crazy.* "I think I'm being targeted."

"Targeted?" He sounded concerned. This "research" he was brought to Primm to investigate wasn't dangerous, was it? Because Holly expected a different reaction than the one she got. "Targeted by whom?"

"Whom? You sound so formal. The president of the PTA. I think she's out to get me. I know she is."

"Hold on." Holly could hear him walking away from the TV. He must have been going to a quieter place in the house, away from Ella. "What do you mean she's targeting you?"

"She's targeting me. But don't worry. I'm starting to learn how she works. You have to know your enemy to defeat your enemy."

FADE IN:

EXT. DARK ALLEY BEHIND SCHOOL – NIGHT

Shot of MARY-MARGARET emerging from shadows, stepping into the dim light cast by an exterior lamp above an empty soccer field. HOLLY readies for battle.

MARY-MARGARET

(holding a plate of cookies, heat rising from them like a smoking gun)

Cookies?

HOLLY

(sinister laughing)

Who do you think I am? Cookie Monster?

"What happened?" Jack asked.

"She planted that bogus school supply list in Ella's backpack thinking it'll break me."

"School supply list."

"Yes," Holly told him. "It's an awful list. You saw it."

"O-kaaaaay."

"Why'd you say it like that? I'm sure I'm not the only mom that's ever felt a school supply list would do her in." Her forehead felt hot, but Holly refused to let it get the best of her. She could see the side doors to Primm Academy, the doors that led to the cafeteria, where she'd confront Mary-Margaret about the supply list and stage her last stand, telling Mary-Margaret she wouldn't be her secretary.

Leaning her chin against the top of the steering wheel, Holly gazed out at the school. It was breathtaking. Truly. "Primm Academy is so perfect. It's like la-la land. The grounds are manicured; the moms are manicured. They served tilapia in the cafeteria today. Do kids eat tilapia? Ella doesn't eat tilapia. She can't even pronounce it."

"Holly, come home. I'll run a bath. You can unwind."

"I'll stay for ten minutes," Holly told him. "I'm curious about scrapbooking, and I had such a horrible day; I kinda want to redeem myself."

Out her car window, a few Scrapbooking Moms were unloading their supplies. At least Holly wasn't the only one who was late. She wouldn't mind being a Scrapbooking Mom. She'd always wanted to make a scrapbook for Ella but didn't know where to start. "Jack? You said you were brought here to investigate three clients in Primm. Can you tell me who they are?"

"We're on phones, Holly."

"So? Who am I going to tell?"

"I could get in a lot of trouble."

"Jack. We're still using our Boulder City phone numbers. Our phones aren't tapped. You're paranoid."

There was a long pause. And then he said, "Fine. But you have to keep this under wraps." He drew in a long, slow breath and then exhaled. "Okay. There's Edward T. Olive. Antiquities dealer. He's British but has offices in Germany. Deals in maps, books, typewriters. That sort of thing. Owes large amounts of money to the wrong kind of people but always seems to squeak by because he has valuables from antiquity he can sell. Mostly black market stuff. Bethanny is handling his account. I do very little with him."

"Never heard of him."

"Didn't think you would. And then there's Merchant Meek Hopscotch the Third. Goes by 'Meek.' Has this huge dog. A Great Dane."

"I've seen him," Holly said. "On the way to the Topiary Park, the day Ella and I picked up Anna Wintour. Beautiful dog. Wow. I didn't know that was Meek. But yeah, he took the trolley to the Topiary Park. And I think he had a typewriter with him."

"That makes sense because Edward's in town. When Edward needs money, he sells to Meek. When Meek needs money . . ."

"He launders—"

"Hollystop! Jeez-us. We're on mobile phones."

"Well, don't yell at me. I'm sorry." Holly's stomach gurgled. She took another swig of Gatorade.

"The dog is interesting," Jack said. "The whole family is interesting. Meek's great-great-grandfather was one of the original planners of the Village of Primm—he designed the clock tower, the compass, and the town square—similar to what James Oglethorpe did for Savannah. Anyway, Meek is the sole heir to the Hopscotch fortune. He owns half the buildings in Primm, especially those that border the town square. First wife is dead; second wife hasn't been heard from in years; third wife's name is Bedelia. She's a piece of work. But I'm fairly certain he's either in love with the owner of the bookstore or thinks of her as his daughter because she's half his age, and he's always granting her special allowances. She buys all the books she wants and never pays rent, so I'm not sure what's happening there. We're having him followed."

"Hopscotch owns the Topiary Park."

"Right," Jack says. "Incorporated in the British Virgin Islands."

"I know."

"How do you know?"

"I noticed it on the receipt." Holly checked the color of her skin in the rearview mirror. It looked . . . grayish green. Maybe she should go home. "Penelope Pratt lives on Hopscotch Hill."

"Penelope's not involved in any of this. Although her grandmother was Meek's sister. So Meek is Penelope's great-uncle."

"And the PTA president who's targeting me—she's cousins with Penelope. So she must be related to Meek too. They all live on Hopscotch Hill."

"The homes have been passed down through the family," Jack said. "But none of that matters. Penelope's family is prominent in town—but in the clear as far as any of this is concerned. They're not involved. Bethanny and I share Meek's account because it's so large and complex."

"Okay . . . so who's the third person?"

"The third account is the account I'm responsible for," he said. "The reason the company brought us to Primm."

Someone started rapping their knuckles on Holly's car window. *Ratta-tap-tap!*

"Jeez!" She jumped. "Jack. She's at my *window*."

"Who is?"

"The Pink Witch. PTA president. She's right outside my window. Oh gosh, even her scrapbooking tote is pink." Holly cupped her hand over the phone so Mary-Margaret couldn't hear her. "She's the woman I was telling you about. She's the one who's targeting me."

More knocking.

"I better go. Tell me your person later?"

"Sure," he said.

"Wish me luck."

"Wish you luck?"

They hung up. Holly rolled her window down.

"Hip! Hip! Lavender! It's me, Mary-Margaret." Mary-Margaret appeared quite chipper. "Why are you sitting in this car? We need to get inside. There's glitter!" She clapped. "Wait a minute. Whose car is this?" Mary-Margaret looked around. "Is this a rental car? Is that what I smell? It is. I know the smell of something that's rented." She leaned in. "Woo! It smells like feet. Never mind. Don't worry, Lavender. Try not to think about the driver before you. About his feet—or his boogers. Because he probably picked 'em and flicked 'em while he was driving. And now you're sitting in it. It surrounds you." Mary-Margaret squirmed and twitched. "That's so gross. So gross. Epic gross! Lint-from-a-belly-button gross. Bits-of-plaque-that-flick-onto-your-mirror-when-you-floss gross. Steamy-poop-at-the-dog-park gross. Floor-of-a-truck-stop-bathroom gross." Mary-Margaret's eyes narrowed. "Floor. Of. A. Truck—"

"I heard you." Holly focused on her breathing. Inhaling, exhaling. "How are you, Mary-Margaret?"

"I'm fine, Lavender, how are you? Wait. Don't answer that. Do you have any hand sanitizer? 'Cause I'd squirt a bunch on the steering wheel if I were you. You're sitting in a booger car."

She exhausted Holly. She really did.

"It's not a booger car, Mary-Margaret. It's a Buick."

21

Inside the Scrap & Swap

The moment Holly walked into the cafeteria, she was given a clear fourteen-by-fourteen-inch shopping bag from Primm Paper, Primm's premiere paper-crafts studio located on Pip's Corner at the south end of the village square. Katie, who introduced herself as the owner of Primm Paper, smiled brightly as she handed Holly the shopping bag.

"I'm so excited to start scrapbooking," Holly told Katie. "I've never done it before and have been meaning to start."

"I'm hosting a scrapbooking basics class next week if you'd like to join us," Katie offered.

"I will." Holly smiled. *Bingo! My social calendar is filling up.*

Holly was directed to a series of long beautiful tables covered in yellow-and-white-striped tablecloths with chunky black fringe at the bottom. There was an ornately drawn black bumblebee logo from Primm Paper on every table, and at one of the tables, Holly bought her "scrapper's sticky sack," containing all the adhesives she'd need to complete the night's projects. *Scrapper's sticky sack. So cute. Say that ten times fast. Scrapper's sticky sack. Scrapper's sticky sack.*

Next, Holly paid thirty-six dollars for a ticket to craft her way down the length of the kindergarten table, completing twelve total scrapbook pages at an average cost of three dollars per page. The cost covered her supplies, with a little extra left over to raise funds for the PTA. Thirty-six dollars on scrapbooking, and Jack might lose his job.

There were thirteen cafeteria tables, each dedicated to one of the thirteen grade levels at Primm, kindergarten through twelfth grade. The mom next to Holly, Shanequa, who told Holly she had four children, could buy four tickets—one for each grade. Shanequa planned to scrapbook her way down four tables: kindergarten, fifth, seventh, and twelfth grade.

"So how does this work?" Holly muttered to Shanequa, hoping the antigas medicine she took earlier would last through the event.

"Stick with me," Shanequa said. "This is my third year. The trick is to stay focused and stay on task so you don't slow the line. If you think you can't finish, they'll suggest you complete the page at home so the line doesn't bottleneck at one of the projects. Don't take offense if that happens. Just know that the volunteers are here to hand out supplies and help with pacing so the lines move smoothly. It's nothing personal."

Starting at the "entry" end of the kindergarten table, Holly worked her way in single-file fashion through designated "scrapbook stations" that featured a sample scrapbook page so you could see what the page would look like when it was finished. A parent volunteer handed Holly a small bundle containing all the supplies she needed to complete that particular page. If Holly wanted to skip that station and move to the next one, she could take the bundle of supplies home with her because there was a set of clearly written instructions inside each bundle. Holly glanced at the first set of instructions. Clearly, some moms could skip the entire event and simply pay the thirty-six dollars and complete everything at home in their free time. The Primm Paper bag Katie had handed Holly at the door became Holly's new best friend. It contained all Holly's treasures, and she was careful to protect it.

Probably the coolest part of the entire evening was the care that was taken to design the scrapbook pages. Thirteen teams of Scrapbooking Moms—one team for each grade—had met with the teachers in that grade to generate a list of the major school events happening over the coming school year. Three of the twelve scrapbooking pages at each table were designed to have a nonspecific, "general" theme, but nine of the twelve scrapbooking pages were created to specifically highlight a particular grade-level event. So Holly would leave tonight with twelve scrapbook pages for Ella's kindergarten year. All Holly would have to do was add photos to the designated location on each page once Ella attended that event. Presto! Scrapbooking made efficient.

"I'm so excited," Holly kept telling Shanequa. "I can't believe I'm going to have Ella's entire kindergarten year scrapbooked in one night. This is amazing!"

And so worth the thirty-six dollars—even if money was tight. Holly didn't care that she was copying the sample scrapbook pages—this was way better than anything she could create on her own, especially since she'd never scrapbooked. Holly felt a tad bit better about Ella starting kindergarten. She felt like she was commemorating Ella's life, slowing things down a bit. And right now, for Holly, that was huge.

Every few steps, she took a peek into her Primm Paper bag to admire her work. But her stomach was getting progressively worse. Holly was thrilled to have met Shanequa (a new friend!) and thrilled Shanequa's daughter Talia was in Ella's class. Maybe Talia would invite Ella over for a playdate sometime. *Actually,* thought Holly, *maybe I should invite Shanequa over for coffee while the girls are in school. Now there's an idea! Yes, I'm going to do that. Just as soon as I finish unpacking, remove the bedsheet from the living room window, and hang some real curtains.*

About halfway through the line, after Holly had completed about six scrapbooking pages (with Shanequa's help), she started to feel nauseated. Really nauseated.

"Are you okay?" Shanequa asked.

"Um, actually, no. I think I should sit down." Any over-the-counter medicines Holly took earlier had completely worn off. She needed to go home, but first, she wanted to get through this line.

"Drink some water." Shanequa offered a bottle of water from her tote bag.

"No, no . . . I'm good." The Gatorade Holly drank in the parking lot sat on her stomach like a puddle of yuckity. She leaned onto the table for a second to rest, closing her eyes.

"Are you sure you're okay?" Shanequa asked. "Because you don't look so good."

"I ate a batch of bad cookies. I think it might be food poisoning." One of those *E* diseases Mary-Margaret mentioned in one of her phone messages.

I'm going to throw up. It's coming. I can feel it.

"Maybe I should go home." Holly surveyed the scene, wondering how she'd ever get out of the line she was trapped in. There were at least twenty moms in front of her and twenty moms behind her with long cafeteria tables flanking either side of them.

Shanequa signaled a nearby volunteer. "Excuse me. Would you mind collecting the next six scrapbooking bundles for this mom? She's not feeling well and needs to go home right away."

"Thanks, Shanequa." Holly was a bit embarrassed but had to kneel down for just a bit because the pain in her stomach was so intense. She lowered herself to a squatting position between the tables.

The moms in front of her noticed what was happening, so one of them started snapping her fingers above her head. "Excuse me? Excuse me." She signaled the moms in front of her. "Everyone needs to move. Move. Lean over the tables so this mom can get through."

"Can you walk?" Shanequa asked.

"I think so," Holly mustered, trying to uncramp her body. *Freaking Mary-Margaret. I'm so pissed.*

And then she heard it: "Yoo-hoo! Oh, noooooo! What is it, Lavender? What's wrong?" It was Mary-Margaret, the Pink Witch. She was seven people ahead of Holly in the kindergarten line, and she'd just taken notice that it was Holly who needed to leave in a hurry.

"Lavender!" Mary-Margaret cried out, rushing down the line toward Holly like Holly was her pet bunny rabbit and just got hit by a car. "What is it? Are you hurt?"

Holly took hold of Shanequa's arm. "Don't let that woman near me."

"What? Why?" Shanequa leaned in. "Has Mary-Margaret been messing with you?"

"They were her cookies," said Holly, hoping to get her story out before the Pink Witch made her way through the line.

"Mary-Margaret gave you a batch of bad cookies?" Shanequa sounded amused. Concerned, but amused.

Holly nodded, bending forward over the scrapbooking table as Mary-Margaret arrived beside them.

The volunteer arrived, too, with Holly's six scrapbooking bundles. Holly handed the volunteer her Primm Paper bag, and she tucked them carefully inside, beside Holly's completed pages. She said she hoped Holly felt better real soon. Told Holly she could finish them at home and even call her if Holly had questions. Now Holly just needed to get out of this line—fast.

"Come with me, Lavender." Mary-Margaret took hold of Holly's arm. "I've got this, Shanequa. Thank you." Mary-Margaret dragged Holly past the moms who were bent forward across the table, providing a pathway for Holly to exit.

"Stop. Let. Go of me!" Holly shouted—sort of burping—as a little bit of bile rolled up her throat and into her mouth. They were almost at the end of the line, and Holly absolutely could not go any farther. *Please, God. Please don't let me throw up. Not here, not now.* Instead, Holly—um. Passed gas. Essentially, this happened:

*

"Good glory, what was that?" Mary-Margaret gasped. "Was that you?" Her eyes grew wide. "Did you just—tootie?"

"It's the cookies, Mary-Margaret," Holly grumbled. "You gave me bad cookies."

"How many cookies did you eat?" Mary-Margaret asked.

"A lot. I was hungry." *Nom-nom-nom.*

"Oh, no, Lavender, this is terrible." Mary-Margaret's eyes grew wide. "Those were detox cookies. I put solidified coconut oil and chia seeds in them. I make them for my love, My Love, when he's constipated."

"You fed me digestive cookies?" Holly panted, clutching her stomach. "Why?"

"Because they're healthy. Penelope told me you moved into Collette's home on Petunia. I thought you were a Foodie Mom. I thought you'd appreciate sturdy ingredients."

"No," Holly yelped. "I'm not a Foodie Mom. I hate kale." It felt like a confession, a release of a weight she'd been carrying. Holly took a peek around, wondering how many Petunia Moms heard her say *that.*

Mary-Margaret elaborated. "I baked them with wheat bran, oat bran, ground flax seeds. Chia seeds. That sort of thing. Whatever I could find. I soaked the batter in castor oil. I thought the flavor of the peanut butter and all those peanut chunks would help disguise the taste of the ingredients. I put all kinds of stuff in them. Oh, Lavender, come to think of it, you did eat a bunch of them. You're in trouble. You're in big, big trouble." She checked her watch. "Yup! About six hours since your last cookie. Right on schedule." The look in her eyes mirrored the urgency in her voice. "Get to the bathroom." Mary-Margaret stepped aside, signaling for Holly to pass. "Go! Toss those cookies. Blow chunks. Move it. Move it!" To the women around them, "Hurl girl's having a yak attack. Everyone, take cover." But it was crowded, the line bottlenecked.

Holly stumbled a few steps, her neck sweating, her palms clammy. Her stomach sent her crumpling over with shooting pain. "I think I'm really sick," Holly said to whoever might hear her and could help. The anger she felt was almost unbearable. Holly stabbed her finger in Mary-Margaret's direction, grumbling at her through gritted teeth. "You did this. You poisoned me. You freaking poisoned me!"

"Let's get you out of this line, Liverwurst," Mary-Margaret said. "Sauerkraut. Polish Sausage." She added, "Move it, Creamed Corn Squirts."

"Stop it!" Holly snapped. "Quit with the grocery insults."

Holly snatched Mary-Margaret by the arm and pulled Mary-Margaret's face close. "You fed me poisoned cookies. Didn't you? Didn't you!"

Mary-Margaret squirmed, obviously aware of the crowd of onlookers. "Poisoned you? But that wasn't my intention at all," she whined. "I was trying to impress you. It's not *my* fault your body is filled with toxins. A body with that many toxins is hard to detox. Turns detox cookies into little intestinal tornados."

And then—

*

"Lavender! Another tootie? Stop that," Mary-Margaret squealed. "This is a scrapbooking event. Do something. Squeeze your butt cheeks together. Do Kegel exercises."

Holly tried squeezing but couldn't. Her entire digestive system was dying a slow, rancid death, and it was all Mary-Margaret's fault. She did this to Holly. She did it.

Holly sort of coughed.

(=)

Burped, choked. Something.

"Lavender." Mary-Margaret must have seen it in Holly's eyes. "Was that a cough—or an itty-bitty roar with a burp in it?"

"A roar with a burp in it," Holly sneered. "Because I'm dying. But first, I'm going to kill you."

"Stop saying that, Lavender! This isn't *Hunger Games: Mom Edition,*" Mary-Margaret whined, placing both hands on her hips. "Winter isn't coming. This is scrapbooking. Not *Game of Thrones*."

"Oh, yes it is!" Holly coughed, stumbling forward. Moms in front of them gasped, moved quickly to part ways to let Holly through. Holly staggered toward the end of the line. "Your cookies suck, Mary-Margaret."

Mary-Margaret was taken aback. "No. Don't say that." Both hands covering her mouth.

So Holly said it louder. "Your cookies suck."

"Stop that!" Mary-Margaret shook her head no. No doubt she was horrified that others were listening. "You're a Petunia Mom. I thought you'd *appreciate* curdled nondairy vegan milk. Do you know how hard it is to find Medjool dates?"

"You suck at baking!" It felt cathartic. So Holly yelled louder. This time, with her hands cupped around her mouth, so her voice was really amplified. "*Mary-Margaret St. James Sucks at Baking.* Do you hear me, Primm?" Holly pointed. "She sucks at baking."

Mary-Margaret, covering her ears: "*Blah-blah-blah-blah-blah!*" But it was no use. Everyone heard Holly, and Mary-Margaret knew it. Everyone talked in hushed voices, and no one—not a soul—made eye contact with Mary-Margaret. Except Holly.

"You. Suck. At. *Baking*!" Holly roared—

*

With a burp. She climbed her way past the moms, clomping sideways like a cavewoman with a lame and injured leg, still clutching her bag of scrapbooking goodies, toward the side door, toward her salvation. *I need to get outside,* she told herself, panting. *I can't puke on anyone. I can't. I'm okay.* She hadn't thrown up. *I'm okay. I'm okay. I'm okay.* She hadn't thrown up. Yet.

Then *whoa!* Criminy. She crouched down, grabbing her sides. The acid. Her stomach. Someone reached down to help her to her feet. *Think fast. Only ten more feet and I'm outside and away from this crowd. Move it, people. Move away. Oh, please. Oh, please don't let me throw up on anyone. This sucks. This sucks so much.*

A split second later, surrounded by moms and their precious scrapbooking pages, Holly had no choice. She snatched open her Primm Paper shopping bag and—

:-O ====

Puked all over everything.

"No!" she cried to the heavens, hurling chunks of peanuts and castor oil sludge into her scrapbooking bag. "No!"

:-O ====

It burned. Set her throat aflame. Holly heaved chia seeds.

:-O ====

Oat bran.

Dandelion whacky-jikky root. Stuff.

:-O ====

Medjool. Dates. Or whatever Mary-Margaret had called them. Butter-crapped peanut-butter-what-the-fluck. Holly's scrapbook pages were ruined. Her chance to slow time and capture the precious moments in Ella's life, ruined. Scrapbooking, the one thing that made Holly feel better about Ella starting kindergarten, ruined. All ruined! Holly was winded, wheezing, breathless. Exhausted. Someone grabbed her by the arm and ran with her toward the door.

"Thank you," Holly managed, slamming her hip against the metal bar, releasing the door. She slumped into the parking lot, into the night air, cow hocked: legs dragging, bent inward. Head hung heavy like a lead weight. Grateful, she gasped for breath. "I got this," she told the mom who had followed her out to the parking lot. "I'm okay." She panted, hand raised to keep her distance. "I'm okay."

But then *bluuurp*—Holly opened her scrapbooking bag—and hurled a crock of oily stomach jam.

:-O ====

Turtle.

Verrr-rock!

Again.

:-O ====

Vrock!

"This is all *her* fault," Holly sputtered, stumbling toward the Buick, swiping tears from her eyes. "Her fault."

Any pride Holly had felt scrapbooking Ella's kindergarten year turned to cat piddle. Any swagger in her step? Turned to swigger.

Stabbing her key into the door lock, up from the depths of Holly's anger and frustration, she cemented a solemn vow. A vow that took root deep within her heart. A vow—to finish that woman once and for all. *I'm gonna get that Betty Crocker mother frocker. If it's the last thing I do.*

:-O ====

All over the side of the Buick.

Holly didn't know exactly what Mary-Margaret put in those cookies, but every peanut, every egg replacement, every single solitary flax and chia seed Mary-Margaret mixed into that castor oil shitake batter-splat left Holly's body in reverse order. What went in—came back out. Like a recipe read backward.

seikooc rettub tunaep delkcep s'teragraM-yraM
.F seerged 053 ot nevo taeherP
.rehtegot tihs fo hcnub a xiM
.setunim 01–8 rof ekaB
,kcis steg enoemos fI
.lortnoC esaesiD rof retneC SU eht emalb
.tluaf s'teragraM-yraM ton s'ti esuaceB
.tluaf s'teragraM-yraM reven s'tI .on ,hO

22

Wednesday, second day of kindergarten

Holly had been up all night, puking peckled peanut butter cookies into the toilet. The hurling was so loud it woke Ella up, twice. On a school night. Struggle did what Struggle did: kept watch, whining most of the time.

FADE IN:

INT. MASTER BEDROOM – MORNING

Wednesday. Second day of kindergarten. JACK and HOLLY still in bed.

HOLLY

(Tries to sit up. Head aches.)

I need to wake Ella up.

JACK

Holly, sleep. I got this.

But clearly, Jack didn't "got this." Because twenty minutes later, from Holly's warm bed and soft pillow, she heard Bus 13 toot its horn as it approached House 12.

HOLLY
(Springing to her feet.)

Jack! Ella! The bus! THE BUS!

Her head hurt, her stomach was still sour, but she rushed down the stairs nonetheless, intercepting Jack in the front foyer.

"Holly. Stop the bus!" He wrung his hands together, doing that "Jack" thing he did while Struggle did that "Struggle" thing Struggle did: barked. "Ella's not wearing any shoes," Jack blurted. "Stop the bus, Holly. Stop the bus!"

With Struggle by her side, Holly barreled out the front door and onto her porch, ready to grab the bus by its ball bearings. In seconds flat, woman and dog leaped from the top step to the bottom step. Holly, on the grass, running barefoot like a crazed ape across her lawn—arms flailing above her head, dog by her side. "Bus Thirteen! Wait!" she yelled. "Wait!" No bra. Hair not brushed. "Stop. Stop!"

But it was too late. The driver didn't hear her and instead tooted his horn, *toot toot—so long, sucka!*—and headed off up the hill, taking with him the dent Holly had left on his back bumper. Holly stopped chasing the bus, but Struggle kept running.

"Struggle!" Holly yelled. "Get back here!"

The bus driver saw her. Holly knew he saw her.

"Struuuuuu-ggle!" Stupid dog was still chasing the bus. They were halfway up the hill already. "Come, Struggle. Sit! Stop running. Stop! Struggle." *Dang it.*

Holly turned to look down her street. A few moms were stopped on their sidewalks, watching all the braless, ape-haired commotion unraveling at 12 Petunia Lane. None of them had welcomed Holly to the neighborhood yet. Why? Because, as a mom, she was clearly incompetent? Couldn't even get her own kid on a bus?

"Struggle!" *Freaking stop running already, you stupid dog.*

Struggle eventually stopped midway up the hill. Probably got tired and pooped out—Holly was sure it wasn't because Struggle was a good listener. That dog needed to repeat obedience school. Oh, who was Holly kidding? Struggle had flunked the first day of obedience school because she kept biting her leash, thinking the whole time they were in class they were just there to play tug-of-war—not to learn how to *sit* and *stay* and freaking *listen*. All the other dogs paid attention. All the other dogs got treats. The German shepherds, the border collies—Struggle didn't stand a chance. If she'd just given up the struggle, stopped biting down all the time, stopped tugging at every little thing that floated past her nose. But Holly couldn't say they weren't warned. The breeder had Struggle named before they picked her up.

Struggle trotted toward Holly with what looked like a smile on her face. Panting, tongue slopping out the left side of her mouth.

"Git inside, Struggle," Holly spat from behind gritted teeth.

Holly lumbered up her porch steps, hearing a creak in the door she'd never heard before—only to find Ella crying in the front foyer, clutching Pinkie Pie because her parents' desperate attempt to connect her with public transportation had resulted in yelling and irrational behaviors that scared her.

"What happened?" Jack was aghast. "Why didn't you stop it?"

"I tried to, but what was I supposed to do, Jack? Throw my body in front of a moving bus?" *I'm sure the other moms would love to see* that.

Ella said, "Mommy missed the bus again?"

"No, Ella, Mommy didn't miss the bus." Holly pointed at the guilty shoe in Jack's hand. "Daddy missed the bus."

Ella slipped her thumb into her mouth. "I's no wanna goes to school."

"Ella! We can't understand you," Holly snapped, head pounding from a night vomiting detox cookies. "And take that *damn* thumb out of your mouth!"

Ella gasped—eyes wide.

"Really, Holly?" Jack scowled.

"Really," Holly mocked the way he said it. *Jerk.* If she was being truthful, she felt horrible for cursing in front of Ella, but she was so frustrated about that da—*dang* bus it slipped out. *So I cursed—big deal. It's a word. Not a mortal sin.* "I'm sorry I said that, Ella. I am. I made a mistake. I'm human. But you've got to stop sucking. You're in kindergarten now."

"I don't want to go to kindergarten," Ella said, looking straight at Holly.

"Well, too bad," Holly said, rubbing her temples with the tips of her fingers. "We're in school now. And the sooner we all figure out how to fit in and do this thing—the better."

"Fit in?" Jack scratched his head on this one. "Really, Holly? Who's this about?"

Holly snatched Ella's green dinosaur from the banister. Tucked him into her backpack. "We'll do your project tonight. I'll find the thesaurus. If not, I'll buy one from Papyrus, Parchment & Paper."

"I'll drive her," Jack said, kneeling down to help Ella with her other shoe.

"That's probably a good idea," Holly said, holding her head. "But you might want to change your clothes."

"I'm in my pajamas." Jack glanced at the undershirt and blue-and-white-striped drawstring pajama pants he'd slept in. "Why in the *world* would I drive Ella to school in my pajamas?"

23

Later that morning

[FIRST PHONE MESSAGE]

(Beeeeeep.) Hi, Lavender! It's me! Mary-Margaret St. James. Hip! Hip! Although, hmm. I suppose after tossing your cookies last night at the Scrap and Swap you're not feeling the "hooray" in your heart, now, are you? Get it? Tossing your cookies? Ha! No. I guess you were tossing *my* cookies. Oh, well, no feelings hurt. I can always bake more. Silly peanut butter recall. Call the White House! Say, you are coming to today's—[CLICK.]

[SECOND PHONE MESSAGE]

(Beeeeeep.) Golly. What's wrong with your voice mail? [CLICK.]

[THIRD PHONE MESSAGE]

(Beeeeeep.) Now, remember! You are coming to today's PTA meeting—right? The school librarian is using our meeting space to prep for the book fair, so we're moving the meeting to the boardroom at the Topiary Park. My husband is on the board of directors. Finance chair. He's doing everything he can to save Plume. Last year, she almost died of fungal leaf spot. Fungal leaf spot! Now they're worried about chilli thrips. Ha! Chilli thrips. They're bugs, by the way. Can you believe it?

Sounds like a teenager ordering chicken strips after an orthodontist appointment. Chilli thrips with flesh flies, peez. Get it? Chilli thrips?! I'm such a silly girl . . . ha! One more thing: peekaboo! [CLICK.]

[FOURTH PHONE MESSAGE]

(Beeeeeep.) Don't forget the cupcakes! [CLICK.]

~

EMAIL—Time Sent: 9:18 a.m.

TO: Psychic Betty, Psychic Hotline Network
FROM: Holly Banks
SUBJECT: Negative Energy

I'm worried I'm attracting the wrong kind of people. Specifically, PTA narcissists and mothers with addictive behaviors (my mom, actually). Or is it just me? Am I being negatively affected by their energy? I feel like I'M crazy because THEY'RE crazy.

Please look into your crystal ball and answer me this:

1. Will Mary-Margaret ever leave me the frick alone? She dang near killed me yesterday.

2. Will my mom ever settle down and stop gambling? She makes me feel I have no ground beneath my feet. I should be more confident at my age, shouldn't I?

3. Is my husband having an affair or is he telling me the truth and he's "just" involved in a little something that might not be entirely legal?

P.S. This is Holly Banks. A lot has happened since our last email. I've missed you, Psychic Betty. How've you been?

~

EMAIL—Time Received: 9:45 a.m.

TO: Holly Banks
FROM: Psychic Betty, Psychic Hotline Network
SUBJECT: I've missed you, too, Holly Banks.

Scrying, the art of looking into a crystal ball and using its piezoelectric properties, has been in use for thousands of years, but sadly, despite smoking a lot of pot in my youth (and okay, I smoked a little a few hours ago), I lack scrying powers. So here's my hunch, based on years of honing my psychic ability. Just to be sure, I pulled some tarot cards for further enlightenment.

1. AVOIDING MARY-MARGARET: Some relationships are toxic, turn your stomach, and feel like poison to your soul, eating away at your self-esteem and sense of well-being. Have you thought about tuning her out? Maybe raising your frequency?

The Law of Vibration is this: Nothing is at rest. The universe and everything in it, including the creatures of the sea (shrimp scampi, oysters Rockefeller, crab cakes, fried calamari) are in constant motion. Every molecule in your body is held in place because of the programmed resonant frequency applied to it. Create a loving energy for yourself and your world, and you'll raise your personal vibration frequency, reach a higher realm, and ward off negative energies. Like creating an invisible shield or bubble around your body, when you raise your frequency through self-love, in a resolute spirit of self-acceptance and calm, you can block any negative energies she's throwing your way, perhaps even reflect them back onto her. Now that'll twist her panties.

2. WILL YOUR MOM STOP GAMBLING: I wouldn't bet on it. I suspect she's built a good poker face over time and is at peace with the notion that in life, ya win some, ya lose some. Want to loosen its control over you? Try changing or manipulating the colors in your aura and/or chakras. Color is associated with specific vibrational frequencies. When there is a predominance of two colors in one environment or relationship, it affects the balance of the vibrational frequencies, which tends to influence not just the activities in that environment or relationship, but the attitudes of those around it. Seek harmonious colors. Avoid mustard tones. Melancholy, shame, feelings of inferiority and regret serve no one.

3. YOUR HUSBAND? I suspect that with most of my clients, if you're asking the question, the answer is

typically, "Yes, he's having an affair." Psychic powers heighten during times of infidelity when vibrations cross. However, with you, Holly Banks, I sense you are a special case. I say trust him. You're probably simply "out of alignment" right now due to Mercury's retrograde and recent transits in your family life—literally, figuratively, and psychically. Ever smudge your marital bed with white sage? That might help. But don't involve yourself with dealings done while hiding or you're in for a lot of shadow work to ward off psychic attacks from what you find in the dark. Ever do shadow work? I hope you like the smell of frankincense.

Holly, I sense your angst comes from trying to see more clearly while sailing through fog in uncharted waters without a compass. Seek mirrors. Beacons of light. Look at life through a new lens and pay close attention to those already ashore—especially those frantically waving their arms above their head, hollering, "Not there, you idiot!" They may sound brash, but they're trying to help you. You keep bumping into the same rocks over and over again. Once you've seen what you need to see—once you row your boat ashore (Hal-le-luuuu-jah!)—pay attention to what you hear. I suspect you have voices in your head that need purging. Try tuning them out. Silencing them. Better yet, channel them into something. Singing, painting. Something creative. Are you an artist? I sense you're a creative type.

Wisdom from the Tarot:

Mary-Margaret = 8 of Cups (move on) paired with Temperance (find balance)

Your mom = 6 of Pentacles Reversed (debt) paired with Wheel of Fortune (luck)

Your husband = 7 of Cups (either fantasy and illusion or choices) paired with 10 of Cups (happy family)

—Psychic Betty

P.S. Are you a big fish in a small pond? Find you're always swimming with sharks? Wish you had other fish to fry? Great news! There are plenty of fish in the sea. So don't be a fish out of water. Enter Dizzy's Seafood fishing for compliments—leave with a fish-eating grin!

P.P.S. Atlantic cod fillet sandwich battered in craft beer and served with crispy lettuce, locally grown tomatoes, "special recipe" tartar sauce, and a side of pub pickles with gourmet coleslaw. (Coleslaw has touches of black peppercorn, dried cherries, and granny smith apples. Delish!) $8.95

Don't be a clod! Eat Beer Batter Cod!

24

A few hours before lunch

"I think you need a new router," Caleb told Holly while sliding a stack of Disney DVDs away from his work space as Struggle closed in on him, trying to lick his neck, hoping for another treat. "This shouldn't take long."

"Do whatever it takes. I just need *something* to work in my life." Holly sighed, wishing she could find a good spot to place a metal rooster she'd just pulled from a moving box. It was midmorning on Wednesday, the second day of school, and she missed Ella something awful. "Do you think the paint color in here has mustard tones in it?"

Caleb squinted, then shrugged. "Looks fine to me. But maybe you're red-green color blind."

"Red-green color blind?" Seriously?

"It's possible."

"Oh, no." Holly tilted her head to study the paint. *I do see mustard. Spit cakes! Maybe I am color blind.* Holly wandered toward the living room toting the metal rooster beneath her arm. "Yesterday was a disaster," she told Caleb, returning empty handed from the living room. "I hit Ella's school bus with my car."

"Whoa." Caleb's eyes widened. "Anyone hurt?"

"My ego." Holly slurped her coffee. "I ate some cookies. But the cookies were tainted." She stared intently at him. "Actually, I was poisoned."

"Ha!" He must have thought it was a joke. Must have thought Holly was telling a story. "Are you serious?"

"Dead serious. The president of the PTA is trying to kill me."

Okay, so maybe she embellished. Holly didn't think Mary-Margaret was really trying to kill her. Did she?

Perking up a bit, Caleb gave her his full attention. "So let me get this straight. You're saying there's a killer mom in the Village of Primm?"

"Yup." She wasn't sure she wanted to go *that* far. Maybe not a killer . . .

"What's her motive?"

Holly smiled. "Your film school is showing." She paced the floor, twisting a strand of hair around her fingers. "I don't know what her motive is. Maybe she's a bully? Maybe because I'm a newcomer . . . I'm an easy target?"

"Do you threaten her?"

"I doubt it."

He lifted an eyebrow. "Maybe you do."

"I do push back sometimes. Been known to wear yellow." Holly plopped down on the sofa, toppling a pile of folded laundry. Struggle was still bothering Caleb for a treat. "Struggle, sit." Holly snapped her fingers. *Please obey me.* "Come 'ere, Struggle." Struggle didn't move. "Struggle!" Struggle stared blankly at Holly like she had no earthly idea what Holly wanted her to do.

"You're probably disrupting the status quo," Caleb offered.

"Her name's Mary-Margaret St. James. She *is* the status quo," Holly grumbled. "And I assume she owns a television. You know her?"

"Mary-Margaret? Oh, sure. Everyone knows her. She's related to Meek. He owns the cable company. They've lived on Hopscotch for what? Four, maybe five generations?"

"Well, I heard about Mary-Margaret before I even moved to the Village of Primm. Penelope Pratt told me about her."

"They're cousins."

"I know. And there's a chance I moved to Primm because of Mary-Margaret. I don't know. Maybe it was the school. Definitely the school." Holly gathered the collapsed pile of laundry, contemplating the idea she may have made a major housing purchase based solely on a rumor about a woman who did amazing things at a local school. "Do you know I almost bought a house in Southern Lakes?"

"Here we go." He rolled his eyes.

"What."

"All of the moms in the Village of Primm talk about Southern Lakes."

"They do? Why?" Holly watched him fuss with her TV.

"Grass is always greener on the other side of the fence."

"Maybe, but Southern Lakes has crabgrass," Holly pointed out.

"How would you know?"

"Someone told me."

"Well, then. Must be fact." He tossed a wrench-looking-tool-thingy into his tool bag. "If you don't mind my asking, if Primm is so great, why's everyone looking over the fence?"

Holly didn't have an answer. She wondered if anyone had an answer for that.

Caleb got back to work while Holly cleared a few dishes from an end table to set them in the kitchen sink. So far, Ella hadn't spilled her juice glass once. Holly considered telling Caleb this, but she didn't want him to know his sippy cup inquisition had gotten under her skin a few days ago. Since he was busy working, Holly sat down at the kitchen table to text Jack a burning question.

HOLLY: Hey. Sorry to text you during work. Gotta second?

JACK: I'm with Bethanny.

(Pause.)

JACK: I'm kidding! What's up?

HOLLY: Who's the third person? The client you're investigating. You never told me.

JACK: You want me to text that?

HOLLY: Sure. Why not?

(Pause.)

HOLLY: Hello? You still there?

(Pause.)

HOLLY: Seriously, Jack? I'm sure your phone's not tapped.

JACK: Okay, but you have to promise me you'll delete this.

HOLLY: Of course.

JACK: Michael.

HOLLY: Last name?

JACK: St. James.

My Love? *My Love?* Holly didn't know if she was surprised it was My Love, thrilled it was My Love, or sad it was My Love. Maybe she was all three. But wow. *If My Love did something that causes him to go to jail—I mean, pris—I mean, if Michael St. James has to sit in a time-out chair, it will hit Mary-Margaret like a freight train.* The reign of the Pink Witch in Primm would surely come to an end. Wouldn't it? And if it was Holly's husband responsible for sending Mary-Margaret's husband to the slammer . . . oh, good gravy. This could get ugly.

Holly put her phone down when Caleb walked into the kitchen. He scribbled something on the top of his aluminum Primm Cable storage clipboard.

"You know, if you wean your daughter off *My Little Pony*, you can cancel the premium channel bundle and save a ton of money. You do know about the Hub Network, don't you? Cronies from the Chinese government hacked into it in a plot to gain territory in the South China Sea. If you support the Hub Network, you're supporting the militarization of China. The money you're spending is lining the pockets of weapons dealers. From Switzerland."

"*My Little Pony*? The militarization of China? Wait a minute." Holly held a hand up. "Hold up. Time-out. First you go after my daughter's sippy cup. You have Jack thinking she's going to sprout a speech delay overnight. Now you're telling me the Hub Network has been infiltrated by Chinese hackers? And subscribers are lining the pockets of Swiss arms dealers?" Holly narrowed her eyes at him. "How much of what you say is total bullspit?"

He grinned.

"I don't believe it." Holly grabbed her head, then covered her face. "This is insane. You're a real piece of work; you know that? Do you have any idea how much anxiety you've caused me? Sippy cups causing speech delays?"

"That part is true," he pointed out. "My sister is a speech therapist."

"Do you do this to all the moms?"

His smile spread to such a point it gave him away. "Actually, yeah, I do." He laughed. "Every day. All the time. To everyone. All across town."

Holly leaned way back in her chair, mind blown. "And that Area 51 business—messing up my cable connection. That was a load of crock too. Wasn't it?"

Holly was just making sure, because Psychic Betty had gotten her thinking all sorts of things lately. Mercury retrograde, vibrations, beer-battered cod.

"You're good. No interference from Area 51. Primm's too far away." More chuckling from Caleb. "Sorry."

"You know you're torturing women who are trying really hard to get through the day."

"I know." His laugh was a harmless, jovial sort of laugh, not a mean-spirited laugh. "But I can't help it. And Holly," he sputtered, "you're not red-green color blind. Your paint color is fine." Now he was really laughing. "I use that one all the time. You should see the look on their faces when I suggest that one! They start rethinking the paint on their walls. It's epic! You gotta see it."

"You're a bad person."

"I know." He laughed. "But I can't help it. I'm so bored with this job. I once told a mom excessive temper tantrums were a sign of early-onset Tourette's syndrome."

Seriously? He couldn't stop laughing.

"Ahhhhhh-ha-ha-ha-ha! Ahhhhhh-ha-ha-ha-ha!"

Holly banged her head on the kitchen table a few times. "Oh, Caleb. Caleb! You're going to hell. You do know that, don't you?"

"Yes," he gasped, holding his sides. "And that's okay. At least I'll go down laughing." He caught his breath. "Oh, but it's so worth it." He settled down, sighed, and then asked with a devilish grin, "So, you wanna see that pinhole spy camera I was telling you about?"

25

Late morning, almost lunch

There's an old saying: Just because you can, doesn't mean you should.

Holly could think of multiple reasons why she shouldn't let Caleb hide a pinhole camera and mic in the neckline of her lightweight white sweater set, but none of those reasons held a candle to the myriad reasons Holly *wanted* to hide a pinhole camera and mic in the neckline of her lightweight white sweater set.

If she was being completely honest, she wanted to experience life as a documentary filmmaker—if only for an afternoon. She wanted to feel she had a snowball's chance of creating *something* for the Wilhelm Klaus Three-Minute Film Festival in October. Because why not. Why not her? And to be honest, if Jack was in this much trouble, Holly needed that prize money. Desperate times called for desperate measures.

"I can't believe I'm doing this," Holly told Caleb. He should have left two hours ago, but she convinced him to stay awhile so she could fire questions at him from a long list. *Do you ever screen before a live audience? How do you meet other filmmakers? Are there any film clubs in Primm I could join?* And now, as he was pinning a tiny camera and mic to her clothes, "Are you sure this will work?"

"Sure I'm sure," he said. "But are you ready for this? This is a bold act."

"I'm ready." *Ready to take Mary-Margaret down.*

When Holly thought of all those conversations she'd had where Mary-Margaret completely ignored her, pretended she wasn't even there, and then—*poof!*—talked right over her, it thrilled Holly to know she'd be amplifying her voice through film. Technology put to use to benefit the underdog for a change.

Caleb installed a wireless, one-inch mini–pinhole spy camera powered by a nine-volt battery inside Holly's sweater. It was so tiny you could hide it just about anywhere. Holly wore leather sandals, soft linen slacks, and a casual white, short-sleeved twinset. One part of the twinset was a sleeveless sweater shell; the other looked like a matching lightweight short-sleeved sweater, buttoned at the neckline by the top button. Big improvement from her piggy days. She looked like a modern June Cleaver and should blend right in at Primm Academy. The tiny mic pinned beneath the neckline and the camera stitched behind the second buttonhole meant no special lighting was required, no boom mic, no nothing. The setup was brilliant.

"There," Caleb said. "Finished. Just act normal."

"I can't act normal. I'm a walking, talking camera." Holly exhaled, thinking of all the things that could go wrong.

"It'll be great. When you get worried, remind yourself why you're doing it."

"Right." Holly gave him a thumbs-up. And then, "Why did the rooster cross the road?"

"I give up. Why?"

"To prove he wasn't a chicken."

"Now remember." He pointed. "When you're capturing the footage, brainstorm. What are you trying to say with this film? Is it a revenge story? Comedy adventure? Underdog disrupts the status quo?"

"I don't know." She really didn't. "Suburban satire?"

"That's okay. It'll come to you. If anything, it'll feel good working with a camera again."

"Caleb." Holly touched his arm. "Is it mean what I'm doing? Filming Mary-Margaret without her knowing it?"

"You're conducting research. Journalists do undercover reporting all the time. Film her only in public settings and then don't worry about it. Holly"—he deepened his voice to make his point—"we're living in a digital age. People record other people with their phones—all the time. I think you're good."

"I don't know. But okay." Holly supposed Mary-Margaret had acted undercover with those cookie ingredients. She manipulated others through speech. And she'd married My Love. Deception surrounded her. "With the Wilhelm Klaus in six weeks," Holly added, "and that ten-thousand-dollar grand prize . . ."

"Stop worrying about it." Caleb gave the side of Holly's arm a friendly slap. "You're a filmmaker. Tell the world your story."

Am I a filmmaker? Me? Holly Banks? The thought of it gave Holly the chills.

"Okay, then." She gave him another two thumbs up. "Let's do this thing."

26

After lunch

About thirty minutes after Caleb left her house, Holly wolfed down a ham and swiss and hopped in the Buick for a cruise through the Village of Primm, feeling bold, feeling invincible, feeling a bit—bad to the bone—like the motley crew of criminals about to pull a triple-casino heist in Soderbergh's film *Ocean's Eleven*. Most heist movies had a scene that depicted feelings of empowerment before the characters were put into peril, and that was exactly how Holly felt right now. She was thrilled the camera was catching her hands on the Buick's steering wheel as she drove. Because the driver's seat sat so low, the camera captured an angle of her hands, steering wheel, and view beyond the windshield that Holly knew would add artistic flair to her film—her film about . . . she wasn't sure what.

She did know she wanted badass music in her opening scene, and she could hear it playing in her head as she walked into Primm's Coffee Joe on her way to the PTA meeting at the Topiary Park. But when she pushed open the door to the coffee shop, a little bell on the handle rang, drawing everyone's attention to Holly and, presumably, to her white lightweight twinset.

Holly nodded, and Gary-Gee nodded back at her, though he didn't stop strumming from the Beatles playlist posted on a chalkboard beside him. At the moment, he was singing "We Can Work It Out," which wasn't exactly the badass song Holly had in mind, but nothing could shake the confidence Holly felt being wired with a camera that would expose the Pink Witch for who she was: a conniving, manipulating, passive-aggressive bully. And her husband! My Love! Holly wasn't sure what My Love had done, but if My Love's actions were hurting Jack, well then, that wasn't okay. Holly sauntered across the coffeehouse, past gazing eyes, past moms with preschool-age children and babies in strollers, up to the counter, where she ordered herself a badass coffee—black.

From a table behind her came a familiar voice. "Holly?"

"Shanequa—from the Scrap and Swap Fund-Raiser. Hello." Holly smiled, extending her hand. "So nice to see you again."

"Likewise." Shanequa shook Holly's hand. "Oh, hey, how are you feeling? Last night was a rough night."

"Yes, well, I . . ."

"After you left, I got with Katie at Primm Paper and gathered a fresh set of scrapbooking supplies," Shanequa offered. "I saw you got sick in the one the volunteer gave you."

A bit embarrassed. "Thank you." Holly smiled. "That's so nice of you."

"But hey, sorry." Shanequa winced. "It's at home. But maybe you can come over, and we can scrap together." Big, hopeful smile. She wrote her phone number on a piece of paper, then handed it to Holly.

A mom friend? To scrap with? Aw, heck yeah. "Thank you," said Holly. "I'd love to."

Holding a paper cup with a name written in permanent marker, "Molly?" said a man from behind the coffee counter.

"Seriously?" Holly rolled her eyes.

"Maybe he didn't hear you," Shanequa suggested.

"Story of my life," said Holly. "Oh, well." She shrugged. "Whatcha gonna do."

Collecting her coffee, Holly said goodbye to Shanequa, promising to come over early next week to scrap together. She tucked a zip-a-dee-doo-dah-dollar in Gary-Gee's cup, then headed to the Topiary Park.

27

Ten minutes later

Coffee in hand, camera in sweater, Holly passed through the wrought iron double-gated doors at the entrance of the park, purple wisteria hanging in a beguiling manner with pendant, bean-like seedpods signaling the end of summer. Carved into the limestone mantel above her, she saw the words *Cnaeus Matius Calvinus*, and this time, she knew what they meant because she had looked them up on Wikipedia. Tucking her chin to her chest to whisper into the mic, "Cee-nay-ay-e-us May-tie-us Calvin-us"—or something like that—"introduced topiaries to Roman gardens during the time of Julius Caesar." She waltzed on, realizing she could narrate all sorts of things into the mic. "And here we have a white-flower bush plant," she announced, pointing the camera with a quick pivot of her torso. Reading from a metal plant stake, she added, "Otherwise known as 'near-ee-um o-lee-an-der.'" *Oleander? Isn't that toxic? And so close to the wisteria Ella wanted to touch. Who's the horticulturist making these decisions?* And why such a poisonous entryway into something as beautiful as the Topiary Park? Like her first visit to the park with Ella, the day they bumped into Caleb (or rather, he bumped into them), it was a glorious day, the kind of day that could only be described with clichés: clear blue skies, fluffy white clouds.

Strolling along a topiary-lined sidewalk laid with clay brick in a herringbone pattern, Holly stopped short to avoid getting hit by a raucous plague of birds—common grackles, who appeared to be fighting in midflight. Holly tapped a few times on her mic, felt the contours of the pinhole camera, confirming everything was still in place, in working order, and, more important, on. She walked around a bend, and as she approached an opening in the sidewalk before a large courtyard, Holly stopped, stunned by a flurry of activity surrounding a peacock—*the* peacock—er, peahen. *Plume!* The peahen the town was so proud of, the peahen she and Ella didn't get a chance to see during their visit earlier in the week. Plume—it was Plume. And wow, oh wow, oh wow, was she magnificent.

Employees of all rank and order were huddled around her—maintenance and groundskeepers carried ladders, buckets, and rags; others from the horticulture office wore white aprons embroidered with the Topiary Park logo in gold thread. Clearly, it was "all hands on deck" to save the giant bird. A cluster of three, one woman and two men in suits, consulted with a horticulturist as the horticulturist pointed to the peahen's crest. Frantic, the horticulturist gripped a stapled pack of tattered papers, pointing to something on the paper, apparently explaining to the two in suits the insurmountable task that lay before them.

This magnificent twenty-five-foot-tall peahen stood proud in her greenery, with an outrageously long tail that cascaded the length of her body, spilling out onto the sidewalk; a plunging waterfall of delicate flowers tumbled in breathtaking sweeps of emerald, vibrant blue, and gold—with only the occasional touches of white flowers and red pepper berries. Plume was more than topiary. Plume was sculpture. Art. The peahen's elegant neck was positioned with a slight turn over the shoulder, like a bride posing for a portrait. Plume's head was angled as if to glance back in response to the slight touch of someone in the courtyard behind her. Perhaps, on another day, that touch would come from a child or a patron, someone mesmerized by her beauty, held captive by her vibrant covert feathers and eye-spotted tips that graced the length of her tail. But today, that touch came from a team of specialists, assembled for triage. Men and women working overtime to install scaffolding and netting, others readying rag-draped buckets to wage war against—what did Mary-Margaret call those bugs? Chicken strips?

"Excuse me." Holly touched the arm of an apron-clad woman standing before the peahen. The woman held a ladder and was pensive, worried.

"What's happening?" Holly asked.

"We took her drape off last night to reattach what we could of her stomach. Now we're wrapping her up again. She's completely infested."

"With chilli thrips?" Holly asked.

"Yes." The woman paused. "How did you know that? Only park officials know that."

Holly shrugged her shoulders. "I don't know. Rumor, I suppose."

"Well, it's horrible. Horticulturists far and wide have dedicated *years* of their lives tending to the upkeep of this peacock, and then whoooooooosh"—her fingers snapped—"a flying yellow bug from Asia shows up. And no one can figure out how the bugs got here. We contacted State Ag, and they have no record of them. It's like someone walked up and shook a box of them on Plume."

"I'm so sorry," Holly said. And she was. "I wish there was something I could do. They won't infest the whole town, will they?"

One look said it all: *If they haven't already, they soon will.*

"For the most part, the bugs that are on Plume now will stay on Plume. But yes, other bugs are infesting other topiaries. Blythe and Peloton seem to be bearing the brunt of it," the woman said. "But there has to be a source where the bugs are coming from. A tree. Another plant. Fruit. Something is causing the bugs to travel across the village. I keep thinking it's the vineyard. But they seem to be up in arms about this whole mess. And who can blame them? They risk losing award-winning vines. Maybe the insects came from the pumpkin patch in

Southern Lakes, but it's a bit early for pumpkins. Maybe they'll leave when the pumpkins are on the vine. I just don't know if Plume can wait that long." She sighed, shaking her head. "I need to get back to work. Sorry. If you'll excuse me?"

"Yes, sure, of course," Holly mumbled, unable to pull her eyes from the magnificent bird. *Poor Plume. Poor peahen—peacock—doesn't matter.* What was happening to Plume was so unfair. *Pumpkins?*

The woman flashed a quick smile, then gestured for Holly to keep walking so they could clear the area and return to work. So Holly moved along, curving her way around the outer perimeter of the courtyard, arriving at the front side of Plume's face. Half of it was sunken in, dried, and browned. And a sickness had crept down her neck, killing everything in sight. Holly didn't wish ill on a pumpkin patch, but the sight of Plume was so utterly sad. One-half of her face was completely gone, nothing but dark-green wires revealing facial contours where flowers once were.

For a brief moment, Holly imagined Plume the way she assumed most children imagined her—alive and well, strutting around the park. Holly lifted her chin and glanced back, over her shoulder, her posture now matching Plume's. Holly thought of Anna Wintour, back home on their kitchen table. Thought of Jack. Of Mary-Margaret and My Love. Plume, the face of the Village of Primm, for all its beauty, was caving in on itself, and somehow, they were all at the center of it.

28

At long last

The PTA meeting was being held in the atrium in a Topiary Park boardroom that overlooked handcrafted bookshelves filled with landscape design books. Mary-Margaret had positioned herself at the door, greeting moms as they entered. At the front of the line near Mary-Margaret, Holly saw Pie Moms Jhone, Peyton, Suong-Lu, and Emily.

"Emily! Sweet, eager-to-please Emily," Mary-Margaret cooed, grabbing Emily by the shoulders to give her a little *kiss-kiss* on the cheeks. "Welcome, welcome. I hope you're baking!"

And then, "Suong-Lu. Hey, you." A kiss and a smile. "Have a seat. Have a seat." Mary-Margaret moved her along. "There you go . . . yup. Buh-bye. So long, Suong-Lu!" chimed Mary-Margaret. "You too, Peyton. Why ya waitin', Peyton? Have a seat. Have a seat."

Holly narrowed her eyes at Mary-Margaret, thinking of Clint Eastwood in every gritty western he'd ever starred in. Holly wished she had a piece of straw to chew on, wished she had a hat like Eastwood—and maybe some dusty cowboy boots—but she didn't. It was just her, little ole Holly in her twinset and film gear, sipping a badass cup of coffee from Primm's Coffee Joe.

"Jhone!" Mary-Margaret pulled her close. "Jhone, whose name used to be Joan but, at my suggestion, is now spelled with an *h*, Jhone.

How are you, Jhone?" Mary-Margaret smiled. "Life's more exciting as a Jhone, isn't it, Jhone?" She winked. "Husband more attentive?"

Why do they put up with this? Why doesn't anyone stand up to her?

"Bree! Bree-with-an-E! Hello, my lovely." Kiss, kiss. "What is it, Bree?" Mary-Margaret asked. "What's the matter?"

The two began quietly discussing something, and then Mary-Margaret looked over Bree-with-an-E's shoulder and pointed directly at Holly. "Lavender! Come quick." She signaled. So Holly walked to the head of the line. Once there, Mary-Margaret eyed her with suspicion, taking a step back. Did she sense something?

"Do I frighten you, Mary-Margaret?" Holly asked, emboldened by her hidden pinhole camera and wanting to catch good footage.

"Bree-with-an-E has to leave," Mary-Margaret announced. "Right away. She has chicken pox!"

Holly gave Bree-with-an-E the once-over, wondering if she'd followed through with Mary-Margaret's request from yesterday to file an article about the bus incident with the *Primm Gazette*. "Where's my photograph?" Holly asked Bree, taking a few steps toward her. "Can I have that photograph?"

Bree backed away.

So Holly confronted Mary-Margaret. "You took the photo with her camera. Tell her to destroy it. Better yet, give it to me. I want that photograph."

"Bree-with-an-E has to go home, Lavender. Right away! She can't be around the children, and she certainly can't be around any of the moms who might be pregnant." Mary-Margaret looked at Holly's stomach. "Oh, gosh. Are you pregnant?"

"What? No!" *That's ridiculous.* "No, of course I'm not pregnant. Thanks, Mary-Margaret."

Mary-Margaret waved Bree away. "You go home, Bree-with-an-E. I'll take care of this."

Holly called out, "I want that photograph, Bree!"

Mary-Margaret grabbed Holly's shoulders. Shook her. "You have to run the Crayons-to-College Symposium this weekend on Bree's behalf. You're the secretary." Shake, shake, shake. "You have to step in when these things happen."

"No way. I won't do it." Mindful of the camera stitched behind her buttonhole, Holly rolled onto tippy-toes and pointed her left breast in Mary-Margaret's direction, hoping to capture a face shot. Holly spoke loud and clear, knowing the mic was picking up their conversation. "I'm not on the PTA executive board, Mary-Margaret. I said no, but you signed me up against my will." Holly made a mental note to insert a Beethoven instrumental *duh-duh-da-dummmm* during film editing. *Duh-duh-da-dummmm.*

"What? Well, that's ridiculous." Mary-Margaret lifted her nose into the air. "I didn't sign you up against your will."

"Oh, yes, you did."

"Fine then, Lavender, you're dead to me. If that's the way you want it, I'll remove your name from the polka-dotted lines. You're no longer a school volunteer. Because you're a quitter. A PTA dropout. No longer welcome at this meeting. Goodbye."

Whoops. Wait a minute. Holly wasn't expecting *that.* How was she supposed to film Mary-Margaret if she didn't have access to her? How was Holly supposed to tell the tale of well-oiled apple brigades and volunteer school moms if she wasn't one of them? How was Holly going to capture a grand-prize-winning mockumentary about schools that exploited an unpaid labor force of volunteer school moms if she didn't have access to the underground world of school moms in the first place?

"Wait," Holly stammered. "Maybe there's something I can do."

Mary-Margaret placed her hands on her hips. "I don't want to pressure you, Lavender. Goodness knows, you've had a lot on your plate in the last twenty-four hours."

"Maybe if I just sit in on today's meeting, have another look at the clipboards, maybe I'll find something that fits my unique talents and family schedule."

Mary-Margaret narrowed her eyes at Holly. So Holly thrust her left breast out, hoping to catch a close-up of that little wedge of pink bubble gum always hiding at the back of Mary-Margaret's pearly whites.

"Fine," Mary-Margaret said at last, stepping aside. "You may enter. But if you can't find a volunteer job that suits you, please leave. Nothing frustrates hardworking volunteer school moms more than a nonvolunteer mom eating all of our *snacks*."

Holly slipped past her, entering the boardroom.

"Speaking of snacks," Mary-Margaret reminded her. "Where. Are. Your. *Cupcakes*!"

Holly took a seat beside Emily at a long conference table. Volunteer clipboards from Parent Orientation Night lined the center of the table, perched prettily on gilded gold display stands.

"Those poor moms," said Emily, nodding toward the clipboards, "thinking they were attending a harmless back-to-school function. They probably didn't know what hit them."

"Don't I know it," Holly agreed. "I was there."

"Oh, I'm sorry," said Emily, her dainty hand resting on Holly's arm. "I didn't realize. When I saw you posting the volunteer sign-up sheets outside the school office yesterday, I assumed you were already an Academy Mom."

Over Emily's shoulder through a bank of glass that brought the hallway beyond the conference room into full view, Holly noticed the horticulturist she'd spoken with fifteen minutes earlier when she had first met Plume in the courtyard. The woman rushed the length of the hallway, extended arms punctuating words spoken in what appeared to be an intense conversation with whomever it was following behind her. *But who is it?* Holly wondered, and then she saw him. It was the man from the vineyard. The G-Class visitor from her driveway who'd delivered the envelope for Jack.

Hoping to get a better shot, Holly shifted in her seat, angling the pinhole camera just so, but the thickness of the glass obstructed their conversation. Muffled words spoken with heat and urgency. Down the hallway they went, horticulturist out front, G-Class in hot pursuit. They continued arguing until they were both out of view.

Returning her attention to Emily, "So what are we supposed to do?" Holly asked, taking a clipboard from the center of the table because other mothers were doing the same.

"Each clipboard is a complete PTA-sponsored project," said Emily, flipping through the stack of signatures on hers. "Read the description and timeline, then try to determine if the committee is in need of more volunteers. In a few minutes, we'll take turns discussing each clipboard. Some will be more complete than others. Some will need handouts attached." She pointed toward tidy stacks of handouts at the head of the table. "Next step will be contacting the person who signed up to be committee head, offering support from the PTA, and answering any questions they might have. We're trying to assemble complete packets of information before passing the clipboard to the lead volunteer. I have Field Day. What do you have?" Emily gave Holly's clipboard a once-over.

"Village Outreach," said Holly, showing Emily her clipboard, which was painted white and featured a large Village of Primm crest on the back.

"Then you're looking out for that project this year," explained Emily, "making sure things get done."

"Would you like to have coffee sometime?" Holly asked, hoping she wasn't imposing. "To discuss pies and clipboards and things." She broke eye contact with Emily, glancing down at her clipboard, pretending her invitation for coffee meant less to her than it did.

"I'd love to." Emily smiled.

"Really?" *Yes!* thought Holly. "Oh, that's great. Maybe we can—"

Clap! Clap! Clap! "Yoo-hooo. Lavender!" Mary-Margaret swept quickly into the room, clapping her hands in the air, signaling above the collective chatter that she wanted, specifically, Holly's attention. "Stop the chitchat. Pay attention, please." To everyone else, as she arrived at the head of the table, she gave a toothy grin, a "hip, hip," and a gentle hand placed across her heart, implying that she, like them, felt the "hooray" within.

Meeting called to order, Holly settled in, slipping her phone from her bag to sneak a quick text with Jack.

HOLLY: Hey, Jack. It's me. Second day of school and I'm in another PTA meeting. First, Friday night's New Parent Orientation sponsored by the PTA and now this: Volunteer Clipboards. A room full of volunteers volunteering to review volunteers who volunteered to volunteer. I have "Village Outreach." Sounds humanitarian. Like a "volunteers without borders" sort of thing. Guess what else I'm doing.

JACK: Things aren't good.

HOLLY: I know, but they're going to get better. I've devised a plan to take Mary-Margaret and her husband down.

JACK: Holly, I have news.

HOLLY: I'm wired with a mic and camera. But don't tell anyone. I'm on assignment filming the secret lives of moms. I think I can gain access to Mary-Margaret's husband and help you with your investigation.

JACK: I think I'm losing my job today.

(Pause.)

JACK: Holly—you there?

HOLLY: I heard you.

(Pause.)

JACK: Say something.

HOLLY: I don't understand. What does this mean? You can find another job, right?

JACK: Not in Primm. Maybe not anywhere. At least, not anytime soon.

HOLLY: But what about the house? We can't sell it—we paid above asking to outbid that couple from Houston. OMG. What are we going to do?

(Pause.)

JACK: Let's talk about it when I get home.

HOLLY: When will you know?

JACK: They're making announcements at five. I'll call when I can.

HOLLY: Okay.

(Pause.)

HOLLY: Jack?

JACK: Yes?

HOLLY: I love you. We'll get through this.

JACK: We won't die in the end?

HOLLY: Are you talking about Mr. and Mrs. Smith? No. No way. It's all choreographed.

JACK: I find that hard to believe.

HOLLY: Then believe in happy endings.

JACK: This isn't the movies, Holly. This is reality.

Holly whispered to Emily, "Sorry, but I have to go." She pushed her chair from the table. "Family emergency."

"Yes, of course," said Emily, reaching down to pull her handbag beneath her chair so Holly could get out.

Leaving the Village Outreach clipboard with Emily, a moment later, Holly was out the door.

From the head of the table, "Oh. Em. Gee," said Mary-Margaret, hands on hips. "She's at it again, isn't she. You're not getting away with this, Lavender!"

29

Rushing

Holly left the PTA meeting, hurrying through the Topiary Park to get to the Buick. Butt dragging, camera and mic still recording, Holly drove through Primm, eager to get home, determined to get through as many boxes as she could before Ella's bus arrived and Jack got home. Nesting instincts in full swing, she wanted some semblance of control in her life.

Once there, she heard Struggle out back, barking. Holly knew she should let her in, but instead, she rushed upstairs and started to unpack. Jack might lose his job? That didn't make sense. *We just got here. We can't lose this house—not if it's unpacked, picked up, and prim, right? They can't do that to us, can they? Of course they can. Employers can do whatever they want.*

It wasn't five o'clock yet, so announcements hadn't been made at Jack's work. They were still a Primm family. Still lived on Petunia. Ella still attended kindergarten at Primm Academy. And Holly? At the moment, by virtue of living in Petunia enclave, it was assumed she was a Foodie Mom. Holly was also a Pie Mom, possibly the K-9 Room Mom, probably the secretary of the Primm Academy PTA, and maybe the Village Outreach coordinator, too, if that clipboard was any indication. Not so bad for her first week in Primm. With a résumé like that, it could be said Holly's volunteer work helped make Primm Academy what it was today: one of the finest schools in the country—the school Holly's daughter attended to learn, to grow, to make new friends. And by golly, even if it killed her, Holly would soon bake the first of many pies for that school. *And you know what? It's my pleasure to do so.*

Unloading a box of Ella's toys onto a shelf in Ella's room, Holly heard something. From downstairs. "Hello?" She set a tiara and magic wand on Ella's bed. "Jack? Is that you?"

No response. She knew she'd heard something.

"Jack?"

Struggle was out back. Barking intensified. Holly walked to the top of the steps. Something inside her felt strange—like every instinct she had told her something was wrong. The camera and mic . . . she reached into her neckline and flipped the switch to on.

Holly slipped out of her shoes to make her way downstairs, moving carefully to avoid the step that creaked. Struggle's barking stopped. Maybe she'd seen a squirrel. Maybe Holly had imagined this whole thing. She heard a bang—*nope*. Not imagining it.

Holly froze, pressing her back against the wall at the bottom of the steps, wishing Struggle were inside with her. The noise came from the kitchen. Like someone was trying to get in the window above the sink. Holly dipped around the corner into the living room, scurrying to crouch behind a chair, waiting. Praying.

Bang!

The sound came from the kitchen. Holly was certain. She'd watched many horror films, told herself, *I'm not the dumb blonde who gets killed in the opening scene. I'm not.*

Bang!

I'm the dumb brunette *who gets killed in the opening scene.*

"My name is Holly Banks, and I'm so scared," she whispered into the mic. "I don't know what's happening."

Bang!

Someone is breaking into my house!

Holly crawled across the living room floor toward the couch, snatching from the table the metal rooster she'd unpacked when Caleb was over. She hid, shaking.

She didn't hear glass breaking but did hear someone hoisting the kitchen window open; then she swore—she swore she heard him jump from her kitchen counter onto her kitchen floor.

Whoever it was, he was now walking through her kitchen. Footsteps—on *her* hardwood floors. Those weren't Jack's footsteps. She knew Jack's footsteps. And they couldn't be Ella's. And they didn't know anyone in the Village of Primm who would attempt to gain access to their house like that. No one else had a key, so a window entry because of a lost key was out of the question.

Holly stayed crouched behind the sofa, wishing she had run out the front door when she had the chance. She steadied herself in case she had to leap out and defend herself. *I can do this. I can do this.* She clutched the rooster, hoping today wasn't the day she'd have to prove she wasn't a chicken.

Whoever it was walked through the foyer and past the steps to stand in Holly's living room—a mere six feet from where she hid behind the couch. He must have heard her because he wasn't moving. He just stood there, breathing heavily, probably messing with her like Hannibal Lector in *Silence of the Lambs.*

Holly couldn't take it any longer. She had no choice: kill or be killed!

She strengthened her grip on the rooster, decided she'd mount her attack with the rooster's feet sticking out. If she was lucky, maybe she'd stab her attacker in the face a few times, gouging his eyes out until his face fell like Plume's.

She'd attack on three. *One, two, THREE!*

"Ahhhhhhhh!" Holly charged, hoisting the rooster above her head, rushing as fast as she could toward the attacker. *"Ahhhhhhhh!"*

She stopped midattack.

Because sure as spit, it was her. All five feet two inches of her. "Mom?" Holly lowered the rooster. "What are you doing here?"

"I'm here to see Ella."

Intruder, yes. Killer, no. Killers didn't wear flowered gypsy dresses and puka beads around their necks. A killer's hair wasn't long and wavy, tucked beneath a floppy hat, face weathered from a lifetime dissing sunscreen. Killers didn't attack while holding a ukulele, and killers didn't laugh like that—at Holly. At Holly's expense.

"It's not funny, Mom." Holly handed Greta the rooster, then gave her a hug. "Why didn't you call? Forget that. Why didn't you knock?"

"I did, but no one answered."

"So you broke in?"

"So I broke in." Greta shoved a newspaper into Holly's ribs. "Looks like you made the front page."

Holly snatched the *Primm Gazette* from her mom. Huge photo of a piggy-wearing, red-faced, enraged Holly reaching through a car window toward the camera. [CLICK!] Caption read: *Petunia Mom caught carpooling in pajama bottoms: a first for the Village of Primm.*

"Well, I suppose it could be a lot worse. They didn't mention me by name."

Holly held the paper in front of her left breast, moving it up and down, slowly, so the camera could capture the news coverage.

"What on earth are you doing with that front page?" asked Greta.

"I have to stop the Pink Witch from Hopscotch before she puts another hex on me."

"Cast a counterspell." Greta followed Holly into the kitchen. "You need a new dog, Holly. I won her over with a stale cracker from my pocket."

"No way. Ella loves her." Holly closed the kitchen window and pulled open the french doors. "And I love Struggle." In ran Struggle, chasing a mangy-looking, furry creature through Holly's kitchen and down the hallway. "Struggle!" Jeez. "What in the hell-o kitty was *that*?"

Holly pointed, ready to panic. "Was that a squirrel?" *In my house? I don't know how to get a squirrel out of my house.*

Holly and Greta followed the commotion and found Struggle in the hallway in a standoff with a cat. Full clumps of fur were missing from the cat's back and hind legs—it had a crazed look in its eyes. Like something out of Stephen King's *Pet Sematary*.

"Charlotte!" Greta cried. "Holly, stop the dog. Charlotte's 'with kittens.'"

"With what?" Holly slapped her leg. "Struggle, come 'ere. Whose cat is that?"

"Mine." Greta crouched low, approaching Struggle from behind. "Didn't I tell you? I'm a cat doula."

"No you're not. Please tell me you're not."

The cat hissed, making an evil, rumbling sound as Struggle cocked her head sideways.

Greta closed in on Struggle, whispering to Holly, "I'm certified to assist with kitten birthing in the state of Nevada, the Virgin Islands, and Guam." She paused to wink at Holly. "Guam! Can you believe it?"

"And who paid for *that*?" Holly knew the answer. Cat doula certification? "Hmm? Who paid for that?"

"Céline Dion."

"Not funny. You're wasting my money."

But Greta didn't listen. Greta never listened.

"That money was for tires. I thought you ordered them. *Mom*!" Holly clapped. "Where are the tires?"

With Holly's clap, Greta sprang into action, tackling Struggle like a rodeo hand taking down cattle. *Eowwww!* Cat howled, springing a foot into the air before scampering across the floor to dive beneath Holly's couch.

"Mom!" Holly stomped. "Stop. Being. Such. A screwup!"

Greta, on the floor now, rolled herself into a seated position, giddy smile on her face. "What's wrong with your curtains?" she asked, pointing to the king-size, pale-blue flannel bedsheet with fluffy white clouds hanging by thumbtacks in Holly's living room window. Struggle's tail wagged wildly as she licked Greta and tried climbing on top of her.

"We can't afford curtains because you're building professional credentials to birth cats in Guam. You're such a screwup," Holly repeated, only softer this time. Not as harsh. Holly offered her hand, but Greta was busy scratching Struggle's belly. From her wrist, Greta slid a plastic grocery bag. "Here you go."

"What's this?" Holly opened the bag. "Ella's library books? I asked you to return these."

"I know." Greta blinked. "I just did."

"To the library. In Boulder City."

Phone rang.

"Now what?" Holly stomped over to the phone. *"Hello?"*

"Mrs. Banks? It's Rosie McClure from the school office. I think you'd better come to school. It's Ella."

30

Out the door

Holly drove to the school, but it was Greta's wild gray hair that led the way into the school office. Once there, Greta introduced herself to Rosie. "I'm Greta, Ella's grammy. What seems to be the problem?" Greta slid vintage pilot goggles from her eyes to her forehead. She looked like Snoopy on the top of his doghouse, dressed as the Red Baron.

So this is my sidekick for the day? My partner in crime? This might not end well.

"It's nice to meet you." Rosie offered her hand to Holly's mother. "My name is Rosie McClure. Your granddaughter, Ella, is a very sweet little girl."

"Well, she has a great mom." Greta winked at Holly. "It's nice to meet you, Rosie McClure."

Holly was shocked. Her mom? Nice to a woman on the other side of a counter? Now there was a first.

Rosie led them through a narrow hallway to a small conference room, then called Miss Bently.

"Thank you for coming, Mrs. Banks." Miss Bently entered the room, checking her watch. "My apologies. I only have a few minutes. The children are in the library with Mrs. Holiday."

"Thank you for calling," Holly began, her emotions a tight knot in her throat. "Is everything okay?"

"I'm Ella's grammy." Greta extended her hand, shaking Miss Bently's with vigor. "Anything you want to say in front of Holly, you can say in front of me."

Okaaaay, thought Holly. *Then take off the aviator goggles, Mom. You look ridiculous.*

"Ella failed her vision test," Miss Bently announced. "We routinely check incoming kindergarteners for vision, as many pediatricians don't check at this young age. A child who can't see the board has difficulty in most subjects."

"Ella's vision failed?" Holly was shocked. Second day of school and Ella flunked her first test? "So what does this mean?"

"It means she's blind!" Greta threw her hands in the air. "Oh, this is terrible!"

"It means she probably needs glasses," Miss Bently said. Distracted by Greta's shenanigans, she focused on Holly. "You should take her to an ophthalmologist."

"Yes. Yes, of course," Holly agreed. "Right away."

A vision problem? Ella? Holly hit rewind. Scrolled back through her memories, searching for evidence of a vision problem she might have missed. Holly told Miss Bently, "She does stand close to the television . . ."

"Ella watches a lot of television?" Miss Bently opened a folder, wrote something down.

"What? Um . . . no. You see, I—um." Now Holly was flunking a test. "Rarely, if ever. Ella never watches television. We don't allow it. Nutrition . . . literacy. And cello! I mean . . . she plays the violin." Holly crossed, then uncrossed her legs. "Suzuki method. So no time for TV. Sorry. Ella hasn't watched it in days. Weeks! It's been weeks." Holly glanced at Greta. "Months, actually."

"Are you sure?" A crooked grin spread across Greta's face. "I believe I saw her watching the Science Channel. Astrophysics, was it?"

"Ella tells me she enjoys watching *My Little Pony*," Miss Bently offered. "She's made quite a few friends talking about Pinkie Pie and Applejack."

"Really? Ella's making friends?" *Oh, sweet Ella.* Holly was so happy she thought she might cry.

"Yes, of course." Miss Bently positioned her pen above her notebook. "Does that surprise you?"

Greta leaned in. "Yeah, Holly. Why are you surprised?"

"Well, because we're new in town." Holly blinked. "I assumed making friends would be difficult."

"Ella doesn't seem to think so," Miss Bently reported. "She's making lots of friends."

"See, Holly?" Greta brushed it off with the wave of her hand. "You worry too much. The kid may be blind—but she's got plenty of friends to point the way."

"Mom, stop." Holly reminded herself she needed to forgive her mom. Start doing that "forgive us our trespasses" thing.

"Holly was a mess growing up," Greta explained to Miss Bently. "Always so anxious. Slow to trust people." Greta whispered, "Let's just say she's not the best judge of difficult circumstances."

"Mom!"

"And she acts impulsively," Greta muttered. Eyebrows tipped toward Holly. "Never thinking things through. She's like a bull in a china shop. With vertigo." Greta shrugged her shoulders. "Oh, well. What can you do?"

"Seriously, Mom?"

"You hate change, Holly. Own it. But it's not Ella's fault."

"No one's saying it is." Holly turned to Miss Bently. "Will you excuse us?"

She motioned for Greta to join her in the hallway, but Greta refused.

"I'm not going with you." Beneath aviator goggles, Greta delivered an incredulous look. "You look angry. I'm staying with her!" She pointed to Miss Bently.

Holly grabbed Greta's ukulele and left the conference room. And just as Holly thought, Greta followed. Holly spoke through clenched teeth. "You're sabotaging my parent-teacher conference. Maybe you should wait outside."

"But Holly," Greta pleaded her case, "that woman is trying to make you feel bad. She called you all the way to school for something that could be sent in an email."

"Stop," Holly hissed. "This is none of your business."

"Sure it is." Greta had no expression on her face. "Ella is my granddaughter."

"But she's my daughter." Holly poked a thumb into her own chest. "My daughter. My business. You got that? Stop telling her teacher bad things about me." Rosie was listening from the front office. She had to be.

Greta remained quiet. Something in the way she held her shoulders told Holly she'd been cruel.

"I understand." Greta took the ukulele from Holly. "She's your daughter." She rested the ukulele against her leg. "And she's in an unfamiliar world, probably wondering where she fits in. You're worried about her."

"Yeah. So?"

"So you check in on her. Want her to be happy."

"Of course I do. She's my daughter."

Greta touched the tip of Holly's nose. "I'll wait with Rosie while you're finishing with Miss Bently. I wouldn't want to interfere."

"You're not interfering."

Greta said nothing.

Ugh! "Fine." Holly stomped her foot. "You can come in. But be quiet, and let me do the talking. You hear me? Don't say a word."

Greta trailed behind Holly into the conference room, promptly forgetting everything Holly just said. "So Ella's adjusting to school, yes?" Greta asked Miss Bently.

"Oh, sure," Miss Bently said. "She cried on the first day, but when her dad dropped her off this morning, she was fine. Walked right in with the other children."

What? No. Holly's shoulders slumped. *No.*

"Is something the matter, Mrs. Banks?" Miss Bently set her pen down.

"No. I mean—yes. Actually." *So the headband woman was right?* "Is it true what they say?" Holly shifted in her seat. "Children stop crying once the mother leaves?"

"Usually." Miss Bently thought about it. "Typically . . . yes."

So Holly was the reason Ella didn't want to go to school. Ella did fine this morning with Jack, no problem. With Jack, she never sucked her thumb. With Jack, she cleaned her plate at dinnertime. With Jack, she brushed her teeth without protest. With Jack, she walked boldly into school. With Holly? Ella was a mess. Fell behind. Stayed little. Didn't progress. *Have I done this to her?*

Greta reached over to rub Holly's back. Greta's hand, though small, felt so big.

"Loving someone is easy," Greta explained. "Separating from them is the hard part."

Holly lowered her head, refusing to cry. Down to her core, she missed Ella. And she knew it was "just" kindergarten, that she'd get over it, but she missed her. Intensely. "Psychic Betty said feelings are neither right nor wrong. They just are."

"I'm sorry." Miss Bently leaned in. "Did you just say 'Psychic Betty'?"

"Who?" Holly tried to divert, not sure she should be telling her daughter's kindergarten teacher she was seeking guidance from an online psychic named Betty. Holly glanced at Greta for help, but Greta didn't know about Psychic Betty. Greta had no clue what Holly was talking about.

Greta offered, "She said 'Sidekick Sweaty.'"

"I'm confused. Who is Sidekick Sweaty?" Miss Bently readied her pen.

Help!

"I am," Greta said quickly, lifting an arm to smell her armpit. "I'm Sidekick Sweaty."

"Here's the problem," Holly confessed. "I don't want Ella to start kindergarten. I'm not ready. Am I, Sidekick?"

"No. No, of course not," said Sweaty.

They stared at Miss Bently, waiting.

"Um." Miss Bently stared at her pen. Checked her notebook for a clue of what to say.

From Holly: "I want Ella home with me. I don't want a quiet house—I want Ella *in my house*. On Petunia. And I'm *fine* that there's no storage. Or curtains. I just want Ella. And I want ponies—*My Little Pony* ponies. But I don't want a pregnant cat!" She got stern, shook a finger at Greta. "Send Charlotte back to Vegas. You're not a cat doula. There's no such thing." Holly returned to Miss Bently. "I do want watered-down white grape juice." Holly smiled. "Lots of it. And I don't care if it's in a juice glass, or a sippy cup, or a sports cup because Ella's already lost a tooth—but she doesn't have a speech delay; don't write that down—and she didn't lose it because of thumb-sucking. It's buried beneath Anna."

"What is?" Greta asked.

"Ella's tooth."

Miss Bently lifted her pen. "Who is Anna?"

"Our topiary."

"I'm sorry, but I'm *really* not following you." Miss Bently exhaled.

Holly would have explained, but it was too late. She'd already turned to face her mom. "This feels cathartic," Holly said. "It's like, I'm okay"—she touched her chest—"and you're okay." She pressed her hand against Greta's chest. To Miss Bently, Holly said, "I'm a hot mess." Then she returned to Greta. "And you. You were a hot mess at the fence that day—I saw you. You were all drunk and trench coat—but I walked away, spinning my Hula-Hoop. You were like: *Ais me, hit's your mom, Holly. Comes to me. Comes to Mommy.*"

Holly stopped. Shoulders slumped. "Oh, Mom. I'm so sorry. I remember—Dad was always pulling you into court. Calling you 'unfit.' But you fought. You fought for me. Me? I hit a school bus. And I'm not going through a divorce—at least, not anymore. Turns out it was just a combo meal. Jack and me? We're fine. Great, actually. Except there might be some legal trouble. But don't worry. We won't die in the end. Brad and Angelina didn't die in the end—well, okay, maybe sort of. But not in the movie. In the movie they were fine. Perfectly choreographed."

"Oh, thank goodness." Greta moved her ukulele to pull Holly close. "Shhh, it's okay, Holly Tree . . . gimme a bear hug." And then, with a lisp and a croak in her throat, Greta imitated a crazed drunk person—who was actually her, way back when. *"Ais me, hit's your mom, Holly. Comes to Mommy."*

Holly leaned into Greta, resting her head on Greta's shoulder as Greta wrapped her arms around Holly. "Dad moved away." Holly sniffed. "He took his fish tank. Little Poops. Big Poops. The puffer fish . . . and Bubba." Holly smiled beneath tears. "Don't forget Bubba. But I don't blame—"

"Excuse me?" Miss Bently waved a hand, lifting her pen in a sign of surrender. "What's going on here? Am I being punked? Am I on hidden camera?"

Wait. What?

Holly and Greta separated.

"Oh, it's nothing," Greta explained. "Just another moment brought to you by our sponsor, Lifetime television."

Holly smiled. "I went to film school."

"Yup," said Greta. "It's true. She went to Northwestern."

"Mostly student loans," Holly explained. "But go on, Miss Bently. What were you saying?"

Miss Bently said nothing at all for quite some time. Just looked at Holly and Greta, presumably still wondering if she was being punked. Wondering if there was a hidden camera in the room. Which in fact there was. "Professors warned me about losing control at a parent-teacher conference." She scrawled something in her notebook. "Here. Dr. Sue Melo. Pediatric ophthalmologist. Her office is one town over."

"Let me guess." Holly read the contact information, and sure enough: Dr. Sue Melo—*Southern Lakes*. "Anyone closer? Anyone in the Village of Primm?" Because Holly's husband might lose his job in a few hours. Because Holly wanted to pretend her life existed only within the confines of this sweet little village—where porches had potential, where Gary-Gee's "Zip-a-Dee-Doo-Dah" filled the town square as villagers prayed for the life of a peahen.

"I'll check with the school nurse." Miss Bently set her pen down. Ran her hands across the fabric of her skirt. She appeared nervous.

"Uh-oh." Greta nodded her chin in Miss Bently's direction. "I've seen that look before. That's a bad sign."

"Is something wrong?" Holly asked Miss Bently. "Was it something I said?"

"Actually, Mrs. Banks, it was something you did."

She knew about the bus. *"I blame Mary-Margaret!"*

"If you have something you want to tell me, Mrs. Banks, please speak directly to me before going to Principal Hayes."

What? I'm confused.

"I'm sorry, Miss Bently. I don't know what you're talking about."

"You sent an email to Principal Hayes about my supply list. You asked if it was the work of someone who enjoys torturing others."

Greta's jaw dropped.

"Oh, that. Oh, gosh. I feel terrible," Holly gushed. "I thought someone planted a bogus school supply list in my daughter's backpack. Elmer's disappearing purple? Athletic socks? Tennis balls? That was crazy. I was like fu—"

"I'm new here, Mrs. Banks."

"Q."

"I grew up in Southern Lakes, but I'm a newcomer to Primm Academy. I'm trying my best," Miss Bently said. "That list was a rough draft. Something I wrote quickly in a stream of consciousness and was meaning to edit. It was never meant for circulation, but Rosie copied it along with a set of other papers, and well, I put the photocopied packets into the backpacks. When I realized the mistake, I emailed the parents, but I didn't have your email. In fact, I don't have any of your forms. Did you receive a back-to-school manual?"

"Is that the same as the back-to-school handbook?" asked Holly. Same handbook Mary-Margaret mentioned? "Or the *Proper*?" The tip sheet? Because Mary-Margaret mentioned that too.

"No."

"The *Primm Gazette*?" No, that was Penelope. "Wait! Don't tell me." Holly snapped her fingers. "The back-to-school packet!" The packet Rosie mentioned. Was that it?

"No," said Miss Bently. "It's a back-to-school *manual*."

"Oh. Well then, no. I don't have that either."

"At any rate," Miss Bently continued, "it was never my intention to *torture* you with a back-to-school supply list. And I'd appreciate it if you'd speak with me first before alerting Principal Hayes when there's a problem. I love my job, and I don't want to lose it."

"Understood."

"Yes. Well. Thank you. This has been . . . interesting. But I'm needed in the library. The *Little Kids, Little Zoo* play is about to begin."

"Wait. What?" Holly stood too. "I thought the *Little Kids, Little Zoo* play was this Friday."

"No, it was moved to today," Miss Bently said. "I sent an email—oh."

"Ella doesn't have a costume. She knows the book, but does she know her lines?"

"Oh, sure. Ella knows her lines. And the costumes are already made and donated by Mary-Caroline's mom, Mrs. St. James."

Holly's eyes narrowed. "St. James? *Mary-Margaret* St. James?"

"Yes. Why? She's quite nice."

"No, she's not," Holly snapped. "She's like—Glinda the Good Witch. Except don't be fooled. She may be sweet and pink, but she's not good. She's evil."

"Holly!" Greta seemed proud. "You're really tearing this place up."

"Mary-Margaret St. James does a lot for this school." Miss Bently readied herself to leave the room.

Holly rolled her eyes. *Pa-leez.*

"Actually, Mrs. Banks, Mrs. St. James has a large family and remembers well what it feels like to be a kindergarten parent. She told me two weeks ago she wanted to make all of the costumes for the kindergarten back-to-school play so that other families could sit back and enjoy the children and not have to worry about making a costume during a hectic first week of school. Leopard Print's *Little Kids, Little Zoo* play is a tradition at our school," Miss Bently explained to Greta.

Greta smiled and nodded at Miss Bently. To Holly, she offered, "I probably can't pay you back for the cat doula certification, but if you want, I can make curtains for your living room."

Holly pushed Greta and her suggestion aside. "Are you serious?" she said to Miss Bently. "She did that for us?"

"Yes. She did. And from what I hear, she does nice things for people all the time."

Holly reached inside her neckline to kill the mic. *That's not true. Mary-Margaret's not nice. This can't be true. It doesn't fit with my story. That's not what my film is about.*

31

After about fifteen minutes

Holly and Greta followed Miss Bently to the library, taking a seat in the back row of chairs set up for kindergarten parents. They waited about ten minutes as Miss Bently and Mrs. Holiday, the librarian, readied the children behind a bookcase and then led them in single file to their positions in front of the parents. The minute Ella saw her grammy, she waved frantically. Almost as frantically as her grammy was waving back. Holly tugged on Greta's earthen hippie dress to get her to sit down.

As the play began, Holly spotted Mary-Margaret slipping into a seat at the side of the room. Mary-Margaret must have been behind the library shelves helping with costumes. Holly's camera was rolling, but she found herself confused. Typically, a witch didn't do nice things. Although, Holly did notice a change in color today. Mary-Margaret didn't wear pink. She wore purple. Why purple? Was she Glinda, the Pink Witch? Or was she a horse of a different color?

FADE IN:

INT. LIBRARY – AFTERNOON

MISS BENTLY sitting in front of the CHILDREN, holding an oversize cardboard book written and illustrated by Leopard Print. She turns the pages and coaches the children as PARENTS gaze lovingly upon them. Everyone is snapping pictures. The costumes are elaborate. Camera zoom in to close-up:

CHILDREN

Little frog, on a log, who is next to me?

LITTLE FROG
(child dressed as a frog)

Little duck, with a cluck, is quacking next to me.

It continued down the line as each child took a turn stepping forward to recite their line. "Little duck, with a cluck, who is next to me? Little bird, flitter bird, is flying next to me."

Mary-Caroline's mom must have stayed up all night. Holly stole another glance at Mary-Margaret. She waved and smiled at her daughter, Mary-Caroline, as Mary-Caroline stepped forward to recite her lines. Mary-Caroline was the little dog. *If she is anything like her mother, she probably bites.*

Greta poked Holly in the arm, pulling her from her thoughts.

When Ella stepped forward, dressed as a teacher, it occurred to Holly: maybe Ella was Holly's teacher. Maybe what Holly should be learning about Primm Academy she should be learning from Ella, not the other moms.

Was Holly playing nicely in the sandbox? Holly had a spy camera buried in the neckline of her sweater because she planned to decimate the mother of the little girl dressed in a doggie costume.

Ella wore a long dress, a shawl that nearly swallowed her up, a big brown wig resting sideways on her head, and a pair of super huge glasses cut from black poster board. The glasses kept slipping down her nose, so she was constantly reaching up to shove them back where they belonged. Ella looked absolutely adorable, and Holly had no one to thank but Mary-Margaret.

Ella's entire class, in unison, said to Ella: "Teacher, teacher, who is next to me?"

And all Holly could see were the enormous poster-board glasses on Ella's face. Holly could hardly stand it and had to blink away tears. Holly's daughter needed glasses, and Holly didn't have the good sense to notice what was right in front of her and do something about it. The sippy cup. Her thumb. Her sight. *What's wrong with me?*

Ella responded to her classmates with, "Little kids, little kids, sit beside me," and Holly thought, *Great. Now all of the other children are staring at Ella in those big glasses. What if Ella hates her new glasses? What if it's a struggle to get her to wear them? What if she breaks them? Loses them?*

"Relax, Holly Tree." Greta rested a hand on Holly's leg, presumably reading her mind. "Her eyeballs aren't falling out. She just needs glasses."

Ella stepped forward, her poster-board glasses cockeyed on her face. She pointed to each one of her classmates as she prepared to recite the final lines of the play—alone. All by herself. Holly's Ella. Ella the Big Girl.

"It's really long at the end," Holly whispered to Greta. "Ella's facing an impossible task. We haven't practiced. I thought the play was Friday—they're not going to make her say the whole thing—are they?"

"She'll be fine, Holly. She'll be fine."

Greta's eyes, they were smiling, supported by rows and rows of laugh lines. She was completely at ease. How was she completely at ease?

"Little kids, little kids, who is next to me? I see a little sheep, a little fish, a little dog . . ." Ella pointed to her classmates one by one.

Ella was on a roll. "I see a little cat, a little bear, a little horse . . ."

"Thank you, Mom," Holly whispered, reaching over to squeeze Greta's arm.

"A little bird."

"I never say thank you," Holly said to Greta. "And I should. I should say thank you more often."

Greta lifted her arm to smell her armpit. Holly got it: Sidekick Sweaty.

Holly gazed at Ella. "A little duck . . ."

Can she do it?

"And a little frog. Sitting next to me."

Whoo! She did it! Ella did it! Polite clapping from the parents as Holly sprang to her feet. Greta whistled. They clapped like wild women. Clapped like there was no tomorrow. Ella had recited the entire book, backward, and by herself. "That's my baby girl!" Holly hollered. "That's my baby girl! Whoo!"

When did she get to be so big? So calm? So poised? That girl of mine—so grown up. Next thing you know, she'll be tossing her crayons and heading to college.

But not so fast. Because just as Holly was celebrating Ella's achievement, Ella slipped that thumb of hers into her mouth—and started sucking.

"No, Ella!" Holly shook her head, signaling to Ella as the other kids bowed and the parents took pictures. "Take it out! Take it out!" Holly and Greta waved their arms above their heads, trying to get Ella's attention. Holly snapped her fingers, trying to be heard above the clapping. "Take it out. Take it out!"

But Holly might as well have said, "---. ---!" because, beneath her ginormous poster-board glasses, Ella was ignoring Holly. Like Mary-Margaret often did. And right now, Holly supposed, that was okay. Because from time to time, you were not always heard, even when the person you were talking to knew exactly what you were saying.

Holly sensed this was it. Sensed her time in the Village of Primm, however short, was coming to an end before it began. How long was Dorothy in Oz? A week? A few days? The length of a dream?

Penelope Pratt
Feathered Nest Realty

—ENCLAVE ALERTS—

KABOOM!

Plume is dying.

Is death knocking at your door?

Reports from the Blythe and Peloton enclaves indicate a widespread bug infestation will likely sweep the Village of Primm overnight. Park officials recommend cremation to prevent further spread. There's even talk of hiring a crop duster to rain chemicals from the sky over our beloved little village.

Though not yet identified by name, if you find what are described as tiny, flying yellow insects on the leaves of your topiary, KILL YOUR TOPIARY. Douse it with kerosene. And yes, kerosene is a flammable liquid, and yes, the vapors can explode and go KABOOM! But we have no choice. The final hour is nigh. The Apocalypse is upon us.

Incinerate those flying yellow suckers. We have no choice. We can rebuild society when the dust settles.

This is it. This is the end, villagers of Primm.

KABOOM!

32

Wednesday night

Jack arrived home at half past six.

"Well?" Holly rushed to the front door to greet him. "What happened?"

He exhaled slowly, setting his briefcase next to the coat tree. Before he answered, he loosened the clasp on his watch, set it in the mercury glass bowl Holly had placed on the hall table earlier that day. He looked tired. "Don't know."

"What does that mean? 'Don't know.' Do you still have a job?"

"They didn't say. They called a meeting to tell us a team will be coming down from corporate next week to announce the changes. Is that a new rug?" He pointed to the floor runner.

"Next week?" Holly laid her hand across her forehead. "That's so far away."

"Holly. Please."

"Fine. Sorry." Holly swung her gaze toward the wall to stare at a framed portrait taken on their wedding day. She'd hung it earlier without first finding the stud behind the drywall. *Will the portrait hold? Of course it will hold. Of course it will.* "I have a question to ask." Holly held up a finger. "One question."

"What is it?"

"If you lose your job, do we have to sell this house?"

"Most likely."

"So we might have to leave the Village of Primm?"

"That's two questions."

She couldn't get a read on him. The poor guy had dark circles under his eyes. "Are you sure you can't tell me what happened?"

Jack walked Holly to the living room couch, which was positioned beneath the bedsheet Holly had hung in the window for privacy and wanted so desperately to take down and replace with actual curtains. Fluffy white clouds on pale-blue flannel? Holly was pretty sure clouds had never been used as an element of design in curtain decor.

"Sit down," Jack said.

They sat, the couch beige and old and—Holly hoped—not hiding Charlotte beneath it. Jack didn't know Greta was in town; nor did he know she'd brought a pregnant cat from the Vegas Strip.

"The man I'm investigating will most likely be brought up on insurance fraud."

"Michael St. James," Holly confirmed. "Whose wife made a costume for our daughter."

"Yes." He fell silent. Picked at something beneath his thumbnail.

"She calls him 'My Love.'"

"I know."

Holly reached over to hold his hand.

He looked off awhile, toward a mirror leaning against the wall. Then he began.

"I really wish I wasn't part of this because apparently, My Love's a super nice guy. He's a music collector. Albums, clippings, books, authentic posters. That sort of thing. Seems harmless. A family man. But whenever something big comes up at a music auction, it whets his appetite."

Holly heard Greta getting something for Ella in the kitchen. Holly had left them in the family room with a big piece of poster board. Ella's thesaurus assignment was due Friday, so they were cutting yellow circles out of construction paper to draw smiley faces on them. The plan was to glue them around the edges of the poster board and then fill the inside space with words they found in the thesaurus. It occurred to Holly her mom might come barging into the living room before Holly had the chance to tell Jack she was there.

"An auction house in Stockholm announced a large block of rare ABBA memorabilia up for auction at the end of the month," Jack said. "We can confirm at least three instances where Michael St. James has committed insurance fraud and then laundered the money through the offshore shell company, probably to fund his addiction to music and album collecting. We think he's in the process of doing it again. Right now. In the Village of Primm."

"But how? With what?"

Jack exhaled. Heavily. Again. "Okay, so first, we incorporated the offshore companies for them. Mostly in the British Virgin Islands. A place called Devil's Bay."

"Devil's Bay?" Holly remembered that name—from the postage stamps on the envelope the G-Class visitor delivered to the house. "Who was that guy? The man who delivered the envelope. Why'd he deliver the envelope here and not the office?"

"Holly, please."

"Is he with the vineyard?"

"Yes," said Jack. "And he's highly agitated about the bug infestation. They can't risk an infestation. It would kill the vines and lower the appraised value of the vineyard."

Holly remembered seeing him through the glass wall of the boardroom at the Topiary Park. The way he chased that poor horticulturist, he did seem pretty angry. "So is that guy under investigation?"

"No." Jack rubbed his temples. "He's just a pain in the butt because he wants something in the Village of Primm he can't have."

The G-Class visitor had unnerved Penelope, that day on Holly's porch. Why? Was any of this connected? "What was in the envelope?"

"Nothing. That's not connected to any of this. An offshore investor from the group that bought the vineyard wants to buy the Stone House next to it. That's what was in the envelope. An offer to buy the Stone House using the vineyard as collateral for the purchase. But if the vines die, the vineyard won't be worth as much, so the purchase of the Stone House won't go through. But more than that, right now, the offer isn't even on the table because a prominent family owns the Stone House and doesn't want to unearth—in their words—an 'unspeakable thing' that happened on the property. They'd rather let it fall into disrepair."

"Unspeakable thing?"

"Before you get excited, there's nothing left to tell about the Stone House and its history. It only matters to the family wanting it forgotten. All of that, the envelope, the offer to purchase the Stone House, all of that is totally unrelated to what's causing all the trouble at work right now." Jack rubbed his eyes. Cleared his throat.

"Keep going," said Holly. "Go back to what you were saying about My Love wanting to buy ABBA memorabilia at auction to add to his music collection."

"Right. Okay," said Jack, reaching to take three coffee coasters from a stack on the table. He lined them up side by side, three in a row. "Here it is in a nutshell. Three separate issues, but they're all connected. Step one." He touched the first coffee coaster with his finger. "Set up an offshore shell company. Step two." He touched the second coffee coaster. "Break the law. Step three." He touched the third coffee coaster. "Get caught. You following me?"

Holly nodded. "Offshore shell company, break the law, get caught."

"Right. So here's how it works. Back to step one: offshore shell company." Jack picked up the first coffee coaster. "A shell company is like an empty shell of a company. It rarely performs any actual business functions beyond maintaining an office with an address in a foreign country.

So some 'corporate headquarters' are no more than a rented room in an old broken-down building with a file cabinet, a desk, and one employee. The headquarters doesn't have to be fancy or do anything important; it just needs to be on foreign soil because if you're incorporated on foreign soil, you follow the laws and tax code of that particular country."

He continued. "Here's one example why someone from the US would want to set up an offshore shell company. Corporate taxes are high in the United States, so if you're a megahuge company that makes a ton of money, you'll pay fewer taxes by incorporating in a country that has a lower corporate tax rate than what you'd pay if you incorporated in the United States."

"That almost sounds illegal," said Holly.

"It's not," said Jack. "You can incorporate wherever you want, and many companies do because they're avoiding not just the higher tax rate but the regulations on business. The problem comes when you break the law either through insurance fraud, illegal gambling, money laundering—that sort of thing—and then use the offshore shell company to hide the money from the US government. That's step two: breaking the law. With Michael St. James, we're talking insurance fraud."

"How does that work?" Holly'd had no idea this little village held so many secrets.

"Michael finds things to insure. A yacht, racing horses—risky endeavors with big insurance payouts if they fail, like a recent series of Wallops Island rocket launches that went bad. Because offshore companies own the insured assets, the money from the insurance payout never circulates in the United States. Everything's done offshore, where laws and finances are more favorable."

"So the legal offshore shell company gets used for illegal things," said Holly.

"Precisely." Jack held up the first coffee coaster. "Offshore shell company." He picked up the second coffee coaster. "Break the law. In Michael St. James's case, his offshore shell company insures something, and when that something gets killed (racing horses), or wrecked (yachts), or fails (Wallops Island rocket launch), the insurance money is paid to the offshore shell company because the offshore shell company is named as the beneficiary on the insurance policy. Now, typically, money made from an insurance settlement isn't taxed under US law, unless it exceeds the original cost of the asset. In those cases, if you want to avoid paying US taxes on the financial gain, it's best to insure them using an offshore shell company."

So if Michael St. James insured Plume, and Plume is worth more today than she was when she was first planted . . . Holly was still piecing things together. "So what you're implying is that the US government is going to get pretty angry when it realizes it missed out on collecting taxes from an insurance settlement because the entire transaction went through an offshore shell company."

"Exactly," said Jack. "Michael is not *just* committing insurance fraud; he's also evading taxes. Not something you want the US Treasury to find out about. But the thing is, they can't nail him for it unless they prove he broke the law on US soil."

"Prove he committed insurance fraud."

"Correct. Federal Treasury agents and the FBI want to shut the entire operation down. Offshore shell companies aren't illegal, but the insurance fraud is happening on US soil. That's what they'll go after," said Jack, picking up the third coaster. "Michael St. James is about to get caught."

"But you didn't know about any of this until recently, right?" asked Holly. *Please say yes, Jack. Please explain to me how you're not involved in any of this.*

"We're in trouble for the byzantine structure we created for them over a series of years—decades, actually. Offshore corporate structures so complex it's nearly impossible to navigate. In our firm, Michael's account *alone* includes seventeen trusts, countless annuities, and twenty-four subsidiary companies. Only recently did we come to fully understand the scope of the insurance fraud and tax evasion, and the minute we were tipped off, we agreed to cooperate with law enforcement officials. Everything we did was legal, Holly. Opening a business in the British Virgin Islands is perfectly legal, and until corporate law and the tax code change in America—and most parts of the developed world for that matter—there will always be compelling reasons to incorporate offshore. You'd be amazed by the size of the economy that's floating on islands."

Jack looked Holly straight in the eyes. Like he needed her to trust him. And she did. Jack was a good man. But good gravy, this was a lot to swallow.

"We're one of nineteen different law and accounting firms they've used over the years. These guys are brilliant. The best of the best. One hand doesn't know what the other is doing. That's the idea. That's why we're all involved. The IRS considers the complexity of the system—the structure we created—to be a willful attempt to evade taxes and creditors."

"I'm almost understanding." Holly winced, understanding a bit more their sudden move to Primm. Why Jack was so stressed, so secretive—spending so much time with Bethanny. *When the feds are breathing down your back, it's time to act.*

"We set up the system. But we didn't commit the fraud. Pretend I'm an architect who over the years built an enormous vacation home without ever questioning the client's requests. What you end up with is a house with secret portals and hallways and staircases that lead to nowhere. The house that was built offshore was custom built, but our clients are white-collar criminals dealing in high-end luxury, and they're using that structure to build and protect their wealth."

"Plume." Holly rested a hand on Jack's arm. "She's insured. The girl at the ticket counter told me that. And Meek Hopscotch owns the Topiary Park."

"I know. Plume is insured," Jack confirmed. "And she's worth a pretty penny now that she's in full bloom and attracting so much tourism to the Village of Primm. Michael St. James—well, actually, his offshore shell company—holds the policies on every animal in the Topiary Park Petting Zoo. Their insured value today far exceeds their original cost, so there will be financial gains in the insurance settlement. *Taxable* financial gains. If those plants die . . . if those plants were *killed* in an act of insurance fraud and that can be proven . . . the US government won't take too kindly to missing out on taxes because someone committed a crime on US soil. Insurance fraud. Tax evasion."

"But what happens to Plume?" *Beautiful Plume. She never hurt anyone.*

"My guess? If someone doesn't figure this out fast—the bugs'll eat her. She'll rot and die. Other topiaries will rot and die. Michael's offshore shell company will collect the insurance money, evade taxes, and Michael will fly off to Sweden to buy a large block of rare ABBA memorabilia for his music collection."

"The winner takes it all," said Holly, finding the whole thing ironic. Sad. Unnecessary.

Holly heard the refrigerator door close. Ella didn't fix herself things from the refrigerator yet. It was a wonder Jack wasn't asking who was in the kitchen.

Holly picked at a button on a pillow. "Anna Wintour is in our kitchen. Topiaries are a big deal in Primm. They're like family pets. Ella loves Anna. I love Anna. I'm sure the other family topiaries will die too. The chilli thrips are sweeping the village, Jack. It started in the Peloton enclave by the Topiary Park and then spread to Blythe. Peloton and Blythe are completely overwhelmed. They're calling for village-wide topiary *bonfires* to kill the bugs."

Holly remembered watching the horticulturist, witnessing her desperation, her willingness to do *anything* to save that bird. The entire town was devastated. Lil' Molly, Milly, and Billy O'Malley? Their mom,

Sally O'Malley? Botanist Billy O'Malley, lil' Billy, Milly, and Molly's Dillydally daddy, was *hospitalized* after Plume's stomach fell on him. "I can't believe Mary-Margaret's husband is behind all of this. I'm so angry. And Meek Hopscotch! That old man. And it's such a shame because he has such a cool dog."

"How do you know about the chilli thrips? I didn't know about the chilli thrips until I read the Devil's Bay letter and found out why the vineyard offer on the Stone House was in jeopardy." Jack eyed Holly suspiciously. "Has the Topiary Park released that information?"

"No, I don't think so . . . My Love's wife told me. She mentioned the chilli thrips in a voice mail. She said it like a teenager with tightened braces. 'Chilli th-whips.' Something like that."

"Really?" He perked up. "She left that in a voice mail? Do you have a copy of it?"

"I think so." Actually, Holly was pretty sure she'd erased it. "So what happens now? Mary-Margaret's not in trouble, is she?"

"Depends on what she knows and when she knew it."

"Jack? If you ever want to collect something—music, wine, bobble-heads—anything, whatever. Just do it. It's okay. I promise I won't give you a hard time. And if you need a room in the house to display everything—fine. Have at it. I don't care. Just no secrets. Don't feel you have to kill a plant or launder money through an offshore shell company thinking I'll complain because you're buying more ABBA. Because I won't care. I promise. Just no secrets. And don't break the law. And stop hiding things from me. We're in this together."

He took Holly's hand and kissed it. Pulled her close so she could slide into the nook of his arm and lean her head against his shoulder.

"So what now?" Holly asked.

"Right now, no one knows how the chilli thrips got here. Someone's floating the idea they're coming from a pumpkin patch in Southern Lakes."

"Always blaming Southern Lakes."

"I need to prove Michael St. James is trying to kill Plume to collect on the insurance. If I can prove that, then I can prove he's operating outside of the scope of the accounts that I set up. That's the one missing piece that would clear my name from all of this."

"And if your name is cleared, you keep your job, and we keep our life in the Village of Primm?" Holly needed to understand. "But to do so, you need proof My Love is guilty."

"Correct."

"So one family will stay." As Holly spoke the words, she closed her eyes and covered her face. "And the other family will go." Banishment. Banishment from the Village of Primm. That day on the porch, Penelope said keeping up with the Joneses was never the concern. If you lived in the Village of Primm, you were the Joneses. The only thing the Joneses feared was banishment. "What do you need?" Holly suspected she already knew.

"I need My Love's fingerprints—on a *bug* the size of a whisker."

Charlotte emerged from beneath the couch, brushing her pregnant body against Jack's and Holly's legs.

"What the!" Jack moved quickly, lifting his feet. "What is that? Is that a cat? You didn't get Ella a cat, did you?"

"Definitely not." It looked like Charlotte was missing a few teeth. "I had nothing to do with it."

"Then whose cat is that?"

Holly was silent.

"No." He covered his face with his hands. "Don't tell me. Greta's here?"

"Slipped in for a surprise visit. She's in the family room making smiley faces with Ella."

"*Greta!*" Jack yelled.

"*Jack!*" Greta yelled back.

Holly hadn't told Jack her secret—her hidden pinhole camera, her plans to enter the Wilhelm Klaus Film Festival with a three-minute film that would win the grand prize: $10,000. They needed that prize money. But was Holly prepared to throw Mary-Margaret under the bus for crimes committed at school? It seemed there were more pressing issues at stake between the two families. Not the warring colors of pink and yellow—that was Mary-Margaret and Penelope's battle. Not clipboards, car crashes, cookies, or costumes. What Holly and Mary-Margaret had going here was dueling husbands.

Holly knew this: if My Love was behind the bug infestation that was killing Plume, threatening the village wine, and causing bonfires across the village—that would knock the zip-a-dee-doo-dah out of Mary-Margaret so fast—no amount of "hip, hip!" would restore the "hooray" she claimed she felt in her heart. If all of this was true, Mary-Margaret's life? Kaboom!

33

Thursday, third day of kindergarten

Holly woke to a quiet house and the distant sound of Bus 13 outside her window. "Ella!" she hollered, throwing the covers off. "Ella! The bus!"

"Holly, Holly. Shhh. Relax." Jack reached across the bed to grab Holly's arm. Neither of them was dressed, their clothes on the floor, Holly's underwear somewhere between the sheets. "Greta's got this. She's letting us sleep in."

"What?" Bloody heck, was he serious? Holly dashed to the window, dragging a sheet with her to wrap around her body. She threw open the shutters, and lo and behold, there was Bus 13, and there was Greta at the bus stop—strumming her ukulele, serenading Ella as Ella climbed onto the school bus from their driveway for the very first time.

"Holy crow, she did it," Holly mumbled. "My mom actually did it."

Holly turned from the window to climb back in bed. "Do you know what this means? This means Ella's one step closer to a smooth transition into kindergarten. By tomorrow, she'll hop on that bus, no problem." Holly heard the front door close.

"Mom!" She stepped into pajama bottoms, pulled a T-shirt over her head, then ran into the hallway to scramble down the stairs. Thump, thump, thump. "How'd you do it? How'd you get her on the bus?"

"It was easy." Greta shrugged. "We pretended we were penguins and wobbled out."

"That's it? That's all it took?" *Maybe I'll try that with Ella.* "Oh, but I suppose you could have moved faster had you chosen a bird that could fly. Or maybe one that could run fast like the Road Runner. *Meep! Meep!* I think it was Friz Freleng who created—no. Chuck Jones. Definitely Chuck Jones. There was a job opening, once, in the film tape library at Warner Brothers, but I was pregnant, and Jack had that East Coast gig. Warner Brothers." Holly exhaled, years of wistful regret leaving her body. "One of the 'Big Six' film studios."

"Holly." Greta cupped Holly's cheeks. "You gotta let it go." Then she swirled her curly gray hair into a bun. "And if you can't, then do something about it. You've always had too much in that head of yours."

"Arcus cloud."

"What?"

"Never mind." Holly bit the corner of her thumbnail. "Holy frack! Mom. Today's Thursday. Listen to me: we need pies. Lots of them. Like, thirteen. And we need cherries stuffed in them. In, like, the next twenty-four hours."

"Sure thing, kiddo. Just need to put some finishing touches on a YouTube video. Teaching *Lion King*'s 'Hakuna Matata' on the ukulele. Chords C, F, G, D, G7, and A minor." Greta pointed the butt of her ukulele at Holly. "You should learn, Holly. It's good for the soul."

34

Pie Committee meeting

The Pie Committee met beside the North Gazebo on The Lawn in the town square.

About fifteen moms took a seat on bright-white folding chairs. Holly sat front and center, wired with her mic and spy camera and in a good position for turning her body so that her left breast pointed straight at Mary-Margaret. If Mary-Margaret said *chilli thrips*, Holly's left boob would record it.

Emily arrived.

"Hi, Emily!" Holly waved. "Hi, Suong-Lu." Lucky for Holly, they sat beside her. Because why not. They were on the Pie Committee together. Made perfect sense that Emily and Suong-Lu would sit beside Holly. "Where's Peyton and Jhone?"

Mary-Margaret took her place beside the gazebo, holding a sleek black megaphone that was so large and high tech it looked like Mary-Margaret held the head of Darth Vader.

"Helloooo!" she tootled into the back of Darth's head as his mouth amplified her voice. The megaphone was so sensitive it picked up Mary-Margaret's breathing. Just like Darth Vader.

"Pie Committee. Listen up." Mary-Margaret snapped her fingers at the moms who were still talking. "We don't have much time—our ovens are hot. First, some announcements from the PTA."

Here we go. Holly settled in.

"As many of you know, Bree-with-an-E is plagued with chicken pox and can't run this weekend's Crayons-to-College Symposium. Unfortunately for the whole town, Holly Banks of Petunia Lane, who is fresh—fresh!—like lavender-scented fabric softener, has dropped the ball and won't be running the Crayons-to-College Symposium on Bree's behalf."

Nnnope. Holly raised her hand. "Excuse me, Mary-Margaret? I didn't drop the ball." Holly cleared her throat. "Because I never picked it up."

Mary-Margaret continued. "Bree-with-an-E, stricken with chicken pox, stricken with itchy pink constellations all over her body—the Big Dipper, Cassiopeia—asked Lavender to run the Crayons-to-College Symposium, but Lavender refused. So I'm sorry, moms, your children probably won't be admitted to the college of their choice, because there will be no Crayons-to-College Symposium this weekend." She clicked a button on Darth, raising the volume. "I repeat: There will be no Crayons-to-College Symposium this weekend. Visits from the Ivy League colleges have been *canceled.* Which is probably a good thing, since the whole town is infested with *bugs.* Thanks to Lavender."

"I didn't infest the town with bugs," Holly announced. "That's such a lie. You're starting rumors. And I never agreed to run the Crayons-to-College Symposium." She didn't. She never agreed to that. *Mary-Margaret better shut the hel-icopter up about those bugs, or I'll take her @ ss down right here.*

Emily whispered in Holly's ear, "If you promise not to tell anyone, I never agreed to be the Pie Committee chair. Mary-Margaret's son plays on my son's travel baseball team. Team jerseys arrived—all wrong. But it was too late. Coach opened the box before the game? Teenage boys played the season opener—not with the words *PRIMM ROCKETS* on their backs like it was supposed to read but *PROM ROCKETS.* The bleacher dads couldn't resist. Jokes were horrible. Not at all age appropriate. And Mary-Margaret blamed me! Suggested I should do community service as the Pie Mom. So ridiculous. Community service? For a mom? Whoever heard of such a thing?"

"No one can do everything, but everyone can do something." Mary-Margaret's mouth was so close to Darth's head, the megaphone took up half her face. Holly imagined David Prowse, the actor who played Darth Vader in *Star Wars*, stomping around the Pie Committee meeting in long black robes. "Unless, of course," Mary-Margaret was saying, heavy breathing into Darth's head, "you're Lavender."

Holly shot a look of dismay at Penelope, sitting a few seats away. *Help me, Penelope. You got me into this. She's* your *cousin.*

"She's insane," Holly grumbled under her breath to Emily. And okay, yes, Holly might have been tucking her chin down to speak into her left breast. "She's trying to ruin my life," Holly told her boob. "But I refuse to be manipulated. I *will* be heard."

Holly stood to confront Mary-Margaret, because why not? Holly was fed up and emboldened by her hidden camera. She was a filmmaker. She needed to capture great footage, or no one would subscribe to the YouTube channel Holly planned to create. Problem was, when she was done recording all of this, she still had to figure out how to retrieve the film footage from the MP3 file Caleb set up, import it to iMovie, somehow make a movie out of it, upload it to YouTube, and then splash it all over social media. Caleb had told Holly all about it. Made it sound so simple. That was how you broke into the world of indie film. Through social media. Which Holly knew nothing about. So there was that.

Mary-Margaret pressed Darth to her mouth. "Will everyone in the town square, everyone on The Lawn, please sit down?"

No. Holly refused to sit down. *I'm going to be heard. I did not volunteer to run Crayons-to-College, nor did I infest the Village of Primm with bugs.*

"Will everyone who's wearing a light-purple Bill's Pizza T-shirt and a pair of white jeans please sit down?"

Great. Now all the moms were staring at Holly's Bill's Pizza T-shirt. What if they noticed the pepperoni on her left breast had a tiny camera lens poking out of it where Holly's left nipple sat?

"If you're holding a cup of coffee," Mary-Margaret continued, "if you have brown hair and need a root touch-up, will you please sit down?"

"I didn't drop the ball!" Holly cupped her hands around her mouth. Her hands weren't Darth, but hopefully, they'd do the job. "It's not my ball. I don't *have* any balls!"

Penelope clapped. Winked. Gave Holly an enthusiastic two thumbs up.

Mary-Margaret: "If you're fresh, fresh like fabric softener . . . if you're wearing a sports bra, will you please sit down?"

"Excuse me?" Holly stretched to wave both arms above her head. "Mary-Margaret?"

But Mary-Margaret ignored her. So Holly walked over to stand next to Mary-Margaret on the bluestone patio that circled the North Gazebo. *I won't be ignored,* thought Holly. *I won't be the "---" in the script any longer.*

"Mary-Margaret. Listen to me."

Holly was a foot away from Mary-Margaret, about to tap her on the shoulder to get her full attention, when suddenly—*buuuuring*—Mary-Margaret swung around and pointed Darth right in Holly's face. Now, Holly hadn't really paid attention in college when they went over the concept of phase and how different miking setups interacted with each other. Sine waves, stereo mics, mono compatibility, blah, blah, blah. But she did know the mic she was wearing disagreed with Darth—because another shrill *buuuuring* let out.

"Whoops!" Holly took a step back as the crowd of moms reacted, covering their ears.

"If you're standing beside me. And you're looking at me right now. Will you please sit down? If your eyes look like Muppet eyes. If you've been known to say, 'Me eat cookie. Nom-nom-nom.' Please sit down."

That's it. Those damn peckled peanut butt—Holly snatched at Darth, but Mary-Margaret pulled him away. So Holly lunged at Mary-Margaret, taking hold of Darth to wrestle him out of Mary-Margaret's hands. Success! Oh, but so many buttons. *How do you work this thing?* Holly banged Darth against her hand. Pushed a button, squeezed a red bar.

"I didn't drop the ball," Holly announced into the back of Darth's head. "I'm sorry Bree has chicken pox"—*buuuuring*—"but I never said I'd run the Crayons-to-College Symposium. And I didn't sign up to be PTA secretary either." Her voice was so loud Holly wondered if they could hear her down The Lawn on Pip's Corner. "I'm not PTA material. I signed up for napkins."

This felt so good. Having a voice gave you power. But WHOO! *Ouch.* With all that technology in close proximity, phase was out of whack, disrupting the two signals.

Mary-Margaret snatched at Darth as Darth let out another glaring, blaring, high-pitched ring. *Zzzpt! Buuuuring!* The moms gasped. Cried out. Covered their ears. But Holly had a good grip on Darth, so as Mary-Margaret and Holly wrestled, tugging Darth back and forth, Holly was able to keep talking. "I'm sorry that Plume is dying!" Holly said. "But I have information about Plume that might surprise you!"

Mary-Margaret's eyes grew wide. "You wouldn't," she snarled.

Wouldn't what?

Confess, Mary-Margaret, say something. Anything. Let me record it. Let me save Jack's job, so we can live in the Village of Primm forever.

Mary-Margaret hauled off and whacked Holly in the shoulder with an open hand, probably hoping Holly would drop Darth, but she didn't. So Mary-Margaret lunged for Darth, arms out like a flying bat, but Holly was too fast for her.

"I have to tell you all something very, very important!" Holly yelled into Darth's bald black head. "Something you all need to know, Pie Moms. Listen up! It's about Plume."

More wrestling. Growing more desperate by the moment. A mom from the crowd yelled, "Girls! Stop that. Use your words." And like an echo, another mom finished with, "That's it. Go to your room!" Mary-Margaret pulled Holly's hair. Stomped on Holly's feet. Holly worried Mary-Margaret might haul off and bite her.

Holly squeezed the red bar on Darth's neck. "I want you all to know!" she shouted, throwing an arm up to block Mary-Margaret. "That Plume . . ."

"Noooooo!" growled Mary-Margaret.

"Plume. Is a peahen." There. She'd said it. "She's not a peacock. I repeat! Plume is not—A PEACOCK." Felt so good to get that off her chest.

The struggle for Darth ended when Mary-Margaret prevailed, ripping him violently from Holly's hands—but Mary-Margaret fumbled, dropping Darth. He hit the bluestone patio facedown, smashing into a dozen pieces. Mary-Margaret's mouthpiece, like Darth himself in *Return of the Jedi*, was destroyed.

"Hip! Hip!" *Hooray!* Holly clapped. "Hip! Hip!" *Hooray!*

"Sit down!" Mary-Margaret clapped her hands in Holly's face. "Sit. Down!"

Holly folded her arms across her chest, staring at Mary-Margaret as if they were kids on a playground. *You want me to sit down? Try and make me. I dare you.* Hidden mic. *I double-dog dare you.* Hidden mic *and* hidden spy camera. *I triple-dog dare you.* They locked eyes and stared at one another.

Penelope stood. "I'll run the Crayons-to-College Symposium—not Holly. My son is a junior at Primm Academy, so it wouldn't hurt if I learned a few things while chairing the College Crayons Committee. I'll run it if it gets postponed until spring."

Mary-Margaret pulled herself from her stalemate with Holly to take control of the meeting. "All in favor, say aye. All opposed—you know what? Don't even bother. Don't anyone *speak*."

And so no one did.

Until at last, "Fine! I'm done," Mary-Margaret announced. "Penelope runs the Crayons-to-College Symposium in the spring. Emily? Pie announcements? Like maybe—don't use store-bought pie filling in your pies?" Mary-Margaret glared at Holly as she marched to her seat.

"Ladies, ladies, please." Penelope motioned for everyone to stop squabbling. "Mary-Margaret, before you sit down, may I remind you? Holly lives in Petunia enclave. I can assure you everything she does is organic."

"It's true." Holly nodded to the crowd before sitting down. "'Frigerator's filled with kale. And grass-eating cows. With good lives before we eat them. Goji berries! And . . . hmm." She thought a moment. "Ed-a-my-me." *That's how it's pronounced?*

Emily rose from her seat to take control of the meeting. "I want to start by thanking everyone for the exposure on Instagram. Great effects and filters. Cherries everywhere, wow. Thanks also for liking and sharing the cherry pie auction on Facebook."

Facebook? Instagram? Was Holly supposed to do something on social media?

"But the activity on Twitter has been a bit lean," Emily reported. "I was hoping we'd trend in the top five locally during the Cherry Festival, so if everyone would head to their buffers . . ."

Head to their buffers?

"And stagger a series of tweets to release during the festival, that'd be great." Emily smiled. "I'll email tweetables later tonight."

Tweetables?

"Holly." *What? Why's she singling me out?* "I don't have your Twitter handle." Emily readied her pen.

Do I tell her my Twitter handle is @EndofRope?

"Go on," Mary-Margaret urged with a slight fire in her eyes. "Tell us your Twitter handle."

Emily explained, "I'm only asking so I can include your handle in a few tweets. That'll make it easier for you to retweet it to your followers."

Followers? "Um . . . well, I. Um." Holly cleared her throat.

Mary-Margaret smelled blood. "Emily, ask Lavender how many followers she has on Twitter."

Emily didn't ask outright, but she did look at Holly, anticipating a response.

Spit cakes! Holly didn't want to answer. "Why does this matter?" Holly asked.

"I'll answer that." Mary-Margaret stood. "Knowing how many followers you have on Twitter gives us an indication of your influence as a mom. Top mommy bloggers and social media influencers like me have thousands and thousands of followers across many platforms."

"Okay, then." Holly folded her arms across her chest. "I'm sorry, Emily, but I don't have a mommy blog. Or a gazillion followers on Twitter. My Twitter handle is how I feel most of the time: at EndofRope. So I'm sorry. I guess I'm not an influential mom." Was this a condition of signing up for the Pie Committee? Holly needed to be a mover and shaker on social media?

"Of course you're influential," Penelope interrupted. "All moms are influential. Moms are probably the most influential people on the planet." Penelope scowled at Mary-Margaret, mouthing the word *yellow* at her.

"Well, some moms are more influential than others!" Mary-Margaret added. "That's all I'm saying. I have so many followers I'm running Tide commercials on my blog."

"You don't need a website to bake a pie." Penelope addressed Mary-Margaret directly. This was starting to look more and more like the Land of Oz: a Pink Witch and a Yellow Witch, warring factions in a prolonged conflict.

"Oh, no," Emily said, jumping in. "I never meant to imply she needed a blog to bake a pie. I was just asking about her Twitter handle so I could include her."

"Don't worry about any of this nonsense, Holly. Focus on the pies." Penelope took a read of the other moms. "We're just glad you're here." Penelope looked around, pausing to make eye contact with certain moms. "Let us all remember that Holly moved to the Village of Primm about a week ago. Not only is she new to the ways of our village, but on Tuesday, she sent her only child to kindergarten. *Kindergarten.*" Penelope paused for effect, then continued. "I think we should all give Holly a break about social media and instead welcome her to the Village of Primm. Holly"—Penelope spoke to Holly but looked directly at Mary-Margaret—"welcome to the Village of Primm. And welcome to the Pie Committee. We're so glad you're here."

"Thank you," Holly said. "And I'm sorry, Emily." Holly hoped Emily knew she was sincere. "About the Twitter thing. I'm just not comfortable disclosing the amount of followers I have on Twitter. Not yet. I'd like to keep that information private—for now."

"Ha!" Mary-Margaret snorted. "Private?" Hands on hips. "Private?"

What? Was I being rude? "I promise I'll tell you later," Holly said to Emily, who looked confused. *Maybe I've hurt her feelings.* "I'll call you tonight. I'll tell you over the phone."

Holly didn't want the entire Pie Committee to know she had exactly three followers on Twitter. Her mom, Jack, and some guy whose Twitter handle Holly couldn't remember but whose name was apparently Piz, which, she understood by reading his tweets, was short for *lápiz*, the Spanish word for pencil. When Holly had looked him up, his profile page indicated his name was Pablo Diego José Francisco de Paula Juan Nepomuceno María de los Remedios Cipriano de la Santísima Trinidad Martyr Patricio Clito Ruíz y Picasso. When this Twitter account had opened, this guy's full name—144 characters with spaces—didn't fit inside a single tweet because Twitter, at that time, limited tweets to 140 characters, so he cubed them all together over a series of tweets. Twitter was hard to follow. Strange at times, almost surreal.

Suong-Lu placed a hand on Holly's arm. She informed Holly that except for rare circumstances on special accounts, Twitter followers were public. Not only could you see the follower numbers plain as day, but anyone who wanted to could click on your list of followers and see exactly who those followers were. Apparently, nothing about Twitter following was private. *So, clearly,* thought Holly, *I'm an idiot.*

Holly tried to read the look on Emily's face. *Does she think I am doing this on purpose? Acting the fool, so everyone will laugh and the meeting will fall apart?* Because that was never Holly's intention. Emily appeared disappointed in Holly. Holly could tell. And Holly couldn't help but wonder: Did Emily regret inviting Holly into her inner circle? Because if she did . . .

Emily could stick it.

A part of Holly didn't care anymore.

Holly would bake the dang pies because she said she would—but she refused to feel bad that she didn't also tweet about pies. Because, in the end, they were freaking pies.

35

Thursday afternoon

Holly's meeting with the Pie Committee ended. She got Ella out of school and drove her all the way to Southern Lakes to see Dr. Sue Melo (pronounced "mellow," not "milo"). Turned out, Ella did need glasses. Like, a long time ago. They got her fitted and were told her glasses would be ready for pickup Saturday morning. Holly decided they'd pick the glasses up before heading to the Cherry Festival on The Lawn. Holly wanted Ella to *see* the thirteen pies her mommy had baked for her school.

Holly drove Ella back to school, then ran home for a quick strategy meeting with Greta. Holly needed to shop for groceries, then be back in time to meet Caleb to discuss the film footage Holly had collected.

Walking into her family room, Holly caught Greta doing yoga wearing nothing but her underwear. No bra, no nothing. "Mom! Jeez. Put a shirt on." Holly shielded her eyes from the most disturbing thing she'd seen in a long while. "At least wear a sports bra."

"Sports bra? Total rip-off. For two bucks I can strap the twins in with an Ace wrap. Works just as well." Greta snickered. "Now hold yer horses, Holly. I'm an old lady stuck in a downward dog. This'll take a few minutes."

Holly heard Greta grunting and moaning and gathered Greta had somehow flung herself sideways against Holly's family room couch and was now rolling out of the thing she called the downward dog. Didn't look like no downward dog pose to Holly, but whatev.

"I need to increase my followers on Twitter," Holly told Greta. "And I need to send out some tweets with the hashtag 'cherry pie' in them." Holly hoped Greta had picked up some hashtagging skills along her path to becoming a social media icon in the world of ukulele. "Emily likes hashtags. She wants me to start using hashtags. And links. Links and hashtags." Links and hashtags. Sounded like something you'd order off the breakfast menu.

They went into the kitchen and sat down at Holly's computer. "I can't believe I'm learning Twitter from my mom. I'm so lame."

"Why? Because I'm old and you're young?" Greta was still stretching, but at least she'd put on a tank top and some yoga pants. "You have to change with the times, Holly. Life is about change. If you don't change, you'll never grow."

"Sounds cliché."

"Truth often is."

Greta fired up Holly's computer, double-clicked the Google Search icon, and typed.

"Mom. Stop. You're typing *YouTube*. I need Twitter. Blue bird, not red play button."

"I know, I know. I thought I'd show you some of my ukulele concerts first."

"Mom, please."

"Holly Tree! I almost forgot." Greta grabbed the collar of Holly's shirt and pulled Holly toward her till they were nose to nose. "The most beautiful man on the planet came to your front door. You missed it."

"Was he driving a G-Class Mercedes?" Holly freed herself from Greta's grip and reached over to pull an apple from a bowl on the table.

"No. No, he didn't drive a Mercedes. He was driving a UPS truck."

"Oh my." Holly took a bite of the apple. "I saw him too. At the school." Holly got serious. "Wasn't he amazing? Like something off the cover of a romance novel."

"I was thinking hard erotica."

"Of course you were."

"So what'd he bring?" Holly surveyed the kitchen table and the counters, looking for a package.

Greta pointed to a stack of about twelve boxes in the family room. "He brought all that."

"That?"

"My stuff. I shipped everything before I left."

"Hold up. Everything?" Holly's hand went limp, still holding the apple. "What happened in Vegas? You didn't pay your marker, did you? Mom. That's a felony. You can't move in. Jack will freak."

"But Holly. Where's your compassion? Charlotte's 'with kittens.'"

"So?"

"So I'm a cat doula. Do you really expect me to practice my trade while homeless? Charlotte's so close. For all we know, she's birthing ten kittens under your couch right now."

Felony? Kittens? Greta and Jack—under the same roof? Was it Friday night yet? No? Holly closed her eyes. *Gevrey-Chambertin. Gevrey-Chambertin.* "Mom? You can't decide to move in without asking. I have a family. The answer is no. No way. Absolutely not."

"Why not?"

"Because I don't want you ripping through Primm. You think dealing with all of your shenanigans is fun for me? How is this my problem?"

"You think I'm a screwup?"

"Yes . . . sometimes." Holly felt bad admitting this to her. "I do."

"Well, I disagree."

"Mom. You broke into my house. You called me in a pickle. I've got a dog, and yet, because of you, I also have a cat under my couch ready to give birth."

"Holly," Greta assured her, "I can handle Charlotte's delicate state. I'm a—"

"Don't say it."

"Cat doula."

"There's no such thing as a cat doula!" Holly set her apple on the table. "You have to hide those boxes." She pointed. "Now. Before Jack gets home."

"Fine," Greta muttered, moving toward the boxes. "I'll find a convent for wayward girls. Maybe the nuns will shelter us until the kittens arrive."

"Why are you limping?"

"I forgot to stretch before my yoga." Greta turned toward Holly, legs bowed. "My kuter hurts."

"Mom, wait," said Holly. "Let me help."

"Is this about the money I owe you?"

"No." Holly exhaled, reaching for her first box. "I mean, yes, partially. But no." She looked around. "I don't even know where to hide these."

"Maybe he won't notice I'm here."

"Not notice his mother-in-law and her pregnant cat?"

"We could try." Greta shrugged. "We might get away with it."

"You know what, Mom? I think that's your problem. You somehow *always* get away with it."

Greta smiled.

Holly didn't.

36

Thursday night

It was Thursday night around eight, and Holly was finally home from the grocery store. Holly had taken the camera and mic off earlier after watching a few of Greta's ukulele concerts on YouTube. Recording a video of a video on a video channel felt a bit like walking a staircase in an M. C. Escher lithograph. Holly couldn't get her head around it.

"I got Lucky Charms, and I bought two percent." Holly set the bags down. "Hold up. What's that?" she asked, pointing to the monstrosity splayed across her living room windows. If you weren't paying attention, they might have passed for—

"Curtains," said Greta. "One-of-a-kind, custom-made curtains. I'm pretty handy with the scissors." She twisted a hair tie into her curly gray mane. "My way of paying you back for the cat doula classes." She winked. "Now we're even."

"No. No, that can't be," said Holly, panic rising from her chest. She moved quickly toward the front windows. It was one thing to have a bedsheet thumbtacked to a window for privacy when you moved in, an entirely different thing to have it fashioned into actual curtains. "That's a bedsheet," said Holly. "A used, worn-out flannel bedsheet. Mom. That sheet's from Jack's first apartment."

"Not anymore!" said Greta. A clap of her hands showed her delight. "Ta-da! You wanted curtains? Now they're curtains."

"I don't even know what that is," said Holly, eyes wide, wanting to cry. "It looks like an amateur rope artist trying"—Holly was stunned into disbelief—"but failing to perform some sort of a swinging-rope act. Like something out of Cirque du Soleil. But more 'cirque' than 'soleil.'"

"Nope! Wrong again, Holly. What you're looking at is called a *cascading jabot*. See how it swoops down and then swoops back up? That's 'jabot.' It's French! It means 'crop of a bird.'"

"It's not French. It's flannel. And it's freaky looking," said Holly, pressing her fingertips against her temples, hoping to find a pressure point to relieve the stress that was welling up inside her. "*Flannel curtains?* Mom. There's no such thing. That's never been done in the history of curtain making."

"Aw, come on. Where's your sense of adventure? I think it's nice to have fluffy white clouds cascading across and down both sides of a living room window. Look on the bright side. It might be dark and rainy outside, but inside, nothing but clear blue skies!"

"Are those shoelaces?"

"I needed something to tie it all together."

"Where'd you get the shoelaces?"

Greta winced, crouching down a bit, fumbling a smile. "From the family shoes?"

"Mom!"

"I needed piping along the top edge—something white to match the clouds, so I washed all the shoelaces in bleach and then braided them. You should be happy, Holly. Those shoelaces saved you a lot of money."

"What'll the neighbors think?" *Those are Collette's windows. Collette's!*

"Well, I think it's pretty." Greta pouted, admiring her work in spite of Holly's reaction. She crossed her arms, appearing a bit defensive. "No one else can say they have curtains like that."

"They need to come down. Right now."

Holly reached up and with one big yank—"Holly, wait!"—tried stripping her window of its public shame. It felt cathartic—except the curtains didn't budge. They held fast.

"Don't!" Greta spoke with urgency. "They're nailed to the trim. Wait till Jack gets home. Maybe he has a tool we can use. A jackhammer. Or something."

Breathing like a bull from flared nostrils, still clutching the fluffy-cloud curtains overhead, Holly stood steadfast for a moment, heart pounding, trying to calm down. Staring out her front window—nothing but manicured homes, hella mulch, and windows framing custom drapes. "You know what?" she said at last. "I have the perfect solution for Ella's thumb-sucking."

She unclenched her fists from the curtains, abandoning the fandangled window treatments to march over to the grocery bags and rummage through them. She held up a bottle of no-bite nail polish. "Goes on clear, tastes horrible."

"Then let's go find Ella," said Greta, pulling Holly by the arm, ushering her quickly toward the family room and away from the front window. "No sense taking your frustrations out on the curtains."

~

Ella agreed she'd let them paint her nails, but only if Greta and Holly painted their nails too. They agreed, and before long, all three of them had painted all ten of their respective fingernails. Assuming it would only work if they really glopped it on, they were ridiculously liberal with the polish, painting second and third coats. As an added bonus, Greta twisted into another one of her yoga poses (this time fully clothed) and painted her own toenails. She winked at Ella as she was painting. "In case I get the urge to suck my foot's thumb."

"Okay, Ella." Finished with the nail polish, Holly held up a *Merriam-Webster Dictionary of Synonyms and Antonyms*. She even found a copy of the *Oxford American Writer's Thesaurus*. "Let's get that 'Happy' poster done."

Everyone spread out on the kitchen table beneath Anna Wintour. Poster board, pencils, markers. And the two thesauruses. Thesauri?

"Ella, I love your smiley faces." Jack pointed to the row of construction paper smiley faces that bordered Ella's poster. "They turned out nicely." He pulled up a chair.

"So, Ella. Let's look at this book. Okay." Holly thumbed through the pages, opening to the entry for the word *happy*. Holly scooted closer to Ella. "Alphabetically, the entries read: *happily*, *happiness*, *happy*. Followed by *happy go lucky*."

"I like that word—*happy go lucky*," Greta said. "Read that one."

"Says here that other words for *happy go lucky* include *easygoing*, *carefree*, *casual*, *free and easy*, *devil may care*, *blithe*, *nonchalant*, *unconcerned*, *untroubled*, *unworried*, *lighthearted*. And *laid back*," Holly said.

"Those are nice words," Ella said.

"Yes," Holly said, distracted by the same thought. "They are nice."

Holly scanned them again, silently. She wished she could be like that. More lighthearted and laid back. She decided to try it. Make a concerted effort to be happy go lucky. Greta had learned how, so Holly figured so could she.

"Okay, so. Let's look up *happy*." Holly took Ella's finger and slid it to the entry. "That's *happy*," Holly told Ella. "That's what *happy* looks like. It reads: *adjective. Cheerful, merry, joyful, jovial, jolly, jocular, gleeful, carefree*."

"Are we supposed to write these down?" Jack asked. "On the poster. Isn't she supposed to write them down?"

"Just a sec." Holly held a finger up. "Let's read them first, okay, Ella? Figure out what all the fuss is about *happy*." Holly touched the tip of Ella's nose. "Everyone's so hung up on being that word these days." Holly squeezed Ella's cheeks. Bent over to kiss Ella's lips.

"Read the words, Mommy." Ella tapped the page. "Let 'er rip."

"Untroubled, delighted, smiling, beaming, grinning." Holly checked on Ella. Ella grinned. *"In good spirits, in a good mood."* Holly checked on Jack, and he smiled. "What? I'm in a good mood . . . ," she told him. *"Lighthearted, pleased, content, contented, satisfied. Gratified."* Holly checked everyone's faces. Greta gazed at Holly like she was remembering something or hoping Holly'd remember something or learn something about something. Holly didn't know. Didn't know what was going on inside Greta's head. "Should I keep reading?"

"Yes, yes, most definitely," Greta said. "That book's a treasure. Who knew there were so many options for being happy?"

"Ella, you think of the words you like," Holly instructed. "And when I'm finished reading them, we're going to copy the words onto the poster."

Ella covered her eyes with the palms of her hands. "Yes, I know, Mommy. *Read.*"

"Okay, okay. *Thrilled, elated, exhilarated, ecstatic. Blissful.*" Holly reread them. "Good gravy. That's a lot of pressure," Holly said to Jack. "Ecstatic? You have to be ecstatic to consider yourself happy?"

"I don't think that's what it's saying," Jack said.

"Miss Bently says feelings are a lot and all over," Ella explained, using her hands in grown-up fashion to demonstrate how Miss Bently spoke to the classroom. "And they're everything. Like that milk," Ella suggested, pointing to the glass. "It's not just *milk*. It's a drink. So it's two things. Milk, drink. No." Ella looked at Jack. "Wait."

"I think that's close, Ella," Jack said. "Great job. But I think, maybe . . ." He checked with Holly to see if he was on the same page as the assignment. "What Miss Bently wants you to do is to learn about different types of words for different ways that you might feel."

"She wants you to be in touch with your emotions," Greta offered. "Like when you're playing with Pinkie Pie. Pinkie Pie makes you feel happy inside. You're in good spirits. Delighted."

Holly chimed in. "Yes, good point, Mom. So, Ella, there's more than one way to be happy." Holly pulled Ella's attention back to the thesaurus. "You can be glad; you can be pleased. You can be delighted or willing. Or you can just be content." Holly shrugged, acting content. "Like you're telling the world: *Hey, everybody, look at me. I'm content. I'm not* ecstatic. *Because I don't have to be* ecstatic *to be happy. I can just be content. Content*'s a synonym for *happy*—just like *ecstatic* is."

Jack, Greta, and Holly exchanged glances.

"This is a pretty cool assignment," Jack said.

"Yes, well. It's a pretty cool school," Holly pointed out.

"Keep going." Ella nudged Holly.

"*Not unhappy,*" Holly read. "I like that one. Tell yourself, *Today, I'm not* un*happy. Therefore, I'm happy.* This is fun. Says here, *a sense of well-being.*"

Well-being. Something Ella didn't have all of a sudden because she sat up in her chair, looking for something. "Where's Happy?" she asked. "My dinosaur?"

"Isn't he in your backpack?" Jack asked.

"No . . . I was playing with him . . ." Ella left the table for the family room—stopped dead in her tracks when she saw what was happening to Happy—and Ella let out a wail, a howl, a bawl. Shriek, scream, cry. Something. It was loud.

Everyone jumped, asking, "What is it?" and "What's wrong?"

"Struggle!" Holly yelled, sliding her chair out from underneath her. "Let go of Happy!"

Ella screamed. She was a few pages after *happy*. She was hys-ter-i-cal. Jack and Holly moved swiftly to the family room to surround Struggle. Greta swooped Ella into her arms to comfort her.

"Struggle, drop it." Jack crouched at the waist, arms extended.

Holly and Jack circled the wagons, so to speak, moving like someone had choreographed the scene, like Brad and Angelina at the end of *Mr. and Mrs. Smith*; both Holly and Jack were ready to pounce on Struggle if she tried bolting from the room with Happy in her mouth. Holly could barely see Happy. Just a lime-green tail jutting out from the side of Struggle's mouth. Struggle had really sunk her teeth into it this time. Holly wondered if she'd ever let go. Holly thought perhaps Happy's head might fall off.

"Drop it," Holly muttered through gritted teeth. "Struggle, please."

"Struggle, sit," Jack tried, then, "Stay, Struggle. Stay."

But nothing worked.

"Hold hands!" Greta shouted. "Form a wall against Struggle."

Jack and Holly clasped hands, crouched down, then walked slowly toward Struggle. Struggle lowered her head and began growling.

"I'll try to hold Struggle down," Jack told Holly, "so you can get a grip on Happy."

"Got it. Good plan." They closed in on Struggle, pinning her between the television and the stack of moving boxes that leaned like the Leaning Tower of Pisa. There was nowhere left for Struggle to go. If Holly were Struggle, Holly would surrender and release Happy.

"You can do it!" Ella cheered.

"Team Banks!" Greta shouted.

"On the count of three," said Jack.

Holly counted, "One, two . . . *three*!"

Jack leaped onto the dog. Holly took hold of the dinosaur, and together, perfectly choreographed, they ripped Happy from the jaws of Struggle.

37

Later that evening

Holly prepped the kitchen for pies while Greta put Ella to bed. Caleb showed up with his laptop, wearing cargo pants and a faded Walnut Film Festival T-shirt. "You busy?" he asked.

"Yes, why? I'm about to bake some pies."

"I noticed you hadn't uploaded any of the film footage yet. I thought I'd come by and help."

Holly let him in, confessing she had no idea what he was talking about when he told her he'd transferred a raw file to somewhere and then shared it with Holly and now Holly was supposed to retrieve it from someplace and somehow download it somewhere else and, as if by magic, find it again and then add her footage and then create a movie out of it somehow so it would be ready for upload. Somewhere. She didn't know where. Probably YouTube.

"I went to film school, Caleb. I did. But that was before Ella was born. Heck, I wasn't even married when I went to film school, so that was, like, almost ten years ago. I was young then. I was hip."

"But now you're not? That's what you're telling me?"

"Need proof? I'm wearing Ella's no-bite fingernail polish." Holly held up her hands, wiggled her fingers.

"Well, I think you're totally hip. For one, you're super bold wearing spy gear. I bet none of the other mothers in Primm wear spy gear."

"True."

"So don't beat yourself up. The digital world thrives on change." He pointed to his T-shirt. "You can join my film crew at next year's Walnut if you want."

"Another film festival?" Holly twitched an eyebrow. *How many can there be?*

"Teams have forty-eight hours to make a short film. You'd be great at it, Holly." His eyes were kind. His smile, genuine. But good gravy, wasn't the Klaus enough?

"We can do this another day," Caleb offered.

"Right now is perfect," Holly insisted. "I want it done. I need to see it finished. I definitely don't think it's Wilhelm Klaus Film Festival–worthy, but it's a start."

Caleb showed her everything. Better yet, he was patient. They loaded everything into iMovie, started building a timeline, pieced everything together, clip by clip. They added sound, royalty-free public-domain music, motion graphics, overlays. They finished around ten o'clock, and truthfully? Holly would have gladly worked through the night and into morning on this. She. Had. A. Blast. Felt high as a kite. It was awesome.

"I can't believe we produced a film at my kitchen table using laptops and a soundtrack we downloaded from the internet." Holly refreshed their decaf coffees. "If it's this easy to produce a short film, I *should* get back into it."

Shoot, if Holly could figure out how to do this on her own, maybe she could start a small business. Call Pinterest moms like Collette and convince them to hire her to film their craft and decorating videos. If Jack got laid off, it would help them pay some bills. Hopefully stay in Primm.

Holly wasn't sure what she'd expected when she started filming thirty hours ago . . . but this was what she'd ended up with now that it was finished. Her amateur, scratch attempt to reconnect with who she once was and who she hoped to become—a filmmaker.

~

The film opened with Holly's hands clutching the Buick's steering wheel as she cruised through Primm—past the road that led to Southern Lakes, past shops, past countless topiaries across town. The camera had caught all sorts of things. Bree-with-an-E's face covered in bright-pink polka dots. Shanequa, at Primm's Coffee Joe, exchanging phone numbers, inviting her to scrapbook. The G-Class visitor in the hallway outside the Topiary Park boardroom, arguing with the horticulturist. The *Little Kids, Little Zoo* play. The camera had caught the metal rooster filling the screen as Holly screamed "Ahhhhhhhh!" and charged an intruder during a home invasion. It had caught poignant moments like her text exchange with Jack when he announced he might be losing his job. And Plume, the moment Holly first laid eyes on her and witnessed the devastation. The camera had captured the horticulturist speaking to Holly: "Horticulturists far and wide have dedicated years of their lives tending to the upkeep of this peacock, and then whoooooooosh—a flying yellow bug from Asia shows up." And from the horticulturist, an ominous warning: "Something is causing the bugs to travel across the village."

As Holly watched her life unfold on film, she choked up. This montage of seemingly unrelated parts, when lined up, told a compelling story of her life during Ella's first week of kindergarten. Holly wasn't sure what she thought of it. It was a lot to take in.

Cut to Holly telling the Pic Committee, "I don't have a mommy blog. Or a gazillion followers on Twitter. I guess I'm not an influential mom." Cut to Sidekick Sweaty smelling her armpits during the meeting with Miss Bently. Cut to Ella beneath those ginormous black poster-board glasses.

There was plenty of footage of Mary-Margaret being Mary-Margaret, and it would have been perfect if the film stopped with a clip of her mouth held wide open, film credits and words rolling between her lips and into her mouth, across her tongue, and toward the wad of pink bubble gum at the back like the opening crawl of *Star Wars*: *A long time ago in a village far, far away* . . . but it didn't. It ended with two bonus blooper scenes, and those, Holly loved.

One of the blooper clips was a montage of Greta's ukulele concerts on YouTube. Holly remembered how strange it felt to be recording video of a video on a video channel. Now she was watching a video of a video of a video on a video channel, the sound in the blooper montage a mix of ukulele playing from Greta's YouTube concerts. Greta, the true dancing queen, apparently believed a good concert should feature her spinning around while playing, wearing a flowery dress and daisies tucked throughout her curly gray hair. Despite her age and hardships, Greta was wild and free and everything Holly hoped to be. The final clip of the blooper montage was Greta skipping around a meadow of wildflowers, just a-strummin' away. *You go, girl.* Holly had gone to film school—but Greta had made her first indie film before Holly did. *Well, would ya lookee there. That mom of mine is something else.*

The final scene of the entire film was a still shot of Greta—stuck in downward dog with no clothes on except her underwear. You could see a hint of what should be covered by a shirt, and if not a shirt, then at least a sports bra. It was first and foremost a butt scene, so Caleb and Holly added the words THE END in big bold letters across her butt cheeks.

And that was pretty much it. Holly's first film post–film school. She wasn't sure it would win the Wilhelm Klaus Film Festival, but for Holly? She was satisfied. Very satisfied. *Immensely* satisfied. Time to open that Gevrey-Chambertin and toast the three-letter word she'd been chasing for years: *fin*.

But there was one problem.

"Wait. What are you doing with the camera and mic?" asked Holly, watching Caleb collect what belonged to him. He packed everything up, then tucked it neatly into the side pocket of his cargo pants.

"I need it for another project," he said.

And just like that, Holly's access Hollywood—gone.

But I was using that, Holly wanted to say. "Oh, sure, sure. I understand," she said instead, trying her best to act chill. She needed that equipment. To entrap the Pink Witch, expose My Love, and save the Village of Primm and Plume from ruin. Then again, it was more than that; it was personal. *I need it to save my family.* Dreams of saving the day, dreams of winning prize money at the Wilhelm Klaus—*poof!*—shoved into the pocket of some dude's cargo pants. *Now what am I going to do?*

Holly followed Caleb to the front door. Caleb pausing at the threshold of her living room. "New curtains?" he asked.

And with a deep breath and a long, slow exhale, Holly said, "You might say that."

38

Late Thursday night

With Holly's lifeline in his pocket, Caleb left, so Holly and Greta started the pies, mixing the crust with their bare hands. The plan was for each of them to make seven pies. Thirteen to go to the Cherry Festival and one to eat at home now that Ella claimed she liked pie. They had to stand to make the piecrusts, using all their strength and arm muscles to dig in and knead each dough ball into submission.

"This is really hard," Holly whined. "Feels like every muscle in my hands is on fire." She had dough between her fingers, dough all over the counter, dough all over the floor. Greta was no different. They were up to their elbows in piecrust.

Just as they were finishing the fourteenth piecrust, Holly pleaded with Greta, "Let's stop. My hands are killing me. We can straighten up and get a few hours of sleep. I'll get Ella on the school bus tomorrow morning, and then we can crank this out. It'll be fine. We can bake them two at a time."

"We might be able to fit four." Greta opened Holly's oven to have a look. "Actually, that might be tight." The house in Southern Lakes had a double oven. *Dang it!*

They cleaned up, washed up, then headed for bed.

But first, Holly logged onto her computer, hoping Psychic Betty was awake.

~

EMAIL—Time Sent: 11:49 p.m.

TO: Psychic Betty, Psychic Hotline Network
FROM: Holly Banks
SUBJECT: Is Mercury a Bully?

What did I (me, Holly Banks) do to offend Mercury? Because a lot of what you said has come true. I've had transportation issues, problems communicating, feelings I'm being sabotaged. But I live in the Village of Primm and Primm is like, really far away from Mercury. I looked it up. Depending on the planets' orbits around the Sun, at any given time, Mercury can be anywhere from 48 to 130 million miles away from Earth. Shouldn't Mercury be more concerned with what's happening on the Sun? The Sun is only 28 to 43 million miles away from Mercury. Much closer than Earth. So what gives? Why pick on Earth? Is Mercury a bully?

I did learn that one day on Mercury is like 59 days on Earth. Lately, my days have seemed long and challenging. I sometimes wonder what planet I'm living on. Earth? Or Mercury?

Your friend,
Holly Banks

P.S. I made a film tonight. It felt good. Really good. Made me feel alive and excited and filled with possibility. Made me feel I found something I'd lost while being Jack's wife and Ella's mom. A set of keys to a unique treasure. Something I locked away. Set aside. Said, "I'll get back to that when I'm done being a mom." Me. Holly Banks! I made a film. Psychic Betty, I feel so overwhelmed. Why did I quiet that side of myself? Why did I ever tell myself it was something that could be postponed—until Ella was grown and my job as her mother complete? Because without my art—I'M not complete. I love film. I love creating. When I was doing it, it felt like my soul swelled—way beyond the limits of my body. Beyond my bones. Beyond my skin. I was everywhere—all at once. I was sky. I was ocean. Earth. Mercury. Psychic Betty, I was the SUN! Fully connected. Centered. Happy. I'm so glad I found you, Psychic Betty. You're my best friend.

~

EMAIL—Time Sent: 11:52 p.m.

TO: Psychic Betty, Psychic Hotline Network
FROM: Holly Banks
SUBJECT: Whoops! Hit "send" too soon.

By "best friend" I mean—I appreciate you. That wasn't creepy, was it? Telling you you're my best friend? Because I want you to know—I have lots of friends. Tons of friends back home. My mom.

(When she's not driving me crazy.) Jack. (When he's not driving me crazy.) And there's a few moms I've met in the village that might make great friends. One step at a time. I'm still getting my feet wet.

Say, I've been thinking. Maybe if I started paying attention to myself, you know, take my interests in film more seriously, I'll feel better about Ella starting kindergarten. I felt so good making that film—like I had the gift all along—like Dorothy's red ruby slippers in the Wizard of Oz. There's no place like home.

How are you, Psychic Betty? You good?

~

EMAIL—Time Received: 12:12 a.m.

TO: Holly Banks
FROM: Psychic Betty, Psychic Hotline Network
SUBJECT: Your Location in the Solar System

You live on Earth. At least, I think you do. (The way you've been talking, I'm not so sure.)

Your questions about Mercury are valid. Maybe Mercury is a bit of a bully. But Mercury doesn't mean to be. Sometimes, it can't help itself. Mercury retrogrades. You can't blame it for retrograding—it's Mercury. That's what Mercury does. The question becomes: How are you going to handle yourself when Mercury retrogrades?

And by the way, have you stopped to consider Mercury's feelings? Maybe having an orbit that—when viewed from Earth—makes it appear as if it stops, and then travels backward for a while, makes Mercury feel like everyone else thinks MERCURY is crazy. Maybe Mercury is crazy; I don't know. Maybe Mercury is a bully; I don't know. But maybe, just maybe, Mercury means well but is misunderstood. Maybe Mercury feels like an outsider.

Holly, may I ask? Who is Mercury? I sense it's someone in your life. Someone you're having trouble getting along with. Someone you're trying hard to understand, but that understanding is eluding you. Mercury isn't traveling backward in the night sky when it retrogrades. It only appears that way. Mercury's doing the same thing Earth is: orbiting the Sun.

And I thought your saying I was your best friend was nice. It wasn't creepy at all. It brought a smile to my face, and I thank you for that, Holly Banks. A relationship with a psychic adviser should feel special. But I encourage you to look for friendships with people in your "real" life, in addition to your "online" life. I suspect there are many women just like you seeking friendship. My advice? After you've "broken the ice" by discussing your children, focus the conversation on each other. Discover who you each are, outside of your roles as wife and mother. It's at that deeper level where you'll find true friendship.

You mentioned living in the Village of Primm. I'm so sorry to hear about Plume. She was a lovely peahen and an inspiration to so many. Have you heard what's been happening at Dizzy's? Piles and piles of pickled beets and alfalfa sprouts were just added to the salad bar. All you can eat. Now THAT'S something to celebrate! Although, I don't understand chickpeas on salad. But I do like hummus!

Psychic Betty

P.S. Why did the pescatarian go deep-sea fishing? No reason. She went for the halibut.

Click HERE to ask another question.

Click HERE to answer our "What is your favorite salad topping?" survey.

Click HERE for directions to Dizzy's Seafood.

~

EMAIL—Time Sent: 12:15 a.m.

TO: Psychic Betty, Psychic Hotline Network
FROM: Holly Banks
SUBJECT: Wait. Where is YOUR location in the Solar System?!?!?!?!?!?!!

I clicked on the link for directions to Dizzy's Seafood, but nothing came up. The link must be broken. How do you know about Plume?! Do you live in Primm? No. Let me guess. You live in Southern Lakes. You do, don't you? How is life in Southern Lakes? Is it normal? The way it should be? I bet it's wonderful.

Mind if I ask? Do you have crabgrass?

39

Friday, fourth day of kindergarten

The alarm rang. Six thirty.

"Ella, sweetie, wake up." Holly kissed Ella's cheeks. "It's Friday. Our first week of kindergarten almost complete." Ella looked so cozy beneath the sheets. Holly couldn't help herself. She climbed under the covers and snuggled in. "We need to get up, Ella-Bella Cinderella. Let's get you to school." Holly yawned. It was so warm beneath the covers, and Ella's body was so soft and tiny, and she smelled like kid shampoo. Holly rolled over to snuggle Ella into her arms, and before she knew it . . .

"Holly Tree! Ella!" Greta shook them awake. "The bus'll be here in ten minutes."

"What?" Holly sprang up, realizing she fell asleep in Ella's bed. "How'd this happen?"

"I'll get her backpack." Greta rushed downstairs.

Holly threw back the covers, swooped Ella into her arms, and ran with her into the bathroom.

Jack was shaving. "Oh, no. Not again."

"Why didn't you wake us up?"

"I thought you were downstairs." He snatched his watch off the counter. "Oh, no. *No*—Holly. Bus'll be here in ten minutes." Jack did that "Jack" thing.

"I know, I know." Holly set Ella down, wet a washcloth, and wiped her face. Poor kid still had her eyes closed, and her hair was absolutely wild from a night of tossing and turning. Lumped up in the back. Tangled. Looked like she hadn't bathed in weeks, like she was starting dreadlocks—in kindergarten. "Jack. Where's Struggle?"

"Backyard."

"We've got to make that bus, Jack. We can't blow through the entire first week of kindergarten missing the bus."

"She rode it yesterday."

"My mom did that. You and I didn't do that." Holly made eye contact with Jack. "I want her on that bus. We have to get her on that bus."

"Okay," he said. "Laser focus. Let's do this!" He clapped like he was in a locker room. "What should I do?"

"Get me an outfit."

Holly squeezed bubble gum–flavored toothpaste onto Ella's *My Little Pony* toothbrush. "Open up, sweetie. Open up for Mommy. We're going to catch that bus. We're going. To catch. That. Bus."

Ella was so groggy she had trouble keeping her head straight. Holly placed her hand at the back of Ella's neck for support so she could get the toothbrush inside her mouth, but Ella's head kept swinging to the side. "You can do this, baby girl. Wake up, sweetie. Wake up."

Jack returned with a pair of Holly's jeans and a T-shirt.

"What's this?" Holly asked.

"You said to get you an outfit."

"Not me." *You idiot.* "Ella. Get Ella an outfit!"

"Crap! Okay."

Ella's eyes sprang open. Her head lifted from Holly's hand, and she turned to stare at Jack, mouth hung open. "Dad." Ella furrowed her brow. "You said a bad word."

"That's not a bad word, Ella," Jack rushed to explain. "I mean, it is. I guess. Sort of. Because *you* can't say it. You're too young. But some people think that particular word is okay to use—you see, Ella. Um. It's hard to explain . . ." He scratched his head. "It's like this. There are different types of bad words. Like *hell*, for instance. It's the name of a place. It's in the Bible." His eyes pleaded with Holly, but Holly wasn't helping. She let him squirm. "But don't say that word, Ella. Even if Jesus said it—and I'm not saying Jesus did. He may have; I don't know. But you can't. Because you're not Jesus. Holly?"

"Oh, for criminy's sake, who gives a split, Jack? We have a bus to catch." Holly waved him off, saving his ass from the wrath of Ella. "Get me an outfit!"

Off he ran.

"Ella. Spit."

Ella spat. Holly grabbed a washcloth. Wiped her mouth. Wiped her face.

Now, Holly had wanted to help the guy out, she had. The thing was, Holly didn't have time to explain to Ella the nuances between curse words, cuss words, swear words, profane words, obscene words, and vulgar words. Because they were all slightly different, and sometimes—well, they slipped out. Nonetheless, after that thesaurus assignment, Holly had grown even more impressed with the power words possessed. *If there's a way to play with language and avoid using actual "bad" words—while still harnessing their power—then sign me up. Can't say I'll be perfect all the time. But I'll give it a shot.* "I love you, Ella." She touched the tip of Ella's nose. "Know this: *hate* is a bad word. It's worse than all the others."

Jack returned with a pair of purple-and-orange plaid leggings and a worn-out pink dress with a banana-eating monkey on it.

"Seriously? That doesn't even remotely match," Holly told him.

"What are you talking about? Ella loves this outfit." He pulled her pajama top off while Holly slid her bottoms down.

"It's fine," Holly said. "Just get her dressed. Wait. Jack. We need shoes—for *Ella*."

Jack ran off again, shaving cream on half his face, and to Holly's horror, he came back with a pair of red boots. "Noooo, Jack. That's a crazy outfit." Holly was so overwhelmed. "Pink monkey dress? Purple-and-orange leggings? Red boots?"

Ella brightened. "I'll look like Dora the Explorer!"

"Grab your backpack," Holly said. "Let's go!"

"Vámanos!" Ella squealed, as Holly swung Ella into her arms and raced with her to the foot of the stairs, where Holly saw Ella's actual backpack and a packed lunch bag leaning against the front door. Charlotte was curled up beside the backpack. She lifted her head to hiss at Holly but saw Ella in Holly's arms and stopped mid-hiss to instead swing her tail in a show of pleasure at the sight of Ella. *So Charlotte likes Ella?* Maternal instincts, Holly supposed.

"Mom?" Holly hollered. Where was she? Was she in the kitchen?

Charlotte slunk away, and Holly found a banana and a bag of crackers on the top of the backpack. "Ella, breakfast." Holly handed Ella the banana and crackers. "You can eat them on the bus. Now listen to me. We have to run."

Holly opened their front door, heard the bus—heard brakes being applied, a loud whoosh!—and Bus 13 came to a stop, its doors opened wide at the end of their driveway. Holly found that so odd. Odder still, the bus wasn't moving. It idled in front of their house. "Mom?" Holly yelled over her shoulder toward the kitchen. "Where are you?" For some reason Holly couldn't explain, she wanted Greta to see this. Wanted Greta to watch her put her child on a bus to kindergarten. It felt important. It felt . . . Holly didn't know . . . full circle. Something. Where was she? "Mom!" *Where are you?* "Let's go, Ella. You and me? We're going to catch that bus."

Holly took Ella's hand, her backpack, and her lunch, and then shuffled her quickly down the steps and across the front lawn. Miraculously,

Bus 13 sat patiently waiting at the end of their driveway. Holly couldn't believe her good fortune. Why was he being so nice to her this morning? It almost felt like cheating.

Holly kissed Ella. Stuffed her lunch bag into her backpack, zipped it, and then hoisted Ella's backpack onto Ella's shoulders. "I love you, sweetie. Go get 'em." Holly hustled Ella onto the bus steps, and then up Ella went, hardly awake, and without time to file a complaint or protest the fact she didn't want to go to school in the first place. "Have a great day at school!" Holly said, feeling like a mom in a Mary Blair illustration.

"I did it," Holly whispered. Placing her hands flat against her cheeks. *I freaking did it! Ella's on the bus. Unfreakingbelievable.* How many more times would they have to do this before kindergarten was over? 176? *See Jane? See Jane master motherhood?*

Holly thanked the driver, wondering if she should say something about the fender bender, but he didn't seem interested in Holly at all. Instead, his eyes were fixed squarely on the road ahead, as if he saw a dead animal and was contemplating rolling over it or driving around it. Holly watched as Ella walked down the aisle and took a seat next to a little girl who was wearing a headband. The bus door closed, but the bus wasn't moving. Was everything okay?

"Is she on?" Holly heard Greta say.

"Mom? Where are you?" Holly walked toward Greta's voice, toward the front of the bus. "Mom?"

Lo and behold, smack in the middle of Petunia Lane stood Sidekick Sweaty. Both arms stretched in front of her, the grille of the bus mere inches from the palms of her hands.

"Mom! What are you doing?"

"I'm catching the bus," she said, her curly gray hair made wilder from a night of sleep. "What does it look like I'm doing?"

Holly pulled Greta by the sleeve of her pajamas onto the grass.

Toot! Toot! Bus 13 pulled away, taking Holly's sweet little Ella with it. As it headed up Petunia Lane, Holly pointed to the dented fender and streak of red paint from her Suburban Godzilla. "See that, Mom? I did that. Me." It looked like a bite mark.

"You did? Well, I'm proud of you, Holly Tree," said Greta. "You left your mark. Way to show this world you were in it."

Greta smiled at Holly. A toothy smile, the kind that spread the cheeks and crinkled the eyes.

"What is it?" Greta asked, as the expression on Holly's face fell.

"I forgot to brush Ella's hair." *Dang it.*

40

Still Friday

With Ella on the bus, Greta and Holly grabbed coffee, then sat at the kitchen table with Anna Wintour to begin pitting cherries. Jack came downstairs, witnessed the fiasco that was already underway, then announced he'd get breakfast on the way to work.

From her chair, Holly leaned her head back to kiss him. "Jack?" said Holly. "Greta's moving in with us."

"No she's not," he said.

"See? Point-blank refusal," said Holly to Greta. "What'd I tell you?"

"Then consider it a long 'visit,'" offered Greta.

"Good luck today," Holly said to Jack, knowing he headed into a tough day at work.

"You too," he said. Then to Greta: "Six weeks and not a day more. And that cat of yours better not have kittens under my sofa. Speaking of sofa, did we get new curtains?" And with that, out the door he went. Probably picking up his usual: coffee black with a corn muffin. Funny, Holly was no longer concerned about Bethanny. If Bethanny learned Holly's husband liked his coffee black with a corn muffin, so be it. Holly wasn't jumping to conclusions based on that.

An hour or two passed, and they were still pitting cherries. "This is killing me," Holly told Greta, stopping to rub some of the stains out of her fingers. Holly couldn't find cherry pitters at the grocery store, so they were using paring knives to cut a slice around the cherries, then using their fingernails to pry the cherries open to extract the pits. "This is unbelievably messy." Holly had cherry juice on her lap, on her hands, up her arms. "This has to be the messiest, most labor-intensive pie ever created. Why couldn't these be apple pies?"

"Apple pies are too easy for this town," Greta said. "If it was easy—it wouldn't be Primm."

They pressed on and, just before lunch, finished pitting what felt like two thousand cherries. "Okay," Holly said, "let's get the cherries off the kitchen table so we can start rolling the piecrusts. After that, we'll dump everything onto the bottom crusts and start on the latticework for the top."

"Latticework," Greta stated.

"Latticework is pretty. They have to sell at auction."

"Holly." Greta held a hand up to stop Holly. "We're never going to be finished by five o'clock. What happens if we're not finished by then?"

"That's not an option."

"What would you say if I told you I have a backup plan?"

"Not interested," Holly told Greta. "Stay focused. You clean the table, and I'll get the piecrusts."

Hours later, enough pie filling for fourteen pies was made, and the bottom layer of crust was rolled out and pressed into the bottoms of fourteen glass pie plates. Holly had found the glass pie plates at a dollar store in Southern Lakes and had decided to splurge, thinking it might class up her pies for the auction.

"Okay. Let's spoon the pie filling in."

"Let's skip the latticework," Greta said. "Please. I'm begging you. We're already past the deadline."

"Stay focused! I won't hear talk of defeat. We're too close."

They preheated the oven, fired up YouTube to watch a few cherry pie–latticework tutorials, then set out to construct the latticework piecrusts—Holly with a burning desire to achieve celebrity status among the Pie Moms by turning out perfectly Primm pies.

"Move fast, but take your time," Holly told Greta. "The latticework is what'll sell the pies. It's gotta look good."

"Move fast, but take my time," Greta mumbled. "Right." She gave a cherry-stained thumbs-up.

Working side by side, Holly and Greta finished weaving latticework across four pies and then took a pastry brush and painted the lattice with a mixture of raw eggs and melted butter. Next, they sprinkled brown sugar and a little bit of cinnamon, nutmeg, and allspice across the tops of the pies. Ella had been home for almost two hours already, and it was after five o'clock—the final, final last minute for dropping pies off in the Primm Academy cafeteria.

"So they're late. Doesn't matter. I'm sure they'll still take them," Holly told Greta. "Just pop these four in the oven so we can finish the latticework on the other ten. Cram as many in as you can, and let's start baking."

"This is never going to work," Greta said. "They're never going to fit."

"Cram them in."

"But it's almost six," Greta said. "Each pie has to bake for an hour, and then they have to cool."

"Mom." Now Holly was really frustrated. "Stop talking."

"Holly, this is crazy. At best, you'll get four pies to the school by six thirty. What if the Pie Committee's not there anymore? It's Friday." Greta pointed to the clock. "The school will be closed by then. Let's stop. Let's move to plan B."

"Plan B is not an option. Cram them in. Four at a time."

Greta tried, but they weren't fitting.

"Fine," Holly said. "Move over, Mom. I'll cram them in." *I can't stop now. I'm so close.*

Holly managed to squeeze four pies into the oven, placing them diagonally on the racks. She set the timer for fifty minutes. At this rate, she should have all the pies finished by midnight. Maybe she could drive them over to Emily's house then and leave them on her porch.

"Holly," Greta started up again.

"Mom, stop." Holly held her hand up to stop Greta from talking. "I don't want to hear about your backup plan. This is fine. They'll be late, but it's fine. The festival isn't until tomorrow, and I'm sure the Pie Committee will still accept them even if they're a few hours late."

"Okay . . . ," Greta said, her voice trailing off.

It angered Holly that Greta was challenging her. Holly was a grown woman. This was her project, and she didn't need a plan B. She was late; that was all. No biggie.

~

Eventually, the timer went off on the first set of pies. Holly opened the oven, and the smell of glory and fresh-baked pies filled her home. *Welcome to Primm,* thought Holly. *I've arrived. I've arrived!*

Holly placed each pie carefully on a cooling rack. Perfection.

They popped four more into the oven while the others cooled.

"Pie baking is almost fun," Holly told Greta, as they clinked their coffee cups together. "If it wasn't so dang stressful."

Greta gave Holly a fist pump. "I'm proud of you, Holly. This is a huge accomplishment."

"Should we taste one?" Holly suggested. "We made an extra . . ." Holly picked a pie. Carried it over to the table.

Greta clenched a fork in her fist, anticipating her first bite.

"I almost don't want to wreck it," Holly said, letting her knife hover above the pie. "It looks so pretty."

Greta agreed. "It's flawless. Picture perfect."

"No." Holly gazed upon the glorious pie they'd created. "It's Primm!"

Holly cut a slice, laid it on Greta's plate. Holly cut another slice and laid it on her plate. Then Holly grabbed a fork and broke off a piece of pie. Before taking a bite, they marveled at what they saw: cherries plump and fresh. The consistency of the filling like something out of a magazine. It held up beautifully and spilled the right amount onto the plate. "Smells amazing. Looks so good."

"Like a work of art," said Greta.

"Well?" Holly smiled. "Are you ready? Shall we taste it?"

They clinked their forks like champagne glasses and then slid the first bites of pie into their mouths.

What the—? The taste. It sort of . . . stung on Holly's tongue. And then. Holly couldn't describe it. She looked at Greta. Greta's eyes, once closed, snapped open the moment she tasted the pie. Greta bent over and spat everything in her mouth onto her plate. Holly did the same. A second later, they were choking. *Pah! Pah! Pah! Blech.*

"What the criminy was that?" Holly cried, eyes welling with tears.

Greta dragged a napkin across her tongue.

Holly snatched coffee. Glug, glug, glug—desperate to rid her tongue of that horrid taste. "What was that? What happened?" *What's wrong with my pies?* The taste was horrendous. Holly felt it in her nose. Greta rubbed her eyes—she couldn't stop.

And then Holly realized . . .

Holly took hold of Greta's wrist, holding Greta's hand in front of Greta's face.

"Ella's no-bite fingernail polish. Mom," Holly said. "It's everywhere. We kneaded it into the dough. We spread the cherries apart with our fingernails to pit them." Holly wanted to cry, scream, she didn't know. "Mom. What am I going to do?" Pies covered every single surface of her kitchen, but none of them—not a single one—was edible. "The Cherry Festival is in the morning. I can't bake another thirteen pies."

Greta busied herself unfolding napkins to cover their pie slices. Like it hurt her to look at them, like she was holding a funeral, encasing the pies in a napkin burial cloth.

"How am I going to face Emily?"

"Stop worrying, Holly." Greta opened countless napkins like she planned to cover every single pie in the kitchen. As the napkins hit the cherry filling, red juice stained the white paper. Like blood. Like Holly's pies were the scene of a murder. After all that. After all that Holly'd been through. Holly wasn't a Pie Mom. Holly was a Napkin Mom.

"Mom, stop with the napkins. You're killing me."

"Relax, Holly Tree. I told you I had a plan."

"What. Quit? Drop out of Primm Academy? Sell the house? Move to Southern Lakes?"

"When you were at the eye doctor with Ella, I went on Google and found a bakery. Placed an order for thirteen ready-made cherry pies. They've been ready since twelve."

"Bakery? What bakery? Where?" On second thought, Holly held her hand up. Stopped Greta from telling her what she already knew. "You know what? Don't tell me. I know where it is. But why didn't you tell me you ordered pies?"

"I tried—but you wouldn't listen." Greta tugged on Holly's earlobe. "And besides, for a while there, it looked like we might pull it off."

"We almost did, didn't we?" Holly surveyed the kitchen. Their mess, their project, their win, their defeat. "I admit I fell in love with the *idea* of baking pies. You know those retro-looking advertisements of a 1950s mom pulling a warm pie from the oven for her smiling, expectant family? I wanted that," Holly confessed. "I wanted what that represented: a perfect, ideal motherhood."

"But that's not real," Greta said. "You're a great mom, Holly. You were trying to help Ella break her thumb-sucking habit in a supportive way." Greta squeezed Holly's fingers, held one of her hands up to inspect the no-bite polish residue on Holly's nails. "If pies represent motherhood, then I'd say you're the best mom in town. You baked the love you feel for your daughter into each and every one of those pies."

Holly pulled Greta close. Hugged her. Squeezed hard. "This 'mom' thing is so hard, and I've had the worst week ever. I'm sorry, Mom. I'm sorry I judged you so harshly. I shouldn't have done that. I was wrong."

"Wrong?" said Greta, still tucked inside their hug. "Never mind that. Something's wrong with Anna."

"What do you mean?" Holly pulled herself from their embrace to look at Anna. "Oh, no!" Holly covered her mouth. *Poor Anna. Our beloved Anna Wintour.* Holly didn't know how she'd missed it, but Anna was crawling with bugs. It was so bad you'd think the editor in chief of *Vogue* magazine had head lice.

"Mom. What am I going to do? Now I have to kill Anna Wintour. Torch her. Burn her at the stake." The thought was almost more than Holly could bear. "Ella's tooth is in there."

41

Friday night

Greta stayed home with Ella while Holly drove to the bakery to pick up the pies. It was dark out, so dark Holly couldn't see the toy clutter on the Southern Lakes lawns and could barely make out the pink flamingo lawn ornaments as she drove through town. When the sun wasn't shining on the other side of the fence, Southern Lakes looked a lot like the Village of Primm.

Jack called. "Leaving work now. Repair shop said your Suburban is ready. We can pick it up tomorrow. Where are you?"

"Headed to a bakery in Southern Lakes before they close. Picking up pies."

It was quiet on the other end until Holly heard a chuckle from Jack as he pieced it together. "Well, at least you tried."

"Anna Wintour's on the front porch. *Covered* in bugs." It hurt just saying it. "Hey, Jack, can we switch cars? I don't want to deliver pies for a school auction in a smelly rental."

"Sure. Leaving now. But what do you want to do with Anna Wintour? Burn her to death and then bury her in a ditch?"

"Stop. Don't talk like that. It's sad, Jack. But yes, we probably should. But I don't want Ella knowing her parents burned Anna to death. When you get home, put her in a trash bag. There's a burning at the Topiary Park tonight." So sad. It was horrible just thinking about it. "Meet me at the bakery? It's on Main in Southern Lakes."

~

The Southern Lakes Bakery was a freestanding one-story building with bright-green awnings and a bright-white door. Holly parked in front of its left window, beside a patch of grass and a fence lit by a superbright light so strong it lit up most of the parking lot.

For a bakery that was closing at eight, it was a bit crowded. Holly told the girl behind the counter she was there to pick up thirteen pies, and the girl returned with fourteen, packed in plain white bakery boxes. When the girl winked, telling Holly she'd left the gold Southern Lakes Bakery sticker off the top of the boxes so no one would know the pies were store bought, Holly felt bad telling her she'd only ordered thirteen. At the cost of $22 per nine-inch pie, Holly was about to fork over $286—never mind the cost of ingredients for the fourteen pies she screwed up in her kitchen. She couldn't afford to buy the fourteenth pie for her family to enjoy. There was no more room on the credit card.

"There must be some mistake," Holly told the girl behind the counter. "I'm pretty sure my mom said she ordered thirteen."

"Actually," Holly heard a voice behind her say, "that's my cherry pie. The extra pie is mine. I ordered it."

Holly turned, and—

No. Flipping. Way. It was Mary-Margaret St. James, still wearing an apron, fingers stained cherry red, hair an absolute mess with small chunks of pastry clumped throughout. She looked utterly defeated—like she'd just walked through a tornado.

"It's like you said." Mary-Margaret shrugged, her voice so small Holly could barely hear it. "I suck at baking."

"You suck at a lot of things, Mary-Margaret," Holly said gently, touching Mary-Margaret's arm. "But it's okay. We all do." Holly tipped her chin toward the pies. "Your secret's safe with me."

"Me too." Mary-Margaret twisted her fingers in front of her mouth. "My lips are sealed."

They paid for their pies, and because Holly had so much to carry, Mary-Margaret offered to help her load her pies into her car.

Holly had wanted to transport them in Jack's car, but Jack hadn't arrived yet.

"I'll take it from here," Holly told Mary-Margaret once they'd reached Holly's Buick and had set the pie boxes on the pavement near the back tire. They were both late getting their pies to Emily. "But thank you."

Afraid the cat hair from the back seat would cling to the pie boxes, Holly decided the trunk of the Buick was the best option for transport. She'd call Jack in a few minutes. He probably got held up.

Holly stabbed the trunk key into the keyhole, popped the trunk, and up from the trunk—flew thousands and thousands of tiny yellow insects. CHILLI THRIPS.

"*Aaaaaahhh!*" they screamed, frantically swatting the insects from their arms. They were everywhere. Tiny and yellow—almost transparent. Awful flying insects, crawling the walls of the trunk, weaving their way up and around the interiors until at last, they took flight and filled the airspace around the Buick—a buzzing, terrifying cloud of wings, legs, and exoskeletons. Like something out of a Hitchcock movie. Like the fog in Dickens's *Bleak House*. Chilli thrips everywhere. Chilli thrips up the trunk wall, where they flowed among red metal and black carbon parts; chilli thrips down the trunk wall, where they rolled on top of each other, unencumbered except for an open cardboard shipping box inside a great and dirty trunk. Chilli thrips on the rear taillights, chilli thrips on the Buick logo. Chilli thrips creeping into their clothing; chilli thrips flying out across their arms and hovering about their ears;

chilli thrips dropping off the fender and onto the pie boxes. Chilli thrips everywhere, as if forming a balloon, hanging as a cloud all around them. And at the very heart of the chilli thrips? Evidence of Michael St. James, Lord of Insurance Fraud, Killer of Plume—his name and signature on a delivery slip from China. The ferroequinologist who'd rented this car to Holly had mentioned a man of Panamanian descent with business dealings in China. Maybe that Panamanian man worked for My Love.

After most of the chilli thrips had taken flight to smother the skies above Southern Lakes, Holly reached into the trunk to retrieve the invoice and handed it to Mary-Margaret. Both of their hands were stained with cherry juice. Their boxes of cherry pies, ordered in secret, lay about their feet.

"What?" Mary-Margaret blinked, as she steadied herself to read the invoice. "Michael? Michael, my love?" She seemed small, lowercased. Weakened, diminished. Something.

"Your husband must have ordered the killing of Plume," Holly told Mary-Margaret, searching her eyes for any semblance of understanding. "Your *husband*, Mary-Margaret, your love. He did this." *Didn't she know? Yesterday—at the pie meeting on The Lawn when she was trying to grab Darth out of my hands—she knew something. Or at least suspected something. Didn't she?* Holly shook her head. *Maybe she's in shock.*

"But why would he want to kill Plume? Plume is the town mascot. Plume is loved by all." Mary-Margaret kept blinking. Why was she blinking? Was she trying to unsee what had been seen? Was she trying to stop the tears from falling? Because it wasn't working. Tears wet Mary-Margaret's soft pink cheeks. "But. Plume is beautiful. Plume is perfect. Plume makes the Topiary Park the Topiary Park. Without Plume, it's just a garden. Why would he do this? Doesn't he love her?"

"I don't know." Holly reached out to brush a chilli thrip from Mary-Margaret's lip.

"Shouldn't he at least *appreciate* Plume? Plume never did anything to hurt him. Plume wouldn't hurt anybody."

"Are you sure?"

"What?"

"Nothing." Holly picked a chilli thrip from her ear.

"Maybe Plume was too Plume. Maybe Plume plumed too much." Mary-Margaret's voice was barely audible. It dropped to almost a whisper. "But Plume shouldn't have to die for being Plume, should she? Since when does being perfect warrant death? Why would someone want to kill perfection?"

"I don't know," Holly assured her. "Plume was just doing what plumes do. They plume." *What in the hell-o kitty are we talking about?*

And then Holly saw him: Jack. Car blinker signaling a right turn into the bakery parking lot. He waved as he pulled into a parking space about fifty feet away.

"Mary-Margaret." Holly spoke quickly, grabbing her by the arms to peer into her eyes as Holly asked her next question. "Do you know anything about this? Are you behind any of this?"

"What?" Mary-Margaret's voice was high pitched, a bit squeaky. She sounded utterly confused and a bit surprised by what Holly was asking.

So Holly clarified. "My husband has been investigating your husband."

"What? Why?"

"Your husband used my husband's law firm to set up an offshore shell company."

"What?"

"Your husband is laundering money through an offshore shell company. He's committing insurance fraud."

"What?"

Jack turned his engine off, closed his driver's side door, and paused a moment to check his phone.

Holly needed to make a decision. *Fast.* "Mary-Margaret. Did you know about the chilli thrip shipment?"

"No," she whimpered. "At least, I don't think so . . ."

"What? What does that mean? Did you know or didn't you?"

"I don't know what I know," Mary-Margaret whined, her exasperation with the matter made quite clear. "I thought I overheard something about a block of ABBA memorabilia, but he never tells me anything. And the chilli thrips? I suspected there was something shady going on, but whenever I asked, he always had the perfect excuse. He's on the board of directors for the Topiary Park. I figured that's how he knew about them. But—"

"But what?"

Mary-Margaret assumed a defensive posture, folding both arms across her chest—presumably in an attempt to put a barrier between herself and what she was about to say. She confessed in a hushed whisper, "I knew the pace of our spending outpaced his income, but I also knew I needed an addition built on the house for a mudroom." Her eyes, doe-like and submissive, blinked at Holly. "So when I asked if we had the money to build the addition, he said yes, of course, he'd take care of it. And when I asked how, he said don't worry about it. So I reached out to our architect and had the plans drawn up. But Holly," Mary-Margaret added, an earnest look on her face, "I love Plume. I do. I would never want something like this to happen to her."

"So let me get this straight," said Holly, hands signaling a time-out. "You weren't a part of any of this, but you knew something weird was going on, but you didn't ask questions—because you wanted a *mudroom*?"

"Oh, no, no, no. That's not it at all. I didn't *want* a mudroom. I *needed* a mudroom."

Holly, stunned. Jack, fast approaching.

"Well, it's not my fault," Mary-Margaret whined. "The homes on Hopscotch Hill are old. They didn't build mudrooms back then, and I needed more room for backpacks. I needed built-ins—like the kind you see in the Pottery Barn catalog. I needed cubbies and brushed nickel hooks for hanging a stylish rain jacket when it rains. You've seen their catalog. Where will I put my boots if I don't have a copper boot tray to hold them? It's not my fault," she said again. "I'm a mom. All moms need a stylish mudroom." She reached out to touch Holly's arm—to connect with her, to see each other, eye to eye. Woman to woman. Mom to mom. "You understand, don't you?"

Jack was twenty feet away. He'd be here any second. He'd see what was left of the chilli thrips in the trunk. He'd see the invoice. He'd know it was My Love—and Mary-Margaret's homelife would be ruined. *What should I do? What should I do?*

When Mary-Margaret placed her hand across her left breast, when she started pointing over and over at her left breast, Holly worried Mary-Margaret knew she'd used *her* left breast to hide a camera these past few days. That Holly had tried to exploit her so she could launch a career in film at the Wilhelm Klaus Film Festival. But instead, Mary-Margaret hung her head and whispered, hand still patting her left breast. "My Love. *My Love!* Had I known—maybe I could have stopped him. Oh, Holly. I feel so betrayed." She spoke softly. "Me, Mary-Margaret St. James, I used to feel *hip, hip!* Now I feel drip, drip. It's true," she said with a sniffle. "I've lost the 'hooray' in my heart." And with that, a single tear from the Pink Witch fell.

Holly slammed the trunk, snatched the invoice from Mary-Margaret's hand, and shoved it into her back pocket. "I'll protect you. But don't say a word, you hear?"

Jack arrived.

"Jack!" Holly said. "Just in time. Do you have Anna Wintour?"

"She's in the trunk."

Mary-Margaret straightened her back, tried reclaiming her composure.

"Mary-Margaret," Holly announced, "this is my husband, Jack."

Mary-Margaret smiled a hesitant, humble smile. Extended her delicate hand to shake his.

"Jack, this is Mary-Margaret St. James, president of the Primm Academy PTA." Holly suspected he already knew who Mary-Margaret was, but he didn't let on. "She's the tireless philanthropist Penelope Pratt was telling us about. Property values in the Village of Primm are strong because Mary-Margaret draws top-notch families to the area. Aren't we enjoying our strong property value? Jack?"

Jack and Mary-Margaret shook hands, regarding each other. Holly wasn't sure why she had said all these nice things about Mary-Margaret after all Mary-Margaret had done to her, but if Holly's family were about to collapse the way Mary-Margaret's family was about to collapse, Holly hoped someone would be around to at least give Holly a dignified exit.

Holly said to Jack, "Aren't you proud that our daughter, Ella, is starting her education at the prestigious Primm Academy?" It had been a rough first week of kindergarten, but Holly needed to give credit where credit was due. "Do you know who makes everything prim at Primm Academy? This woman standing before you: Mary-Margaret St. James."

"I've heard a lot about you," said Jack. "It's so nice to finally meet you."

"It's nice to meet you too," Mary-Margaret said. "Welcome to Primm." To Holly, Mary-Margaret said, "Thank you, Holly. Holly Banks. I really appreciate your kind words." Mary-Margaret lowered her head. Dabbed a tear with her pinkie finger.

"Aw, Mary-Margaret, don't do that." Holly touched Mary-Margaret's arm, giving it a little shake. "It'll be okay."

It was Mary-Margaret's husband who would face charges if and when Holly handed the invoice in her pocket over to Jack, who would certainly hand it over to the authorities. But the emotional toll the death of Plume would take on the Village of Primm would forever be pegged to Mary-Margaret. It wasn't fair, but it would be Mary-Margaret's fall from grace the villagers would remember. Not My Love's.

Mary-Margaret bent to retrieve her pie box from the pavement. Holly had once marveled at Mary-Margaret's perfectly coiffed hair and diamond-studded earlobes. Now, she looked like Holly: completely average in every way. Mary-Margaret was presentable in her pink yoga pants, raspberry T-shirt, and cute white apron but also a bit frumpled at the edges, her hair an afterthought, pulled into a crooked ponytail with escaping stray wisps. Her thin nose, dotted with dried piecrust, showed she was battle worn; she had fought the good fight. Must have had one heck of a wrestle with that cherry pie she attempted to bake back home. But she sucked at baking. Holly was sure Mary-Margaret's kitchen would never be the same. Holly knew hers wouldn't. She was thinking about painting her kitchen walls a cherry red to commemorate the time she had spent baking pies with Greta. Crayola's parakeet blue would look nice with cherry red. A color palette even the almighty Collette hadn't thought of. A color palette that was uniquely Holly's, never done at 12 Petunia Lane. A color palette that would warm Holly's home, making it supercalifragilisticexpialidocious.

Mary-Margaret pointed to the strip of grass that lined the bakery parking lot. "Oh, look," she said. "Crabgrass."

Holly wondered if Mary-Margaret was contemplating a move to Southern Lakes. Holly hoped not. The Village of Primm could always use the same topiary frame to raise another Plume. But the Pink Witch? They broke the mold when they made her. She was the real deal. Mary-Margaret was the mascot of Primm. A town hero. Not Plume. Plume was just a plant.

Holly wished it hadn't been her home that, when swept up in a cyclone, eventually fell on top of the Pink Witch. Mary-Margaret had turned the sepia tones of suburbia into Technicolor. Odd: Holly thought she might miss the *hip, hip*s, the *poof*s, and the "---s." The Land of Oz just wouldn't be the same without Mary-Margaret.

"Holly?" said Jack. "It's time to go. We need to get Anna to her final destination."

Holly gave Mary-Margaret's arm a gentle squeeze. "Are you going to be okay? Can I walk you to your car?"

Holly walked Mary-Margaret to her car as Jack loaded the thirteen pies into his car. Holly figured she'd leave the smelly red Buick in the bakery parking lot until morning. After what she had seen come out of that trunk, she sure as heck wouldn't be driving it tonight. And then: *Oh, no. No!* Holly covered her mouth, looked back at the smelly red Buick.

The horticulturist at the Topiary Park had said the bugs on Plume would stay on Plume.

Did that mean . . . ? Was Holly to blame for the widespread chilli thrip infestation in the idyllic little town of Primm? *No. Please, no. That smelly red Buick?*

"Mary-Margaret." Holly spoke quickly, a bit stunned by what she was about to say. "The trunk. The chilli thrips." If Mary-Margaret was an accessory to My Love's criminal act, then so was Holly. In a roundabout way. "I drove that car all over town. I spread the chilli thrips across Primm."

Mary-Margaret nodded, touching a gentle finger to the tip of Holly's nose. "Yes, I know," she said softly. Not in a mean way. But in a way that said she understood. "And when you opened your trunk, you spread them across Southern Lakes too."

"It was an accident."

"Yes, of course."

Holly felt horrible. *I spread devastation across the Village of Primm. And Southern Lakes. This can't be!* "I know I've been a bit noncommittal," Holly said, "but I'm ready to commit. I owe everything to the Village of Primm. Mary-Margaret?"

"Yes?"

"I'm ready to serve. I'm ready to officially join the Primm Academy PTA." She placed her right hand over her heart and pledged, "I, Holly Banks, will be your secretary."

"I know."

I know? How'd she know?

So what now? What's next? wondered Holly. Did all roads lead to this? To this moment? Now they both harbored a secret about the other. *Do I out Mary-Margaret to the authorities for wanting a mudroom paid for with dirty money? Does Mary-Margaret out me for driving a smelly red Buick? Or do we both zip it and serve out our penance working tirelessly on behalf of the Village of Primm and its inhabitants?* As far as Holly could tell, the only other option? Banishment.

"Thank you, Holly." Mary-Margaret opened the back door of her platinum-gray Lexus, placing her cherry pie on the back seat. "For what you said a moment ago in front of your husband. And for what you didn't say."

So there it was. Both guilty. Both with information that would damage the other. Their only way forward—was silence.

Mary-Margaret's words left Holly speechless.

Poof!

42

Hours later

They were killing Plume tonight.

Lighting torches. Setting her on fire.

Any remaining topiaries in Primm had been summoned to the bonfire. By morning, there would be nothing left. All the topiaries in the Village of Primm would be dead. None would be saved.

Holly placed Anna Wintour beneath Plume. She considered digging around in Anna's soil to retrieve Ella's tooth but in the end decided against it.

Holly and Jack stood back from the fires as one by one, every animal in the Topiary Park Petting Zoo was doused with gasoline and set on fire. The air—orange. Crackling. Hot. Smoke and heat that burned her nose. Dads silent. Children crying. Mothers covering their mouths in sad disbelief, unable to take their eyes off the glowing inferno. A town paying quiet homage.

Smaller fires burned throughout the park, throughout the enclaves, throughout the great land of Primm. But the view from where Holly stood—watching Anna, watching Plume, with Mary-Margaret on a hill not far away—was of the brightest fire in the night sky, which raged long into the night: the burning of the town mascot, the idol they all worshipped, the goddess that dared them all to believe. In a village bewitched with many magnificent peahens, the grand cru of all peahens—Plume, the peahen with whom all things rested—was dying a slow and painful death. The burning at the stake continued long into the night. By morning, the Village of Primm peahen—dead.

Rest in peace, Plume.

Rest in peace, Anna Wintour.

Rest in peace, Mary-Margaret St. James.

And let us not forget: rest in peace, Holly Banks.

KABOOM!

Penelope Pratt
Feathered Nest Realty

—ENCLAVE ALERTS—

I know it's late, but this just in:

My cousin, Mary-Margaret St. James, President of the Primm Academy PTA, philanthropist, prominent member of both the Primm and the Magnolia Societies, publisher of the Proper Tip Sheet, and long-standing resident of Hopscotch Hill, announces the sale of someone-she-is-no-longer-speaking-to's entire music collection, valued in the low seven figures. Effective immediately.

Proceeds benefit the rebuilding of the Topiary Park and the birth of a new Plume.

It is with a heavy heart that Mary-Margaret also announces her immediate separation and pending divorce from that-person-who-is-now-living-in-a-cut-rate-motel-in-Southern-Lakes.

In consideration of recent events concerning our beloved Plume, Mary-Margaret St. James will also donate thirteen high-value albums by Swedish pop group ABBA for use as Frisbees in the next Great F.U.—the F.U. Frisbee Tournament at tomorrow's Cherry Festival on The Lawn. Though Mary-Margaret prefers clear blue, the F.U. may take place beneath ashen sky. It is her prayer that prevailing winds blow Plume's plume of soot toward Southern Lakes and away from the skies above Primm.

Text "INNOCENT" to read Mary-Margaret's press release and Statement of Truth.

Text "GUILTY" to read about that hemorrhoid-of-a-man-she-used-to-be-associated-with-but-isn't-anymore.

I, Penelope Pratt, leave you with a direct quote from my cousin, Mary-Margaret St. James:

"Plume will live forever in our hearts, and I, Mary-Margaret St. James, at one with the phoenix, will take flight from the ashes, and rise again."

I, Penelope Pratt, #1 in Sales at Feathered Nest Realty, leave homeowners in the Village of Primm with this thought: if Mary-Margaret's attempt to rise like the phoenix fails, if she, indeed, flutters about but can't take flight, she intends to sell her home on Hopscotch Hill and move to Southern Lakes, where she will work tirelessly to elevate the status of their school and town beyond that of Primm. Should this occur, brace for declining property values. Should this occur, the Primm Academy PTA will need a new president—preferably someone already on the executive board—ready to work and, hopefully, undaunted by increased competition from our neighbors beyond the fence. Competition, the likes of which we've never seen.

43

Saturday

The best thing that happened yesterday according to Holly? Baking fourteen pies with Greta, then tossing them all in the trash before driving to Southern Lakes to pick up thirteen more to deliver to the outstretched arms of Emily the Pie Mom. Emily smiled sweetly, even hugged Holly. Said the pie auction wouldn't be possible were it not for the hard work and dedication of volunteers like her. When Emily handed Holly a gilded certificate acknowledging Holly as the top pie producer in Primm, Holly didn't feel it was necessary to confess to not baking the pies she donated, having bought them from—of all places—Southern Lakes. What did it matter, these harmless sins of omission? Emily got her pies.

The worst thing that happened yesterday according to Holly? Watching the burning deaths of Plume and Anna Wintour, knowing Holly might have driven the vehicle that led to the widespread bug infestation across Primm. All of the topiary animals in the petting zoo, dead. Hundreds of family pet topiaries across all enclaves, dead. Peloton hit especially hard. Blythe a close second. Holly hadn't told Jack about the trunk, the chilli thrips, or the invoice with the signature of Michael St. James. She didn't know why she hadn't told him, but she would—later today. And she would call the ferroequinologist to alert him to the infested Buick. Holly knew Jack didn't receive Penelope's Enclave Alerts. And as far as Holly could tell, Bethanny hadn't called to inform Jack that something was fishy in the St. James household. Holly wondered what had gone on inside Mary-Margaret's home on Hopscotch Hill last night. Wondered what the Pink Witch had said to My Love.

The best part about today according to Holly? It was Saturday, so there was no bus to catch. *Toot! Toot! Sucka.*

Despite the sadness that cast an ugly shadow across the village last night, today Mary-Margaret's prayers must have been answered because the Village of Primm woke to a glorious day. Seventy-two degrees, and a sky that looked like Twitter: birds chirping, everything a brilliant shade of Crayola's parakeet blue, with only the occasional drift of Plume's gray smoke and ash. Who needed 140 characters—or 280 characters, for that matter? Holly could say it in twenty-eight: I LOVE THE VILLAGE OF PRIMM! And yes, Holly counted the spaces between words, especially around *love*. Spaces around *love* should be counted. As should the punctuation, when a sentence about love came to an exalted end.

Before heading to the Cherry Festival, Jack returned the smelly red Buick and picked up Holly's Suburban while Greta and Holly drove Ella in Jack's car to Southern Lakes to pick up Ella's new glasses. The other day, Ella had chosen a pair of lavender glasses with a little bit of sparkle on the edges, and now that she was wearing them, she couldn't look cuter. She even decided lavender was her new favorite color, and Holly was okay with that. So long as Ella never let another girl tell her there was a difference between lavender and lilac. Neither was superior. Both were purple.

Ella sat sideways on Holly's lap when she was getting fitted for her glasses. Ella waved at Holly in the mirror and said, "I look like Twilight Sparkle." Then she turned to wrap her arms around Holly's neck and pulled up for a kiss. When Ella pulled back, she smiled up at Holly, and Holly could see the space where Ella's tooth once was. It brought Holly back to that night in Ella's bedroom when Holly had played tooth fairy for the first time and all her worries had crept in, feeling arcus-cloud and mustard undertones.

"You can be my Pinkie Pie, Mommy. I'll be Twilight Sparkle for a little while."

"Okay, Ella." Holly kissed the tip of Ella's nose. "I'll be your Pinkie Pie."

Ella turned back to look at her reflection in the mirror, and Holly held her place behind Ella in that reflection. Holly hoped when Ella was older and looked back at this time in her life, she'd see Holly and her best efforts through her Twilight Sparkle glasses, not Holly with her imperfections and blemishes through a pair of ginormous black poster-board glasses. *Little Kids, Little Zoo*.

"I can see everything now with perfect clear-ity," Ella said, seeing the world for the first time through lavender-rimmed glasses. Ella pointed at Greta. "Grammy's smile is pushing up her eye wrinkles." Ella pointed to Holly's face. "And you have a big black dot on your chin."

"It's a blackhead, Ella." Holly gave her baby girl a hug. "It's just a blemish. Happens sometimes."

Holly felt Greta's hand on her shoulder. All three shared the same mirror.

~

They met Jack on Petunia, then all piled into Holly's Suburban to drive up the hill past the magnolia grove and out onto the main road on their way to the center of Primm. At a stoplight near the bus stop at Dillydally and Castle Drum Tower, where Holly had tried to board Ella onto Bus 13 on the first day of school, they rolled to a stop beside a G-Class Mercedes. *The* G-Class Mercedes. Jack stopped in such a way that it positioned him, as the driver of their car, in the blind spot of the man driving the G-Class. Jack kept his head straight, never looking at the G-Class driver, so as not to engage. "He wasn't involved," said Jack, as if reading Holly's thoughts. "Just a man worried his vines would get eaten."

"But the Stone House—"

"Let it go."

Holly watched the steady expression on Jack's face as the light turned green and the G-Class turned left as they continued straight. Was Jack lying? Was there more to learn about the job that had led their family to the Village of Primm?

"There's nothing to figure out," said Jack, cocking the rearview mirror to have a look at Ella and Greta in the back seat. "Just an offer to buy a house."

"If you say so," said Holly, reaching out to hold Jack's hand, willing to let it go since Ella and Greta were sitting behind them. She suspected he was telling a white lie. A half truth. There probably *wasn't* a connection between the Stone House and the killing of Plume, so she was prepared to drop it. But then, Holly suspected, in the coming weeks and months, there'd be more she'd uncover in the secretive little village they now called home. And when that time came, if Jack was at the center of it, he'd tell her. Of that she felt certain.

~

With the Cherry Festival in full swing, the village square bustled with Primm families. In memory of Plume, flags were being flown at half mast across the village, and fresh white flowers with cherry-colored ribbons replaced last week's gold, black, and white start-of-school ribbons. Shopkeepers with tables displayed their wares. Kids played tag and ran around with jump ropes and Hula-Hoops. Everywhere you looked, folks were dressed in cherry-themed clothing and gathered to socialize and enjoy the beautiful weather. Gary-Gee strummed away outside of Primm's Coffee Joe, back to his "Zip-a-Dee-Doo-Dah" followed by "You Are My Sunshine." There were jugglers and face painters on loan from the Topiary Park. Everyone wanted to be happy despite the village-wide fires that had consumed a piece of Primm's heart the night before. There was still smoke overhead as a juggler twisted balloons into elaborate shapes: pink ponies, blue birds, and yellow school buses.

The first thing Ella spied was an old-fashioned candy stand, where the whole family enjoyed their first taste of cherry-flavored cotton candy, followed by waters for Ella and Jack, cherry sodas in tall glass bottles for Greta and Holly.

"I'm going to check on my pies," said Holly, leaving Ella, Jack, and Greta to enjoy the cotton candy.

Off in the distance, at the south end of The Lawn near the bookstore on Pip's Corner, Holly saw the old man and his blue Great Dane. Merchant "Meek" Hopscotch III. She wondered what would become of him. Wondered what would become of Edward T. Olive, the antiques dealer. And My Love. Holly wondered what would become of him.

Events like the Cherry Festival were the reason Penelope and Feathered Nest Realty thrived, as families visited the village and then fought to outbid each other for real estate in the gilded glow of Primm Academy. Holly was proud to say she owned a home on Petunia with no storage in it, that a Pinterestworthy front porch had charmed her into buying it. Primm was la-la land, and Holly now had a piece of it. The price to live there was high, but on days like today, it was easy to convince yourself it was worth it.

Caleb caught up to Holly as she passed a pretzel stand. "Hey there."

"Oh, hey, Caleb."

"Where's Ella?"

"South Gazebo. She's with her dad and grandma heading for the live petting zoo near the magnolias. The minute Ella saw a miniature pony walking by on a leash, she went nuts thinking the pony's owner might know Pinkie Pie and Twilight Sparkle."

Caleb smiled. "Did you upload to YouTube yet?"

"No. Not yet."

"Oh."

"I got caught up with some pies."

"Maybe this afternoon," he said.

"Yeah, maybe."

"You don't sound very convincing."

"I'm sorry, Caleb. I just don't know." Holly tipped her head to look over his shoulder. She thought she saw Rosie McClure from the school office. "The truth is, I don't think I want my first full week in Primm splashed all over the internet. Everyone's so caught up with tweeting and posting and going viral; I don't know if I want all of that right now. I'm kind of enjoying my privacy."

"I get it." He bobbed his head, acknowledging her concerns. "I totally get it."

"Oh, but hey—I almost forgot," Holly said. "I was talking with Jack, and he suggested I take another film class. Get up to speed on the latest technologies. I was thinking I might start a film studio in my dining room. Shoot home-decorating or crafting videos for Collette and some of her friends. You know, start small. Help Etsy moms and mommy bloggers produce video for their websites while Ella's at school."

"Yeah, yeah," Caleb agreed, "that's a great idea."

"I'm not ready for the Wilhelm Klaus, Caleb."

"Hey, I get it," he offered. "But you're taking huge steps forward."

"Yes, well. I have you to thank for that." Holly smiled, reaching out to touch his arm. Something caught her eye. "Rosie!" She signaled for Rosie to come over.

Rosie was barefoot, wearing a pretty yellow sundress. Her hair was pulled back, fastened with a flower at the nape of her neck. She looked totally different now that she was out from behind that counter.

"Rosie, this is Caleb. Caleb, this is Rosie McClure."

Caleb moved quickly to wipe the palm of his hand on his pant leg. He offered it to Rosie, who smiled, placing her hand in his.

One look at Rosie, and Caleb grew fidgety. Caleb the Cable Guy, who tortured unsuspecting moms across the village, appeared nervous in Rosie's presence. He cleared his throat. "Nice to meet you, Rosie McClure."

"Rosie works at Ella's school," Holly told Caleb, thinking he might be too young for Rosie. "Don't you, Rosie?"

Rosie was wearing her pink freshwater pearls, a truly exquisite necklace. "Rosie," said Holly, "Caleb is a documentary filmmaker."

"Really?" Rosie took a step closer.

Holly could smell her perfume and assumed Caleb could too. Gardenia.

"You're a filmmaker?" Rosie tipped her head and smiled a flirty smile. "That's so interesting."

"If you'll both excuse me," Holly said, "I need to check on some pies."

She left so she could swing by the pie auction, surprised to find her pies were actually selling. They weren't earning top dollar like some of Emily's pies, but they were selling. To Holly's relief, so far, no one had accused her of entering Southern Lakes pies into a Village of Primm pie auction, and Holly wasn't about to tell anyone her secret. Emily had wanted pies to sell. Emily got pies. Thirteen of them plus fourteen more in a trash can on Petunia. Holly was a card-carrying volunteer school mom now. Even had the certificate to prove it.

Emily was helping a man with a pie purchase. She spotted Holly watching from afar and lifted her hand to wave. Holly smiled and waved back. So what if Holly had baked pies almost as bad as Mary-Margaret's peckled peanut butter cookies? She came through in the end. She volunteered, and by golly, she finished the job. Hoped it was good enough. If it wasn't, oh well. At least she tried.

A buzzing sound overhead drew Holly's attention to the Twitter-blue sky, where an old-timey airplane flew over the Cherry Festival, pulling a long lettered sign behind it:

COMING SOON: TOPIARY PARK HOSTS FIRST ANNUAL SCRABBLE TOURNAMENT.

Scrabble? Since Holly was a little girl, she had loved Scrabble. From the moment her mom taught her about anagrams. That *great* was an anagram for *Greta*.

"And *Vogel* is German for *bird*," whispered Holly.

Of all the birds Holly had met during her short time in Primm—Plume, now in ashes; Mary-Margaret, rising like the phoenix—all this time, the greatest of birds was Greta. The signs were there all along. Holly just hadn't seen them.

God willing, Jack would keep his job, and Holly would have more adventures in the Village of Primm, more time to figure out if the Wilhelm Klaus Film Festival was indeed something she'd submit to, because despite what she had just said to Caleb, as far as Holly was concerned, the verdict was still out. A lot had happened in the past week. Like standing at the end of a novel, thumbing back to an earlier chapter, Holly'd have to look back to decide how it all shook out. Read it again. Uncover clues missed in the first reading. She shielded sunlight from her eyes with her hand, noticing the fluffy white contrails from the plane. They looked like dash marks. If they were set into dialogue, what would they say?

~

Holly set off for the live petting zoo, where Ella, Jack, and Greta were waiting. Primm Paper had a yellow-and-white-striped lemonade stand at the festival. Katie was handing out small decorative bags with the Primm Paper signature bee printed on them. Inside the bags were chocolate-covered cherries. They were so delicious, and as Holly licked her fingers, wondering if it was impolite to ask for a second bag, she spotted a display outside of the Drunken Plaid Gift Shoppe. A whole table filled with cute things Holly could put on her front porch. She walked over to have a look and, lo and behold, found everything Pinterest Collette had once had on her porch on Petunia Lane. *Bingo!* Collette must have shopped here. All this time, Holly had thought Collette possessed a secret knowledge hidden to Holly.

Walking among the merchandise, Holly decided she'd pick up a large swirly letter *B*, a gorgeous silk ribbon, and a hook to hang the ribbon and letter across her front door. She bent down to search through Drunken Plaid's collection of rubber rain boots. Maybe she'd even buy a bouquet of white flowers from the florist to tuck into the rain boots. They had a great selection of welcome mats too. Holly decided that was the place she'd start. She'd pick up a welcome mat for the porch she'd fallen in love with on Petunia Lane.

"Hip! Hip!"

Holly's back bristled. No, please. Not her. After reading Penelope's Enclave Alert, Holly suspected Mary-Margaret had cut ties with her husband to distance herself from scandal. "Hello, Mary-Margaret," Holly said.

"Shopping for porch decor?"

"Yup."

"Can I help?"

"Nope."

Mary-Margaret pouted, reaching out to fondle a mailbox flag. "Let Mary-Margaret help you."

"Nope. Don't need your help."

"I'm sorry how things turned out between us."

"No, you're not." Holly folded her arms across her chest. *She thinks she's a phoenix? Thinks she'll rise again?* That meant nothing would ever change.

"What kind of look are you going for?" Mary-Margaret wanted to know. "Enclaves and porches are celebrated destinations in the Village of Primm."

Apparently, so are mudrooms. But then, Holly wasn't going to mention Mary-Margaret's indiscretion unless Mary-Margaret mentioned hers. So Holly ignored her. Focused on buying things for her porch. Holly's place of welcome to create. Not Mary-Margaret's.

"Well?" Mary-Margaret asked. "Are you going traditional? Contemporary? Or cute?"

Holly figured, *If I drill holes in the bottom of the boots for drainage, I can buy two daisy plants before leaving the festival and plant them in the boots when I get home.*

"Because I think 'cute' would be a great look for your porch," Mary-Margaret was saying, trying to slip inside Holly's psyche and become a voice inside Holly's head. *Peekaboo!* "All of the houses on Petunia are so cute. Doing 'cute' on Hopscotch Hill is difficult. We have fewer choices. Must maintain the status quo."

Holly didn't respond. Like Ella with her new glasses, Holly could see with clear-ity now. Mary-Margaret wasn't going to clutter this up. *This is my porch and my home.* For as long as Jack still had a job, and they still lived in Primm.

"Have you thought about flower planters? Maybe mount a flag?"

Holly said nothing. Scratched slowly behind her ear again. Tugged gently at her earlobe.

"Lavender," Mary-Margaret whined. "Why are you ignoring me?"

Because I've learned a lot this week. About letting another woman get inside my head. Voices. They're like the volume button on a remote control. Turn 'em up; turn 'em down. And when you really need a break, press mute. Or simply hit the power button and enjoy the silence.

"Lavender, are you listening?"

Maybe I'll buy some exterior paint from Primm Paint this weekend and paint my door cherry red to match the boots, thought Holly. Right now,

Holly's house was white with black shutters. A red door might look nice. No, maybe she should go for lime green, like Happy the dinosaur. Or chocolate, like Struggle. Or maybe Crayola's parakeet blue like the sky over the Topiary Park when Plume was still alive. Yes, blue. Holly liked blue.

Holly walked over to the bins that held the monogram letters, flipping through to the *B*s to see what colors they had. Mary-Margaret followed.

"You can always buy a miniature initial to hang from your mailbox," Mary-Margaret said. "Or maybe get an initial on your welcome mat. Instead of the word *welcome*."

Welcome was the last word of Mary-Margaret's Holly let slip inside her head. Funny, that was the one word Holly would have appreciated hearing from the president of the Primm Academy PTA on Ella's first day of kindergarten. *Welcome.* Seven letters. Two syllables. One simple word that was never said. Never felt.

Holly held up a white letter *B*, wondering if it would get dirty hanging outside.

"---."

What's that? Did someone say something? Holly put the white letter back and pulled out a parakeet-blue one. If she painted her door cherry red to match the cherry-red boots, and her house was white and her shutters black, maybe a parakeet-blue initial was the way to go.

"---."

Did someone say something? Is the Pink Witch giving unsolicited decorating advice? No, must be the wind. Must be the rustling of dash marks and punctuation moving through the trees. Holly stayed focused on her thoughts, not letting anything or anyone distract her. The words she heard needed to be her words. Because Holly was in control. Holly decided that yes, the parakeet-blue letter was the way to go, but that maybe a white ribbon would add some nice contrast.

"---!"

I can't hear a thing. I can simply tune it all out if I want to. If the white ribbon was the wrong choice, Holly could always change it later. She picked up a hardware kit so she could mount the hook and hang her letter as soon as she got home today.

"---."

If someone's getting frustrated with the choices I'm making, I'm certainly not worrying about that right now. Why should I care what other people think? Holly pulled aside the cherry-red rubber boots with white polka dots. She'd plant white daisies in each boot, and before the weekend was up, she'd paint her door cherry red to match the boots, and she'd hang this parakeet-blue letter *B* by this white ribbon. Now for the most important part, the thing Holly had been missing since moving to the Village of Primm: a welcome mat.

Welcome mats were on the table overlooking The Lawn.

Holly walked over, aware that she was being followed.

"---!"

Ho hum. Don't hear a thing. With the view of happy families enjoying the Cherry Festival, Holly used both hands to flip through the welcome mats, holding each up to find the perfect one. At last, she found it. At the bottom of the pile. It was a soft brown, with lovely scrollwork around its edges. In bold white raised letters was a simple word that meant so much: *Welcome.*

With no clutter in Holly's head, with no extraneous words, voices, or fluff to fluster her, Holly paid for her porch decor, then proceeded to leave. No more Pink Witch. La-la-la. *Poof!* Mary-Margaret's hold over Holly vanished. Holly released it. And hoped it would stay that way once PTA meetings resumed next week. *Secretary.* Holly would pay her dues to the Village of Primm for one school year and then return to private life.

~

After a few hours of watching all the synonyms of *happy* play out in a buoyant, joyful Ella as she ran around with some of her new classmates, Holly and Jack decided it was time to leave the Cherry Festival on The Lawn and head for Petunia Lane. They told Ella she could run around the magnolia tree one more time, and then they were leaving.

"With my new friend, Talia," Ella announced, poking Talia in the shoulder. "She's in my class."

From behind Talia came Shanequa, waving as she approached. "Hey there, Holly. How's it going?"

"Great!" said Holly. "Shanequa, this is my husband, Jack. My mom, Greta."

The three exchanged greetings.

"Looks like the girls are becoming fast friends," said Shanequa.

They all watched as Ella and Talia took off to play beneath the magnolia.

"Yes. I think that's great," said Holly. "I'm so glad to learn they're in the same class. We should get them together for a playdate."

Shanequa turned to face Holly, big smile on her face. "I'd like that."

"Maybe Wednesday after school? You're welcome to stay for coffee."

"Wednesday works, yes. It's a date," said Shanequa.

"A playdate!" offered Holly, jovial smile, acting silly. Feeling silly. "We're number twelve Petunia."

"We're on Dillydally. So I'll see you then. Wednesday," said Shanequa, offering her goodbyes to Jack and Greta before walking toward Talia and Ella playing beneath the magnolia tree.

Yes. I'll see you then. Holly smiled.

"I don't think I've seen Ella suck her thumb once today," muttered Jack.

"Come to think of it, neither have I," said Holly. "Mom? Have you?"

"No, I haven't seen it either."

So the no-bite nail polish worked? Could it be? The end of Ella's thumb-sucking? Ella rounded the magnolia tree, tripped on a root, and came up crying. But she didn't reach out for Holly like she typically would. Instead, she consoled herself with a few quick sucks of her thumb, then gave it up and got right back to playing with Talia. *Oh, well. Can't win 'em all.*

Heading toward their car, Holly spotted a lonely-looking Mary-Margaret St. James sitting on the ground beside a wagon filled with ABBA albums. Holly left Jack, Ella, and Greta to walk over. "You okay, Mary-Margaret? Need anything?"

"Me? No, I'm okay. I don't need anything."

"It looks like you're gearing up to play a concert."

Mary-Margaret exhaled. "You might say that." Beside her, next to the wagon filled with ABBA albums, was a turntable powered by a battery pack and a fairly large set of speakers.

"I'm sorry I ignored you. Earlier," Holly said. "At the shop. That was mean. I'm not like that. I'm sorry."

"That's okay. I deserved it." Mary-Margaret kicked at the dirt. "Would you like to do the honors?" She handed Holly *Arrival*, ABBA's fourth studio album. "Song number two." A slow smile returned to Mary-Margaret's face. "I think you'll like it."

Holly did as she was told, pulling the album from the cardboard sleeve, setting it on the turntable, lifting the needle, and placing it carefully at the start of the second song—essentially, the world's first Europop disco hit: "Dancing Queen."

As ABBA singers Anni-Frid Lyngstad and Agnetha Fältskog layered their vocals, paying homage to discotheques and the euphoric, unbridled joy and freedom of dancing, Holly offered her hand to Mary-Margaret, helping her to her feet.

"Thanks." Mary-Margaret smiled, a small wad of pink bubble gum tucked at the back of her teeth. She turned up the volume as F.U.

Frisbee Moms across the Cherry Festival looked up, located the source of the music, then began to gather. "See you around?"

"Yes, of course," Holly said, hoping the coming weeks and months would be kind to Mary-Margaret and My Love. "I'm looking forward to it. Lilac." Because why not. Lilac was high end. Lilac was couture. Lavender gave Lilac her due.

Upon hearing that word, Mary-Margaret moved quickly to pull Holly into a warm embrace. "Thank you," she said. "I really am Lilac." Holly hoped she'd remember that should My Love ever cause her to question.

Holly left Mary-Margaret to join up with Jack, Ella, and Greta, stopping one last time to watch Mary-Margaret tend to family business: the throwing of My Love's ABBA collection into the crowd of F.U. Frisbee Moms. Everyone seemed to be having a great time. Team Buttercream, the Pink Erasers . . .

"Hip! Hip!" Holly said quietly. Hoping the "hooray" would, in time, find its way back to Mary-Margaret's heart.

44

On the way home

Holly and her family left the Cherry Festival and drove through Primm, arriving at their home on Petunia Lane a little past three o'clock. They all climbed out of the Suburban Godzilla, satisfied by the festival but a bit exhausted from a week of turmoil and change. Ella took her grammy's hand, and the two of them dashed off down the sidewalk toward the house to do each other's hair in Ella's *My Little Pony: Equestria Girls* mirror, presumably while also admiring the cherries they had painted all over their faces.

Pulling her porch treasures from the back of her SUV, Holly stopped in the driveway to take in the beauty of their little cape on Petunia Lane. So what if it didn't have any storage? It was their home, and Holly loved it.

"Holly?" Jack walked over. "Are you okay?"

"I'm fine. Just having a moment."

"We don't know if anything's changed yet, Holly. I won't know until next week."

"I know." Holly smiled. "It's all good."

"And who knows, if there are changes, maybe I'll be able to find work close by. I hear there's a block of commercial development coming to Southern Lakes. That's just one town over. We could live here, and I'll commute."

"Jack?" Holly touched his arm. "I have proof My Love arranged for the chilli thrips. I found an invoice in the trunk of the Buick I was driving. Michael's signature was on it."

"I know," he said.

"You do? How?"

"The ferroequinologist told me everything when I dropped the Buick off this morning. We were checking for dents and other signs of damage as per the rental agreement—opened the trunk—and saw the infestation. The train guy told me everything."

"I should have told you last night. I'm sorry." Holly searched his eyes for signs of disappointment but didn't find any. "It's just—Mary-Margaret was so devastated. She was just standing there in the night sky like planet Mercury, and her life appeared to be moving backward. And she seemed so, I don't know . . . weakened. There was no more 'hooray.' Her 'hip, hip!' went bye-bye. She wilted, Jack. Right there before my eyes—like Plume, who went up in smoke. A fragrant, majestic, legendary topiary died last night, covered in bugs. Torched by villagers." *And me? I was at the center of it.* Seat hung low, butt dragging, devastating Primm from the trunk of a smelly red Buick.

"If I were a betting man? I'd put all my chips on Mary-Margaret," said Jack. "She's been knocked down, but she'll get up again." He kissed Holly's forehead. "See you inside?"

"Sure," she said. "Be there in a minute."

Porch items gathered in her arms, Holly walked the length of her sidewalk slowly, seeing her naked front porch with fresh eyes. She thought she'd leave the columns white but paint the floor of her porch and the tread of the stairs black to match the shutters. If it worked, great. If it didn't, she could always paint the floor a different color and leave the treads black. *If I learned anything this week, it's this: nothing's permanent; everything changes. And there's more than one word for happy.*

Lime green. Maybe she'd paint her door lime green.

She certainly wasn't the naive new homeowner seeking the promise of perfection in a village filled with zip-a-dee-doo-dah, persnickety plants, and charming enclaves. No. Holly's front porch didn't look like the front porch she'd first seen when coming to look at this house with Penelope Pratt by her side. It was different now, changed. It was definitely *not* Collette's porch anymore. It was Holly's porch, the porch that led to Holly's home, where Holly's family lived.

Holly climbed the porch steps, placing her new welcome mat beneath her front door, where it belonged. Where Holly belonged. Greta opened the front door to let Struggle out to sit beside Holly on the top step. Then Greta closed the front door, giving Holly time to be alone.

"Hey, Struggle. You a good girl?" Holly pulled Struggle close, scratching behind her ears. "You're always right by my side, aren't you?"

When they were leaving the festival and driving past the Topiary Park, a smoldering arcus cloud loomed overhead as Eva Cassidy's rendition of "Somewhere over the Rainbow" played on the radio. Holly had imagined the Village of Primm as one big movie set with her as the main character. Was she Dorothy? Was the Village of Primm her Land of Oz? In this movie playing out in Holly's mind, Greta was the scarecrow, Caleb the tin man of industry, and Jack the courageous lion. Ella was Toto. She'd like that. And Struggle too. Struggle was Toto. Two Totos. Why not?

One thing was certain: If this was Holly's movie, Holly's screenplay, Holly's novel? She'd open with the snap of a clapboard slate. *Welcome to Primm: take one.* Her story would mash quirky, woebegone, and prim, but it would be her story, as only Holly could tell it. In it, she'd give voice to a less-than-perfect mom and her pursuit of mostly happy in a pretty good life. At least, that was how she'd pitch it to Wilhelm Klaus.

And when there was nothing left to say, when all the words and all the dash marks had whooshed and poofed away, Holly'd write the word she most longed to see:

FIN.

ACKNOWLEDGMENTS

Writing a book is harder than I thought, takes longer than I'd like to admit, but is more rewarding than I ever could have imagined.

I am indebted to my literary agent, Joëlle Delbourgo, bringer of life-changing news, who took a chance on an unknown writer who made her laugh. This novel wouldn't be what it is without the skill, support, and hard work of my editor, Alicia Clancy, and the entire spectacular team at Lake Union, to whom I extend unending gratitude. I especially want to thank those who were instrumental in getting me there: Samantha Stroh Bailey, Arielle Eckstut, Francine LaSala, and Kris Spisak. Early readers Sara-with-an-A Allen, Sarah-with-an-H Sneed, Josie Brown, Meredith Schorr, and Pauline Wiles.

I am blessed beyond measure by family and friends who have been there for me in countless ways. My parents, Bill and Jeanne Breitbach, for a lifetime of patience, encouragement, and support. I couldn't have stepped out if you hadn't stepped in. My sisters, Sarah Sneed and Jill Taylor, with their husbands, Skip Sneed and JT Taylor, for listening when I shared my thoughts and for putting up with me when the road was long. My sister, best friend, and companion on the Appalachian Trail, Beth "Crème Brûlée" Cuzzone, for a lifetime of getting lost before reaching the summit. My brother-in-law Jamie Valerie, for always asking when it would be ready and for always letting me know he couldn't wait to read it.

Fierce women who lead the troops, jump off cliffs, and always have your back: Tracy Craddock, Karen Kinslow, Kathryn Rust. "Beach Babe" partners in crime, six writers who epitomize sisterhood and know where the bodies are buried: Samantha Stroh Bailey, Josie Brown, Eileen Goudge, Francine LaSala, Meredith Schorr, and Jen Tucker. Pauline Wiles, for your loveliness, elegance, and friendship—you inspire me. Rhonda Richardson, beautiful soul, for your spirit-filled friendship. Influencer Melissa Amster and bright sunshine Dany Drexler, champions of writers. Anne Burt and Stephanie Morecraft, wherever you may be.

To my comrades on the 85K Writing Challenge, members of James River Writers, and the talented authors at Lake Union: every writer needs a tribe, and I'm so honored to be a part of yours. To the women in the Kinloch Book Club, whose love for books is infectious. I wish to thank the faculty and staff at my children's schools—Agape Preschool, Saint Bridget Elementary, Saint Bridget Middle, Saint Gertrude High School, and St. Christopher's School—fine institutions with parking lots that became my office while I was waiting in carpool line. And I wish to thank the countless volunteer parents with whom I've served. Hip! Hip!

Four children who grew quicker than the writing of this book, Emma Elizabeth, Noelle Kathryn, Holden Thatcher, and Porter Finn—setting my pen aside to watch you grow has been the highest honor and greatest privilege of my life. You are my light, my life, my whole world.

For believing in me, for being patient, and for knowing how truly important all of this is to me, this book is dedicated to Andy, college sweetheart, husband, father of my children, love of my life, best friend. No one more than you created the space I needed to grow as a writer and achieve my dreams. You moved mountains. Made sacrifices every day. Thank you doesn't begin to cover it.

To my readers, the mere thought of you inspires my every word.

BOOK CLUB DISCUSSION QUESTIONS

1. When Holly relocates to the Village of Primm, she must cope with the challenges of being a newcomer in a village with established rules and hierarchies. Have you ever had to adjust to an entirely different culture? How would you describe your experience?

2. The drive to belong to a community can be a powerful one. How do the concepts of welcome, belonging, and banishment play out in the novel?

3. Why is Holly so invested in her struggle to belong in Primm? At times she reflects on her hopes for Ella's belonging to this idealized community, but at one point Jack asks Holly who this is really for. Who do you think Holly is working for? Are Holly's unrealistic ideals imposed on her or self-imposed?

4. In what ways do moms strive to present themselves as perfect mothers to mask underlying flaws they hope no one will notice?

5. Much of the book concerns the fear of making mistakes that hurt our children. To what degree is there a connection between a parent's foibles and a child's well-being?

6. Does Holly come to terms with her mother's failings because her mother has grown or because Holly has, or both? What events have occurred in your life that have led you to reevaluate the mothers you have known, either more or less favorably?

7. The book depicts characters connecting through many different mediums: script writing, texts, email, voice mail, Enclave Alerts, school correspondence, even security cameras, Western Union money transfers, messages from a psychic, and a recipe spelled backward. Do these differing means of communication facilitate understanding and connection or detract from it? What do you think about the author using depictions of these kinds of communications in the book as a supplement to in-person character dialogue?

8. Holly often lapses into fantasy sequences and film references. Is this an escape for Holly or a reflection of her desire to connect with her art?

9. What are some ways the loss of Holly's "voice" is depicted in the novel? In what ways does Holly attempt to reclaim her voice? At novel's end, was Holly successful at silencing others, or was she silencing something else?

10. Is Mary-Margaret justified in pressuring other mothers to volunteer? How do we look upon mothers who lead and make demands? Have you ever taken on the role of a leader of parents? What was your experience?

11. Mary-Margaret offers plenty of observations and advice in the book. In many ways, she serves as the manic tour guide to the school mom subculture. Does Mary-Margaret give good advice? Is she insightful or misleading? Do you love her or hate her?

12. Central to the book are school moms represented as a societal subculture. Can you think of other works that have explored this subculture? Which type of mom featured in this book resonated with you? Do you play a particular role in a particular societal subculture? Does the role you play ever differ from the role you wished you played?

13. In what ways do cousins Penelope and Mary-Margaret work for and against each other on behalf of the Village of Primm? How do their respective roles within the community elevate the status of the Village of Primm?

14. Why was Plume, a topiary peahen, so beloved in the Village of Primm? Was she more than a tourist attraction? What did she represent? The role of women in society? The meaning of beauty? Of conformity? Perfection? Mastery over nature or natural instincts? In what way did topiaries like Anna Wintour make a larger statement about community?

15. When the topiaries were threatened by insect invasion, what was your emotional response? Was this a trivial or humorous matter or a threat of deeper emotional impact? What makes the importing of the predatory insects a crime, not just legally but otherwise? What is it a crime against?

16. Would you rather live in the Village of Primm or Southern Lakes? Does living in a community like Primm come at a cost? If yes, in what ways is that cost an investment? Are the costs worth it?

ABOUT THE AUTHOR

Photo © 2018 Kim Brundage

Julie Valerie is the founder of the 85K Writing Challenge and serves on the board of directors of James River Writers. Julie earned an editing certificate from the University of Chicago Graham School and has a master's degree in education, a bachelor of fine arts in fashion, and certification in wilderness first aid. She enjoys books, the study of wine, hikes on the Appalachian Trail, and travel. Julie married her college sweetheart, and they live in Virginia with their four children and two English labradors. *Holly Banks Full of Angst* is her debut novel. Follow Julie Valerie's Amazon author page, and be the first to learn of author updates and new releases in the Village of Primm series. Learn more about Julie and subscribe to her newsletter at julievalerie.com. Connect with Julie on Twitter and Pinterest at Julie_Valerie, on Facebook and Instagram at JulieValerieAuthor, and on Goodreads at JulieValerie.